THE
DEVIL'S
SANCTUARY

Marie Hermanson

Translation by Neil Smith

D0313348

TRAPDOOR

First published in Sweden in 2011 as *Himmelsdalen* by Albert Bonniers Förlag
First published in Great Britain in 2013 by Trapdoor
This paperback edition published in 2013 by Trapdoor

Copyright © Marie Hermanson 2011
Translation copyright © Neil Smith 2013

The moral right of the author has been asserted.

A CIP catalogue record for this book
is available from the British Library.

ISBN 978-1-84744-577-3

Typeset in Bembo by M Rules
Printed and bound in Great Britain by
Clays Ltd, St Ives plc

Papers used by Trapdoor are from well-managed forests
and other responsible sources.

MIX
Paper from
responsible sources
FSC   FSC® C104740

Trapdoor
An imprint of
Little, Brown Book Group
100 Victoria Embankment
London EC4Y 0DY

An Hachette UK Company
www.hachette.co.uk

www.littlebrown.co.uk

Evil is merely a form of ineptitude.

BERTOLT BRECHT
The Good Woman of Setzuan

PART ONE

1

When Daniel received the letter, at first he thought it came from Hell.

It was a thick envelope, made of yellowish, coarse-fibred paper. There was no sender's name, but Daniel's name and address were written in the lazy, almost illegible capitals that were characteristic of his brother's handwriting. As if they had been written in haste.

But the letter could hardly be from Max. Daniel couldn't recall ever getting a letter or even a postcard from his brother. On the rare occasions that Max had been in touch, he had phoned.

The stamp was foreign. And obviously it didn't say Hell, as he first thought with a shudder. The poorly printed postmark read: Helvetia.

He took the letter with him into the kitchen and left it on the table while he sorted out the coffee machine. He usually had a cup of coffee and a couple of sandwiches instead of dinner when he got home. He ate lunch in the school canteen and, seeing as he was single, he never really felt like cooking just for himself later on.

As the old coffee machine rattled into action, he started to open the envelope with a bread knife, but stopped when he noticed that his hands were shaking so much he could hardly hold the knife steady. He was having trouble breathing, as if he'd tried to swallow something far too large. He had to sit down.

The way he felt about the as yet unopened letter was the same way he used to feel whenever he and Max met. Great joy at finally seeing him, an urge to run up to his brother and give him a big hug. But at the same time something holding him back. A vague, rumbling unease.

'I can at least read what he's got to say,' he said out loud to himself in a voice that was steady and firm, as if a different, more sensible person were talking through him.

He took a firm grasp of the bread knife and opened the envelope.

2

Gisela Obermann was sitting facing the big picture window looking at the rocky mountainside on the other side of the valley. Its surface was smooth, yellowish-white, as if a sheet of paper had been stretched out, and there were elements of something black. She realised she was trying to discern letters.

At the top, the rocky wall was crowned by a fringe of audacious fir trees. Some of them had got too close to the edge and were hanging there like broken matches.

The faces around the conference table faded away into the light shining behind them, their voices like a radio that had been turned down.

'Any visits this week?' someone asked.

She felt tired and thirsty, washed out. It was the wine she had drunk last night. But not just the wine.

'We've got one relative's visit booked in,' Doctor Fischer said. 'To see Max. I think that's all, though.'

Gisela woke up.

'Who's coming to see him?' she asked in surprise.

'His brother.'

'Oh. I didn't think they were in touch with each other.'

'It's bound to be good for him,' Hedda Heine said. 'It's the first visit he's had since he's been here, isn't it?'

'Possibly.'

'Yes, it's his first visit,' Gisela confirmed. 'That's nice. Things are looking much more positive with Max right now. He's struck me as very happy and harmonious lately. It's bound to do him good to get a visit from his brother. When's he coming?'

'He should get here this afternoon or evening,' Karl Fischer said, glancing at the time as he gathered his papers. 'Are we done?'

A man in his forties with a red beard waved his hand anxiously.

'Brian?'

'No news about Mattias Block?'

'I'm afraid not. The search is still going on.'

Doctor Fischer gathered his papers and stood up. The others followed.

Typical, Gisela Obermann thought. Max's brother is coming today. And no one bothered to tell me, his doctor.

That was the way things worked in this place. That was why she was so tired. Her boundless energy, which had always cut like a knife through all resistance, was impotent here. It glanced off the walls that surrounded her and turned in on herself.

3

Daniel went with the flow towards the exit of the airport, where a small gaggle of taxi drivers were holding up hand-written signs with people's names. He glanced at them, pointed at the one bearing his name, and said in German:

'That's me.'

The taxi driver nodded and led him to a minibus with eight seats. Daniel appeared to be the only passenger. He got in as the driver took care of his luggage.

'Is it far?' he asked.

'About three hours. We'll have a break on the way,' the driver said, sliding the door shut.

They left Zürich and headed round the side of a large lake surrounded by forest-clad mountains. Daniel would have liked to ask the driver about things they passed en route, but there was a glass screen separating them. He leaned back in his seat and ran his fingers through his beard, a gesture he repeated several times during the journey.

It wasn't only fraternal interest that had made him agree to the visit, he had to admit. His finances weren't in great shape. His temporary post at the school would come to an end in the autumn when the usual teacher returned from maternity leave. He might be able to get a bit of work as a supply teacher, and maybe some translating. He couldn't afford to go away on holiday anywhere this summer. Max's offer to pay for the ticket to Switzerland had been very tempting. After visiting the clinic he could stay on for a week in a small hotel in the foothills and spend the days doing some moderately strenuous hiking in the beautiful surroundings.

Outside the car window the greenery flashed past. Elm, ash, hazel. There were neat houses with sloping gardens along the shore of the lake. Large brown birds sailed slowly above the road.

In recent years Daniel had had little contact with his brother. Like him, Max had lived abroad, first in London and then other places, where, to the best of Daniel's knowledge, he had been involved in some sort of business.

Ever since they were young Max had always seemed to be on a rollercoaster ride of success and failure, invariably of his own making. He could be impressively inventive, almost inhumanly energetic when he started a project. Then, suddenly, when he had got what he wanted and more besides, he would lose all interest and walk away with a shrug of the shoulders while his colleagues and customers tried desperately to contact him via switched-off phones and abandoned offices.

On several occasions the brothers' long-suffering father had had to step in and rescue Max from various scrapes. Maybe it was the turbulence surrounding his unpredictable son that had led to him collapsing on the bathroom floor one morning from the heart attack that ended his life shortly afterwards.

A psychiatric assessment conducted in conjunction with a court case had concluded that Max suffered from bipolar disorder. The diagnosis explained much of the mysterious chaos that Max always seemed to be surrounded by, his daring business ventures, his self-destructive behaviour, and his inability to maintain long-term relationships with women.

Every now and then Daniel used to get a phone call from his brother. On those occasions Max always sounded slightly drunk, and the calls usually came at strange times of day.

When their mother died Daniel went to great lengths to get hold of him, but without success, and the funeral went ahead in Max's absence. Somehow the news must have reached him anyway, because he called a couple of months later wanting to know where their mother was buried so he could take some flowers. Daniel had suggested meeting up and going together. Max promised to get in touch when he got to Sweden, but never did.

The glass screen slid open. The taxi driver glanced round and said:

'We'll reach an inn soon. Do you want to stop for something to eat?'

'Not eat, but I'd like a cup of coffee,' Daniel replied.

The glass screen slid closed again. Shortly after that they stopped at the small inn and each had an espresso standing at the counter. They didn't say anything to each other, and Daniel was grateful for the cheesy pop music blaring from the speakers.

'Have you been to Himmelstal before?' the driver eventually asked.

'No, never. I'm visiting my brother.'

The driver nodded as if he already knew that.

'Do you often drive people there?' Daniel asked cautiously.

'Now and then. More in the nineties when it was a plastic-surgery clinic. Christ, I used to drive people who looked like mummies. Not everyone could afford to stay until their wounds had healed. I remember one woman, you could only see her eyes through the bandages. And what eyes! Swollen, crying, sadder than you can imagine. She was in so much pain that she couldn't stop crying. When we stopped here – I always stop here, it's exactly halfway to Zürich – she sat in the car and I had to get orange juice and a straw for her, and she sat there in the back seat slurping it up. Her husband had a younger mistress and she'd had a face-lift to get him back. Christ. "I'm sure it'll all be fine. You're going to look beautiful," I said as I held her hand. Bloody hell . . .'

'And now? What sort of place is it now?' Daniel asked.

The driver stopped with his little espresso cup in mid-air and gave him a quick glance.

'Hasn't your brother told you?'

'Not exactly. I think he said it was some sort of rehab clinic.'

'Right. Yes, that's it.' The driver nodded eagerly and put the cup down on the saucer. 'Shall we carry on?'

Daniel dozed off as the car started again, and when he next opened his eyes they were in a valley of green meadows lit up by the evening sun. He'd never seen such an intense green colour anywhere in nature before. It looked artificial, created by chemical additives. Maybe it was the result of the light.

The valley got narrower and the scenery changed. To the right of the road an almost vertical rock face rose up, shading the sun and making the inside of the car darker.

Suddenly the driver braked. A man in a short-sleeved uniform shirt and peaked cap was blocking their path. Behind him was a lowered barrier. A little further on was a parked van, from which a second uniformed man was approaching.

The driver rolled down his window and exchanged a few words with one of the men as his colleague opened the rear door of the car. The glass screen between the front and rear seats was still closed, so Daniel couldn't hear what was being said. He opened the window in his own door and listened. The man was chatting amiably enough with the driver, apparently about the weather. He was speaking a German dialect that was difficult to understand.

Then he leaned in through Daniel's window and asked to see his ID. Daniel handed him his passport. The man said something he didn't understand.

'You can get out,' the driver translated. He had turned round and opened the screen between them now.

'I have to get out?'

The driver nodded encouragingly.

Daniel got out of the car. They were standing right next to the rock face, which was covered in moss and ferns. There was water trickling down it in various places. He could smell the mountain, cool and acidic.

The man held out a metal detector and ran it quickly over Daniel's body, front and back.

'You've come a long way,' he said in a friendly voice, returning the passport.

His colleague put Daniel's suitcase back in the car after going through it, and closed the door.

'Yes, I caught a plane from Stockholm this morning,' Daniel replied.

The man with the metal detector leaned inside the car and ran it quickly over the rear seat, then indicated that he was done.

'You can get back in,' the driver said with a nod to Daniel.

The men saluted and the driver started the car as the barrier slid upwards.

Daniel leaned towards the driver's seat to ask a question, but the driver pre-empted him:

'Routine check. Swiss thoroughness,' he said, then pressed the button to close the glass screen in Daniel's face.

Through his open window he saw the mossy rock face rush past, and heard the reflected, amplified sound of the engine.

He was squirming. The security check had reawakened his anxieties. He didn't imagine that this was just a social visit. If Max had chosen to get in touch after all these years, there had to be a good reason. Max needed him.

The thought both moved and saddened him. Because how could he help his brother? Max was, you had to admit after so many years of disappointed hope, beyond all help.

He consoled himself with the fact that his visit in itself was a sign of goodwill. He had come when Max had called. He would listen to him, be there for him. And then, after a couple of hours, he would leave again. There was no question that there would be any more to it than that.

The minibus went round a sharp left-hand bend. Daniel opened his eyes. He saw sloping meadows, a forest of fir trees and, some way off, a village and church spire. A woman was working in a market garden, bent over in a sea of dahlias. She straightened up as they approached and waved with a small trowel.

The driver turned off on to a smaller road leading up the hillside. They passed through a patch of forest and the climb got steeper.

Shortly after that Daniel saw the clinic, an imposing nine-teenth-century building surrounded by a park. The driver drove right up to the main entrance, took out Daniel's suit-case and opened the passenger door.

The air that flooded into the vehicle was so clean and bright that his lungs trembled with surprise.

'Well, we're here.'

4

Max and Daniel were identical twins, but they had almost been born on different days. When their mother, thirty-eight years old and a first-time mother, finally managed to free herself from one twin after ten hours of hard labour, the second, Max, was still inside her, and evidently planned on staying there for a while longer yet. It was late in the evening and the midwife, who was also starting to get tired of the whole business, sighed and said to the exhausted mother: 'It looks like you'll have to organise separate birthday parties for these two.'

While Daniel was being washed and weighed, and fell sweetly asleep in his little bed, the obstetrician took out the suction cup, which however failed to get a grip on his resistant, evasive brother, and instead sucked hold of their mother's innards, threatening to turn her inside out like a tangled sweater. When the suction cup was eventually attached in the right place, Max seemed to realise that this was serious, adapted to the situation and made the first of many rapid bursts of speed that he would later employ to surprise those around him.

'Now we've got him . . .' the doctor said, but had no time to finish the sentence before his catch, entirely on its own and without the need for any suction, slid out on a waterslide of blood and slime, building up a bit of speed and flying into the doctor's lap.

It was then five minutes to midnight, so the brothers were able to celebrate their shared birthday after all.

Five to twelve. How should that be interpreted?

That Max was struggling to be unique and wanted at all costs to avoid being born the same day as his brother, but changed his mind at the last minute and prioritised solidarity over integrity?

Or should it be interpreted the way those around Max often did when he arrived late – but not *too* late – to a meeting, train or airport check-in desk, and asked his nervous friends with a laugh what they expected from someone born at five minutes to midnight: a high-wire act, balancing on the edge, a way of getting people's attention?

The boys spent their early years in their parents' house in Gothenburg. Their father was a successful businessman with his own electronics company, and until the boys were born their mother had rather aimlessly studied various arts subjects at university.

From the outset the two twin boys were quite different.

Daniel ate well, seldom cried and stuck to the projected growth forecasts in an exemplary way.

Max was a slow developer and, when he still hadn't uttered a word by the time he was twenty months old, nor made any effort to move independently, his mother began to get worried. She took both boys to see a well-regarded female paediatrician in her home city of Uppsala. When the doctor saw the boys together, she decided there was a simple explanation. Whenever Max so much as looked at any of the nice toys the doctor had laid out for the purposes of the experiment, Daniel scrambled off on his stubby little legs and fetched it for him.

'You can see for yourself,' she said to the twins' mother, pointing in turn at the boys with her pen as she went on: 'Max doesn't *need* to walk, seeing as Daniel fetches everything for him. Does he speak for his brother as well?'

Their mother nodded and explained that Daniel would work out in an almost spooky way what his brother wanted and felt, and would transmit this to those around them with his limited but skilfully employed vocabulary. He would say if Max was thirsty, hot, or needed his nappy changing.

The paediatrician was concerned about the brothers' symbiotic relationship and suggested that they be separated for a while.

'Max has no natural motivation to walk or talk so long as his brother keeps providing him with everything he wants,' she explained.

At first the boys' mother was uncertain about this separation, which she realised would be painful for both of them. They had always been so close, after all. But she had great confidence in the doctor, who was an authority in both paediatrics and child psychology, and following lengthy consultation and discussion with the boys' father, who thought the idea made sense, she gave in. They decided that the boys should be separated for the summer, when their father was on holiday and could look after Max at home in Gothenburg while their mother took Daniel to visit her parents in Uppsala. And according to the doctor, the summer was when children develop fastest and are most open to change.

Both boys spent the first week crying in despair with their respective parent in their respective city.

By the second week Daniel moved into a calmer phase. He seemed to realise the advantages of being an only child and began to enjoy the undivided attention of his mother and grandparents.

Max, on the other hand, went on crying. Day and night. His father, who was a novice when it came to looking after children, sounded more and more desperate in his phone calls to Uppsala. Their mother thought they should abandon the experiment and called the paediatrician, who encouraged them to carry on with it. But the father would need the help of an au pair.

Getting hold of an au pair in the middle of the summer turned out to be tricky. And the mother obviously didn't want to hand her son to just anyone. There was no way she was going to accept a sloppy, immature teenager desperate to earn a bit of money over the summer.

'I'll see what I can do,' the doctor said when the mother explained her concerns, and a couple of days later she called to recommend an Anna Rupke for the job. She was thirty-two years old and had experience of nursing children with physical handicaps, but she had become so interested in children's mental development that she had gone on to study psychology and pedagogy, and was now working on her doctoral thesis. The doctor had taught her on a specially tailored course, and Anna's talent and engagement had made a lasting impression on her. Of course she lived in Uppsala, but if the family could arrange accommodation for her in Gothenburg she was prepared to move down there for the summer to look after Max.

Two days later Anna Rupke moved into the guest bedroom of the family home. Her presence made life considerably easier for the boys' father. The young woman seemed quite unaffected by the child's cries, and could sit and calmly read an interesting research article while Max sat on the floor howling loud enough to make the walls shake. Now and then the boys' father would pad into the nursery and ask if this really was normal. Maybe the boy was seriously ill? Anna shook her head with an expert's smile.

16

But surely he must be hungry? He hasn't eaten anything all day.

Without looking up from the report, Anna gestured towards a Singoalla biscuit placed on a footstool a few metres away from the boy. Max loved Singoalla biscuits. His father resisted the instinct to get the biscuit and give it to him. He left the room and put up with the screaming for another hour or so from his office upstairs, then, just as he couldn't bear it for another second, there was silence. He hurried downstairs, worried that the boy had passed out from exhaustion or hunger.

When he reached the nursery he saw his son half-shuffling, half-crawling towards the stool, his eyes fixed on the biscuit, concentrating hard, and extremely angry. Max got hold of the stool, and with a furious jerk he heaved himself up and grabbed the biscuit. He took a big bite, and with his mouth full he turned round with a triumphant grin that was so wide that half the mouthful fell out again.

Anna Rupke gave his father a pointed look, then went back to her reading.

The following week was intense. With the help of strategically positioned Singoalla biscuits, Max raced through the stages of shuffling, crawling, standing and walking.

The next week Anna got to grips with speech. To start with, Max communicated in his usual way, which meant pointing and screaming. But instead of rushing round and desperately trying different things that Max might possibly want, Anna sat there calmly with one of her books. Only when he said the correct word was he rewarded. Max actually had a large passive vocabulary, and understood an almost alarming amount of what other people were saying. It had just never occurred to him to say anything himself.

Towards the end of the summer it was time to reunite the two brothers again.

They didn't appear to recognise each other.

Daniel behaved the way he would have done with any stranger, and was shy and reserved.

Max appeared to view his brother as an intruder, and reacted aggressively when Daniel put his hands on toys Max regarded as his private property. (A not entirely unexpected reaction, seeing as 'mine' was the first word Max uttered, and his first two-word sentence had been 'Have it!')

During the period of separation the parents had unfortunately come to regard the twin in their respective care as 'their' boy. Every time the boys came to blows the family was therefore divided into two camps. On one side stood Daniel and his mother, with her parents in the background. On the other side stood the boys' father, Anna Rupke and Max. Their mother thought Max was treating her little Daniel badly. Their father and Anna thought that Max's aggressive behaviour was a positive sign of his liberation from his brother.

In light of the unsuccessful reunion it was agreed, in collaboration with the paediatrician in Uppsala, to separate the boys once more.

Anna Rupke was supposed to be going back to work on her thesis, but decided to take a break and carry on as Max's nanny. Or pedagogical instructor, as she preferred to call herself. The boys' father expressed his sincere thanks, well aware that Anna had put her promising career on hold. But Anna assured him that Max was such an interesting child that he was more of a benefit than a hindrance to her research.

The boys' mother once more took Daniel to her parents in Uppsala, and in this way the parents lived apart the entire autumn, each with their own twin, with daily phone calls about the boys' progress.

When Christmas came, it was time to make a new attempt at reunification. But the split in the family was now so deep that it seemed impossible to repair. Besides, during the couple's long separation, the father had embarked upon a relationship with his son's nanny.

He wasn't entirely sure how it had come about. It had started with him being *impressed*. By the way Anna dealt with Max, her certainty, her calmness, her intelligence. He concluded with some satisfaction that she, like him, had a pragmatic researcher's nature, and wasn't an indecisive, emotional creature like the boys' mother.

Without him really noticing, he went from being impressed to being *attracted*. By Anna's high Slavic cheekbones, the fresh smell of shampoo she left after her in the bathroom, the thoughtful way she twined her necklace, and the audible yawns from the guest bedroom before she fell asleep.

Maybe there was no more to it than a man being attracted by the woman living in his house and looking after his child.

During the autumn the mother had made a life for herself in Uppsala. While her mother looked after Daniel, she spent a few hours each day working as a secretary at the Institute of Classical Languages where her father still worked as a professor.

One year later this arrangement was confirmed. The boys' parents divorced, the father married Anna and the mother moved into a flat just ten minutes' walk from her parents.

So the twins grew up with one parent each, and only met once a year on their shared birthday, 28 October.

Everyone was always nervous in advance of these birthday encounters. Did the brothers still look similar? What did they have in common? What were the differences?

It was clear that the brothers, in spite of being twins, had retained their differences. Max was sociable, outgoing, talkative. Daniel was reserved and cautious. It was odd to think that Max had once been entirely dependent on his brother for all that he wanted in life.

But while their behaviour grew more and more different

19

with every meeting, they became more and more alike in their appearance. Max, who to start with had been both shorter and skinnier than his brother, soon caught up, and from the age of three the boys' height and weight matched each other down to the last millimetre and gram. Their facial similarities also emerged more clearly when Daniel's features were no longer concealed by pink puppy fat, and Max's voice, which in his early years had been shrill and piercing, sank around the age of five to the same pleasant, soft tone as Daniel's. When the boys met on their seventh birthday, they felt a mixture of delight and horror when they realised they were staring at their own mirror image.

Birthdays were the only time each year when the two camps met, Max-Father-Anna and Daniel-Mother-grand-parents, and all sorts of feelings were stirred up. The grandparents regarded the father as an adulterer and marriage wrecker. The mother criticised the way Anna was raising her son. Anna, who regarded herself as an expert in the field, wasn't prepared to take advice from an amateur. And the boys' father felt confused at suddenly seeing his son in duplicate.

While the adults talked and argued the two boys would run out into the garden, down into the cellar, or somewhere else exciting. They were drawn to each other, curious and full of anticipation. They would fall out, keep their distance, then converge again. They fought, laughed, cried and comforted each other. During one single intense day the boys were sub-jected to such a tumult of emotions that they were left utterly drained for a week afterwards, and often suffered bad bouts of fever.

Although the adults disagreed about almost everything else, they were in complete agreement about one thing: *one* meet-ing a year was enough.

5

Daniel found himself in what looked more like the lobby of a fashionable old hotel than the entrance to a health clinic.

He was met by a young woman wearing a well-cut, light blue dress and shoes with a slight heel. The way she was dressed, her straight posture and her smile made him think of an air hostess. And she did actually introduce herself as a 'hostess'.

She appeared to know who Daniel was straightaway, and who he was there to visit. She asked him to write his name in a green, felt-covered ledger, then showed him to some armchairs grouped in front of a magnificent open fireplace in the art nouveau style. The wall above was adorned with a crossed pair of old skis, with stuffed animal heads on either side: an ibex with enormous ridged horns and a beard, and a fox with its top lip pulled back, baring its teeth.

'Your brother will be here shortly, I'll go and tell him you've arrived. My colleague will take your luggage up to the guestroom.'

Daniel was about to sit down when a blond man in a short-sleeved steward's shirt and tie appeared and took Daniel's suitcase away.

'But I'm not staying. I'm going on to a hotel later,' Daniel protested. 'Can't I just leave my case down here for a couple of hours?'

The man stopped and turned round.

'Which hotel are you going to?'

'I don't really know. The closest one, I suppose. Can you recommend one?'

The woman and man exchanged an anxious glance.

'You'll probably have to go a fair distance,' the woman said. 'Most of the hotels up here in the mountains are health resorts. They have their regular guests, and are usually booked up months in advance.'

'But there's that village down in the valley. Isn't there anyone there who has a room to let?' Daniel wondered.

'We don't recommend that our visitors stay in the village,' the woman said. 'Has anyone offered you a place to stay there?'

She was still smiling, but her expression had hardened slightly.

'No,' Daniel said. 'It was just a thought.'

The man cleared his throat and said calmly: 'If anyone does offer you a room in the village, just say no. Politely but firmly. I suggest that you stay in one of our guestrooms. That's what most visitors do. You can stay a few days, we've got plenty of rooms at the moment.'

'I wasn't planning on that.'

'It won't cost you anything. Most relatives live a long way away, so it seems reasonable for us to let them stay here a few days. That way people are able to settle a bit and can spend time together in a more natural way. You've never been to Himmelstal before?'

'No.'

The man, who had been holding Daniel's case in his hand throughout this conversation, appeared to regard the matter settled.

'Perhaps you'd like to see your room and get unpacked? We can take the lift over here,' he said, leading the way across the thick carpet.

Daniel followed him. Maybe, he thought in the lift on the way up, it wasn't a bad idea to spend one night here after all. It was getting late, and he wasn't looking forward to chasing round trying to find a room nearby late at night.

The guestroom was small, but bright and pleasantly furnished. There was a vase of fresh flowers on a white, painted table, and the view of the valley and the mountaintops in the distance would have matched any tourist's expectations of a holiday in the Alps.

Himmelstal. Heavenly valley. A beautiful name for a beautiful place, Daniel thought.

He washed in the basin and changed his shirt. Then he lay down on the bed and rested for a few minutes. It was a good-quality, modern bed, extremely comfortable, he could feel that at once. He would have liked to stay and have a nap for an hour or two before seeing his brother. But the hostess downstairs had already told Max he was here. He could sleep later.

In the lift down to the ground floor he realised what had been so odd about the conversation he had had a short while ago. He had been aware of it the whole time he was talking to the man and the hostess, but hadn't been able to put his finger on it: they had been speaking different languages. He had addressed them in German, seeing as he assumed that was their mother tongue, and they had responded in English.

He was so used to switching between different languages that he had hardly noticed. It had just made a slightly jarring impression, a sort of disconnect.

He had always found languages easy. As a child he had spent a lot of time with his maternal grandfather, who was a linguist.

He and his mother used to eat dinner with his grandparents pretty much every day. While his mother and grandmother did the washing up in the kitchen, Daniel and his grandfather would go off to the large, tobacco-scented study.

Daniel loved sitting on the floor leafing through books full of pictures of Egyptian tomb paintings, Greek sculptures and medieval engravings, while his grandfather told him about languages that were still alive and languages that were dead. How languages were related to each other the same as people, and how the origins of words could be traced far back in time. Daniel thought this was absolutely fascinating. He was always asking his grandfather where different words came from. Sometimes he would answer at once, and sometimes he would look the words up in a book on his desk.

To Daniel's astonishment, he realised that the words he used and took so much for granted were considerably older than him, older than Grandfather, older than the old house with its creaking wooden floors. They had travelled a long way, through different countries and ages before suddenly landing in Daniel's little mouth like a butterfly on a flower. And they would continue their journey long after he himself was gone.

He had retained this respectful delight in language. He studied classics at high school, then went on to study German and French at university, and eventually got a job as an interpreter for the European Parliament in Brussels and Strasbourg.

Using his own voice to express another person's thoughts and opinions, which often completely contradicted his own views, stimulated him in a strange and exciting way. If what was being said had a strong, emotional charge, spoken language wasn't enough and he would use gestures and facial expressions to convey the message of the person whose words he was interpreting. Sometimes he felt like a puppet with someone's else's hand inside him. As if his own soul had been pushed aside. He heard his voice change, and could feel himself using facial muscles he never used otherwise. 'Ah,' he would think in fascination, 'so this is what it feels like to be you!'

Occasionally, when he finished interpreting a particularly intense discussion, there would be a little gap before he landed back in himself again. For a few giddy moments he would experience what it felt like to be no one at all.

On several occasions he had been mistaken for the person he was interpreting for. People who disagreed would be abrupt and offhand with him, because they regarded him as an extension of their opponent.

The reverse was also true: that sympathy for the person he was interpreting for would spill over on to him as well. He suspected that this was how he had managed to arouse the interest of the woman who later became his wife.

Emma had been a lawyer, specialising in international environmental law. Daniel's job had been to interpret a conversation between her and a German expert in water conservation, a stylish, middle-aged gentleman with a very definite erotic appeal. While he was interpreting, Daniel had a strong sense that he was merging into the German, to the point where in an almost creepy way he felt he knew what the man was going to say before he spoke.

Emma, too, seemed to have regarded them as one and the same person, because even after the man had left she carried on discussing water conservation with Daniel, as if *he* had been the person she had been talking to, instead of his shadowy mimic. Several times he had to remind her that he didn't actually know anything about water. But the conversation was underway by then. They moved on to other subjects, went on to a little Italian restaurant, and then, rather drunk, they went back to her hotel room together. A couple of times while they were making love she jokingly addressed him as 'mein Herr', which unsettled him.

Even after they were married Daniel had been unable to shake the idea that his wife had got him mixed up with someone else, and that she was constantly disappointed when reminded of her mistake.

Then he discovered that she was being unfaithful with a biologist from Munich, and they got divorced.

The year after the divorce Daniel had suffered a mental breakdown. He didn't really know why. He had got over the divorce surprisingly quickly, and thought in hindsight that it had been the right thing to do. He was well regarded within his profession, he had a good salary, and lived in a modern apartment in the centre of Brussels. He had short-term flings with career-orientated women who were as uninterested in a serious relationship as he was. He didn't really feel he was missing out on anything. Until one day when everything changed from one moment to the next, and he realised that his life was utterly empty and meaningless. That all his relationships were wholly insubstantial, and that the words he expressed in the course of his work belonged to other people. Who was he really? A glove puppet who performed tricks for a few hours each day, and was then discarded and tossed in a corner. He was only alive when he was interpreting, and that life wasn't his, it was borrowed.

This shattering insight had struck Daniel one morning when he was on his way to work and had stopped at a kiosk to buy a paper. He stood there with the money in his hand, as though he'd been turned to stone. The newsagent asked which paper he wanted, but he couldn't answer. He put the money back in his pocket and sank down on to a nearby bench, exhausted. Although he had an important job that day, work suddenly felt quite impossible.

He was on sick leave for two months. For depression, according to the doctor's note. But he realised it was about something more than that: terrifying clarity. A revelation of an almost religious nature. Like converts who had seen the light, he had seen the darkness, and it had given him precisely that sense of an absolute truth that he had heard such people describe. The shabby veil of existence had been yanked aside, and he had seen himself and his life exactly as they were. The experience had come as a shock, yet at the same time he was deeply grateful for it, and the thought that he might have gone on living a delusion made him shudder.

Daniel had resigned from his interpreting job, moved back to his hometown, Uppsala, and got a temporary job as a language teacher in a high school. The pay was obviously much worse than his previous job, but it would do until he worked out what he was going to do with his life.

When he wasn't working he played computer games. World of Warcraft and Grand Theft Auto. To start with it was just a way of passing the time, then he started to get drawn in. The greyer his real life became, the more vibrant those fictional worlds seemed. The classroom and staffroom became waiting rooms where he would spend impatient hours, reciting verb conjugations like a sleepwalker and engaging in small-talk with his colleagues. At the end of each working day he would close the blinds in his cramped one-room flat, switch on his computer and immerse himself in the only life that could make his pulse race with excitement, his brain flash with ingenious insights. When he stumbled off to bed in the small hours, exhausted by hard fighting and breathtaking escapes, he was always surprised that he could feel so strongly about something that didn't exist, when what did exist made so little impression on him.

6

Daniel had just got out of the lift and was on his way to the armchairs in front of the fireplace when the front door was thrown open and Max headed over towards him.

This was the moment he had been worrying about. Although he had been through it so many times before, he never got used to it: walking towards himself, looking into his own eyes, seeing his own facial features.

To his great relief that didn't happen this time. The man heading towards him under the crystal chandeliers seemed familiar in a distant, elusive way, but no more than that.

Daniel ran his fingers through his beard as if to reassure himself that it was still there. The soft but effective visor that protected his sensitive face.

Max was suntanned, dressed casually in Bermuda shorts, sweatshirt and sandals, like a tourist. His hair was cropped short and his smile was so broad and dazzling that Daniel immediately placed him at the manic end of the spectrum in which his psyche constantly moved. Of course that was also the impression he had got from the letter, but the letter had been written a month ago and Max's moods changed quickly.

In just a few hours he could switch to pitch-black lethargy or aggressive irritation. But for now he was clearly in an ebullient mood. As long as Daniel didn't have to take any responsibility for the consequences, that was at least better than its polar opposite.

Max's embrace was heartfelt, almost passionate, and was followed up by macho slaps on the back and playful shadow boxing.

'Bro! Hey! You came. You *actually* came! Yesss!'

He laughed out loud as he clasped his clenched fists together in victorious gesture, and looked up at the ceiling as though he were thanking some invisible god.

Daniel smiled back cautiously.

'Of course I came,' he said. 'Good to see you. You seem to be doing well.'

'The default setting is pretty stable. How about you? God, you've still got that ridiculous beard! It's worse than ever. I'm surprised they let you on the plane. You look as though you're in the Taliban.'

Max grabbed hold of Daniel's beard and gave it a quick tug.

'I like it,' Daniel said, taking a step back.

'Really?' Max laughed. 'And those glasses! Who knew you could get second-hand frames! Where did you find those? Why don't you have contact lenses, same as everyone with any sense?'

'I really don't care for the idea of sticking things in your eyes.'

'Bollocks. It is a bit of a nuisance, though. I've been wondering about laser surgery for years, but I haven't found the right opportunity. You need to have a fortnight free for everything to heal up again. And when would I have time for that? OK, let's get your stuff down to my room and then we can have dinner in the restaurant. They've got trout on the menu today, I checked. Where's your luggage?'

'The staff took it up to the guestroom.'

'Guestroom? Nonsense! You're *my* guest, and no one else's. So obviously you're staying with *me*.'

'Where do you live?'

'I've got a little cabin nearby. Simple but comfortable. Guestroom! Is that the key?'

Max took the room key with the brass fob out of Daniel's hand and disappeared off towards the lift.

'Wait here!' he ordered, impatiently pressing the lift button.

After waiting three seconds he gave up and took the stairs instead, two steps at a time.

Daniel stayed where he was, bemused and at something of a loss. Caught off guard already, dominated and overridden. How quickly it had happened.

A few minutes later Max returned with his case, and rushed determinedly with it through the front door, down the ornate flight of steps and off across the park. Daniel trotted obediently after him. What else could he do?

'This seems a reasonable place,' he said to make conversation when he had caught up with his brother. 'The staff are nice. No white coats.'

'No, why should they have white coats? As far as I know, no one's ever been cured by a white coat. I like the outfits the hostesses wear. They're quite stylish. And sexy. Don't you think?'

'Yes, maybe.'

On the far side of the park was a cluster of little cabins built of rough timber, in the Alpine style. Max opened the door to one of them and gestured to Daniel to go in.

'This is where I live. What do you think?'

The cabin consisted of a single room with rustic pine furniture and benches fixed to the walls, covered with throws with traditional folklore patterns. There was an open fire, a basic kitchen and a curtained alcove containing the bed.

'You can live more grandly here if you choose, but I prefer to live like this, simple and frugal,' Max said, putting Daniel's case down with a thump. 'You can sleep on that bunk over there. That'll do for one night, won't it?'

'Do you live here on your own?' Daniel asked in surprise.

'Obviously. I don't want to live with anyone else. Apart from you now, of course. No, I want my own space. That's the advantage of a place like this. You have more choices. Let's go and have dinner. I hope you didn't eat anything at that terrible place the driver always stops at. I think he must have some sort of contract with them.'

'No, we just had coffee.'

'Good, then you'll be hungry enough to appreciate the fresh trout and a chilled Riesling. Or whatever you'd rather have. But I'd recommend the trout.'

Before they had dinner Max wanted to show his brother round.

The clinic was bigger than Daniel had realised at first. Besides the old main building, it consisted of several tall, modern, glass-fronted buildings. The whole place was surrounded by the beautiful park, where people were walking about with a spring in their step. Most of them were dressed in casual leisure wear, and looked more like healthy holiday-makers than patients at a rehab clinic. Daniel guessed that their problems, as in his brother's case, were mostly mental in nature.

'By the way, do you play tennis?' Max asked. 'We can book one of the courts and have a game first thing tomorrow morning.'

'No, thank you.'

'Otherwise there's the fitness centre over there. The sports hall. Table tennis. And a pretty good gym, actually.'

Max gestured towards a large building they were walking past.

At its rear was a swimming pool. A couple of patients were lying on white recliners, soaking up the afternoon sun. Daniel shaded his eyes with his hand and looked at them in surprise.

'When you wrote that this was a rehabilitation clinic, I imagined something completely different,' he said. 'More like a hospital.'

Max nodded.

'This is a private clinic, as I'm sure you're worked out. For people who can afford it.'

'So what does it cost to stay here?'

Max screwed his face into a grimace and shook his head, as if it was far too painful to talk about it.

'Too much for my budget, really. I can manage it for a while. But if I'm not declared well soon, things will come to a head. That's why I behave as normally as I can. I keep my distance from the worst psychos, flirt with the female staff and have learned conversations with the doctors. And I hear them talking behind my back: "What on earth is *he* doing here? He seems sound as a bell." Obviously there's a risk of them keeping you here to get more of your money. That's why I've made it very clear to my doctor, Gisela Obermann, that my resources have almost run out, and that I'd appreciate it if they could declare me fit again soon.'

They carried on through the park. The air was cool and smelled of the forest below. From the direction of the tennis courts came the regular sound of balls being hit.

'What sort of treatment are you getting?' Daniel wondered.

'None at all.'

'But you're still getting your usual medication here?'

A man was approaching along one of the paths. He looked as though he wanted to talk to them, but Max put his arm round Daniel's shoulders and steered him quickly in a different direction.

'Gisela cancelled all my prescriptions when I arrived. To see how I function without them. She always wants to see what patients are like without any medication.'

He stopped, stood in front of Daniel with one hand on his shoulder, and went on in a firm, didactic tone, so that every word got through:

'Examining a medicated patient is as bad for a psychiatrist as it would be for a doctor of the body to examine a patient with their clothes on. After all, the clothes could be covering up a skin complaint or tumour. The main purpose of psychotropic medication is the same as clothes: to *conceal* things. They don't cure anything, they're not like penicillin, they don't kill off harmful bacteria and so on. They just sit like a protective layer of clothing over the illness.'

Daniel nodded in agreement and backed away slightly to avoid the saliva spraying from Max's lips as he spoke.

'Or like one of those blasting mats,' his brother went on, 'those things that muffle explosions and stop stones and debris flying about and hurting anyone. Nice and safe for anyone nearby, obviously. But . . .'

Max jutted his head forward, fixing his eyes on Daniel's and lowering his voice to an intense whisper:

'What sort of damage do muffled explosions like that do on the inside?'

He paused, his gaze still firmly fixed on Daniel, then started to walk on again.

A young man in jogging clothes ran towards them and they stepped aside to let him pass.

'And how does your doctor think you're doing without medication?' Daniel asked cautiously.

'Fine, I presume. The last time we met she said she couldn't see any reason to prescribe anything.'

'Really?'

Daniel was surprised. As far as he knew, ever since he was

a teenager Max had been on regular medication. Periodically he had given up taking it, which everyone, him included, had realised was a big mistake. As long as he took his medication he felt pretty well and could live a relatively normal life. Yet here he was, saying that his doctor had taken him off all the drugs. Strange.

Max laughed.

'Don't look so horrified. There's such a thing as self-healing, don't you know? That's what they mainly focus on here. The healing power of nature.'

Max made a sweeping gesture towards the sloping lawn, the glass-fronted buildings and the mountains.

'Good, nourishing food. Clean air. Peace and quiet. Tried and tested therapies that got forgotten when we came up with all those chemical treatments. People often seem to think it takes a huge amount of effort to help or bring someone down. That we're these massive, steel constructions, difficult to knock over and then just as difficult to put back on our feet after we have fallen over. But think what a bit of stress can do to a person. There are several people here at the clinic suffering from exhaustion. Have you ever seen someone like that? One woman could only sit there staring in front of her, she didn't even know her own name. She had to be fed, because she'd forgotten how to use a fork. You might think some sort of terrible trauma had made her like that, war, or torture. No. It was nothing more than ordinary stress. Too many demands, pressure from all sides. It's odd that you can be so completely crushed by that. But in actual fact, we human beings are fairly uncomplicated constructs. It doesn't take much to make us fall apart. And it doesn't take that much to put us back together again. Time. Peace and quiet. Natural surroundings. Simple things, but often overlooked.'

Daniel nodded thoughtfully.

'So you've . . . healed yourself, then?'

34

Max turned towards him with a broad smile.

'Well, I'm well on the way, according to Dr Obermann.'

'I'm very glad to hear it.'

Max gave a quick nod, then clapped his hands together noisily to signify that the subject was closed.

'Well, *now* we definitely need some food!'

7

To Daniel's great surprise, the clinic contained a restaurant that looked much like any other high-class establishment. It was located in attractive premises on the first floor of the main building, with an ornate plaster ceiling and oriental carpets. There were white tablecloths, slender glasses and linen napkins. Apart from one solitary elderly man at a table in one corner, they were alone.

'Is this for the patients?' Daniel exclaimed in amazement as Max made his way towards a table and sat down.

'What patients? There are no patients here. We're customers, paying a fortune to have a bit of a rest. Some decent food in a nice setting is surely the least we can ask for? We'll have the trout.'

Max waved away the waitress who was trying to hand them menus.

'And a bottle of Gobelsburger. Chilled.'

The waitress gave him a friendly nod and went off.

'So, how are things with you, Daniel, or have I already asked? If I have, I can't remember what you said,' Max said.

'Things are fine. You know I'm living in Uppsala now. Life

at the EU got a bit too stressful. I was in a pretty bad way towards the end. With the divorce and everything. Well, you know.'

'Here comes the wine!'

Max tasted the sip of wine that the waitress had poured and nodded happily.

'Taste this, Daniel. I have a couple of glasses most days. Maybe it doesn't go with everything, but I don't really give a damn.'

Daniel took a sip of the wine, which was dry and fresh, actually very good.

'Well, like I said. It got too much,' he went on.

'Too much? Have you been drinking already?' Max said in surprise.

'No, no. Too much ... Never mind. The wine's great. Fresh. Invigorating.'

'Invigorating! That's the word! You always have such fantastic words for everything, Daniel. But I suppose you are a linguistic expert.'

'No, no. I'm an interpreter. Or was, anyway.'

'If interpreters aren't linguistic experts, I don't know who is.'

Daniel gave an embarrassed shrug.

'I find languages easy, that's all,' he admitted. 'Really I'm just a parrot.'

'A parrot? Yes, there's probably something in that. You like mimicry, Daniel. But at the same time you're absolutely terrified of being the same as anyone else. Me, for instance. What are you frightened of?'

'I'm not frightened. I don't understand why you'd think that,' Daniel protested, sounding more upset than he meant to.

'Well, let's not start arguing when we've only just met. We don't want to upset Marike, do we?'

He smiled at the waitress, who was standing beside the table with two plates.

'Go ahead, Marike. He looks dangerous but he doesn't bite.'

The trout was fried whole, and served with new potatoes, melted butter and lemon.

'She's a pretty little thing, isn't she?' Max said when the waitress was no more than a few steps away. She was in her forties, and hardly a little thing.

'Not in the conventional sense, obviously,' he went on. 'But she's got something, don't you think? Did you notice how big her backside was? All the women born round here are like that. You can tell at a glance if a woman is actually from the mountains or has moved here. Well, I'm talking about the ones whose families have lived here for generations, of course. They've all got an excess of subcutaneous fat, mainly concentrated around their backsides and hips. The men are thickset as well, but you see it most clearly in the women. Do you know why that is?'

'Why you see it more clearly in the women? Probably because you look at them more than the men, I suppose,' Daniel said.

'Very funny. I mean: what makes people up here in isolated mountain regions fatter than people down on the plains? It's the same in all the mountainous parts of the world. But not just there. People on islands, in the Pacific, or deep in the jungles of South America, exhibit the same solid, fleshy body shape. Whereas people who live on plains, like the Masai in East Africa, for instance, are tall and thin. Why? Well,' Max said, pointing at Daniel with his fork, 'when there's a famine, the people on the plains can walk to new areas to find food. People with long legs, the ones who are most mobile, survive, while the little fat ones are left sitting on their big arses and starve to death. But in isolated places there's no advantage to having long legs, because you're still not going to get any-where. On an island, or in thick jungle or snowed-in alpine valleys, it's no use being agile. The ones who survive periods of famine are the ones who have an extra layer of fat to live off.'

Daniel nodded. He always had trouble keeping up with Max when his thoughts veered into uncharted territory like this.

'That sounds plausible.' In an effort to shift the conversation into calmer waters he added: 'This trout is excellent. It seems very fresh. Do you suppose they caught it nearby?'

'The trout? Of course. In the rapids. Who knows, it might have been me who caught it.'

'You?'

'Or someone else. I catch more than I can eat, so I give the rest to the restaurant. But it's interesting, isn't it? In this age of globalisation. That genetic predispositions like that survive. You can travel all round the world, but nature has still pro-grammed you to live in an alpine valley where you might be forced to live off the fat you've built up. It's quite attractive. Women with big backsides, I mean. It piques your imagina-tion. Don't you think?'

He glanced at the waitress who was passing their table on her way to the solitary diner at the corner table.

'Maybe.'

The waitress cleared the man's table and went past them again with her hands full of dishes. Max quickly stuck out his hand and gave her a light slap on the buttock. She turned round with a slight grimace but said nothing.

'That was completely uncalled for,' Daniel said disap-provingly.

Max laughed.

'A madman has to permit himself a few moments of mad-ness. You have to live up to expectations. It's all about knowing what the boundaries are. Otherwise they'll have you strapped down in a straitjacket before you know it, your life of luxury replaced by the torture chamber in the cellar.'

'Is that true?' Daniel said, then realised it was a joke.

To cover up his mistake he quickly went on:

'So why are you really here, Max? You seem to be doing very well.'

Max's taunting smile vanished. He stretched, then said seriously:

'I'm working in Italy these days, maybe you know? With olive oil.'

'No, I didn't know, actually,' Daniel said in surprise.

'It's a tough business. Particularly for a foreigner like me. I've done pretty well, if I do say so myself, but success has its costs. It's not exactly a forty-hour week. Recently I've been working round the clock.'

'Oh,' Daniel said quietly. He knew what it usually meant when Max worked round the clock.

'I hit the wall, as the saying goes. The same's true of most people here at the clinic. The working environment for business executives is completely inhumane these days. And I'm not talking about Sweden here, which is a kindergarten compared to the rest of Europe. Down here no one manages to stay at the top for long. No one talks about it openly, but most people fall apart every so often. It's built into the system. We're like Formula One cars, we have to go into the pits at regular intervals to change tyres and take on more fuel. Then we're ready to get going again.'

Max made a rolling gesture with his finger and laughed, pleased with his own imagery.

'So this is the pit stop?' Daniel said, looking round the restaurant, where they were now the only guests.

'Yep. Himmelstal is a pit stop. Possibly the best in Europe. Now for coffee and something stronger.' Max slapped his hand on the table. 'But not here,' he added. 'I know a nice little place down in the village. Come on.'

He screwed up his napkin and stood up.

Daniel looked round for the waitress. He felt he should pay for dinner, but wasn't sure how things worked here.

'In the village?' Daniel said. 'Can you really leave the clinic just like that?'

Max laughed.

'Of course. That's the whole point of Himmelstal. Put it on my tab, darling,' he called to the invisible waitress, then marched towards the exit.

8

Mosel wine. Cool, refreshing, as if it had been drawn from a well deep in the earth.

Gisela Obermann wished she still had the Bohemian crystal glasses she'd inherited, instead of the dull, mass-produced glasses of the staff quarters. But she'd given the glasses away to charity, where they had been sold to raise funds. She had given everything away when she got the chance to work at Himmelstal. She had got rid of her beautiful flat and put an end to a damaging, long-term relationship. The only things she kept were a few decent items of clothing, some psychiatric textbooks and her cat, Snowflake.

'I've burned my boats,' she said to herself.

She loved that expression. In the past generals would burn their boats so that their men wouldn't be tempted to set off for home when the fighting got too tough. She could see the burning boats before her, flames reflected in water. A beautiful, terrifying sight.

Gisela lay down on her bed and curled up beside her long-haired cat, breathing in its faint, clean smell. Unlike dogs, cats always smelled good. She'd have liked to have a cat-scented perfume.

The cat purred, its soft white coat vibrating gently against her face.

The window was ajar. A blackbird was singing outside. She could hear voices, and the sound of metal scraping against stone. Then she picked up the smell of burning charcoal. Yet another staff party. She wasn't thinking of going.

She closed her eyes, letting the cat's fur caress her cheek and pretending it was Doctor Kalpak's hand.

She would never see Doctor Kalpak at a staff party. He didn't go to parties. She had felt his hand when she arrived at the clinic and introduced herself to him. She had never forgotten the touch of his hand. Slender and brown, with the longest fingers she'd ever seen. It was more like an independent object than a hand. Some sort of animal. A quick, agile, silky animal. A polecat, maybe.

His lilting accent fitted in well up here in the mountains, soft, with a rising note to it, like Austrian or Norwegian. But his expressive hands were his true language: when you saw them you almost forgot to listen to what he was saying.

Gisela Obermann had let go of most of her dreams. One by one she had let them fall and drift off on the harsh winds of life. Yet the dream of one day feeling Doctor Kalpak's hands on her naked body remained, and she would take it out and enjoy it when she was alone.

She shut her eyes again and felt the wine drawing swirling patterns in her brain. She remembered that Max had had a visit today. From his brother. Max was the only one of her clients who still gave her a glimmer of hope. What would a visit like this do to him?

The cat's purring motor speeded up.

43

'I love animals because they are alive without being human.'
Who was it who said that? Mayakovsky? Dostoevsky?

Gisela went back to thinking about Doctor Kalpak's hands.
Two silken polecats padding over her body. One on her
breasts, and the other on her stomach and down between her
thighs.

9

It was dark outside now. Sporadic outdoor lights illuminated the paths in the park surrounding the clinic. Max and Daniel were heading down the hillside towards the village.

'You seem to be able to come and go from the clinic as you choose,' Daniel remarked.

'Of course. The clients here would never accept anything else. As long as I go to bed like a good boy each night, I can do pretty much whatever I want during the day.'

They had reached the bottom of the slope and come to a narrow tarmac road where the lighting was brighter and more regular, like a jogging track. A funny little electric car, bright yellow, was coming towards them with a gentle hum. The driver said hello as he glided past. He was wearing some sort of uniform, like a janitor or hotel porter, and there was a similarly dressed man sitting beside him in the cramped vehicle. Daniel guessed that they belonged to the clinic staff. Absent-mindedly and without comment, Daniel returned the man's greeting, then quickly crossed the road.

They passed a few houses, went round a bend and suddenly

found themselves, without Daniel realising how it had happened, in the centre of the village.

Houses with flower-covered balconies surrounded a small square with a well at its centre. There was a cosy glow from the lead-panelled windows, and from somewhere there came the sound of voices and a dog barking, echoing between the rocky walls of the narrow valley. It was strange to think that people lived their lives in this fairytale world.

Max turned off into an alley and stopped in front of a brown house set in a small garden where coloured lanterns hung from the trees.

'Hannelores Bierstube,' Max explained rather unnecessarily, seeing as the name was written above the doorway like icing, in looping, ornate white lettering.

'And there was me thinking it was the witch's gingerbread house,' Daniel said.

'Who knows?' Max said. 'Are you brave enough to go in?'

'I'd love a beer. Let's forget the idea of coffee and liqueur. A large tankard of cold German beer is exactly what I need. Come on, let's go in. It looks nice.'

'That's what Hansel and Gretel thought too. Well, if you like,' Max said, gesturing to Daniel to go first.

It seemed Max was a regular customer in the gingerbread house, because as soon as they got in he settled down in a corner of the dimly lit room, then turned towards the bar and ordered beer for them both without saying a word, by just holding two fingers in the air. His order was received with a nod by a thickset older woman, and a moment later she was on her way over to them with two huge tankards. She set them down firmly on the table. She had arms as big as a lumberjack's and a mouth like a bulldog's.

'What did I say?' Daniel whispered with a shudder. 'Do you suppose she's going to gobble us up?'

Max shrugged.

'I've been OK so far. I think she's waiting until I get a serious beer belly first. She usually pinches my waist to see how it's coming along. Well, cheers, bro! It's really good to have you here!'

They raised their tankards.

'I feel the same. Much better than I thought, in fact. I never imagined—' Daniel said, but was interrupted by an unexpected 'cuckoo', and only now did he notice the large cuckoo clock on the wall beside them.

The clock played out an entire scenario. Apart from the cuckoo emerging from its door, there was an old man chopping wood and an old woman trying to milk a goat. But the goat kept kicking its hind legs, knocking over the little pot, and the old woman kept having to stand it up again.

'Bloody hell,' Daniel said, taken aback, once the performance was over and the cuckoo had disappeared behind its door.

Max seemed untroubled. He was gulping his beer greedily, and some of the froth ran down on to the table. A skinny man in an apron with thin, back-combed hair appeared out of the gloom like a ghost and wiped the table with a cloth. As the man leaned over into the light of the candle Daniel thought that his jutting cheekbones resembled a skeleton's.

'I take it that was Hansel?' he said after the man had withdrawn with a silent bow. 'He's doing a good job of not letting himself get too fat.'

'There's a Gretel as well. I don't know if she's here today,' Max said, looking round the room. 'Maybe she's been gobbled up already. It wouldn't surprise me. She's fairly tasty. If I didn't have my little Giulietta I might have been tempted to have a nibble.'

'Who's Giulietta? Your latest conquest?'

'Latest, last and only. A stunningly beautiful twenty-two-year-old olive farmer's daughter from Calabria. She still lives at home with her parents, but we're engaged.'

'A twenty-two-year-old! You're thirteen years older than her,' Daniel objected.

'That's not unusual in Calabria. Her parents are very happy with me. I'm mature, experienced and comfortably off.'

'And burned out. In a rehab clinic. But perhaps you haven't told them that?'

'No, I've told them I'm in Sweden on business.'

'What about Giulietta? Is she happy with you as well?'

'She's crazy about me.'

'And does she think you're in Sweden on business too?'

'Yes. But I'm planning to take things a bit easier from now on. When I leave Himmelstal we're going to get married and settle down in Calabria. We're going to have our own olive farm. Children. Seven or eight.'

He nodded happily to himself, as if this was a decision he'd just taken. Then he looked up and asked:

'You don't have any children, do you?'

'No, you know that perfectly well. Emma wanted to wait, and then we got divorced.'

Max put a calming hand on his shoulder.

'There's no rush. Us men have time on our side. It's different for women. Shall we have another beer?'

'I haven't got through this one yet. You have another. I'll pay.'

'You're not paying for anything. You're my guest,' Max said, gesturing with his hand to order a tankard from the bulldog woman.

The room had filled up and the noise level had increased. Most of the clientele were men, but it was hard to form any idea of what sort of people they were seeing as the lighting was so dim. Apart from a few spotlights on the bar, the only lighting was the candles on the tables.

'Your stay here seems to have done you good,' Daniel said. 'I was quite worried when I got your letter.'

'As I said, this is the best clinic in Europe for nervous exhaustion. You should have seen me when I arrived.'

Max tilted his head to one side, stuck his tongue out and crossed his eyes.

'Nervous exhaustion,' Daniel repeated. 'You've never been diagnosed with that before.'

'No. Weirdly enough. Because if you think about it, all my breakdowns occurred following periods of seriously hard work. The last time I was in hospital was after I'd spent a while working twenty-four hours a day. I never slept. It's hardly surprising I got exhausted.'

'But,' Daniel said, 'that sort of hyperactivity is a *symptom* of your illness. Not one of the *causes*.'

'Are you sure about that? Maybe we've been getting it wrong. Maybe we haven't understood what was the chicken and what was the egg. Maybe I've been wrongly diagnosed all these years. The more I think about it, the more likely it seems that I've simply been suffering from recurrent bouts of nervous exhaustion. Exhaustion can express itself in any number of ways.'

'Well,' Daniel said with a yawn, 'if we don't go home to bed, *I'm* going to end up with nervous exhaustion. And I wouldn't like to imagine how that might express itself.'

Just as he said this a few long notes from an accordion broke through the noise of the room, and a moment later a woman started to sing in a low voice with a clear, lilting rhythm. Daniel looked round in surprise.

In the glow of a newly lit spotlight at the far end of the room a young woman had appeared, and was standing there singing, dressed in some sort of peasant costume with a laced bodice and puffed sleeves. She was accompanied on the accordion by a middle-aged man wearing a flowery waistcoat, tight knee-length trousers and a ridiculous flat hat with flowers stuck under the brim.

'Look at that, tourist entertainment,' Daniel exclaimed. 'I thought we were well away from the tourist trail. Maybe I could find a hotel nearby after all.'

'I'm not sure I'd call it tourist entertainment,' Max said nonchalantly. 'More like locals entertaining other locals. They're here a couple of evenings each week. Do you want to listen, or shall we go?'

'We can't go as soon as they've started. Let's wait a bit,' Daniel said.

The woman sang with exaggerated clarity, emphasised by gestures with her hands and eyes, as if she were singing to children. Yet Daniel still understood practically none of her Swiss German. Every now and then she rang a cowbell. It was a long song, with an amusing, narrative text, he understood that much, and after a few verses he found he was able to predict when the cowbell was going to be rung.

'They carry on like that for ages. Come on, let's go,' Max said in his ear, but Daniel shook his head.

There was something about the singer he found fascinating. She had narrow brown eyes, bright red lipstick and a stubby little nose with a scattering of freckles. Her hair was chocolate brown and cut in a short bob with a fringe as straight as a ruler.

Daniel looked at her, trying to work out the nature of her beauty, because it wasn't at all obvious. She was pretty in an enchanting, doll-like way, but beneath the prettiness there was an entirely different sort of face, with heavy, peasant features that could only be seen from certain angles. Daniel could guess what her older relatives looked like, and what she herself would look like one day. There was something enticing about this solid core beneath the pretty exterior, and in no way did it detract from her appeal.

But really it was her eyes that formed the foundation of her beauty, he suddenly realised. They glittered like pulsating stars, and when she held her head still and moved her eyes from side to side, it was as if the glitter flew out and landed on the audience.

Her singing voice was nothing remarkable, and the whole performance was rather ridiculous. Exaggerated. Absurd. The staring eyes moving left and right like a toy's. The overblown gestures: arms folded, head tilted, hands on hips. The red, rubber-band mouth.

And the pudgy, red-cheeked man with the accordion and the stupid hat had to be some sort of joke, surely? A parody of the worst clichés of alpine culture.

The paradox was that the performance, in spite of its over-emphatic nature and childish simplicity, was utterly incomprehensible. Daniel had never heard such a peculiar dialect. It was something to do with cows, he grasped that much. Cows and love. Mad! Mad and tasteless, yet simultaneously, Daniel was forced to admit to his own surprise, deeply fascinating. He sat there enchanted, unable to tear his eyes from the girl.

When she had finished singing, she accepted the feeble applause with a curtsey, holding her skirt coquettishly between forefinger and thumb. Daniel thought the audience was being churlish, and himself applauded loudly. The girl looked in their direction and blinked at him. Or possibly at Max?

'OK, let's take our chance before they start up again,' Max said, getting up.

He walked quickly towards the door. Daniel followed him, walking backwards, still clapping and without taking his eyes from the singer.

When they reached the door the accordionist played a long, drawn-out note, and they started to sing a duet, but Max had already dragged Daniel into the garden, where rows of red and green lanterns swung among the leaves of the trees, then out into the alley.

'I'm sorry if I'm rushing you, but we have to be back in our rooms and cabins by midnight at the latest. That's the only rule at the clinic.'

'Who is she?' Daniel asked.

'The singer? Her name's Corinne. She's at Hannelores Bierstube pretty much every night. Sometimes she sings, sometimes she serves drinks,' Max replied.

They turned off the road and on to the path leading up through the patch of fir trees towards the hospital. It soon got dark when they left the lights of the village behind them, and the smell of the trees was intense. All of a sudden Daniel felt extremely tired.

'Do you think the clinic could help me get a taxi first thing tomorrow morning?' he asked. 'To take me to the nearest railway station?'

'You're leaving tomorrow? But you've only just got here!' Max exclaimed in disappointment, stopping on the path. 'Most relatives stay a week.'

'Well, I only planned . . .'

'Yes, what had you planned? A free holiday in the Alps at my expense? Spend an hour visiting your crazy brother, then go off and have some fun?'

'No. Well . . . I don't know.'

Daniel was so tired now that he couldn't think straight. He couldn't see how he was going to make it back up the hill to Max's cabin. His legs felt soft, like jelly. And the way his brother was talking was making him feel guilty. It was true that Max had actually paid for his trip.

'Do what you want. But I'd really appreciate it if you stayed another day. There's so much I'd like to show you,' Max said, suddenly sounding gentle and beseeching.

They carried on up the steep path. Through the trees they could make out one of the modern steel-and-glass buildings of the clinic. Only the upper floor was lit up, which made it look like a hovering spaceship.

'It really is lovely here,' Daniel said. 'Do you know, to start with I thought your letter came from Hell. I misread the post-mark.'

Max burst out laughing, as though Daniel had said something incredibly funny. They were weaving through the trees and Daniel almost stumbled over a tree root, but Max caught hold of him, still laughing.

'Wonderful! That's wonderful! Do you know the story about the man who rowed the boat to Hell?'

'No.'

'Anna used to tell it to me when I was little. There was this man who was doomed to row the dead across the river to Hell. Back and forth, back and forth, for all eternity. He was utterly sick of it, but he couldn't think how to escape it. Then one day he worked it out. Do you know what he did?'

'No?'

'He had to get someone else to take over the oars. Do you get it? As easy as that. He just needed to get one of his passengers to row for a bit. And then he'd be free and could get away, while the other man was left to row for all eternity.'

Max couldn't stop laughing at his own story.

They had reached the park now. Moths were fluttering round the lamps. Then they were blinded by headlights and a moment later one of the funny electric buggies came rolling down the path. A young man leaned out and called cheerily as he glided past:

'So, this is where you've got to, is it? Evening round in twenty minutes, Max, don't forget!'

'Oh God, we'd better speed up,' Max muttered.

Five minutes later they stepped inside the little cabin at the top of the slope, out of breath.

Without getting undressed, having a wash or brushing his teeth, Daniel lay down on the bench by the wall that Max had said would be his bed. He felt ready to pass out. Max tossed him a blanket and pillow.

'You'll have to forgive me, but it's been a long day,' Daniel muttered, already drifting off to sleep.

A loud knock woke him up with a start.

'Coming!' Max shouted from the bathroom, where he was brushing his teeth.

In only his underwear, with his toothbrush still in his mouth, he went over to the door.

'The evening round,' he explained as he went past, his mouth full of foam from the toothpaste.

Through half-open eyes Daniel watched as a woman in a pale blue dress (a 'hostess', as they were evidently called) and a man in a pale blue steward's uniform (a 'host'?) took a couple of steps inside the room and then stopped and nodded with a friendly smile. They glanced quickly round the room, caught sight of Daniel under his blanket on the bench and the man whispered:

'Your brother's already asleep? Sleep well, Max, and have a good day together tomorrow.'

Max said something inaudible with his toothbrush in his mouth. The man and woman quickly slipped out again. Daniel heard them knock at the next cabin and exchange a few words with its resident. Then another knock further away.

He closed his eyes. Everything he had experienced during this long, peculiar day was rushing through his brain, all out of order and muddled. Voices, sensory impressions, little things he didn't even know he had noticed.

On the edge of sleep a memory popped up, crystal clear in every detail: the uniformed men who had stopped them at the roadblock. Their faces below the peaks of their caps. The metal detector. The deserted, shaded road. The rock face with its ferns, the trickles of water and the smell of rock and damp. For a moment his brain was utterly awake, full of an anxiety he hadn't felt at the time.

Then he tumbled helplessly off into sleep. As he might have expected, his dreams were restless and confused. Only one of them etched itself into his consciousness and would stay with him for most of the following morning: Corinne in her laced-up dress. She was standing on the isolated road beside the rock face, and was blocking his path by swinging her cowbell high above her head. He stopped the car – he was driving, there was no taxi driver in the dream – and got out.

She rang the bell and the sound was thrown back by the mountains. Then she came across to him and ran the cowbell over his body, first the back, then the front, playful and laughing.

As she held it over his chest she suddenly became serious, as if she had discovered something. (He was bare-chested now, unless he had been the whole time?) She pressed the cowbell to his skin, right where his heart was, then frowned in concentration, her eyes narrowing to slits as she listened, trying to detect something vibrating.

He knew what she had picked up on, he could hear it himself now: his heart was pounding so hard and fast that it was close to bursting.

She's found out! Everything's lost! he thought, as if his heart had been a stowaway he was trying to smuggle past, but which had given itself away.

Except, in the dream the woman wasn't called Corinne, but *Corinte*, he knew this even though neither of them had uttered a word. It was do with her eyes.

10

The smell of fried bacon was the first thing he noticed when he woke up the next morning. When he opened his eyes the cabin was lit up by strong sunlight. Max was standing by the stove.

Daniel squinted at his watch and saw to his surprise that it was twenty past nine. He almost always woke up at quarter to seven, weekdays and weekends alike, with or without an alarm clock. It was hard to believe he had been able to sleep with the sunlight flooding the room and the sound of Max clattering about in the kitchen.

'Breakfast in five minutes,' Max said in a slightly stressed voice as he got plates out and slammed the cupboard shut.

Daniel hurried into the bathroom and had a quick shower, then, with a feeling of having fallen behind the curve he sat down at the table where Max was already sitting eating. Through the window there was a view of the steep, shaded mountainside to the south.

'Well, there's certainly nothing wrong with your sleep,' Max said, pouring coffee into Daniel's cup. 'But it's good you've had a proper rest, because we're going on an adventure today. We're going to cycle up into the mountains and go fishing at my favourite spot.'

'Cycle?'

'Yes, and don't try to get out of it by saying you haven't got a bike, because I sorted that while you were asleep. And I've asked for a packed lunch from the kitchen as well. I could have made it myself, but I haven't got much in the fridge right now and I didn't think we should waste time going shopping in the village. They'll put together something nice, and we can pick it up before we set off.'

Daniel couldn't recall them planning an outing for today.

'You do know I'm leaving today? I did say,' he reminded Max.

So as not to seem ungrateful, he quickly added: 'Yesterday was fun. Dinner was first rate. And I liked that bierstube. But it didn't feel right, you paying for me.'

His brother waved away his objections, saying:

'I didn't think we'd had enough time together. And you've hardly seen anything of how lovely it is round here. Have you ever been trout fishing?'

'No.'

'You're really missing something. It's incredibly tense. Total concentration. You must try it. Anyway, now I've asked for a packed lunch, and arranged rods and bikes for us. So I'd be very disappointed if you decided to leave straightaway.'

Daniel gave up.

'OK, then. If you've already got it all planned, I'll come with you.'

Outside the cabin stood two mountain bikes with panniers strapped to them, and out of each bag stuck an oblong case that Daniel guessed contained a fishing rod.

They walked the bikes up to the main building of the

clinic, where Max slipped round to the kitchen and returned shortly afterwards with some plastic tubs and bottles of beer that he stowed away in the panniers. With Max in the lead they rolled off down the slope, then turned to the right and followed a narrow road that ran above the village.

They soon got away from the houses and now the valley lay before them, such an intense green that it gave Daniel a feeling of unreality, as if he were in some sort of computer game.

And their speed seemed somehow unreal as well. Had he always been able to cycle this fast? They really were racing along. It had to be the bike, its gears were excellent, overcoming all resistance. They were flying.

Maybe it was something to do with the air as well. Everything around him was so clear and distinct, down to the smallest detail, he could see every flower in the distance.

They were cycling through a narrow glacial valley. On the side they were on, the mountain rose up in sloping meadows and forests. Above, the mountainside was steep and bare, covered with fallen debris that made it resemble a huge gravel quarry.

On the other side of the valley there was no slope. The mountain rose vertically like a wall in a very peculiar way. A road clung to the mountainside and Daniel could see a van driving along in the distance. Of course, that was the road he had arrived on the day before. And that was the rock face that had been covered with moss and ferns.

Max was cycling ahead of him, leaning forward as if he was in a race. Every now and then he looked back and smiled at Daniel. He had a beautiful smile, with white teeth and a masculine bone structure. He looks handsome, Daniel thought, then realised at the same moment that he himself ought to look handsome as well. As identical twins, they had an opportunity denied to most people: seeing themselves from every angle. From behind, and in profile, and at speed on a bicycle.

It was quite different to looking in a mirror, and seeing your-self the wrong way round, right and left reversed, observer and observed at the same time.

'So that's what I look like without a beard,' Daniel thought, and immediately decided to shave his beard off as soon as he got home. (He looked ten years older with it, he had once been told by an unguarded female colleague.)

The beard had its own story. Daniel had started to let it grow when he was nineteen years old, and he could remember the circumstances and reason very well.

He had been in London visiting Max, who was living in a sublet flat in Camden. His brother had been an attentive host, taking him out on the town.

When Daniel bought a rude T-shirt from a market he hardly had time to pay before Max bought one just like it and put it on. Daniel hadn't wanted to, but Max had insisted that they both wear their T-shirts, so he had reluctantly agreed. Max had his arm round Daniel's shoulders, and laughed whenever people looked at them and pointed. Daniel had felt uncomfortable, as if their similarity were some sort of defect.

They reached a street lined with pubs and restaurants. Daniel wanted to go into one that looked interesting, but Max had led them instead into another pub that was big, smoky and noisy, where they were showing football on wide-screen televisions.

While Daniel jostled at the bar with Max and his friends, he caught sight of a girl sitting at a table and eating alone. She was platinum blonde, thin, almost transparent somehow, like milky glass. There was something about the way she moved, the way she raised her fork, looking straight ahead without actually focusing on anything. Something determined, self-aware, almost aggressive.

Max noticed his interest at once.

'Bet you she's Swedish,' he hissed close to Daniel's face. It was hard to make yourself heard in there. The televisions were at full volume and the clientele were shouting and yelling in response to the match.

'There are loads of Swedes here, you can spot them at a glance. And I'll bet you something else.' Max leaned even closer, so that their noses were almost touching. His eyes were twinkling from intoxication, beads of sweat stood out on his forehead, and he had bad breath. 'She's a virgin.'

Then Max's friends had wanted to move on somewhere else, but Daniel didn't want to go with them.

'You go,' he said to Max. 'I'm going to stay here a bit longer.'

Once they had gone he went over to the girl's table and asked if he could sit down. She was eating fish and chips, it looked greasy and unappetising, but she was gamely struggling through mouthful after mouthful.

'Are you actually enjoying that?' Daniel asked in Swedish.

'Oh yes, I really . . .' she began to say in a tense voice, then stopped herself. 'You're Swedish! Well, er, no, not really. But I'm trying.'

She was an au pair for a family with three children. She had graduated from high school that spring, from the science programme, and wanted to become a chemical engineer. But first she wanted to get some experience and see a bit of the world. She was hating it and longed to go home. She had one day off each week, but it was hard to make friends, she didn't know where to go. And to her despair she had discovered that she was bad at English. She'd had top marks at school, but the people here didn't sound anything like they did in British television programmes and she could hardly understand a word.

Daniel had asked why she didn't just go home if she was having such a bad time. She had straightened her back, stuck her chin out and said she wasn't going to give up. She never gave up. She was her parents' only child and they were very proud of her.

'It's tough being an only child,' she said. 'Sometimes I wish I had brothers and sisters. Have you got any?'

To his surprise Daniel heard himself say 'No.' He didn't know why, but at that moment he didn't feel like going into the whole business of being a twin. It was a subject that always drew attention to itself, and threw a shadow over everything else.

'So you know what it's like,' she said.

They spent ages talking, maybe a couple of hours. The girl said she hadn't talked so much in months. She was evidently very lonely. No boyfriend, no female friends.

There was something special about her. Something fragile but at the same time strong and unyielding. A girl of glass and steel, Daniel had thought. She had the sort of very blonde eyelashes that most girls would have made darker with mascara, but she wasn't wearing any makeup at all. She was quite excitable. Her pale face would turn bright pink and her pupils would expand and reveal a blackness that was both enticing and scary.

To his astonishment Daniel realised that he was falling in love. In a painful, fateful and wonderfully absurd way that was entirely new to him. He felt great respect for this girl, almost adoration, and at the same time a desire that threatened to burn him up.

He had drunk a lot of beer over the course of the evening, and when he had to excuse himself to go to the toilet, he had a chance to think through what seemed to be happening. What was he going to do? Should he ask for her phone number? Would they stay in touch after he went back to Sweden? Maybe he could move here, study at some English university or get a job, washing up or something? His

61

thoughts were racing round his head as he stood in the jostling queue for the toilet. He was worried about having to wait so long. She wouldn't think he'd just left, would she? What if she got tired and went home?

When he finally returned he saw that his seat was taken. Max was sitting there talking to the girl. He had left his friends and come back. Presumably he had been standing somewhere in the crowd at the bar watching Daniel and the girl. And had taken the chance to step into his place when he went to the toilet.

The girl was completely absorbed in the conversation, laughing out loud. Daniel would hardly have recognised her, she suddenly seemed much prettier. He realised he had never seen her laugh. During her long conversation with Daniel she hadn't laughed once. But Max was evidently saying something extremely funny, because the whole of her thin, pale face was transformed by laughter.

And then, still laughing, the pair of them had stood up and left the pub together without so much as a glance in Daniel's direction.

With his heart pounding with humiliation and anger he ordered a beer, downed it, then went off to another pub, the one he had wanted to go in to begin with, which looked nice and old-fashioned. But a bouncer had stopped him, and with a frosty look had uttered the peculiar words:

'You're never coming back in here, you know that. Not after what you did.'

Taken aback, Daniel went to another pub, where he was let in without any problem. He drank until he could hardly stand, then, hours later, took a taxi back to Max's flat. But there was no answer when he rang the doorbell, and he had to spend the night on a park bench.

The next day Max let him in, and said with a triumphant smile:

'I was right. She was Swedish. *And* a virgin.'

When Daniel had showered and got his razor out to tidy himself up after the night's carousing, he suddenly changed his mind and angrily wiped away the shaving foam. He wasn't going to shave. He was going to grow a beard. He never wanted to be confused with his brother again.

11

'Here it is,' Max said breathlessly. 'This is my favourite place.'

He pointed with his rod as he moved among the rocks in a dam-like, still section of the rapids. All around him the water tumbled down small waterfalls and drops.

'There's a little pool behind these rocks. There are usually five or six of them here, floating motionless. You just have to fish them out. I haven't shown this place to anyone else. Only you.'

During the next couple of hours they were completely absorbed with fishing. Daniel wasn't used to it, but he was a quick learner and by lunchtime his casting technique was pretty good. He had had no idea that his brother was a keen fisherman. He guessed it was the element of gambling that appealed.

'Do many tourists come up here?' Daniel asked when they'd sat down on a flat rock and Max had got their lunch from the bikes that they'd left in a clump of fir trees nearby.

'Tourists? In Himmelstal?'

Max handed him a ham sandwich and laughed as if Daniel had said something funny.

'I mean, it's so beautiful here,' Daniel added.

'Not beautiful enough. The valley is narrow and shaded and the mountains are too steep for skiing or hiking. No, no one comes to Himmelstal for the scenery. They come here to avoid being seen.' Max opened a bottle of beer and held the cap in place to stop the frothing liquid from escaping. 'This valley is a hideaway.'

'A hideaway?'

Max took a deep swig of beer, then sat there, one leg raised, with the bottle in his hand. He gazed out over the rapids and said:

'This has been a hiding place since the Middle Ages. There used to be a convent here where they looked after lepers. Right where the clinic is now. The convent is long gone but the old churchyard is still there at the bottom of the hill. Only lepers could be buried there, no one else. Banished even in death. Unclean.'

He picked up a pine cone and threw it angrily into the water, where it was caught by the current and twisted round and round.

'A vile disease,' Daniel agreed. 'I can imagine that there might have been a sanatorium here as well. After all, the Alps are full of old sanatoriums that have been turned into hotels and private clinics.'

Max snorted.

'Oh, no. Tuberculosis patients were a completely different class. They never came to Himmelstal. It was far too inaccessible. No railway. And no vehicle access before the 1950s.'

'How do you know all this?' Daniel asked, impressed.

'I got sent a brochure when I signed up for the clinic. Sometime during the 1800s the convent was rebuilt as a home for the disabled. For people with learning difficulties, the mentally ill and handicapped. In other words, new groups of undesirables that society wanted to hide out of the way. The staff lived in the village, or in the home itself, and they were pretty much self-sufficient. It must have been like its own little world. Then the whole place burned down. A number of patients died. One of the patients is rumoured to have started the fire.'

There was a pause as Max took another swig of beer, and Daniel saw a series of unpleasant images in his mind's eye. To get rid of them he said:

'Didn't it used to be a cosmetic surgery clinic as well? That's what the taxi driver who drove me up here said.'

'That's right. The perfect hideaway for freshly operated faces. Christ, what a place. A dumping ground for poor bastards for hundreds of years. Sometimes I think you can sense it back there at the clinic. Bad vibes. That's why I try to get away as often as I can. Down into the village or up here to the rapids.'

A fish jumped out of the water. Like a discarded knife it arced past and landed in the bubbling eddies of one of the higher pools.

'They're amazingly strong,' Daniel exclaimed.

Max smiled grimly.

'They don't get far. There's a sluice just up there. That's what makes this such a good spot for fishing. Right, let's carry on.'

Max got to his feet and grabbed his rod.

Daniel was able to manage without instruction now and Max moved to a rock further out in the rapids. Twenty metres apart they each stood and fished on their own. They shouted to each other every now and then, holding up their catches whenever they caught something, congratulating each other. Otherwise they were silent, concentrating on the fishing and their own thoughts. The air was full of the smell of fir trees, and above the noise of the water Daniel imagined he could hear the sound of cowbells every so often. It sounded like the cowbell the girl in the bierstube had rung during her song.

The two brothers had now been together for the best part of twenty-four hours. And so far nothing had happened. No violent flashes of temper, no malicious remarks, no stupid practical jokes. Max seemed harmonious, happy. A bit restless, maybe, but that was part of his character.

Daniel was also discovering that he had become more tolerant of his brother's slightly pushy manner, his self-absorption and inability to listen. He didn't find it upsetting, as he had done so often when he was younger. Max was evidently pleased to have him there. He'd taken him out to dinner, and here they were, fishing together. That was what Max had to offer, and these days Daniel understood the value of that sort of gift. Maybe they had finally found a frequency on which they could communicate as adults, as independent people.

The monotonous roar of the rapids, the whispering trees and the distant cowbells put Daniel into a sort of meditative state. He hardly even noticed that Max had left his stone and was now cleaning the fish at the edge of the water. He only woke up when Max shouted at him to go and fetch some wood for a fire.

There was wood under the trees, covered by a waterproof arrangement of branches and tarpaulin. The cut sections of wood had the letters 'T O M' written on them in bright pink spray paint.

'This wood's been marked. Is it OK to take some of it?' Daniel called.

'It's fine. I know the farmer,' Max said from down by the river.

He had clearly made a lot of new contacts at the bierstube in the village.

A short while later they were sitting by a small fire, and

while they were waiting for the flames to die down Max said:

'Can I ask a favour?'

He said it in a breezy tone of voice. Maybe it was to do with passing him something he couldn't reach, or getting something, more wood perhaps. But these simple words, so gently and pleasantly uttered, struck Daniel like a punch. The air went out of him and he had to take several deep breaths before he could talk again.

'Oh?' he said stiffly.

Max stirred the embers with a stick, and seemed preoccupied with this for a moment. Finally he said:

'I've got some problems.'

'What with?'

'I've been at the clinic for a while now and the bill has mounted up badly. Personal trainer, tennis lessons, mental coaching, massage, food and wine. No one ever mentions money, it simply gets added to the invoice. In the end it feels like it's all free, even though you know it's absurdly expensive.'

'You can't pay the bill, is that what you're trying to say?'

'One of the hostesses handed it over in a pale blue envelope during the late-night round. Discreet, smiling. I didn't open the envelope until she'd gone. I almost fainted.'

Daniel felt upset. He found the clinic's payment methods very odd, and in Max's case distinctly inappropriate. Maybe they weren't aware of his problems? But he composed himself and said as calmly as he could:

'I can't pay to get you out of the clinic, if that's what you're thinking. I work as a supply teacher, and I'll be unemployed as of this autumn. I just don't have the money.'

Max crushed some glowing pieces of wood with his stick.

'I'm not asking you for money,' he said tersely. 'I've got money.'

Instead of being reassured by this response, Daniel felt even more anxious.

'So what's the problem?'

'The problem is that I can't get at my money. I can't leave the clinic without paying the bill. And I can't pay the bill without leaving the clinic. Catch 22.'

'But you're away from the clinic now, aren't you?' Daniel said. 'You come and go as you like.'

'Only as long as I'm in my cabin at eight o'clock in the morning and twelve o'clock at night. The staff make daily rounds. To keep an eye on us, as they put it. But in reality they're making sure that no one tries to get away without paying.'

'So why do you have to leave the clinic? Can't you just transfer the money over the internet or something?'

'The money isn't in a bank account. It's somewhere where it needs to be moved to somewhere else. In person. Not digitally. In cash. The mafia are a bit old-fashioned when it comes to that.'

'Oh,' Daniel said, taken aback. 'I'm not sure I'm quite with you now. Are you doing business with the mafia, Max?'

Max shrugged his shoulders beseechingly. Far in the distance came the quirky, clanging sound as the cows moved. Sometimes there was only a solitary little ring, sometimes a whole peal.

'Not if I can help it. But in this case I had no choice. I won't bore you with the details. But I've got money to collect there. An investment I made that's paid off, so to speak. Not strictly legal, as you can probably imagine.'

Daniel wasn't particularly surprised. Max had got mixed up in things before. There had been proceedings and court cases. But, as far as Daniel was aware, they had all been in the civil courts. He had never actually been accused of breaking the law. Had he?

'This is positively the last time I ever do a deal like this, you can be sure of that,' Max said through clenched teeth. 'I hate those criminal bastards. They've got no morals at all. The problem is that I'm in debt to those scum.'

'The mafia?'

It felt unreal, and almost rather thrilling, to use that word in conversation with his own brother.

'Yes, I was forced to borrow some investment capital. And I would have paid off every last penny if things hadn't got messed up and the profit been delayed. You don't need to know the details,' Max said quickly when Daniel looked as if he was about to ask a question. 'I worked day and night to be able to repay the debt. You don't miss a payment when you've got creditors like that. I asked for an extension, but they wouldn't even talk to me. And then I collapsed and signed myself in here. Not long after I arrived I got a letter from the guy I borrowed the money from. I don't know how he got hold of the address. Clinics like this are supposed to be protected by all sorts of confidentiality, but he knew exactly where I was. He gave me a new deadline for repayment of the loan. A date. And a threat.'

'He threatened you?' Daniel said, horrified.

Max shook his head.

'Not me. Giulietta. In a few brief lines he implied that he knew that Giulietta was my fiancée, and the times when she usually goes to the market, and said he hoped that nothing bad ever happened to her.'

'Bloody hell.'

'Now I've heard that my investments have come good, exactly as I thought they would, even if it's taken time. I could repay the debt straight away. The problem is, I'm in debt here at the clinic as well, and they won't let me go and get the money. Do you see my problem?'

Daniel was starting to realise what Max wanted to ask him.

'I can't get your money for you, Max. I want to help you, but I'm not going to get mixed up in anything criminal. There's a limit to how much help I'm prepared to offer.'

Max stared at him in astonishment, then burst out laughing.

'No, no, Daniel. I'd never ask that of you. You wouldn't be able to do it. Dealing with the mafia is a science in itself.'

To his surprise, Daniel felt hurt. Somewhere deep down he had already made up his mind that he might just let himself be persuaded to take this on, something entirely new in his life.

'But you said you wanted to ask a favour?' he reminded Max. 'What do you want me to do?'

'Nothing, really. No more than you've been doing today and yesterday. Have a beer at Hannelores Bierstube. Cycle up here and go fishing. Wander the alpine meadows. The sort of thing you were planning to do anyway during your holiday in Switzerland. But without having to pay for a hotel.'

'I don't follow.'

'No? I'm asking you to stay here while I sort things out. Three, four days at most. You take my place.'

Max looked Daniel in the eye and went on:

'I leave here as Daniel. You stay here as Max. We're identical twins, had you forgotten?'

Daniel sighed and raised his eyes.

'Like those stupid games we used to play as children? Or when you took a girl from me in London? Do you think it's as easy as that? Besides, we're not even particularly similar any more. No one's pointed out how alike we are since I got here, have you thought about that? Not at the clinic, or in the bierstube. No second glances, no whispering, no comments. "Oh, are you twins, that's great!" No one's so much as raised an eyebrow.'

Max smiled scornfully.

'But how could they see how similar we are when you've got half your face hidden?' With these last words he leaned in close to Daniel, pinching his thumb and forefinger together as if he were thinking of grabbing Daniel's beard.

Instinctively Daniel leaned back, his hand flying up to protect his cheek.

'That's why you grew that ridiculous thing, isn't it?' Max went on. 'So we wouldn't look the same? You wanted a face of your own. It works, actually, I've noticed it too. But beneath the disguise you look exactly the same as me. All you need to do is shave it off, Daniel, and we'd be like two peas in a pod.'

'So, I shave my beard off. And look like you. And your beard grows overnight and you look like me?' Daniel said sarcastically. 'If your beard grows the same rate as mine, it'll take you several months to get one like this.'

'If it's real, yes.'

Daniel let out a short laugh.

'You're thinking of wearing a false beard? Well, that's one way to convince them that you're mad. This isn't one of your silly student pranks. A cheap false beard – assuming you could even get hold of one here, which I doubt – would look ridiculous. It wouldn't fool anyone.'

Max carefully folded a piece of foil containing the bare fishbones. He licked his fingers and put the foil in the pannier beside him.

'Who said anything about a cheap false beard?' he said calmly. 'Here at the Himmelstal clinic we don't do anything on the cheap. Everything, from the toilet paper to the oriental rugs in reception, is of the very highest quality. Are you done?'

He pointed at Daniel's piece of foil, with its few scraps of fish and bones. Daniel nodded, and said:

'And why would a rehab clinic have false beards at all?'

'We have a little theatre, you know,' Max said, taking care of Daniel's foil in the same neat way as his own. 'A proper theatre with a stage and dressing rooms and everything. It's used as an auditorium for lectures, conferences and so on. And also theatrical performances. The clients themselves perform, as a sort of therapy. For instance, I played Sun, the pilot, in *The Good Woman of Setzuan*. Much admired by the audience.'

'I can imagine,' Daniel said tartly. 'Did you have a false beard?'

'No. But when I saw the collection of beards in the costume store, I realised the possibilities. It's quite an impressive stock. The hostess in charge of props buys in hair from a company in Britain. They supply all the big theatres and opera houses in Europe. Crêpe hair, it's called. It's made from wool from Scottish sheep, and is supplied in plaits of various different shades. You stick it on a bit at a time with special glue, then cut it however you want it. There's a particular technique you have to learn. But as a member of the drama group I've got a key to the costume store, so I've been able to put in a bit of practice. As a matter of fact, I've got quite good at it.'

He pointed at Daniel's beard.

'We've got that dark brown, almost black colour in the store, and I reckon I could come up with a beard like yours without too much trouble.'

Daniel wanted to protest, but Max went on calmly:

'Of course the beard isn't the only difference between us. There's the way we move. I've been studying you carefully since you arrived, and I think I've got you pretty well now. That stiffness you had when you were younger is more pronounced. You sort of turn your whole body instead of just your head. Do you have trouble with your joints? A bad neck? No, you're probably just a bit awkward. You ought to do more exercise. And those gestures you make with your wrists. As if you're trying to delineate what you're talking about. Putting. Everything. In. A. Little. Square. Box.'

Max demonstrated with his own hands. Encouraged by his success, he stood up and started strutting around the clearing, stiff and straight-backed, gesticulating and pretending to have a conversation.

'There, that's it, you see? I know what it's all about. All under control. Completely under control.'

He put his hands together elegantly, and nodded sagely.

'Then there's this, I almost forgot!' he cried in delight.

With an anxious expression he raised his hands to his cheeks and squeaked:

'Don't touch my beard! Don't hit me!'

Daniel jerked as if he'd had an electric shock. Max's performance was exaggerated, but disconcertingly accurate, he had to admit.

He himself had always been good at imitating other people's speech, which had been very useful when it came to learning foreign languages. Now he realised that Max possessed the same talent, but to a considerably larger extent. His brother's skill at mimicry went beyond speech to encompass the entire physical register: expressions, glances, gait, gestures. It was impressive, and alarming. Daniel felt a pang of relief when Max went back to his own languid body language.

'What do you think?' Max asked expectantly as he stamped on the ashes of the burned-out fire. 'Did I miss anything?'

'No, I think you got most of it,' Daniel said curtly.

'Great! Praise from the highest judge. Well, perhaps it's time to be getting home. And now you know how to catch trout. You've going to manage absolutely fine for a few days.'

'Don't be stupid. It'll never work.'

'We'll see,' Max said as he fixed the pannier to the bike frame. 'We'll see.'

12

During their journey back through the valley Max suddenly pulled alongside Daniel, leaned towards him and said in a breathless, intense voice:

'I'm begging you, Daniel, please, do me this favour. I'll never ask for anything ever again. But this is a matter of life or death. I mean that literally. Life or death. All I'm asking is that you make sure you're in my cabin every morning and evening when the hostesses do their checks.'

'That's all? Don't you get any sort of treatment?'

Max slowed his pace.

'Gisela Obermann, my doctor, is trying to get me to go for therapy, but I'm not exactly keen. She might try to persuade you while you're here. All you have to do is say no, because that's what I usually do. Anyway, I think she's given up. There's no point unless you're properly motivated.'

'What about the other patients? I mean, you know people here. How am I supposed to behave towards them?' Daniel said, then realised that his question could be taken to mean that he had already agreed to Max's suggestion.

'I don't really socialise with anyone. Maybe a few words

about the weather, that type of thing. You can manage that. And remember: the language at the clinic is English. For patients and staff alike. Don't try to show off with your German or French.'

'But surely a lot of people here have German or French as their mother tongue?' Daniel said.

'Not all. This is an international environment. So stick to English. Otherwise people might get annoyed. There are some paranoid types here who might think you were gossiping about them if they couldn't understand you.'

The sun had gone down behind the mountain and dusk was filling the valley. High up on the northern slope, just before the green meadows were replaced by the part of the mountain that resembled a gravel quarry, Daniel could see a car's headlights moving at low speed. So there was evidently a road up there as well.

'I really don't know, Max,' he said. 'Isn't there some other way I could help you?'

Max shook his head firmly.

'This is the best way. The only way.'

They had reached the village now, and turned up towards the clinic. They parked the bikes at the back of the main building, leaving them unlocked.

'You can borrow a bike whenever you need one. And you can ask for fishing tackle in reception,' Max said. 'Before we go back I'll show you the library. If I remember rightly, you read a lot.'

They headed up the slope towards two of the glass-fronted buildings.

'We might as well check out the fitness centre too,' Max said, leading the way into the first building.

On the ground floor they peered into a sports hall. A lone man was dribbling a ball around the vast space, trying to get the ball through a basketball hoop.

'You don't play any ball games, do you, but maybe the gym might be something for you?'

The gym was large, well-equipped, situated on the first floor in a brightly lit room. The high-tech machines and sweaty, panting people made Daniel think of a factory in a science-fiction film.

'There's everything you could ever want here,' Max said, but was drowned out by a roar that made Daniel jump.

A man beside them was lifting a heavy bar with his muscly, tattooed arms, holding it up precariously as he grimaced with pain.

'And next to the changing room there's a sauna and jacuzzi,' Max went on, unconcerned. 'OK, I'll show you where to borrow books.'

The next building contained a library, classrooms and the combined theatre and auditorium. As they went inside, Max suggested that Daniel take a look around the library while he ran a quick errand.

'You don't need a card or anything. Just give your name to the librarian. *My* name.' he corrected himself, then left Daniel with a pat on his shoulder.

Daniel wandered aimlessly around the library. It seemed unusually well stocked for a hospital library. The journals section was impressive, with publications covering all manner of subjects in various languages. He leafed through a number of them, then carried on his tour of the shelves. Through the glass wall he could see that the lamps in the park were now lit.

Fifteen minutes or so later Max appeared.

'It's good, isn't it? You can even get Swedish books and newspapers here.'

They went out and Max led him past the swimming pool and tennis courts, all deserted at this time of the evening.

'There's not much wrong with it as a holiday resort, is

there?' Max said. 'Don't you think you could put up with it for a few days?'

'That's not the point,' Daniel muttered.

Back in the cabin Max put on some modern jazz and poured them each a glass of whisky. They settled into the armchairs and Max talked about the group on the recording. It was a Dutch jazz ensemble, incredibly talented, he'd borrowed it from another patient.

'I thought you never socialised with anyone?' Daniel pointed out.

'There are a few people here who stick to the right level. Keep your distance. Don't get too involved. People don't mind lending books and CDs to one another. That sort of thing's fine. You don't want to seem unpleasant, after all. Besides, we're all in the same boat. But I'm really not interested in any more serious conversation than that.'

Daniel nodded sympathetically, tilted his glass and looked down at the golden liquid.

'Where did you get the whisky?'

'I bought it in the village. It's not one of the expensive ones. Not bad though, is it?'

There was a knock on the door, and before either of them had time to get up the door flew open and one of the hostesses looked in. She was pretty, like a little girl, with big blue eyes and her hair in a ponytail.

'Good evening, gentlemen. Have you had a nice day?'

'Wonderful. I took my brother up to the rapids. He demonstrated a definite talent for fishing.'

'Really, you went fishing? Did you catch anything?'

The hostess was standing in the doorway while her male colleague nodded in greeting behind her.

'Yes, but we ate them all, so there was nothing left for the restaurant today. But my brother's bloody good at trout fishing. I've been trying to persuade him to stay a while, so we can maintain a steady supply for the restaurant, but he's eager to get away.'

'Don't you like it here in Himmelstal?' The hostess turned her little doll's face to Daniel, and her look of surprise was replaced by one of understanding. 'Well, this is quite an unusual place. Perhaps not as bad as you were expecting?'

'I think it's rather wonderful here,' Daniel said truthfully. 'In fact ...'

But the hostess had already stepped back and was about to close the door.

'Sleep well!' she called.

Her colleague echoed her somewhere out there, and then they were gone.

'More whisky?' Max asked.

Without waiting for an answer he refilled Daniel's glass.

'Just a small one, then. Thanks, that's fine.'

Max turned the music up.

'I love this.'

They sat for a while, listening. The music was soft, relaxed, with an unusual, looping melody.

'And they're Dutch, you said?' Daniel asked.

Max got up and read the group's name from the cover with some uncertainty. Then they carried on listening in silence, sipping their whisky.

'It's been a good day, hasn't it?' Max said.

Daniel nodded.

'A bit like our birthdays used to be.'

'Yes. The first act,' Daniel said.

Their extravagant, carefully arranged birthday parties always used to follow the same pattern: joy at seeing each other again, carefree games that got wilder and wilder and ended in squabbling, tears and, not infrequently, some sort of accident: a fall from a tree, a badly aimed dart, a hard ball to the head.

Max gave a wry smile.

'Do you remember when we jumped from swings while they were still moving, to see who could get furthest?'

'Yes, when I looked to see how far you'd got, the swing hit me in the head and knocked me out, and I ended up with concussion,' Daniel said.

'But we used to have a lot of fun when we saw each other as well. I don't know why we didn't meet up more often,' Max said, getting up.

He dug deep into the pockets of his shorts and pulled out something that looked like a small coil of rope and put it on the table.

Daniel said:

'I think they had some sort of arrangement. Mum and Dad. And I suppose there was a lot of old history between them.'

'You were lucky, getting brought up by Mum,' Max said as he carried on pulling things from his pockets.

He went and fetched a shaving mirror, which he set up on the table, then moved one of the floor lamps. Daniel watched him curiously, but let him get on with it.

'You were OK with Dad, weren't you?'

'You reckon?' Max gave a short, joyless laugh as he adjusted the angle of the lamp so that the light fell just right. 'He was always working. I didn't get brought up by Dad but by Anna. And obviously you know . . . ' – he glanced at Daniel with a demonic grin – ' . . . that all stepmothers are witches.'

'But Anna was the one who taught you to walk and talk and everything,' Daniel pointed out.

'Children learn to walk and talk on their own.'

'She devoted loads of time and attention to you. I remember her having long phone calls with Mum, telling her how you were developing and what progress you were making. She was totally engaged in you.'

Max sat down at the table. He inspected his face in the mirror, fine-tuned the lamp, and said:

'The same way a scientist is engaged in a laboratory mouse, sure. Because she was a scientist first and foremost.'

'She was almost finished with her doctoral thesis in educational science when she married Dad. She gave up her career to look after you and the house,' Daniel reminded him.

'Educational science? Ha!'

Slowly Max started to unroll one of the coils of rope, and Daniel saw it was a sort of tightly wound plait. Max carefully untangled it as he went on:

'What she did was more like dressage. She was only interested in me as long as I did the right thing. But she treated me as if I was nothing whenever I got anything wrong. Refused to talk to me. Made food for herself and ate it while I stood and watched. If I made a fuss to get her attention, she used to lock me in a room in the basement. She never told me what I'd done wrong, I had to work it out for myself.'

Daniel was staring at his brother in astonishment.

'Did Dad know about this?'

Max shrugged his shoulders.

'He was never home, was he?'

An acrid smell was spreading through the cabin. Max had unscrewed the lid of a small bottle and was applying some of the clear contents to his chin with a little brush.

'Didn't you tell him that Anna was mistreating you?'

Max's laugh sounded strained, because he was trying to hold his neck still and keep his chin tilted up. He attached a strand of dark hair to his chin, took a sip of whisky, then turned towards Daniel.

'I didn't *know* she was mistreating me. I thought *I* was the one who was behaving badly.'

Max drank the last of his whisky. The long, dark strands of hair were dangling like a sort of seaweed from his chin.

'Don't worry what it looks like now,' he said as he saw the critical look on Daniel's face. 'It'll be fine when it's finished.'

He attached another strand and went on:

'As I got older I stopped bothering about her. I had my friends. I managed OK. I don't know why I'm telling you this. Maybe so you'll understand me a bit better. I've always had to *fight* to get rights that you took for granted. Do you want more whisky?'

'No thanks. I'm going to go to bed.'

On his way to the bathroom Daniel glanced in amusement at his brother.

'What look are you aiming for, Max? An old troll? A hippy with irregular hair loss?'

Max leaped up and before Daniel had time to close the bathroom door he had forced his way in. He took an electric razor out of the bathroom cabinet and put it down on the basin with a very firm gesture. He pointed towards Daniel's beard and said:

'There you go.'

Before Daniel could reply he left the bathroom and closed the door behind him.

Daniel washed his face and upper body. The whisky had made his limbs feel pleasantly numb.

He thought about what Max had said about his stepmother, Anna Rupke. Was that really true? He remembered Anna as a dependable, plump woman. Strong. Intelligent. Efficient.

Beyond the closed bathroom door he could still hear the Dutch jazz musicians.

'Do you remember your promise?' Max said from the other side of the door.

Had he promised anything?

He could see Max before him as a little boy. Standing in the kitchen doorway as big, strong Anna sat on her own, eating at the table.

He brushed his teeth as he inspected his face in the mirror, rinsed his mouth, spat and then said to himself.

'This is never going to work.'

Then he picked up the electric shaver and turned it on.

'This is never going to work,' he muttered again as he ran the shaver over his cheeks.

When he was done he stood and stared at his naked face in the mirror. The angle of the cheekbones and chin, the little depression in his top lip. His pale skin, the uncovered pores. All the things that had been hidden for so long.

He went out to his brother, who was still sitting at the kitchen table fiddling with his false beard.

'It's not ready yet,' Max muttered. 'This takes time. Do something else for a bit. There's a paperback in the alcove. It's good.'

Daniel went and got the book, an American crime novel. He sat down on one of the wooden armchairs by the open fireplace and tried to read. Eventually the plot of the book forced out his own anxious thoughts and he had just managed to get into it properly when Max tapped him on the shoulder.

Daniel looked up.

Max no longer had only a few random, wispy strands of hair on his chin. He had a thick, full beard of exactly the same length and dark brown, almost black colour that Daniel had shaved off. It covered most of his face, and it looked alarmingly natural. Even the odd copper-red hairs were there, the ones that only showed up in certain types of light and which Daniel didn't think anyone but him had ever noticed.

'I've pretty much got it, haven't I?'

'I'm very impressed.'

'I told you this was professional stuff. And you've done well too, I reckon,' Max went on generously with a quick glance at Daniel. 'Considering that you're not used to shaving. No cuts?'

He took Daniel's chin between his thumb and forefinger and turned his head left and right.

'Fantastic.'

Then he crouched over in front of the shaving mirror on the table and looked intently at himself.

'My hair's far too short, of course. There wasn't a good wig in the store. And if you can't do it perfectly, it's better not to bother. I'll just have to wear a hat.'

Max went and dug through a drawer and pulled out a knitted woolly hat and put it on. He tugged it down over his forehead and ears, then looked in the mirror. He seemed satisfied.

'You don't think it looks a bit odd to be wearing a woolly hat in the middle of summer?'

'Not if you're going hiking in the Alps, which is what you said you were going to do. Up among the peaks it can be really cold. Snowstorms in July aren't unusual. I'd never go up there without a woolly hat.'

Daniel laughed. The whole thing was so absurd. And he was a bit drunk, and very tired.

'I'm going to bed now,' he said. 'All this,' he added, gesturing at Max's face, then his own. 'No, it's not going to work. But it's nice to be rid of the beard. You're right. I look better without it.'

'We look better without it,' Max said. 'You've got one more thing left to do. This.'

He grabbed Daniel by the hair and pulled him towards the bathroom.

'You're trying to cheat, aren't you?'

Max took out a pair of scissors and snipped at the air.

'Is that really necessary?' Daniel said.

'Of course it's necessary.'

Max started cutting Daniel's hair. Then he switched to clippers, and trimmed Daniel's hair until it he had the same cropped hairstyle as Max himself.

'OK. Now can I go to bed?' Daniel said, curling up under the blanket on his bunk. He glanced over at Max with his thick beard and woolly hat and burst out laughing again.

He'd just taken off his glasses and turned to face the wall when Max said in a serious voice:

'There's something I want to show you before you fall asleep.'

Daniel rolled over with a sigh. Max switched on the standard lamp above Daniel's head, crouched down next to him and held a photograph in front of his face.

'They sent this to show me how they do business.' Max's whispering lips were so close to Daniel's temple that it felt like a kiss. 'A traitor's daughter. Seventeen years old.'

Daniel had to put his glasses on again, and found himself looking at a badly beaten face. Both eyes were swollen shut, the eyelids purple and bulging like overripe plums. Her bottom lip was split in two and her cheeks scarred with jagged cuts. It was impossible to tell how she had looked before, but with her long black hair and slender neck she could very well have been beautiful.

'This is what they want to do to Giulietta,' Max hissed in a low voice.

'The mafia?'

Max nodded quickly, put his finger to his lips in a hushing gesture, then vanished with the photograph into the alcove where his bed was.

The next morning Daniel woke up to the sound of the hostesses knocking at the door, then – and he had got used to this now – it opening at once and a cheerful voice said:

'Good morning, campers. Are you still feeling sleepy, Max?'

'My brother will be here in a moment. I'll go and wake him,' Daniel muttered.

He fumbled for his glasses where he had left them the night before, but couldn't find them. He threw off the blanket, stood up and went over to Max's alcove. He had slept in his underpants and felt slightly embarrassed in front of the hostess. She smiled and put a hand up to stop him.

'Your brother's already gone, Max. He left the clinic at six o'clock. He probably didn't want to wake you. Did he have a plane to catch? I'd better get on. It's wonderful weather, by the way. Well, bye for now!'

The door closed and then Daniel heard a knock on the next cabin, and the twittering voice repeating its 'Good morning!'

Daniel went over to the alcove containing the bed and drew back the curtain. The bed had been neatly made.

He opened the door to the bathroom, but it was empty.

He looked around for the clothes he had draped over one of the pine armchairs the previous evening. They were no longer there. He searched the whole cabin, without success. His shoes were gone as well. And, far worse: his glasses had vanished.

And his suitcase. And his toiletries bag. And his wallet, his mobile phone and his passport. And the wristwatch that he had left on the table. Even his toothbrush was gone.

But Max's Bermuda shorts were on the back of the other armchair, and his sweatshirt on the seat. And Max's expensive sports shoes in soft, thin leather were over by the door.

Daniel suddenly realised that the only thing in the entire cabin that belonged to him were the underpants he was wearing. Automatically he put his hand on them, as if to hold on to them.

The other hand he held up, just as automatically, to his naked, clean-shaven cheek.

13

In one of the two wardrobes Daniel found a pair of clean trousers and a T-shirt, and put them on. The light brown sports shoes Max had left by the door were size forty-two, the same as his. So he put those on as well.

What annoyed him most was the fact that Max had taken his glasses. They were an extension of his senses, part of him. Without them life was fuzzy and uninteresting, and reading an impossibility.

In the bathroom he found a large pack of single-use lenses. As children the brothers had the same problems with their sight, and that was evidently still the case, because after half an hour of fiddling about Daniel managed to get them in, and found he could see as well as he usually did with his glasses.

At once everything felt a bit better. Through one of the cabin's small windows he looked out at the hillside and clinic. The mountain on the other side seemed surprisingly close. The clinic had to be in an extremely narrow part of the valley.

So, he was going to be spending three or possibly four days here. It annoyed him that Max had left in such a hurry. He had probably been worried that Daniel might change his mind. His fears would have been justified. Daniel *had* changed his mind. He really had no desire to act as Max's stand-in. Had he ever actually agreed to it? He couldn't remember doing so. On the other hand, he couldn't remember giving an unambiguous refusal either. But he had been utterly convinced that Max's crazy plan would fail and that the staff would just laugh at his false beard and woolly hat.

Should he go to the main building and tell the hostess in reception about the deception? Then Max would be tracked down, arrested and charged with fraud. Maybe Daniel would also have to face possible repercussions. He decided against it.

It was only a few days, after all. He had his own cabin and didn't need to socialise with the patients. If it got lonely he could always go down to the village and have a beer in Hannelores Bierstube. Maybe Corinne would be there, singing and rolling her eyes and ringing her cowbell? He'd go and see if the real woman was anything like the one in his dream. All of a sudden the idea of spending time here seemed easier to bear, if he could see Corinne in the evenings.

But the evening was a long way off. What was he going to do until then?

He started by having breakfast. There were eggs and some sort of sausage in the fridge. Instant coffee. No bread.

By the time he'd finished it was ten o'clock. He opened the cabin door and peered out. It was warm. Outside the cabin sat a fat man of indeterminate age. He was resting his head against the wall, his eyes were closed and his mouth half open. His drooping cheeks slid straight into his broad shoulders with no obvious neck. It looked as though he was asleep, but as Daniel was about to close the door he said:

'Morning.'

The voice was so high it was hard to believe it came from that huge body. The man still had his eyes closed. Daniel looked along the row of cabins, but no one else was outside.

'Good morning. Lovely weather. Really warm,' Daniel said, without getting any further response from the man.

He had no idea what sort of relationship Max had with his neighbour, but if there was no more to it than that, he'd probably be OK.

Daniel recalled having seen a swimming pool further down in the clinic grounds. He unearthed a pair of trunks, sunglasses and a towel, put them in a plastic bag along with the paperback he had started reading the previous evening, and went out. The air outside felt like a tickling caress against his newly shaven cheeks.

He stopped a short distance from the pool and checked it out. He had no desire to bump into anyone who knew Max and be forced into some sort of role-play.

Beside the pool was a paved area where a dozen or so people were sitting on folding plastic chairs. A few had moved them into the shade of nearby trees.

Daniel wasn't entirely sure what sort of clinic this was. Max had described it as a rehab centre for burned-out rich people. A rest home where top executives could regain their strength with alpine air and good food.

But how bad were the patients really? He looked around. The people by the pool all seemed perfectly normal. No tics, no outbursts, no hysterical laughter.

Two of the men were playing cards, using a stool as a table. The others were sunning themselves. There was a faint splash as someone slid into the pool and started swimming round with gentle strokes. It looked like any other holiday hotel.

Daniel strolled nonchalantly into the area of the pool, nodding politely but discreetly at the others, took a free chair and carried it over to a shaded part of the lawn. He adjusted it to the right position, spread his towel over it, took out his book and was about to settle down when he noticed he was being watched. The people around the pool – all men, he now realised – had turned towards him and were regarding him with curiosity.

Daniel remained standing. Had he done something wrong? Was he behaving in a way that Max wouldn't? Maybe Max never came to the pool at all?

He sank slowly on to the chair, made himself comfortable in a half-reclining position and started to read. He peered over the edge of the book. The others were still looking at him.

The men who had been playing cards had got up and were standing close together and talking as they glanced in his direction. One of them, a skinny man in ridiculously tight bathing trunks, left the group and was heading calmly over the lawn towards him.

The man stopped beside Daniel's chair and looked down at him. He was standing so close that Daniel could make out the shape of his genitals under the tight nylon, as well as the ribs that stood out under his dry, hairless skin.

Daniel put the book down and looked up at him questioningly. The man stayed silent. He can see I'm not Max, Daniel thought. He wasn't sure if he should carry on pretending, or admit that the man was right and confess everything. The latter would undoubtedly be easiest.

'I think you took the wrong chair,' the man said.

Daniel looked at the chairs around the pool, and at the ones that had been moved on to the grass. They all seemed exactly the same as his.

'Sorry,' he said. 'I thought this one was free.'

The man said nothing, but started to rub one shoulder nervously. It looked like he was giving himself a massage.

'I can put it back,' Daniel said amiably.

Still the man said nothing. His rubbing had changed into a sort of gentle patting of his shoulder and arm. As if he was trying to calm himself the way you'd calm a startled horse. Daniel didn't imagine the man was one of the burned-out executives Max had mentioned.

He carried the chair back over to the pool and put it down by the edge.

'OK?' he asked.

The skinny man was rubbing his shoulder and the back of his neck faster and faster.

His friend pointed at one of the paving slabs. His body was covered with a thick, steel-grey pelt, and on one finger he had an eye-catching ring with a dark red stone.

'There,' the man said.

Daniel couldn't see anything special about where the man was pointing.

The man gestured vaguely at the chair with his hand as if he were brushing breadcrumbs in the air, then pointed his finger towards the paving stone again.

Daniel moved the chair to where the man was pointing. The skinny man stopped rubbing himself and everyone around the pool seemed to breathe out.

The men sat down and started to talk to each other, ignoring Daniel. The others went back to sunbathing.

The change in the atmosphere was so tangible that only now did Daniel realise how tense it had just been. As if a big carnivore had gone away and the birds had started twittering again.

He didn't dare take another chair, so went and sat on his towel, leaning against a tree trunk, and picked up his book. The sun was warm and it felt good to be clean-shaven with cropped hair.

A tall, slightly crooked older man in a linen suit appeared by the pool. He strolled around purposefully as if he were a landowner surveying his estate, nodding to right and left. The patients sat up and responded.

'Good morning, Doctor Fischer,' the voices from the sun chairs echoed.

'Good morning, my friends. Good morning, good morning,' the doctor replied.

He stopped in front of Daniel and looked down at him.

'Good morning, Max.'

Daniel put his hand up to shade the sun, but before he had time to reply the doctor had moved on.

At one o'clock the pool area started to become less crowded. Daniel heard a few people talking about lunch. He was feeling hungry as well. Where did everyone eat lunch at the clinic? Surely not in the fancy restaurant that he had gone to with Max on his first evening? He could hardly ask anyone because that would reveal him as a new arrival. He decided that the simplest thing to do was to follow the others.

14

The patients' canteen turned out to be a large, open space with modern furnishings and glass walls facing the hospital park. The menu offered a choice of oriental chicken or vegetarian pasta bake, and Daniel took the chicken. There were plenty of seats and he was able to get a table to himself. Several other patients were also sitting on their own.

He had just started eating, surprised at how good it was, when someone said close beside him:

'I saw you by the pool.'

Daniel looked up. Alongside his table stood a man the same age as him, slightly overweight, with a denim waistcoat and his thinning blond hair tied back in a ponytail. He was balancing a tray of food in one hand as he pulled out the chair opposite Daniel with the other. He sat down and grinned:

'I don't ask for permission before sitting.' He began to eat, quickly and hungrily. 'But, then, neither do you,' he added with a pointed look.

Daniel tried to think of a suitable response.

The man held up his hand to stop him. He looked like a small-town rocker.

'It's cool, mate. You did exactly the right thing. It's high time someone used that chair. He's not coming back, is he?'

'Who isn't coming back?' Daniel asked cautiously.

'Block. We'll never see him again. Maybe that's as well.'

Daniel nodded thoughtfully. This was what he had been worried about. Meeting someone who knew Max and spoke to him about things that only Max could know. Or else the man was a complete madman and was talking rubbish.

'Block's been transferred,' the man said with his mouth full, as he stared straight ahead over Daniel's shoulder.

'Oh. Has he?' Daniel said.

Something told him that Max hadn't been entirely honest in his description of the clinic and its patients.

'And we both know why.'

'Of course,' Daniel muttered as he struggled with a troublesome chicken thigh. He would have to avoid this man in the future.

'Block wasn't the man he pretended to be.'

Daniel lowered his cutlery and held his breath. This conversation was distinctly uncomfortable.

'And we don't like that.' The man was following some patients who had just arrived with his eyes. He watched them carefully as they sat down over by the glass wall, then lost interest and turned back towards Daniel as he went on:

'We're the same, you and me. We don't like people who sail under false flags.'

For several unbearably long and silent seconds he stared at Daniel with pupils so sharp that Daniel felt he'd been speared with a fork. Then the man said:

'Maybe it was you who got him transferred?'

'No,' Daniel said, horrified. 'Definitely not. I had nothing to do with it.'

The man took out a toothpick and began to clean his teeth.

He leaned back in his chair and looked at Daniel with an amused expression.

'It's OK,' he said. 'Do you need anything?'

He closed one nostril with his index finger and sniffed through the other.

Daniel shook his head, excused himself and left the dining room.

He walked quickly up the slope towards Max's cabin. He would have to avoid encounters of that sort in the future. He wouldn't be eating in the dining room again.

Max had said that he would be away for three, possibly four days. Today was Tuesday. That meant Max would be back on Thursday evening, or Friday at the latest.

Daniel pulled out his brother's worn Bermuda shorts, which he had carelessly tossed in a wardrobe. He dug through the pockets. The shorts smelled of smoke, and had soot stains from the previous day's campfire. In the back pocket he found Max's wallet. Max could hardly have any objection to Daniel using his wallet, seeing as he had gone off with his.

He decided to go down to Hannelores Bierstube for dinner at seven o'clock. On his previous visit he had noticed that they served some simple food. He would take his paperback, then sit and read over a couple of beers. Until then he would go for a walk and have a look at the village and the surrounding area. He'd be back in the cabin by ten o'clock at the latest, carry on reading, get checked in by the night round, and then go to bed.

And with that his first day as a stand-in patient would be over. It felt good to have his schedule worked out that far.

15

On her way up to the doctors' floor, Gisela Obermann found herself in the same lift as Karl Fischer. He stepped in from the lobby just after she had pressed the button and the doors had started to close. His linen suit was creased and he smelled slightly of sweat. She saw his reflection in the glass, and as the lift rushed upwards his reflection spoke to hers:

'Your contract's due to expire soon, Gisela. I have to warn you that it won't be renewed.'

'What have I done wrong?' she asked.

'Nothing. However, to continue working here takes more than not making mistakes, as I'm sure you understand. This is a research clinic. You haven't come up with any find-ings.'

'Not yet. But I've seen so many interesting things here.'

'And I've no doubt you will have use of that in your future activities. The fact remains, your contract expires in October and I can see no reason to extend it. There are hundreds of researchers who want to come and work here.'

'But Doctor Pierce has been here considerably longer than me. What findings has *he* come up with? Has *anyone* come up with any firm results?' Gisela exclaimed in a voice that had suddenly become unpleasantly shrill.

The lift had stopped and the doors slid open, but Karl Fischer was blocking her exit.

The strong features of his face were marked by deep furrows. Cropped grey hair stood up from his head like nails. Behind him she could make out the doors lining the staff corridor.

'It isn't your concern to evaluate the others' findings,' he said calmly. 'And you lack the most important requirement for working here: vision.'

Fischer was still standing in the way of the doors, stopping them from closing.

'Have you spoken to Max since his brother was here?' he went on.

The lift doors were jerking impatiently, but he ignored them.

'No, I haven't had time. I'll call him in as soon as possible. I believe his brother's visit will have done him good. It will be interesting to hear what he has to say about it. Max is without doubt a most fascinating patient.'

'You think so? I don't agree.'

Karl Fischer stepped aside so that Gisela could get out. As she passed him he said:

'You smell of alcohol, Doctor Obermann.'

She turned round and saw the doors slide shut with Fischer still in the lift. She remained where she was, frozen to the spot, listening to the noise as it rushed down through the clinic.

Doctor Fischer was right. She lacked vision. Both when it came to the patients, and herself. All the other researchers had come to Himmelstal with theories, plans and brilliant ideas lighting up their futures. As for her, she could see nothing ahead of her. She had simply run away from her own tattered life. That was the truth, although of course she had phrased it rather differently in her application. She had felt drawn by the alpine air, the isolation, the narrow valley that held its inhabitants like a womb.

At the beginning she had also been stimulated by the sense of starting afresh at the clinic. The others' enthusiasm had infected her like a virus.

But it wasn't long before life here felt as pointless as life outside. The sense of workplace camaraderie that she had been hoping for never materialised.

In their free time the researchers socialised energetically. There was a party almost every evening in the staff quarters. But when it came to work, each of them clung to their specialist area and guarded it jealously. They were all extremely secretive. Often she didn't understand what people were talking about in meetings. She didn't believe the others understood everything either. Doctor Fischer seemed to be the only person who was kept informed about all the various projects.

He never took part in the parties, nor did Doctor Kalpak. They didn't live in the researchers' residential section. Gisela assumed that they lived on one of the upper floors of the admin building, where the nurses and hostesses had their apartments.

She herself had no project. That was the problem. She had arrived with her mind open to suggestion, assuming that the stimulating environment would make her creative. That it was only a matter of time before she got going. That turned out to have been a mistake.

She had long since stopped listening to what the others said during meetings. Instead she would look at the alpine scenery outside the window, or at Doctor Kalpak, who always sat there with his eyes closed, as if he were asleep. In her head she called him Doctor Sleep. He seemed to be in a permanently drowsy, half-asleep state, even when his eyes were open, and the patients he treated were always falling asleep. No, not asleep. Unconscious.

Oh, to be put to sleep. Gisela had never been put to sleep, but she had heard other people describe what it was like. Everything vanishes: pain, thoughts, dreams. Everything. Like death, but you wake up again. And during this temporary death things get better. Evil gets excised. Maybe something new gets put in. You wake up healthier, more beautiful, happier.

Gisela often wanted to die. Except she didn't want to be dead all the time. Being put to sleep would be perfect. Her evil couldn't be cut out, but she was convinced that the very act of being put to sleep would be good for her.

What would Doctor Kalpak say if she asked him to put her to sleep? For a couple of hours, or maybe a couple of weeks?

No, she had to stop thinking like that. She had to stay alert. She had to stay sober. She had to concentrate on her work.

She had to find herself a project.

16

Daniel was walking along the road that he and Max had cycled the day before. They had raced along it quickly and the whole experience had seemed unreal: the speed, the intense green of the grass, the improbably pure air rushing down into his lungs.

Now he had the peace and quiet in which to look around at his own pace. He was struck by how narrow the valley was. Scarcely a kilometre across, and surrounded on all sides by high mountains. In the middle ran the rapids. Their water was zinc-grey, bubbling like an effervescent tablet dissolving in a glass. Maybe it would be OK to go fishing down here as well? He'd see about borrowing a rod and give it a try.

His gaze was drawn to the southern mountainside, which was dramatically vertical, like an immense wall. Now that the sunlight was hitting it from the side, the details of the surface stood out more clearly. It seemed to be a different sort of rock to the mountain on the north side. Was it sandstone? Limestone? The surface was smooth and yellowish-white. Occasionally there were hollows and caves whose size was impossible to determine, and which no person would ever reach. Some of these indentations appeared to be inhabited by the swallows that circled the rocks. Others formed the mouths of small streams, which had carved themselves a passage through the rock and filtered out through these natural drainpipes and on into little trickles down the rock face. The constant flow had left long, black lines along the yellowish surface. Some of these had taken almost human form, as if the rock face were the backdrop to a vast Balinese shadow theatre where the characters were thirty metres tall.

The north side of the valley, where the clinic was located, wasn't as abrupt and wall-like. The mountain rose gently in grass and forest-covered slopes before stretching up to its full height, grey and naked with drifts of fallen stone.

To the west the mountains opened up like a window at the end of a corridor, and through this opening you could make out a snow-capped mountaintop, sparkling regally in the sun, the way everyone imagines the Alps.

Daniel immediately christened the southern mountain the Wall, and the northern side the Gravel Quarry, then felt rather surprised at himself. Why give names to anything in a place he was going to be leaving soon?

He had been walking in dazzling sunshine, but now reached a narrow passageway that was completely shaded by the mountain. The valley constricted like a cramping intestine. The contrast between light and dark was so abrupt that for a moment he was almost blind. When he suddenly caught sight of a man on a bicycle, it felt as if he had appeared out of nowhere.

The bicycle was pulling a cart laden with a large wooden box. The whole contraption was moving very slowly, with a great deal of squeaking.

When the man was about ten metres from Daniel he

stopped, got off the bicycle and rifled through his shoulder bag.

'Good afternoon,' Daniel said in German. 'Do you know if it's OK to fish down here?' He pointed towards the rapids.

The man looked up.

'I presume so,' he replied.

His face looked almost Mongolian, with pronounced cheekbones, a button nose and a low, wide forehead. His eyes were small and bright blue. Daniel was reminded of a particular breed of cat, but couldn't quite remember which one.

The man pulled on a strange, rough leather gauntlet that he had taken out of his bag.

'I went fishing further up the valley the other day,' Daniel went on. 'It was excellent. But perhaps it's not quite as good down here?'

'Perhaps not.'

The cart rocked slightly and from inside the box came a scratching sound, followed by several shrill squeaks. Daniel stared at it. There was something alive in there. The look on the man's face didn't change.

'What have you got in the box?' Daniel wondered.

Without a word the man loosened a couple of straps on one side of the box, and carefully pulled back a sliding shutter. Out tumbled a confusion of feathers and fluttering wings.

The man turned to Daniel. On his arm sat a falcon. Its head was covered by a leather hood crowned by a little bundle of feathers, and it had a bell attached to one claw. The hood bulged out over the falcon's eyes, making it look like a huge insect.

'Isn't she beautiful?' the man said.

Daniel nodded in agreement.

'Very.'

The falcon was sitting quite still on the man's arm, as if the loss of its most important sense had left it in a state of lethargy.

Mechanically and with almost creepy regularity, the blind head turned left and right, like the lingering reflexes of a dead body.

'And there was me thinking you had fishing tackle in the box,' Daniel exclaimed with a laugh.

'I prefer hunting to fishing,' the man said. 'And this is the oldest form of hunting. Without weapons. I don't like guns.'

He raised the falcon to his lips as if he were about to kiss it, but instead he nipped the cluster of feathers with his teeth and pulled the hood off with a jerk of his head.

A tremble ran through the bird as it came back to life. Daniel was astonished by its eyes, big and glossily black, like wet stones. There was nothing predatory about them. The eyes seemed to belong to a creature in a fairytale, from some dark forest or bottomless lake.

'She can see seven times better than any person,' the man said.

He held the fluttering falcon up to the wind. It rose up in circles, higher and higher on the air current, like an invisible spiral staircase. The little bell rang out faintly up above them.

'Silent and beautiful,' the man said, following the bird's flight with his head tilted back. 'We ought to learn from the animals.'

The falcon held still, hovering, then dived straight down towards the ground like an attack plane. Then it returned at once to its master with something small and grey in its claws. It dropped its prey in his right hand, then settled down on his gloved left arm.

Daniel saw that its prey was a bird, wounded but still alive. Its eyes were blinking in terror and it was flapping one wing without actually being able to move.

The man threw it to the ground, and gave the falcon an imperceptible signal to help itself to its prey.

The little bird's wing was still flapping as the falcon tore chunks from its chest.

'Nature's wonderful, isn't it?' the man said.

Daniel felt distinctly uncomfortable.

'Wonderful,' he repeated with a shudder.

A church bell began to ring. It sounded muffled and tinny, like the clatter from a distant factory echoing off the mountainsides. Hannelores Bierstube would soon be open.

Daniel raised his hand in farewell.

The man didn't react. But the falcon turned its onyx eyes towards Daniel and observed him with its sevenfold sight. Bloody entrails were hanging like worms from its beak.

17

Like most old villages the layout of the streets was confusing, with no straight lines, and Daniel spent a while walking about before he found the brown, gingerbread house. As he wandered around he discovered that the village was fairly small, but nonetheless it boasted a café and a number of shops whose contents it was difficult to determine from outside.

Last time he was here it had been dark and he had formed an impression that it was an old village. Now, in daylight, he took in certain details – building foundations, drainpipes, window frames – that suggested most of the houses had been built recently but made to look old.

Corinne was a waitress rather than a singer this evening. She was still wearing her dirndl. She came over to him and waited for his order as she impatiently and distractedly twined a towel in her hands. When their eyes met she gave him a smile that he couldn't quite decipher.

He asked for the menu.

'Don't be sarcastic,' she said, slapping him with the towel. 'What do you want? The usual?'

'Yes, please,' he said, hoping it was something he liked.

He was served rösti with fried egg, cocktail onions, pickled gherkins and a tankard of beer. When he had finished he ordered more beer and began reading his book.

The room was fairly gloomy and when Corinne saw he was trying to read she came over to his table and lit the candles in the squat candelabra. Small leaves made of red, yellow and orange glass dangled from a black metal frame. When the candles behind them were lit, they shimmered like fire. Beautiful, but not much good as a source of light. With the book open in front of him, he sat and stared at the glowing leaves as they quivered gently from the heat.

Corinne spent most of the time in the kitchen, emerging every now and then to serve customers. He snuck glances at her triangular face and narrow eyes. When she passed his table she reached out her hand, stroked his hair against the grain, and said:

'Have you had a haircut or something? I hardly recognised you.'

She was gone before he had time to think of an answer. Her touch had been so fleeting and light that none of the other customers had noticed anything, yet it continued to send waves of tickling pleasure across his scalp and neck long after she had gone.

He wondered what sort of relationship she had with his brother, and his thoughts began to toy with the idea of somehow exploiting the situation. A belated act of revenge for the girl in London. Max had asked him to step into his place. Well, he ought to do it properly.

Obviously he would never do anything of the kind. Using an innocent woman as a pawn in their old sibling rivalry. That was what had upset him most about the girl in London, that was what he could never forgive.

A hand approached from behind and he felt its caress on his

head again. It ended in a firm grip of his ear. Corinne was at the other end of the room. Daniel gasped with pain and tried to turn round, but the iron grip on his ear made that impossible. Someone leaned over him and a deep female voice, or a high male voice – Daniel couldn't tell which – snarled:

'Amateur!'

The voice slid into laughter and his ear was released. A middle-aged man, slim and fit, with a silly boyish fringe in an improbable shade of dull red, was standing beside him with a tankard of beer in his left hand. With the forefinger and thumb of his right hand he snipped at the air like a pair of scissors, and said:

'Who was it?'

Daniel gave him a questioning look.

'Who is it who wants to take the bread from my mouth?'

He gave Daniel a hard slap over the head.

'You don't have to say. It doesn't bother me. You're the worst advert he could possibly have.'

The man laughed again and took a seat at a table a short distance away. He finished his beer, then left the bierstube.

When he had gone Corinne came over and sat down beside Daniel.

'You really ought to get your hair cut at the barber's,' she said. 'He might take offence if you let someone else do it.'

The barber? Oh, so that was who the man was.

'Surely I've got the right to get my hair cut wherever I want?' Daniel said.

She nodded quickly.

'But he might take offence. Bear it in mind.' She gave him a serious look and added: 'And he's right. It's not as good this time.'

She gazed at his cropped head and smiled apologetically.

'Has your brother gone now?'

'Yes. But he's coming back on Thursday.'

'Is he? What for?' she wondered in surprise.

'He's doing a bit of travelling in the area. Then he's coming back to say goodbye before he goes home to Sweden.'

She nodded and he tried to interpret her smile. Warmer than a waitress's smile. Cooler than a lover's.

'It must have been nice to have a visit from your brother. Did you used to see much of each other before you came here?'

'Not much.'

There was a moment's silence. Daniel wondered if Max had told her he was a patient at the clinic.

Corinne was idly fiddling with a chunky bracelet of multi-coloured stones. Then she let out a sudden laugh and started talking about all sorts of things. Difficult customers, her aching back. How no one appreciated her performances. An endless torrent of complaints, but presented with smiles and jokes, as if she were worried about appearing to feel sorry for herself.

'Tell me something,' Daniel interrupted. 'Why is a talented artiste like you stuck in a dump like this? I saw you sing the other night. You should be on stage in Berlin.'

It was risky. Perhaps Max already knew all this.

She let out a harsh little laugh.

'I *have* been on stage in Berlin. And maybe I would still be there if things hadn't got in the way. But life's the way it is, isn't it? I'm just happy I get to perform here. I don't care about the audience. I do it for my own sake.'

There was a note of sorrow in her defiant statement.

'I'd rather not talk about it,' she said.

'What would you like to talk about, then?' Daniel asked.

'Nothing right now, actually. I have to work.'

She got up abruptly and disappeared towards a group of impatient customers at another table.

*

108

When Daniel found himself back in Max's cabin a short while later, he felt a degree of reluctance about sleeping in his brother's bed. But the bench where he had spent the previous two nights was hard and uncomfortable. He looked for clean sheets in the wardrobes, but found none and decided to make do with the ones Max had used.

It felt odd, lying in that cramped space, a niche in the wall with no room for anything but a bed and a shelf of books that ran around the wall of the alcove. When the bedside lamp was lit and the curtain drawn, it was like a secret childhood den, cosy and exciting.

But when he turned out the light it felt a bit claustrophobic. The heavy drape shut out every glimmer of light, the air seemed heavy and low in oxygen, and the smell, which couldn't be anything but his brother's body odour, suddenly grew stronger and more intrusive. But the bed was wonderfully comfortable and his senses were slightly muddled by the beer. Within a couple of minutes he was asleep.

As if in a dream he saw the beam of light from a torch. It didn't hit him right in the face, but was directed discreetly at the wall. He blinked and saw a figure leaning over him. A woman's face, shining white like a moon, smiling tenderly. The feeling of confusion and fear subsided and was replaced by a great sense of calm. It was only Mum, come to tuck him in.

The curtain fell into place, it was dark again, and outside he could hear amiable whispering and footsteps going away as he slid back into a sleep from which he had never really woken.

18

Wednesday wasn't as sunny and warm as the previous few days. Daniel spent the morning in the cabin with his paperback. By lunchtime he had finished it. He heated up one of the tins of baked beans he'd found in the cupboard above the stove.

As he ate he looked out of the window. A restful mist was drifting over the valley, softening everything. He had always liked summer days such as this, mild but sunless. He gazed at the rock face on the other side of the valley, with its patches of damp that looked almost human. It was odd that nature could come up with something like that. As if the valley had been populated by skinny giants who had walked right into the mountain and left these traces behind. Or like Hiroshima, where people had been burned on to walls like shadows.

Suddenly, in the middle of a mouthful, he remembered the previous night's visit. The beam of the torch by his bed, the woman's face that he had sleepily confused with his mother's. Obviously it was the nightly patrol checking that he was there. Daniel had forgotten that they came every night, and had gone to bed without expecting them. He had a clear memory of having locked the door from the inside, so they obviously had their own key.

After lunch he stopped by the clinic library and borrowed another crime novel by the same author. It all went smoothly. He didn't have to give his name, just showed the book to the male librarian, who said lazily:

'Sure, Max, no problem.'

'You don't want to check the book out?' Daniel wondered cautiously.

'No need,' the librarian said with a friendly smile. 'I never forget a face, or a book.'

He returned to the cabin, saying a discreet hello to his neighbour in the next cabin, who was sitting half-asleep by the wall of his cabin, his face gazing upwards like some huge toad. He spent the rest of the afternoon with the new book, and playing a few games on Max's computer.

He had been pleased to discover that Max had left his laptop behind. But he hadn't managed to get an internet connection. Instead he found some sort of internal network for the clinic. Various links informed him of the treatments, courses and activities on offer. There were even a few adverts for shops and services down in the village. Hannelores Bierstube featured a picture of Corinne in her puffy sleeves and laced-up bodice, with a frothing tankard of beer in each hand. Some of the pages required a password to gain access.

The link *From my corner of the valley* led to a page containing the reflections of the village priest, Father Dennis, who had been photographed in full regalia in front of his church. *He maketh me to lie down in green pastures: he leadeth me beside the still waters* was the heading of this week's observation. Daniel read on: *It struck me that these words from the Psalms could well be about Himmelstal. Where could the pastures be greener than here? Where could there be a more soothing, babbling brook?*

The priest was right, Daniel thought. He had never seen greener grass anywhere.

I like to think of Himmelstal's inhabitants as a little chosen flock that the Lord has shepherded into this particular valley so that we might finally find peace, Father Dennis went on.

Daniel clicked other links, and found a list of that autumn's film evenings, details of circuit-training sessions, the colourful assortment of flowers and vegetables on offer from the market garden, and a course on how to control impulses led by one of the clinic's psychologists.

He logged out of the network and checked to see if there was anything else interesting in the computer. He found a few dull sport and puzzle games, and an internal email program, but that was it. The computer was strangely empty. Max seemed to have purged it of any personal files.

Daniel opened the email without needing a password. There was only one message in the inbox. Under *sender* it said *Corinne*. And the subject: *Meeting?*

He hesitated for a few seconds, then closed the inbox. He went back to the football game he had looked at earlier and spent five minutes playing it, without much interest. Then he opened the inbox again, then the message. It was very brief.

How about a picnic? I'll bring something to eat. Sorry if I seemed cross and whiny last night. I was so tired.
Hugs.
  Corinne

So he had guessed right last night. There was something going on between Max and Corinne. Presumably their relationship was a secret. It could hardly be appropriate for a girl from the village to be seeing one of the clinic's patients.

He had been right about something else as well: Corinne had accepted him as Max without any hesitation.

He had no objection to going on a picnic with Corinne. If it was him that Corinne wanted to meet. But it wasn't. And Max was coming back tomorrow, and Daniel had to stay at the clinic to be there when he arrived, and then leave.

He was longing to be himself again and not have to pretend to be someone else. He really wasn't enjoying his stay here at this luxury clinic. Even though everyone, oddly enough, seemed to accept his false identity, he was still plagued by a gnawing anxiety that he was about to be uncovered. And there were a number of patients here that he didn't care for at all. What had that bloke in the dining room said? 'We don't like people who sail under false flags.'

It would be a big relief to get away from here. How was that going to work, though, in purely practical terms? Would he have to go through the same routine with the beard as Max had done, in order to restore his original appearance? In order, so to speak, to disguise himself as himself? What a peculiar thought. That hadn't occurred to him until now. But Max was bound to have thought of everything.

19

'Good morning. Thursday again,' the blue-clad hostess said, putting a paper bag down on the floor.

'Is that for me?' Daniel asked, still drowsy.

The hostess laughed. It was the little dark-haired one, the one who had shone her torch at him the other evening.

'It's Thursday, Max. Laundry day. Have you got anything for us?'

He peered in the bag. It contained a pile of clean clothes, neatly folded.

'Have you got anything?' she repeated impatiently.

'Your bag?' the other hostess explained when Daniel looked blank. She pointed towards the cupboard where the laundry bag was evidently kept.

'Ah. Just a moment.'

He took out the laundry bag full of dirty clothes and handed it to her. The little dark-haired girl felt it, checking how heavy it was. Her porcelain forehead crumpled into a frown.

'Your sheets? Are they in here?'

'Of course, the sheets.'

Daniel hurried over to the alcove, pulled the sheets off and bundled them into the bag.

'You'd forgotten it was Thursday, hadn't you?' the hostess said with a smile.

No, he most certainly hadn't forgotten. But laundry wasn't at the forefront of his mind.

Once they had gone he unpacked the clean laundry from the bag. Max's clothes and, at the bottom, a set of freshly pressed sheets.

As he made the bed in the cramped alcove, he found that something had fallen on to the floor when he pulled the dirty sheets off. He picked it up and saw it was the photograph Max had shown him the night before he left. The girl with the badly beaten face. The traitor's daughter. The victim of the mafia. Max had evidently kept the picture under his mattress.

Daniel lifted the mattress to see if the threatening letter was there too. But there was nothing else.

He replaced the photograph under the mattress and finished making the bed. Typical of Max to come back on a Thursday when the clean laundry was handed out. He would get to sleep in fresh, clean sheets while Daniel would have to make do with Max's used ones.

He stayed inside the cabin for most of the day. At seven o'clock or so he set off down the slope, past the modern glass buildings towards the old main building.

It was overcast but still warm. The valley seemed filled with stagnant, stale air, like a room that was never aired. Isolated drops of rain fell through the air and he could hear the sound of balls being hit on the tennis courts.

He went up the ornate flight of steps and over to the reception desk in the lobby.

'Excuse me,' he said to the hostess who was sitting at her computer.

She turned to him with a warm smile.

'Hello, Max. Can I help you with something?'

'I was wondering if my brother had arrived. I was thinking I might have missed him.'

Shrill voices drowned out his question and he had to repeat it. Through the open doors of the lounge he could see the skinny man from the swimming pool in the company of an older but very lively woman. They seemed to be playing a game.

'Your brother?' the hostess said. 'The one who visited you a few days ago?'

'Yes, that's right.'

'Was he going to be coming back? I thought he'd gone home to Sweden?'

'No, he's been doing some travelling. He wanted to see more of Switzerland.'

'That's understandable. Himmelstal is beautiful but small ... confined.'

She let out a mischievous and almost embarrassed laugh, as though she'd made a joke and wasn't sure how he would react.

'He's going to pay me another short visit before he goes home to Sweden,' Daniel went on. 'I was wondering if he'd arrived?'

The old woman in the lounge burst out laughing and threw herself back in the heavily upholstered armchair while the man angrily tapped one of the game pieces on the board.

'I haven't seen him,' the hostess said seriously.

'OK, I just wanted to check.'

Daniel went back to the cabin. The rain seemed to have changed its mind.

He waited an hour and a half before returning to reception.

'Sorry, Max,' the hostess said before he had time to say anything. 'Your brother hasn't arrived yet.'

Daniel went outside. He wandered about in front of the main building, gazing down towards the road that the minibus had brought him up a few days before. Darkness fell. He waited until ten o'clock then returned to the cabin. Thursday, or Friday at the latest, Max had said. So it was going to be Friday.

When the night round arrived he was sitting listening to the Dutch jazz music. And when Thursday turned into Friday it was Daniel and not Max who burrowed down between the clean, slightly stiff sheets.

He waited until one o'clock the following day. Then he went over to reception.

There was a different hostess on duty today. A young girl with red hair and black-framed glasses that were too big for her face. It looked as if she'd borrowed them from her father.

'Your brother? Was he coming back?'

He had to go through it all again. His brother's tour of the Alps, and then a last visit to Himmelstal before he went home.

'I hadn't heard about that.'

'I'm worried I might have missed him. I've been out for a bit, so maybe our paths have crossed somewhere.'

'I'll check the register.'

She pulled out the large, green, felt-covered book that Daniel had written his own details in a few days before.

'Hmm. Daniel Brant. Arrived at 18.20 on 5 July. Left at 05.50 on 7 July. He hasn't signed in again. Sorry. Was he supposed to be coming today?'

'Yes, today at the latest.'

Before she closed the ledger Daniel caught sight of his signature, and beneath it, next to the departure date, another signature, also his name. But he hadn't written that one. Max had done that, to confirm his departure. Daniel would never have believed that anyone could write so similarly to him.

The girl tapped at the computer, then shook her head apologetically.

'We've had no notification of any visitors to see you, either today or any other day. And no one has turned up spontaneously at the gate. Maybe you misunderstood? Was he really going to come back?'

'Yes! Definitely!'

'Hmm,' the girl said. 'Perhaps he ... Well, I was on duty here the morning he left, and he looked a bit nervous. He seemed to be in a hurry to get away. Had you had an argument?'

'Not at all.'

'Hmm,' she repeated, frowning in a way that made her look older than she was. 'You know, some people don't like it here. They want to get away as quickly as they can. I had the sense your brother felt that way.'

'But he said he was going to come back. Thursday, or Friday at the latest,' Daniel protested angrily.

'Maybe he didn't dare say otherwise. I mean, he might not have wanted to upset you. He was probably ashamed about not staying longer.'

'If he does turn up, would you mind telling him I'm in the cabin?'

'Of course.'

Daniel had been in the cabin for twenty minutes or so when a mobile phone started to ring. An elegant little tune that could have been the soundtrack to a film of flower buds opening.

So Max had left his mobile! Daniel tried to work out where the sound was coming from. It seemed to be somewhere behind the front door.

He found the mobile in one of the many pockets of Max's fishing jacket, hung up on a hook.

The moment he pulled it out it stopped ringing. Daniel was left standing with the phone in his hand.

Max had taken Daniel's mobile with him. Presumably so he could make expensive international calls that would be charged to Daniel's account.

Daniel dialled his own number. He had a lot of questions for his brother, and he would have called earlier if only he had known there was a phone in the cabin.

As he'd expected, there was no answer. After a number of rings, a recorded female voice informed him that the number he had called did not exist. He dialled the number again, slowly and carefully, with the same result. So Max was in a country that couldn't be reached through this operator.

He looked at the mobile's screen to see which network Max used. He hadn't taken much notice when he dialled the number. Now he saw that the background picture was a snow-covered mountaintop against a clear blue sky. In one corner was the time, the battery level and the strength of the signal. And in the place where the name of the network usually appeared, 'Himmelstal' was written across the blue sky in bright white lettering, as if it, like the mountaintop immediately below, was reflecting strong sunlight. Surprised, he stared at the screen as it slowly faded and went dark.

He almost dropped the mobile on the floor with shock when it started to buzz and quiver like a large insect in his hand. The screen lit up again and the letters of the word 'Himmelstal' pulsed in time with the vibrations. A moment later it began to ring.

With a sweaty finger Daniel pressed the button to answer the call and put the phone to his ear.

'Yes?' he managed to say. 'Is that you? Where are you?'

'Hello, Max,' a woman's voice said. 'This is reception.'

'Oh. Has he arrived?'

119

'No. But I've got a message from Doctor Obermann. She'd like to see you today at four thirty.'

Gisela Obermann. Max's psychiatrist. Max had mentioned her, Daniel remembered.

'Four thirty,' he said slowly. 'Sorry. I can't make it then.'

He could hear how ridiculous it sounded. A mental patient with a full diary.

'What time would you like to suggest?'

'I'd rather not come at all,' he said as politely as he could. 'I'm not feeling motivated. Doctor Obermann knows how I feel.'

There was silence on the line.

Daniel held his breath. 'You just have to say no,' Max had said. But could he rely on that? Maybe it wasn't anywhere near as straightforward as that? Maybe they'd come and get him by force, and shove a suppository up his arse if he protested?

'Would you like me to pass that on to Doctor Obermann?' the girl asked.

'Yes please. That would be very kind.'

'Call Doctor Obermann if you change your mind. I'm sure she could find a time that would suit you.'

'Of course. What's her number?' Daniel asked politely.

'You've got her number,' the receptionist said, and hung up.

Daniel opened the mobile's phonebook. There were loads of names. Most of them just first names. Some had both first and surnames. Some only surnames, with the title Dr in front of them. 'Dr Obermann' was there. He didn't know who any of the others were. Except for one: 'Corinne'.

20

At quarter to five on Sunday afternoon there was a knock at the door. Daniel pulled aside the curtain of the alcove and sat up in bed, but before he had time to get to his feet the little dark-haired hostess was standing in the doorway with one of the male hosts.

'Are you here already?' Daniel said.

He'd dozed off for a while, and didn't quite know if this was the morning or evening patrol. Neither felt right.

'Time for the test,' the girl said.

'What test?'

'Just the usual blood test,' the host said calmly, leaning against the door frame. 'A tiny prick in the arm. And a few new pictures of your brain. Completely painless.'

What was this? Max hadn't mentioned anything about this.

Through the open door he could see some heavily built men in guards' uniforms waiting outside.

'Can't it wait a bit?' he wondered. 'I'd rather do it another day.'

'Apparently you turned down Doctor Doberman as well,' the host said.

He leaned against the door frame and folded his arms, with his pale blue cap pushed back on his head.

'Not at all. I'd rather see her some other time, that's all,' Daniel said. 'I'm going to see Doctor Obermann later.'

'No, you said you didn't feel motivated,' the host pointed out.

'Did I?'

'Maybe we'll have to try to motivate you.'

He grinned again. Daniel felt like asking why he called her Doctor Doberman.

'We're a bit short of time,' the hostess said. 'So let's get on with it nice and quickly, shall we? You'll be back in your cabin tomorrow. It'll be you and Marko.'

She gestured towards the next cabin. Daniel went out on to the step. His neighbour was standing outside his cabin, staring sullenly at his feet.

There were four guards. They stood there looking vacant, inactive, bored, but with a sense of innate power, like harnessed horses waiting for their driver's command.

'You've done this before, Max. There's nothing to it,' the hostess went on. 'But you'll have to move on to one of the wards. We have to keep an eye on you. The MRI scan this evening, and the blood test first thing tomorrow morning. You need to have fasted for twelve hours beforehand. So, no breakfast.'

'But afterwards you get a top-notch lunch in the restaurant,' the host added with a wink. His blond, wavy hair shone like burnished brass in the sun. 'Scrambled egg and bacon. Blueberry pancakes. Exotic fruit drinks.'

'Is smoking allowed?' Daniel's neighbour said.

'Yes. But not on the ward, of course. The staff will go out into the park with you. You only have to ask.'

'I'm not going,' Daniel said firmly.

The host sighed.

'You want to do this the hard way? You'll have to take that up with these guys.' The host gestured languidly towards the guards, who instantly straightened their backs and looked more alert. 'Well, Lydia and I must get on. He's all yours, lads.'

The host and hostess jumped into their electric buggy and rolled away.

'*I'm* not making a fuss,' the neighbour said to the guards, holding his hands up in the air. 'I'm happy to go. Just let me get my cigarettes.'

'Bring your toothbrush as well,' one of the guards said.

The neighbour lumbered into his cabin while a guard watched him from the doorway. The other three gathered around Daniel.

'So, what's it to be? Voluntary or involuntary?'

'I want to talk to a doctor.'

'Sure. But first you need to go to the care centre. Now, get your things.'

Daniel went to get the bag of toiletries that he had bought from reception. A thought had occurred to him. If they take a blood test from me, will they see that I'm not Max? Or are we the same there as well? He had a vague memory that identical twins shared the same blood group. Or even the same DNA. But perhaps there was some other difference between them?

The fact was, it would be quite a relief if their deception were revealed. He didn't want to let Max down, but he'd been gone far too long now. This way maybe their switch would be uncovered without him actually having to spill the beans.

The MRI scan was a sort of X-ray. It could hardly do him any harm.

'OK,' he said. 'Let's get this over and done with.'

Escorted by the guards, Daniel and his neighbour were led towards one of the tall glass-fronted buildings. They took the lift up and headed along one of the corridors. A door opened and a nurse appeared with a stainless-steel trolley full of pads and instruments. Before the door closed behind her Daniel had time to notice a blinding light from a very strong lamp. There was a smell of disinfectant and some sort of sweet-scented soap. Until this point the clinic had seemed more like a luxury hotel, but now there was no doubt that he was in a hospital.

They went into a ward and Daniel and Marko were each shown into a private room with separate toilet and shower.

'Fill this in, please,' a nurse said, handing Daniel a four-page test and a pen.

The questions related to his attitude towards other people and how he usually behaved in certain situations. A lot of the possible responses were silly, and some of them downright absurd.

While he pondered which of the options he should go for, he looked round the room and caught sight of the surveillance camera on the wall opposite the bed.

He filled in the questionnaire as best as he could, then handed it to the nurse who was sitting in an office along the corridor. The guards were still there, leaning against the wall with their arms crossed.

'OK, let's take some nice pictures of your brain. Who wants to go first, you or Marko?' the nurse asked.

Marko wasn't there. Presumably he hadn't yet finished filling in the form.

'It better be you,' the nurse said to Daniel.

The woman in charge of the magnetic scanner introduced herself as Sister Louise.

'Take off your jacket, shoes and belt,' she said. 'And anything metal.'

She was wearing a lilac lab coat, her face was sallow and she spoke in a nasal, lazy voice as if she had said these words many times before. But her hands seemed to have a life of their own and worked at an entirely different speed. Their rapid, efficient movements reminded Daniel of the school nurse who had given him his vaccinations and cut off his verruca – it had all been over before he had time to feel scared.

'Lie down on the couch and relax.'

Daniel lay down on the couch that jutted out in front of the scanner's circular opening, like a tongue sticking out of a mouth.

'I hope you're not claustrophobic,' Sister Louise said as she strapped his head down and put a pair of headphones over his ears with the same matter-of-fact gestures as if she were strapping a baby into a pram.

'Now, lie absolutely still.'

Slowly the bunk slid into the narrow tunnel as classical music streamed out of the headphones. Then the machine started to make a terrible noise. The music went quiet and Sister Louise's voice came over the headphones, whispering, almost sensual:

'Don't worry. It's only the magnet working. Just relax and listen to the music. And don't move. This examination costs over a thousand dollars. Doctor Fischer wouldn't be happy if we had to redo it.'

The music gradually got louder. It was a famous piece of classical music. Tchaikovsky's *Swan Lake*? Daniel tried to think back to his music lessons at school. To concerts he had attended. An opera he and Emma had been to. Where was that? Brussels? Which opera was it? He couldn't remember.

'Happy thoughts?' Sister Louise said over the headphones. 'You're about to get something else to occupy you. Just relax and take it all in.'

On a small screen in the ceiling of the tunnel an image of a landscape suddenly appeared. Daniel thought it looked like the south of England. The landscape faded away and was replaced by a picture of a single, crying child in a street. The pictures went on changing. People, animals, landscapes. They were followed by some words in English. Single words, abstract or concrete, one after the other, without any sort of context.

The banging continued, as if a whole gang of poltergeists were messing about, and the music went on playing.

When the scanner finally fell silent and he slid out again, Sister Louise was standing there with his shoes and belt in a plastic tray.

'See? You survived this time as well,' she said.

Daniel spent the evening watching television with Marko in a small lounge on the ward. Daniel tried to make conversation. He talked about the examination they had both been through, and about the questionnaire. But Marko wasn't interested in social niceties.

'Shut up. I'm trying to watch the film,' he said.

The nurse came over to them.

'Your sleeping pills, Marko,' she said, handing him a little pink tub of tablets. He didn't seem to notice her, so she put it down on the coffee table.

'There's a flask of tea for you over there. You'll have to manage without milk and sugar. Goodnight.'

They were watching an American action film starring Sylvester Stallone, who was speaking German with a voice that seemed to say far more words than his lips did. Marko was leaning forward with his stomach hanging like a heavy sack between his legs, staring at the television screen as if under hypnosis. He was breathing heavily through his nose, and he smelled of stale sweat. Daniel hoped one of the patients in the other rooms would come out. Someone who felt more like chatting. He went and got the flask and two mugs.

'Do you want some?'

Marko didn't answer. Without looking away from the screen, he fished out a packet of cigarettes from the breast pocket of his shirt. He tapped out a cigarette, put it between his lips and lit it.

'You can't smoke in here,' Daniel reminded him. 'You have to ask one of the staff to go out with you.'

'They've gone,' Marko muttered with the cigarette clamped between his lips.

'So go out alone, then.'

'It's locked.'

Daniel got up and went over to the glass doors at the end of the ward. Sure enough, they were locked. He knocked on the door of the nurses' room, waited, then tried the handle. That was locked as well.

'You'll have to wait until the night staff get here,' he said.

Marko blew out a cloud of smoke and tapped the ash into Daniel's mug of tea. Sylvester Stallone was throwing a man through a window, the glass shattering in slow motion.

'I think I'll go to bed,' Daniel said, getting up.

Marko didn't react.

Once Daniel had got into the hospital bed he lay awake for a long time, enveloped by the detergent smell of the crisp sheets and the sound of the television. He found himself longing for the cosy sleeping alcove in Max's cabin. He tried to remember his own bed at home in Uppsala, but kept getting it mixed up with other beds he had slept in over the course of his life, and he couldn't remember what it looked like or how it felt.

When he woke a couple of hours later he didn't know where he was. He sat up, and had to fumble for the bedside lamp before finding it. His heart was racing and he could feel a strong, almost bestial anxiety. Had he been dreaming? Yes,

127

he had been dreaming about skyscrapers at night, fast cars, women with eighties hairstyles. Hangovers from the film on television. A pleasant, inoffensive dream. So that couldn't be the source of his anxiety.

He took a couple of quick, shallow breaths. Smoke. Not cigarette smoke. A fire!

He flew up out of bed and opened the door to the corridor. The smell of smoke was stronger here, but he couldn't see anything out of the ordinary. Little green nightlights glowed along the edges of the corridor floor. The small lounge was dark and deserted, and the nurses' room was locked. There was no sign of any night staff.

Marko must have lit a cigarette in his room and forgotten to put it out. Maybe he'd fallen asleep while he was smoking.

Daniel couldn't remember which door belonged to Marko's room. It didn't matter, all the patients in the ward had to be woken up. Why hadn't the fire alarm gone off? He opened the doors, one after the other. Some were locked, but the ones leading to the patients' rooms were unlocked. He found eight single rooms the same as his own. They were all empty, with neatly made beds. When he switched on the light in the ninth room he discovered Marko fast asleep, snoring on his back with his clothes on. The mattress was billowing with dark smoke like the crater of a volcano.

Daniel hurried over to the bed. A glowing hole, as big as a hand, had opened up around the pillar of ash that had once been the cigarette. Daniel grabbed a folded blanket and beat the glowing mattress to put it out.

Marko's heavy body rocked and his snoring got louder, but astonishingly he didn't wake up. His sleeping pills must have been very strong.

'Wake up, you idiot!' Daniel yelled as he beat the smoking mattress with the blanket.

Marko muttered an oath. At the same moment a flame

emerged from a different part of the mattress. Instead of putting the fire out, it appeared Daniel had managed to encourage it with his beating.

'Get up!' Daniel shouted. 'The bed's on fire!'

Marko groaned and rolled over to heave his big frame out of bed, but he was so drowsy and clumsy that both he and the mattress slid to the floor.

The fire flared up explosively, making Daniel lurch backward. The amount of smoke coming from the mattress was incredible, like a whole factory's worth.

The surveillance camera on the wall glared at them with its hemispherical eye. Daniel stood in front of it waving his arms. Evidently no one was watching these cameras.

He rushed out into the corridor, shouting for help. He yelled several times, but the corridor remained completely deserted. The glass doors were still locked, and beyond them the lift button shone like a red eye in the darkness.

Was it really possible that he and Marko had been left alone in a locked ward?

He rushed down the corridor looking for a fire extinguisher or a fire-alarm button. At the very least, there had to be a fire escape.

In a corner of the television lounge he found a green sign with the crouched, running figure on it. When he managed to get the heavy metal door open he could see a narrow staircase with fluorescent lighting and cool, clean, smokeless air. He took several deep breaths, fighting against the urge to flee alone. Then he let the door swing shut and returned to Marko's room.

In the two or three minutes he had been gone, the scene had changed from alarming to catastrophic. Smoke was pouring from the room as though someone were forcing it out from the inside. It filled the room like a sort of black stuffing that stopped maybe half a metre above the floor.

'Are you still in there, Marko?' he yelled.

He heard a rattling cough.

Daniel ripped off his T-shirt, rushed into the bathroom and soaked it in water. He pulled it over his head so it covered his face, then crept on all fours into the pocket of air under the smoke. Marko was howling in a language that Daniel couldn't identify.

'This way. You have to crawl. Under the smoke,' Daniel shouted. 'Can you hear me, Marko? Crawl this way. I've found a fire escape.'

He had no idea where he was. The smoke and T-shirt made him blind. He got his bearings from Marko's screams and coughing. Sweat was pouring off him. He seemed to be almost at the core of the fire.

Suddenly he felt a firm grip on his lower arm. Nails digging into his skin like talons, and heavy, panicked breathing close to his face. He fought the impulse to pull free and tried to say something to calm Marko, but the wet T-shirt had stuck to his mouth and was making him feel he was suffocating. Still on all fours, he changed direction and tried to lead Marko towards the door. Christ, why was he being so slow? Instead of crawling, Marko was just lying on the floor clinging tight to Daniel's arm as he breathed in shallow, jagged bursts. Was he having a heart attack?

Daniel grabbed him under his arms and tried to drag him across the floor. But he couldn't budge the huge body. How much could the giant weigh? One hundred and fifty kilos? He put him back down, rested for a moment, then tried again. He felt his lower arms slipping about in Marko's sweaty armpits, and pulled as hard as he could. Centimetre by centimetre he dragged the inert colossus through the smoke. He had to reach the door before the fire spread and cut off his escape route.

Then he realised he was no longer sure where the door

was. He tried to remember what the room had looked like before it filled with smoke, and how far he had crawled when he found Marko. It was only a small room. He decided he couldn't possibly have got it wrong. If only Marko weren't so heavy and awkward, and so slippery and wet with sweat.

Daniel struggled on, blind, exhausted and poisoned with smoke, for what could have been hours or days, or possibly no more than a few minutes. By this point he had forgotten where he was, why he was there, and who he was dragging. He was like a mindless animal.

From somewhere came the sound of male voices and heavy boots. Daniel managed to utter a hoarse cry for help. Foam extinguishers and hoses burst into life and a voice close to his ear told him to stay calm.

Afterwards he couldn't remember how he got out into the park. But suddenly he found himself sitting on a bench, breathing in the cool, clean alpine air.

'That was a close call,' one of the guards said.

'How's Marko?' Daniel gasped.

'He's a bit worse than you. They've taken him to intensive care. But he'll be OK.'

He looked around at the nocturnal park. It was all weirdly calm.

'Aren't you going to evacuate the building? It's on fire,' he exclaimed in astonishment.

'The fire's already out. It didn't have time to spread. We have fireproof walls between the wards.'

Daniel looked up at the large care centre. Most of the windows were dark. There was nothing to suggest that a fire had been raging inside a short while before.

'Marko was smoking in bed,' he said. 'His mattress caught light. Is there something wrong with the alarms? They should have gone off the moment he lit his first cigarette.'

'He must have disconnected it.'

'Is that possible?'

The guard shrugged.

'Nothing's impossible if you're good with your hands, as my dad always says. Where do you want to go now? Another ward, or back to the cabin? They say there won't be any blood tests tomorrow. You're not in a fit state for that.'

'I want to go to the cabin. Mind you, more than anything I want to go home to Sweden.'

The guard let out a whistle.

'One step at a time. We'll take you to the cabin.'

When they got there Daniel turned to thank the guards.

The night was clear. Below them the valley slept on in darkness.

But to his surprise the highest peak in the distance was lit up as bright as day. Its glittering, silver-white slopes hovered like some dwelling of the gods above the nocturnal alpine landscape. How was that possible?

Then he realised the moon was lighting it up. It was like a miracle. He began to cry.

One of the guards put his hand on Daniel's shoulder.

'You're tired. Go in and get some sleep now.'

21

There wasn't much to pack. Max had already taken everything he owned. But he needed a change of clothing at the very least. He gathered up a few of Max's clothes and put them in a small rucksack.

It was raining outside, the lobby was gloomy and a fire was blazing in the open hearth. The hostess behind the reception desk glanced up from her files and said:

'Oh, it's you, Max. I'm sorry. Your brother hasn't been in touch.'

Daniel took a deep breath and looked into her eyes with a serious expression. It was time to detonate the bomb.

'My name isn't Max. I'm his twin brother. We switched places.'

The hostess frowned. It was one of the slightly older ones, maybe forty-five, but still attractive in a cool, professional way. He let the information sink in, then went on:

'We look very similar. I shaved off my beard and he put on a false beard. From the theatre. It was his idea. He needed to get money so he could pay the bill. It was only supposed to take a few days, then he was going to come back. Something must have happened.'

'I see,' the hostess said with a cautious smile.

'I'm going to be leaving now,' Daniel continued. 'I can't wait any longer. I just wanted you to know about it. That you made a mistake, and let the wrong person leave.'

'We did?'

He nodded.

'One moment,' the hostess said.

Her voice was neutral and her face expressed nothing but friendly professionalism. She picked up a phone, dialled a number and waited.

The double doors to the lounge were open and Daniel could hear laughter from within.

The hostess quietly repeated what Daniel had told her to someone over the phone. Then she listened for a while without speaking.

'I understand,' she said. 'Of course. Thank you.'

She hung up.

'Maybe you ought to put out an alert for him,' Daniel said.

'I doubt that will be necessary.'

'Maybe not. He could show up at any moment. But I'm going home now. I can't wait any longer. Say hello to him for me. I'm sure he'll understand.'

The hostess smiled and nodded.

'I'm sorry,' he went on. 'I only did this to help my brother.'

'That was kind of you.'

'I just hope he comes back of his own accord.'

'Yes,' the hostess said. 'Let's hope so.'

He put the key to the cabin on the counter, as if he were checking out of a hotel.

'Would you mind helping me call for a taxi?'

'A taxi?'

'Yes. To take me to the railway station. I want to set off at once.'

She looked at the key on the counter as if it were an unpleasant and possibly dangerous insect.

'A taxi?' she repeated quietly, without touching it.

'Yes please. Because there's no bus from the village, is there?'

Suddenly her eyes twinkled and she laughed out loud, as if he had been telling her a joke that she had only just understood.

Without touching the phone she started writing something in a folder.

Daniel waited. The heat from the fire could be felt all the way over to where he was standing at the reception desk. An elderly couple and a teenage boy emerged from the lounge and headed towards the lift.

Daniel cleared his throat and the hostess looked up.

'Yes?'

She seemed surprised that he was still standing there.

'You haven't forgotten the taxi?' Daniel said.

She smiled.

'Of course. The taxi.'

She smiled even more broadly. An oddly stiff smile. If it weren't so ridiculous, he would have said she was afraid.

The firelight was dancing over the stuffed animal heads on the wall, making them look alive. The fox grinned maliciously and the ibex looked like a stern old man with its beard and furrowed brow.

'Well? Are you going to make the call?' he asked.

'One moment, please. Just a moment.' Her smile was wavering and she looked anxiously over Daniel's shoulder.

A male host with greying temples was hurrying towards them across the carpet and polished floor, as if he had been summoned by a secret signal. He exchanged a quick glance with the hostess behind the desk, then gave Daniel a stern look.

'Oh, it's you. You came up here before, I heard. Please don't bother the staff with your pranks.'

'He doesn't mean any harm,' the hostess said in a conciliatory voice. 'He was having a bit of a joke, that's all.'

'But that sort of thing gets very tedious in the long run.'

'They all joke about leaving. Surely he's allowed to do that too?'

The host shrugged.

'Provided it remains a joke. Let me know if it starts to bother you.'

He irritably picked up the key from the counter and held it out to Daniel, as if it were some rubbish he had dropped, then marched off.

The hostess smiled at Daniel. She didn't seem scared any more.

'A taxi, that was it, wasn't it?' she said breezily, straightened her back and raised her hand to salute him. 'Of course, sir. Right away.'

She burst out laughing at her little performance.

Then she calmly resumed work on her files.

22

Daniel was astonished at the reaction of the staff, to put it mildly. At first he had felt relieved that the hostess didn't seem to be taking the matter too seriously. He had imagined that he would be called in to see the clinic's management, where he would be interrogated and then given a severe reprimand. The hostess's nonchalant behaviour and her unwillingness to help him arrange transport was so bizarre that it could only mean one thing: she didn't believe him.

It was his own fault. He had spent a week doing his best to fool her, and he was forced to conclude that he had succeeded only too well.

Now at least he had told them what was going on, and it wasn't his problem if they chose to believe him or not. He wasn't about to spend another minute at this clinic. He wasn't about to allow himself to be put through any more 'tests'. Himmelstal may be a luxury clinic in some respects, but their patient safety was distressingly atrocious. It was probably an oversight that he and Marko had been left without staff overnight in a locked ward, and sheer bad luck that the fire occurred when it did, but even so. That sort of thing simply shouldn't be allowed to happen at a hospital. And clearly the fire alarm should not have been able to be disconnected.

He still hadn't received an apology from the staff, and he wasn't planning to hang around waiting for one. If no one was willing to help him arrange transport from the clinic, he'd have to ask someone in the village instead.

On his way down through the park he met a man carrying a tennis racket in a case. He smiled warmly at Daniel and called:

'Do you fancy a game?'

'I'm afraid not,' Daniel replied. 'It would have been nice, but I'm on my way out of here.'

'Aren't we all? Until then we just have to make the best of it, don't we?'

Daniel nodded and carried on down the hillside.

On reaching the village he stopped by the well and looked hesitantly at the cobbled streets that radiated out from the little square. Where should he go? Hannelores Bierstube was the only place he had been to until now, and that wasn't open at this time of day. He saw a small shop and decided to try there.

The array of goods on offer in the shop was decidedly eclectic. There were shelves of groceries and cosmetics and DVDs, and there was a rack of clothes. A broad-shouldered man was standing idly in one corner. He showed no interest in Daniel, but he was evidently the sales assistant.

'Excuse me,' Daniel said. 'I need to get to the nearest town. I understand that there's no public transport. But do you think I could get a lift with someone? I'd pay, naturally.'

The assistant adjusted a pile of T-shirts and slowly turned to face Daniel. He stood with his legs apart and his strong arms folded, and chewed his gum for a while before saying:

'Are you going to buy anything?'

There was something familiar about him, but Daniel

couldn't pinpoint where he'd seen him before. At the bier-stube, probably.

'Buy anything? No, but . . . '

'This is a shop. If you're not planning to buy anything, I suggest you leave,' the assistant said, pointing at the door.

His shirt sleeve slid up slightly, revealing a tattoo on his lower arm. At that moment Daniel remembered where he had seen him before. He was the man who had been lifting weights in the gym at the clinic. A patient doing work experience in the village shop? Unless villagers had access to the clinic gym, of course.

Daniel left the shop.

It had stopped raining, but the sky was still dark. The streets were empty. He followed the main road out of the village and carried on, hood up, with a firm grasp on the straps of the rucksack.

Veils of fog hung like wet rags over the valley. He could hear the sound of an engine in the distance and saw a car approaching along the wider road on the other side of the valley. Obviously that was where he should be if he wanted to get a lift. But the river was blocking his way, and he hadn't noticed a bridge thus far. The only bridge he could recall seeing was the one he had crossed when he first arrived at the clinic, and that lay some distance to the east. He'd have to go back at least a couple of kilometres, and he didn't feel like doing that. There had to be another bridge at some point.

The rain started to fall again, light but persistent. Leafy thickets of deciduous trees were now lining the right-hand side of the road he was on. A tractor and trailer emerged from a turning in one of these small groves. Both the tractor and trailer were tiny, the sort that are normally used in parks and residential areas. The trailer was heavily laden with roughly chopped chunks of wood.

Daniel waved down the tractor and said:

'I'm on my way to the nearest town. Could you take me part of the way?'

The man driving the tractor had a thin beard, greying, shoulder-length hair, and a large cowboy hat on his head. Daniel had spoken to him in German, but the reply came in American English.

'You're mad.'

'I'm not a patient, if that's what you think,' Daniel said irritably.

The man in the tractor eyed him suspiciously.

'OK,' he said eventually.

Now Daniel thought he understood the reason for the man's reluctance. There was only space for one person in the little tractor, there was no passenger seat.

The man gestured impatiently towards the trailer-load of wood.

Daniel walked round, clambered up and stood at the back, holding tight to a metal pole. The trailer jerked and set off.

After a while the road curved and started to head upwards. Daniel recognised their surroundings. This was where he and Max had gone fishing. Through the fir trees he could hear the rapids, fierce and foaming in this section of the valley. The road grew steeper and more uneven, the trailer shook and it was only with a great effort that he managed to hold on.

He heard the sound of cowbells as they drove past sloping meadows with pale brown cows standing still and grazing in the rain. They were high up the slope now, close to the Gravel Quarry. Fir trees rose up around them through the fog, taller, thinner, more elegantly continental than their Swedish cousins.

Then the tractor stopped.

They were in front of a house that was architecturally very similar to those down in the village: shuttered windows, a balcony with an ornate balustrade, scalloped barge boards. But this house was painted shocking pink, the details picked out in lime-green, bright yellow and purple, apart from the shutters, which were all painted in a black-and-white zebra pattern. On the railing around the veranda was a large hand-painted sign with the words 'Tom's Place'.

The man in the cowboy hat climbed down from the tractor. Daniel jumped to the ground and looked round as he tried to flex his fingers, which had gone stiff from clinging to the metal pole.

Opposite the house was a little sawmill, and in the yard there were stacks of timber, spreading an aromatic smell of fresh wood. On the veranda were grotesque sculptures carved from misshapen logs and tree stumps.

The man went up the steps and into the house. Was he going to get the keys to some larger vehicle? Or phone someone? Daniel waited a moment, but when the man didn't reappear he went in after him.

He found himself in what looked as if it had once been a living room, but which had been gradually transformed into a workshop. Among the dirty upholstered chairs was a carpentry bench, and the threadbare Persian rugs were covered with sawdust and wood shavings.

There were more of the bizarre sculptures in here, and at the far end of the room was a collection of stumps that were presumably intended to become sculptures in the future. The fog and the surrounding fir trees made the room as gloomy as if it were evening. It was cool inside, and there was a smell of old cigarette smoke.

'Did you have something to sell me?' the man in the cowboy hat asked. He was sitting in an armchair whose stuffing was spilling out of the shabby fabric like moss from cracks in a rock face.

Daniel shook his head, confused.

'I just want a lift.'

The man snorted and took his hat off. Under it he was wearing a multi-coloured headband woven from some sort of wool, with tassels dangling off it. He kept his dirty suede jacket and cowboy boots on. He leaned over, lit the standard lamp and began picking at a half-finished sculpture with a knife.

'You've made some lovely things,' Daniel said.

He waited for a moment, then, when he got no response, he went on:

'Do you know anyone who could drive me to a bus or train station? Obviously I'm willing to pay.'

The man was evidently too absorbed in his work to be able to reply. Daniel waited in silence. Once the critical moment had passed, the man looked up and pulled a face.

'You're mad. So fucking mad. I've always known that,' he suddenly said in a voice that managed to express both derision and sympathy.

Daniel gulped.

'You're probably getting me mixed up with my brother. I can see why. We're twins. You might have met him in the village, perhaps? Max?'

The man snorted again and went on with his carving.

'I've been visiting him at the clinic down there, and now it's time to leave,' Daniel continued.

The man had slid off the armchair and come to rest kneeling beside the lump of wood. Squinting, he looked at it from various angles, holding it away from him, then bringing it closer. The whole while his lips kept moving, but the sound they were making was so faint and unclear that Daniel had to take a few steps nearer to make out what he was saying:

'So fucking mad, so fucking mad, so fucking mad . . . '

Daniel pulled back. While he tried to think of something suitable to say, he looked at the strange sculptures. He was simultaneously impressed and unsettled by them. Facial features had been carved out of the contours of the wood with such skill that they seemed to have been there from the start and merely revealed rather than created.

Some of them had exaggeratedly coarse features, others resembled embryos, curled up with their eyes closed, with flat noses and paw-like hands. Over by the door stood an old man, the size of a five-year-old child, but there was something slack and retarded about him. His eyelids were heavy and his jaw jutted out to form a bowl that was evidently used as an ashtray.

Daniel cleared his throat.

'Your name's Tom?'

The question was superfluous. The name was all over the place. It had been carved into every sculpture in capital letters, and had been burned on to all the tools hanging above the workbench. It was also etched into the wooden base of the standard lamp, Daniel realised. It was repeated time after time, from the floor and up towards the bulb itself, like runes on a magic staff. Most striking, however, were the bright pink capital letters spray-painted across the back of the old sofa. TOM. Every object in the room seemed to have been marked with the name. As if the man were worried about someone stealing them from him. Or as if he were himself unsure of his name, and needed to be constantly reminded of it.

'OK, Tom. My name's Daniel.'

He held his hand out towards the man.

Tom looked at his hand as if it were a leaf or a cloud or something else that you notice without actually reacting.

'Completely fucking mad,' he muttered, and went on with his carving.

'Really lovely things.' Daniel let his hand drop and nodded at the room. 'You're an artist?'

'I work with wood,' the man said through clenched teeth.

'So I see.'

Daniel realised he couldn't expect much help from this weirdo. It had been a mistake to get a lift with him. He ought to get away from here as quickly as possible. He was a fair way from the village, but he could use the river to help him get his bearings. He just had to follow it down to the valley bottom.

He picked up the rucksack from where he had left it on the floor, brushed off the sawdust and put it on.

'It was good to see your work, Tom. Now I need to get back down into the valley and see if I can find someone else to give me a lift. You don't happen to know where the nearest railway station is?'

Tom looked up. He stared at Daniel with friendly interest, then said:

'You're not doing so good, are you?'

'Well, OK, I guess. The fact is . . . '

'You'd feel much better if you were made of wood. Then I could have made something nice out of you. Your chin.'

'My chin?' Daniel said, taken aback.

'It's wrong. It sticks out to the left. No, hang on. It starts too early. Way too early.'

Tom screwed up his eyes and held the knife out towards Daniel, taking measurements. He started to make complicated movements in the air with the knife, as if he were carving an imaginary sculpture.

Daniel gave his chin a quick rub and coughed lightly.

'Like I said, it was good to see everything, Tom. Really great stuff. Well, take care.'

He had just left the room when Tom roared with sudden intensity:

'Are you the one who's been stealing my wood?'

Daniel turned round in surprise.

'What did you say?'

'There's some wood missing from my store down by the rapids. Was it you who took it?'

In a sudden flashback Daniel saw the stack of wood down by the rapids where he and Max had gone fishing. The spray-painted letters T O M. He'd assumed that was an abbreviation of something. Max had said it was OK to take some of it: 'I know the farmer.'

So this was the farmer. A paranoid old hippie who had taken a few LSD trips too many and had ended up in a cottage in the Swiss Alps.

There had been hundreds of pieces of wood in that store. Daniel had taken five or six. Did Tom count every single one?

'I haven't touched your wood, Tom,' he said, trying to make his voice as firm and believable as he could.

'I'll cut the throat of anyone who touches my wood,' Tom declared matter-of-factly, drawing the knife in front of his own throat. 'All the wood in the valley is mine. I've got the sole rights to work the forest. If you need wood, you have to buy it from me.'

'Of course,' Daniel said emphatically. 'Of course. I'll remember that.'

Tom seemed satisfied. He went over to an old-fashioned record player in the corner and put an album on. A moment later two loudspeakers roared into life and Jimi Hendrix filled the room with his deep, vibrating electric guitar.

Tom nodded in approval, turned up the volume even further and returned to his carving. He hunched his shoulders and started grinding his teeth and pulling faces, jerking his head back and forth in time to the music like a hen. He seemed to have withdrawn into a world of his own where Daniel didn't exist.

23

It took him almost an hour to walk back to the village.

By this time the valley was completely filled with fog, as if someone had tried to mend the crack between the two mountains with filler. Now and then a gap appeared and part of the landscape became visible, as distinct and surprising as a vision.

For a couple of seconds he saw a car high up by the Gravel Quarry. He hadn't realised there was a passable road up there. And a while later came the sound of another car, driving invisibly in the other direction on the far side of the rapids. Unless it was the same car? Had it been down to the village, and was now taking a different route back?

Either way, both of the roads were much too far away. Evening was falling and he was hungry. He decided to spend another night in Max's cabin at the clinic. Tomorrow he would make a fresh attempt at getting a lift. He'd cross the bridge off to the east so that he was on the right side of the rapids from the outset, and could follow the main road.

Once again Daniel caught sight of a car's headlights high up on the slopes of the Gravel Quarry mountain. It seemed to be the same car he had seen before, driving east and then west on the other side of the rapids, and now heading east again until the fog swallowed it up. If it hadn't been so unlikely, he might have assumed it was driving round the valley in an elliptical circuit.

He was tired, his clothes were damp and when he finally saw the glass buildings of the clinic rising out of the veils of fog on the hillside he experienced a feeling that surprised even him: a sense of coming home. Security. Back to the dear old psychiatric clinic after getting mixed up with uptight villagers and mad recluses. The journey away from here could wait. Now he had to rest and eat.

He had no food left in the cabin, he'd eaten the last of it before he set off. If the canteen was open, he would eat there. He could sit there in peace and quiet, now that he no longer had to pretend to be Max.

The park lay deserted in the grey mist, but as he passed the swimming pool he caught sight of one patient swimming. He stopped. He could see it was a woman. Back and forth she swam with powerful strokes, sinking slightly below the surface only to emerge and take another breath. Her short hair was slicked down on her head and her shoulders glistened with water.

Daniel watched her in fascination until she had finished and pulled her slim frame nimbly on to the edge of the pool. With her shiny bathing costume and slicked back hair, she looked like a sea lion.

'I thought I was alone here,' she said.

'I'm on my way to the canteen. Have you eaten?' Daniel asked bravely.

'You know I never eat in the canteen.'

'I don't know anything. I'm not Max, if that's what you're thinking. I'm his twin brother. Max has gone, and to be honest I don't think he's coming back. He tricked me into

147

visiting him, and now he's just dumped me here. And it seems to be harder to get away than it did to get here in the first place.'

When she laughed Daniel could see how strikingly attractive she was. Her face, body, the smooth, lithe way she moved. It was all perfect. If he'd realised this at the start he'd never have dared talk to her.

'A hell of a lot harder, yes,' she said, wrapping a lemon-yellow bath towel round her shoulders. 'I don't usually like eating that much. Except after I've been swimming. Then I'm hungry as a wolf.'

She bared her canine teeth in a predatory grin.

'And then I want lots of food. Good food. And decent wine to go with it. And perfect service. In other words: the restaurant.'

With one hand she gestured towards the main building, and with the other she grabbed hold of Daniel's upper arm, as if she'd known him a long time. Even though her touch was comradely in nature, almost rough, it still sent an erotic charge through his body.

'Right. But I'm not sure I can afford it,' he muttered.

'Well, I can. I'm rich as anything. I'll go and change, and we'll meet in the lobby in twenty minutes.'

Forty-five minutes later – not twenty – she appeared in the light of the fire by the group of armchairs in the lobby where Daniel was sitting and waiting. She was dressed in a short, tight dress made of some sort of shiny fabric that left her shoulders bare. Daniel felt underdressed in his cotton shirt. On her feet she had leopard-skin patterned vertiginous high heels and, unlike most women Daniel had ever met, she didn't seem to have the slightest difficulty walking in these stilt-like creations, but practically ran into the lobby and across to the armchair where he was waiting. As she leaned over to give him a quick peck on the cheek, he was hit by a pressure wave of perfume.

'Come on. I'm *hungry*,' she whined, tramping impatiently on her high heels as she tried to pull him up from the arm-chair. She turned to the hostess at the reception desk and called:

'What are they serving?'

The hostess shook her head with a smile.

'A surprise, then. Well, at least there are always two dishes to choose between. To give the illusion of *choice*,' she muttered as she hooked her arm under Daniel's and steered him towards the lift.

He let her lead him. He was still feeling giddy from the shock of the perfume.

'Choice!' the woman repeated, pressing the lift button and bursting out laughing. 'Isn't that funny?'

Daniel didn't know if it was because of the fog outside the windows, or because he had the company of a beautiful unknown woman instead of his brother, but the atmosphere in the clinic's restaurant struck him as quite different tonight. The lighting was more subdued, the room seemed smaller, and he couldn't recall those red velvet curtains being there last time, and definitely not the soft music.

The woman walked straight to a small table in the corner, sat down and started to read the menu that was already on the table.

'Venison fillet or duck breast? What do you think? I'll have the duck breast. Duck breast! Don't you think that sounds strange?'

She cupped one of her own breasts in her hand. It was extremely large and strangely spherical. Daniel wondered if it was made of silicone.

'I really haven't got enough cash on me,' he muttered.

'Shut up about that. I've already said I'm rich.'

149

Now that it was dry, her short hair looked much lighter, almost platinum blonde. In her ears she had two huge silver rings, but her cleavage was a blank expanse of skin without any jewellery.

'We need some champagne!' she cried.

Shortly afterwards, as Daniel was clinking his tall, vaguely pink-tinted glass against hers, he wondered how this had all happened. He had been on his way out of here with his rucksack that morning. And now he was sitting in the clinic's restaurant drinking a toast with a beautiful, rich patient. Everything was somehow going too fast for him to keep up with it. But at the same time it felt as if time were standing still.

The food arrived. The woman stamped her heels eagerly under the table like a child.

'*God*, I'm so hungry. I can go weeks without eating a proper dinner. It's not the sort of thing I ever think about really. Then I build up a huge appetite. I turn into a black hole.'

Manic, he thought. But beautiful.

She started to eat, quickly and greedily, washing the food down with large gulps of wine. A trickle of wine ran from one side of her mouth and dripped on to the tablecloth.

'I have got the most fucking awful table manners,' she declared, wiping her mouth with the back of her hand.

'This is very good.'

'Is it? I never have time to notice.'

She took a few more hurried mouthfuls, then suddenly put her cutlery down.

'*God*, I'm so full.'

'Already?'

She thrust the plate away, then dabbed at her mouth with the linen napkin and tossed it aside.

'I saw they've got chocolate tart for dessert,' Daniel said.

150

She shook her head firmly.

'I won't need anything else to eat for a few weeks. I'm like a python. I swallow a whole ox, then spend a month digesting it. Do you want to hear a story? I don't know if it's true. There was a girl who had a python. She fed it rats and guinea pigs, and it slept in her bed every night. It would curl up at the bottom of the bed like a dog. Then one day it stopped eating. Not a single guinea pig for months. The girl got worried, of course, and took the snake to the vet. "Have you noticed anything else unusual about it?" the vet asked. "Yes," the girl said, "it usually sleeps curled up at the bottom of the bed, but it lies stretched out beside me like a person." Then the vet told her that pythons prepare to eat large prey by starving themselves for several months and lying down next to their victim to get the measure of it. Do you suppose that can be true? A friend of mine back home in London told me.'

'I don't think it's true,' Daniel said.

She shrugged her shoulders, pulled a pocket mirror from her handbag and checked her face.

'I ate my lipstick as well. See, I must have been hungry!' she cried, taking out her lipstick and applying a layer of smooth, bubble-gum pink that she hadn't had on before. She pulled a face in the mirror, then tugged at her short hair with her fingertips. Finally she closed the mirror and said:

'Can't we have a romantic evening, you and me?'

'How do you mean?'

'You know. Have some wine. Cuddle up under the moonlight.'

'It's raining,' Daniel pointed out, glancing at the window.

'Good. Then we'll have to seek shelter in your cabin, take off our wet clothes and dry out naked in front of the fire.'

He laughed.

'I don't even know your name.'

'Rubbish. Everyone knows my name.'

'I don't. I'm not a patient here. I came to visit my brother ... '

He fell silent. How many times had he said this now?

'Yes?'

She was leaning interestedly over the table and he could see right down her cleavage.

'Max and I are twins. He asked me to swap places with him for a few days, but he didn't come back. He's abandoned me here.'

'Cool.' She discovered a splash of wine at the bottom of her glass and quickly drained it. 'Do you want to come out for a cigarette?'

'I don't smoke.'

'I didn't ask if you smoked. I asked if you wanted to come out for a cigarette.'

She had already pulled a cigarette and lighter from her bag.

'OK,' he said.

They took the lift back down and went and stood on the steps under the projecting roof. The rain hissed invisibly in the darkness. She lit the cigarette, greedily inhaled the smoke, then blew it out in a short, hard puff.

'It's a lovely clinic,' Daniel said tentatively.

'You won't think that when you've been here as long as me.'

'How long have you been here?'

She seemed to be thinking, blowing some smoke rings that danced off into the darkness.

'Eight years.'

'Eight years! Non-stop?'

She nodded.

'But you do get to go out occasionally?'

'Are you kidding?'

'How old are you?'

'Thirty-three. My own parents are responsible for me ending up here. My own parents!' she snapped bitterly. 'Even though they knew I'd never get out. Unless that was precisely the reason.'

Daniel tried to imagine what it would be like to spend the prime of your life in a clinic.

'It's a bit cheeky of me to ask, and you really don't have to answer, but what's your diagnosis?' Daniel asked carefully.

'The same as you, I imagine.'

'As me?'

'The same as everyone here.'

'I'm not actually ill. It's my brother who's ill.'

'Idiot,' she said, and carried on smoking without looking at him.

He explained the whole story, about the threat from the mafia, the bill, and the false beard. It sounded completely incredible. He hardly even believed his own story. He expected her to shrug her shoulders and blow out some more smoke. But to his surprise she dropped the cigarette and looked at him with eyes that grew steadily larger the longer he went on.

'Is that true?' she asked. 'You're not just standing here making up a load of crap to keep me amused?'

'It's true,' he said wearily.

She looked at him with renewed interest.

'Wow!' she exclaimed. 'That's crazy. Why haven't *I* got a twin who could swap places with me? God, that's so unfair!'

'You believe me?'

'Of course.'

'Why?'

The cigarette lay on the steps, glowing to itself. She crushed it under her high heel.

'Because it's such a useless story. Not even the craziest lunatic would come up with anything that lame. But there's

153

something else as well.' She paused and gave him a sly glance. 'I can tell you're different. I'd almost forgotten what people like you are like.'

'People like me?'

'You're so alive. And you've got a really good aura. Did you know that?'

'No. In what way?'

'I can see people's auras. It's a gift of mine. Some people have strong auras, others' are weak. Yours is strong. Beautiful.'

'Has it got a colour?'

'Green. Emerald green. I haven't seen an aura like it since I got here. Max's aura was white and metallic. Like thunder.'

Daniel laughed.

'Shall we go back up to the restaurant? You look cold, with your shoulders bare.'

'You can put your arm round them if you want.'

'OK,' he said, without doing it. 'But I still think it would be best if we went back up. We haven't paid the bill.'

'So? They know where we are, don't they? The rain's stopped. Come on, let's go for a walk. We're supposed to be having a romantic evening, or had you forgotten?'

She put her bare arm under his and pulled him down the steps and out into the park. The clinic grounds were quiet and still, and the trees were dripping after the rain. Her arm was cold, her hip bumped against his as she walked. But, Daniel thought as they strolled along the narrow footpaths in the damp darkness, you don't spend eight years in a clinic for no reason. As if she could read his thoughts, she said:

'You think I'm mentally ill, don't you?'

'To be perfectly honest, I think the people down in the valley seem considerably crazier than the patients here at the clinic.'

He told her about his failed attempt to get a lift on Tom's timber trailer earlier in the day. She listened, wide-eyed.

'You were in his *house*? What was it like?'

'He had a load of wooden sculptures that he'd evidently made himself.'

'Creepy stuff, eh? Did you see anything else creepy?'

'No, but he seems a bit strange. Do you know who he is?'

'Tom?' She let out a gruff laugh. 'Oh yes. I get wood from him. He brings it to my cabin and stacks it in a neat pile along the outside wall. Even so, I'd think twice before going into his house. God, you really are a little lamb!'

She suddenly looked anxious again.

'Did you tell him you'd swapped places with your brother?'

'Yes.'

'How did he react?'

'He said I was mad. He kept repeating it. Talk about projection.'

'Who else have you told?'

Daniel thought.

'The bloke in the shop. But he wouldn't listen.'

'Any of the clinic staff?'

'Yes. I spoke to the hostesses in reception.'

'And they didn't believe you?'

'No.'

She threw her head back and let out a long laugh.

'They didn't notice anything? But that's brilliant!'

Daniel couldn't see what was so brilliant about it.

'Have you spoken to any of the doctors?'

'No. I was given an appointment with Gisela Obermann, only I turned it down.'

'Gisela Obermann would see through you. She's an expert. She'll see at once that you're not genuine.'

'Do you think she'd help me get a lift out of here?'

'She'll put you in a car to the airport immediately. She'll want to get rid of you fast as fuck, before you tell anyone

155

about their shitty security. God, she's going to be so furious. Have you told any of the other patients?'

'No. I've hardly spoken to the other patients.'

'Good. Don't.'

'Why not?'

She turned towards him, took a firm grip of his chin and cheeks, and looked at him with a peculiar smile.

'Because they'd eat you up, darling. And I don't want that. If anyone's going to eat you up, it's me. You're *my* lamb, no one else's.'

They heard footsteps and voices. Daniel looked up. People were rushing across the park from various directions. Some were on their way to the main building, others heading towards the cabins. He had no wristwatch, but he knew it must be almost midnight. Over the previous few days he had come to recognise the tense atmosphere that always preceded the bedtime round. The clinic grounds that had only recently seemed empty and deserted were now teeming with patients hurrying back to their rooms and cabins. What would happen if they weren't there at the witching hour?

'Looks as though it's time,' he said.

She continued holding his face, her long nails pressing into his skin.

'Once the hostesses have tucked you in I'll come over to your cabin. So you'll get a goodnight kiss from *me*. It'll taste much better, I promise.'

'I still don't know your name.'

She let go of him and politely held out her hand. It was slender but strong.

'Samantha,' she said.

She left him, cutting across the lawn. Her high heels dug into the wet ground, making her lurch every now and then. Then she vanished behind some bushes and was gone.

*

Daniel was hardly back in the cabin before he heard the hum of the electric buggy outside, then the knock on the door. The patrol was evidently starting its round with his row of cabins that evening.

'I see you're still with us, Max. I'm glad about that.'

It was the slightly older hostess who had been in reception that morning. The one who had refused to call for a taxi.

He didn't reply. He was now aware that the bedtime patrol was invariably in a hurry, and didn't expect a response. Their questions and comments were simply a way of saying 'We've checked you're here'. There was always one of them who came in and said something. The other one merely poked their head in, but he had seen that she had a small handheld computer on which she presumably made a note of his presence.

He nodded amiably, and then they were gone. He heard them knock on doors all the way along the row of cabins, then the electric vehicle began to hum again.

Daniel poured himself a whisky and wondered if Samantha had given him an erotic invitation. It could hardly be interpreted any other way. Should he accept or reject it?

He peered out through the cabin window. Where was her cabin? She evidently didn't live in the main building, because she hadn't gone off in that direction. The wind had got up and the trees in the park were swaying in front of the lamps, so that the lighting seemed to flicker.

He had a shower and sat down in the wooden armchair, sipping his whisky and listening for the sound of high heels. After an hour or so he gave up, relieved and disappointed at the same time. He went to bed, but left the door unlocked.

Once he had fallen asleep, he dreamed that someone was lying beside him in bed, breathing deeply. In the faint, flickering light from outside he imagined a thick snake lifting its head from the pillow and looking at him with eyes that were black and glossy as oil.

He woke up and realised it was a dream.

But not entirely. Because there really was someone next to him in the bed. A thin creature dressed in something tight and shiny and black was watching him, leaning on one elbow, then a moment later it snaked across him and attached itself to his mouth.

If it hadn't been for the familiar smell of perfume – heavy, sweet and sickly, like incense or overripe fruit – he would have let out a scream of fright.

'My goodnight kisses are better, aren't they darling?' Samantha whispered, pulling off his underwear.

Although Daniel was still half-asleep, his penis appeared to be wide awake. She sat astride him and rode him slowly and seductively, then faster and faster, and then slowly again, until something seemed to break inside him.

She slipped off him, curled up into a foetal position with her back to him, and whimpered:

'Fuck, fuck, fuck.'

'What is it?' he wondered in alarm.

'I've found a little lamb and now he's going to leave me. You're going to go and see Doctor Obermann and she'll send you away. Fuck.'

She lay there crying and sniffing for a while as he patted her impotently on her black corset.

Then she stood up and pulled on her coat.

'Maybe it won't be that easy for Doctor Obermann to arrange transport at such short notice,' she said rather more confidently as she put her shoes on. She stopped halfway and added: 'It's obvious that you're from a northern country.'

'How?'

'When you come, your aura flares up like the northern

158

lights. It's magnificent. It's a shame you can't see it yourself. Goodnight.'

In the doorway she turned and said:

'I hope you're still here tomorrow night at least. Because if you are, I'm going to come and fuck your brains out, my little lamb.'

24

At first he could see nothing but light. A bright, blinding light that made Daniel stop in the middle of Doctor Obermann's room and put his hand up to shade his eyes. There were large picture windows stretching all the way to the floor, and through them the sunlight flooded in, reflecting off the polished beechwood floor and white walls. (Surprisingly, considering he hadn't noticed any sunshine as he walked through the hospital grounds. Maybe it wasn't strong enough to hit the ground, and only reached the top floors of the building.) When his eyes had got used to it, he saw that the room was large and looked more suited to the director of a big company than a doctor's surgery.

Gisela Obermann and the other doctors had their rooms on the fifth floor, at the top of the modern block behind the main building. The lobby was as lofty as a cathedral. Daniel had to pass through two locked doors and a security guard who called Doctor Obermann to check before letting him into the glass lift. The doctors here were well protected.

Gisela Obermann stood up behind her desk.

'Welcome. I'm glad you changed your mind. Your input is important to our research.'

He couldn't tell if she was being serious or ironic.

'What does my input consist of?' he asked, standing in the middle of the room.

'Being here. Coming to meetings when you're asked, and talking as honestly as you can about yourself. That's your input,' Doctor Obermann explained calmly as she headed over to a group of rigid, block-like armchairs and sofas.

She sat down in one of the chairs, and asked Daniel to sit down in the other. Only now, when he had his back to the light, could he see her properly. She was in her forties, tall and slim, with nice legs but a commonplace face. Her hair was thick, blonde, and parted so that it fell diagonally across her forehead and cheek.

'Let me repeat that: I appreciate your being here, Max. As you know, you've got everything to gain by coming. And everything to lose if you don't. And it's hardly that much of an effort, is it? Just a bit of chat for a while.'

She smiled, and Daniel made an effort to smile back. Could she notice anything? Samantha had said that Doctor Obermann would be able to tell the difference at once.

'Well, let's get started. As usual, we'll be filming our conversation.' She leaned back and crossed her legs.

Daniel looked around. He saw two small cameras, spherical, like eyeballs that had been plucked out, mounted on a frame on the wall. One was pointing towards him, the other at the doctor.

'Is everything OK? You seem a bit distracted.'

'It's fine.'

'Good.'

Doctor Obermann leafed through some papers she had in her lap. Her nails had been bitten to the quick, Daniel noted in surprise. It made her hands look childish and fragile, as if they belonged to someone else. She frowned as she read, then looked up.

'You've been rather unsettled these past few days, I've heard. Has anything particular happened since we last spoke?' When there was no answer, she prompted: 'You had a visit from your brother, didn't you?'

Daniel took a deep breath.

'You and I have never spoken before, Doctor Obermann. You're confusing me with my brother. Which was actually the intention. I'm afraid we set out to deceive you.'

She can tell, Daniel thought. Now she can tell.

'How do you mean?' Doctor Obermann asked in a neutral voice.

'You can probably tell that I'm not Max, even though we are very similar. My name is Daniel Brant, and I arrived here last week to visit Max, my twin brother. He was in a difficult situation and needed to get away from the hospital for a few days to sort something out. Because he wasn't allowed out, I agreed to switch places with him. Well, I'm not entirely sure I ever agreed as such, but that was evidently how Max interpreted it. Because we're identical twins he thought we'd be able to fool everyone here at the clinic and change places. It appears we succeeded.'

'Hold on,' Gisela Obermann interrupted, leaning forward in interest. 'You're not Max but his twin brother, is that what you're saying?'

Daniel nodded and smiled apologetically.

'If you look closely, you can probably tell. Max was supposed to come back on Friday at the latest. And it's now Tuesday. I haven't heard anything from him. Maybe he's sent you a message, Doctor Obermann? Or someone else here at the clinic?'

Instead of answering, Doctor Obermann made a note in her papers and said:

'Could you explain to me a bit more about how this switch took place?'

Daniel explained, and Doctor Obermann listened intently.

'Stop for a moment,' she suddenly said. 'Why are you calling me Doctor Obermann? You usually call me Gisela.'

'But I've never met you before. If you'd rather I call you Gisela, I can do that. And if you'd rather talk German, which I believe is your mother tongue, that's fine too. I speak German fluently. I used to be an interpreter.'

Doctor Obermann sighed and raised her eyebrows slightly.

'Yes, you've been a lot of things, haven't you? But, as you're well aware, we speak English here primarily. That's easiest all round. You can call me what you wish, but I'm going to carry on calling you Max. Apparently you want to act out some sort of role-play today. I know you like pranks, but I'm really not very keen on games.'

'My brother likes pranks. Not me,' Daniel said irritably, slapping his hand down on the arm of the chair. 'All I want is to sort this out and get away from here. My name is Daniel Brant, but I can't prove it because Max took all my official documents with him when he left. You're just going to have to believe me.'

'But I don't believe you.'

She tilted her head to one side and gave him a gentle, almost tender smile.

'Why not?' he asked, taken aback.

'Because you're a pathological liar. Lying and trying to manipulate other people is part of your character.'

'Part of *my brother's* character.'

Gisela Obermann got up and went over to her desk. She tapped at the keyboard, then studied the screen in silence.

'Hmm,' she finally said. 'Your brother arrived on Sunday 5 July. He left here on Tuesday 7 July.'

'*I* arrived on 5 July. *Max* left here on 7 July. He was wearing a false beard he got from the theatre, and I shaved off my beard. Incredibly simple, like something out of an operetta, don't you think? I never believed it would work. But, seeing as we're identical twins ...'

'You're not twins at all,' Gisela Obermann interrupted, spinning round on her office chair so she was facing Daniel. 'Daniel was born two years before Max.'

'That's the stupidest thing I've ever heard. You've got hold of the wrong information.'

'Daniel's date of birth is ...' She turned back to the screen. '... the twenty-eighth of October 1975, it says so here.'

'That's right.'

'And Max was born ... Here it is: the second of February 1977.'

'No, no,' Daniel said. 'That's wrong. Obviously we were born the same day.'

Gisela Obermann gave him a long, impassive look. She stood up, returned to the armchairs and stared out of the picture window in silence. In the strong sunlight she suddenly seemed old and tired.

'What sort of game are you playing, Max? We know all about you here. Outside you might be able to fool people, but it's fairly pointless trying it on me, isn't it? What do you hope to gain from it?'

'I'm hoping that you will believe what I say and help me get out of here,' Daniel said impatiently. 'You've got the wrong information in that computer. I dare say Max lied when he was first admitted. He's good at that sort of thing. Well, I'm not going to waste any more time on this conversation. You can believe whatever you like, but I'm leaving. You've got no right to hold me here.'

He stood up and walked quickly towards the door.

'Just a moment,' Doctor Obermann called.

He turned round. Only now did he notice the stunning view of the valley and the snow-capped peaks in the distance. Doctor Obermann was still seated in the armchair. Leaning back comfortably and with a hint of a smile on her face, she went on:

'Exactly what do you mean by "leaving"?'

'I'm leaving the clinic, of course. Getting out of this bloody valley,' he replied angrily, then put his hand on the door handle.

The door was locked. There was no key, and no obvious lock.

'Out of Himmelstal?' Doctor Obermann said from her armchair.

He turned towards her.

'Yes. I know the communications are useless and the villagers are unwilling to cooperate. They've been given instructions by you lot, haven't they? But I'm leaving, and if it comes to it I'll just have to walk.'

She let out a small burst of laughter.

'You're very convincing. If I didn't know better, I'd be inclined to believe you.'

Daniel tugged at the door handle again, even though he knew there was no point. He wasn't going to get out of here until she let him out. Her pale summer coat was hanging beside the door. He waited with his hand on the handle, studying the coat and the hook it was hanging from. Gisela Obermann remained seated in silence.

'Can't I leave if I want to?' he exclaimed impatiently. 'Do you keep your patients locked up?'

'We don't keep anyone locked up here. You can go when you want. I'm merely keeping other people out. So we aren't disturbed while we're talking. But we aren't finished yet, Max. To be honest, you're making me feel rather concerned today.'

'Concerned?' Daniel turned round. 'One of your patients has escaped. You ought to be worried about him. Put out some sort of alert. Something might happen to him, has that occurred to you? You're behaving very irresponsibly, that's all I can say. Now, will you please let me out?'

'Of course. I hope we can continue our conversation another day. This could lead somewhere.'

She went over to her desk.

There was something odd about that hook. It was made of rough wood, and seemed out of place in the minimalist surroundings. When Daniel studied it more closely he could make out two very thin figures in the carved wood, pressed against each other, back to back. The figures had their crooked arms held tight to their bodies, but their fingers were splayed out into hooks, and it was one of these that was holding Doctor Obermann's coat. At the top were two oblong faces, carved to face in different directions. One of the faces was asleep, its eyes and mouth closed, but the other was awake with its mouth wide open, as if it were screaming.

He was just about to comment on the peculiar coat hook when there was a click from the lock. He pushed the handle again and the door slid open.

'Goodbye, Max,' Gisela Obermann said from her desk. 'You're welcome to come and see me whenever you feel like it.'

In the lift Daniel turned his back on his own reflection and leaned his forehead against the cool glass wall instead. The stone floor and green plants of the lobby were rushing towards him. Why had Max given the wrong date of birth? Had he left the clinic for good?

Suddenly he recalled his brother's story of the man who rowed the boat to Hell: get someone else to take over at the oars.

*

166

Hannelores Bierstube was busy that evening. Daniel had to take a seat at a large table where there were already several people sitting.

Corinne had begun her performance. This time she wasn't wearing traditional costume, and there were no cowbells. She was dressed as a sailor, in bell-bottomed trousers, a jacket with blue stripes on the collar, and a sailor's cap with a small, perfectly round pom-pom. Her accompanist on the accordion was dressed as a captain, with a peaked cap and white uniform. They were performing German sea shanties, and the whole thing was just as theatrical, unsophisticated and charming as the evening with the cowbell.

Daniel was sitting at the same table as on his earlier visit. Over in the corner. He was on his second tankard of beer, there were plenty of people in the dimly lit room, and the glass leaves on the candelabra were shimmering yellow and red like autumn leaves. There must be someone he could get a lift from. As soon as possible, and without the clinic finding out.

Corinne's eyes flitted from right to left beneath her brown fringe, reminding him of jokey cards of characters with moving eyes. With a rolling gait, as if she were on a boat in a stormy sea, she made her way to Daniel's table and seemed to be singing for him alone. In the scant light from the candles he could see her makeup: pale blue eye-shadow, right up to her eyebrows, bright and sparkling like the wings of an exotic butterfly.

Hypnotised, he held out his hand and touched her lightly on the arm. She winked at him and returned to her place beside the accordionist.

How well did she know Max? Could she help him get a lift if he explained the situation to her?

After the end of the performance he sat and waited for Corinne to return. But she disappeared into the back of the bierstube and didn't come out again.

167

When the cuckoo clock struck half past eleven everyone began to leave. Daniel walked out of the bierstube and made his way quickly through the cold rain up towards the clinic. He noted that the majority of the clientele were heading in the same direction.

When he unlocked the door to his cabin he heard a voice in the darkness off to his left.

'You like staying out late, don't you?'

Behind the glowing red eye of the cigarette he could just make out his neighbour as a large shadow, a darker part of the darkness.

'It's good to see you back, Marko. Are you OK?' Daniel said.

There was no answer, so he went on:

'I've been down in the village to have a beer.'

Marko was breathing heavily and loudly through his nose. He sounded more like an old dog than a human being. The projecting roof protected him from the rain that was falling, soft and invisible.

'Do as you please,' he hissed. 'I never go out after dark. I don't take any risks.'

'That's probably wise. Goodnight.'

I wonder if he goes anywhere at all of his own volition, Daniel thought. He seems to be stuck to the wall of his cabin.

He switched on his computer, opened the emails, found Corinne's week-old message, and wrote a reply:

I very much enjoyed your performance this evening. You made a fantastic sailor.

Is the offer of a picnic still open? If it is, I'd love to go with you as soon as possible.

Sorry to be so slow replying. Things have been rather complicated. I'll explain later.

After a moment's hesitation over what name to sign off with, he typed:

Max.

As soon as he had sent it a hostess walked in through the door.

'Everything OK, Max?'

'I've already explained to your colleague that I'm Max's *brother*. Hasn't anyone told you?' Daniel said irritably.

'Not that I can remember,' the hostess said cheerily. 'Do you want anything to help you sleep?'

She opened her shoulder bag and peered down into it.

'No thanks.'

The computer bleeped and when he turned back to the screen he saw he had already received a reply from Corinne.

Daniel opened the email. It was short and to the point:

Be at the well nine o'clock tomorrow morning.

25

The air was cool and clear, and had a smell that Daniel recognised from his childhood but couldn't identify. When the memory finally broke through he realised why the smell was so confusing. It was the smell of snow, which was completely wrong in the middle of July. The grass meadow was radiant green, full of red clover and bellflowers.

But when he looked at the mountain with the etched figures on the other side of the valley, the one he called the Wall, he discovered that its fringe of fir trees was no longer green but white. And when his gaze wandered up above the meadow he saw that the Gravel Quarry no longer looked quite as cheerless and quarry-like as it had, seeing as its upper slopes were now sparkling with what looked like a sprinkling of sugar.

The rain of the previous evening had fallen as snow up there. It was beautiful, and surprising.

They were skirting the valley along a narrow path that Corinne knew. She was wearing a thick green sweater and had a hairclip above each ear. He had hardly recognised her by the well. As soon as she saw him she gave him a curt nod and started walking without saying a word. He had fallen in beside her and followed her out of the village.

'What's that?' he asked.

Corinne glanced across the meadow.

'That's what we in the countryside call cows.'

'No, not the cows. Down there,' Daniel said, pointing at something that looked like a small Greek temple.

'That's the Leper Cemetery. Haven't you seen it before? Come on, let's go and take a look.'

As they got closer Daniel could see blackened, leaning crosses surrounded by a wrought-iron fence. Immediately above them lay the little stone temple that he had seen from the distance. It was slightly smaller than his own alpine cabin, with pillars and some steep steps, and the rear of it seemed to have been built into the hillside. Its front was a solid wall.

'It's an impressive memorial. A proper little mausoleum. Whose is it?'

'No idea. Someone rich and powerful. I suppose they got leprosy as well,' Corinne said. 'The cemetery belonged to the convent. The villagers had their own cemetery down by the church. They didn't want to get their dead mixed up with the lepers.'

Corinne took off her sweater, laid it out on the damp steps of the mausoleum and sat on it. She got bread, cheese and cider out of her rucksack. Daniel sat on his jacket beside her.

'A good spot for a picnic,' she said, pouring him a mug of cider. 'When I first arrived in the valley I often used to come to these steps to sit and think. Now I don't like coming here alone. But with you it's fine.'

She leaned against the stone pillar, closed her eyes and breathed in the fresh air.

Daniel looked at her. It was obvious that she knew Max, but how well, and in what way? Probably not terribly well.

No one knew Max well. Had they slept together? Presumably. How would she react if he put his hand on her thigh?

He remembered the girl in London. He had seen her once more, just before he left, at the dairy counter of a large supermarket. When she recognised him all the blood drained from her face and she had abandoned her basket on the floor and rushed out of the shop.

The sun was warm and the smell of snow was lingering in the air. The cows were wandering across the meadow with the high mountains in the background, like a picture on a box of Swiss chocolates. Daniel closed his eyes and listened to their bells. It was an odd sound, completely unpredictable, random and without purpose. A little clang here, another somewhere else.

'It's such a relaxing sound,' he said.

'At a distance, maybe. But a bell like that makes a hell of a noise close up,' Corinne said. 'That's why I ring my bell so carefully when I perform. I always think of those poor cows who have that awful noise right next to their ears.'

'It's actually cruelty to animals,' he agreed.

Corinne cut a slice of cheese.

'They're probably all stone deaf by now,' she said.

'Or else they've got appalling tinnitus.'

She held out the knife with the slice of cheese to Daniel.

'Try it. It comes from these cows. Himmelstal's own dairy. All their stuff's very expensive, but what can you do? It's the only dairy in the valley. No competition.'

He popped the piece of cheese in his mouth, but before he could say how good it was she went on, almost to herself:

'Oh, I get so sick of this valley sometimes.'

'So why are you here, then?'

She glanced quickly at him.

'I don't ask *you* why *you're* here,' she said.

'Feel free, if you want to.'

'I don't.'

One of the cows had come down to the cemetery and was rubbing its horns against the iron railings, making the bell round its neck ring crazily. He had to raise his voice:

'If you weren't here in Himmelstal, where would you like to be?'

'Purely hypothetically?'

'Yes.'

She looked up at the sky, took a deep breath, then said:

'In some big European city. Where I could work in a small theatre and do my own thing. Put on my own plays. Direct. I trained as an actress.'

He nodded.

'I guessed.'

He felt like adding: I'll come with you, Corinne. I can support you until you find your theatre. I'm an interpreter, I can get work anywhere.

For a moment he saw this imaginary future before him, down to the smallest detail, he and Corinne living in some old apartment next to a park. Corinne in jeans, T-shirt and sunglasses, sitting on the floor with her legs crossed in a ray of sunlight coloured green by the foliage outside, with a bundle of scripts in her freckled hands.

'You had dinner with Samantha the other evening,' Corinne said.

Daniel started. Samantha? The woman who had been at the clinic for eight years. Daniel hadn't seen her since that evening, and he had almost managed to persuade himself that their encounter had been a dream, particularly the latter part of it.

'How do you know that?' he asked in astonishment.

Corinne shrugged her shoulders and cut herself a slice of cheese. The cow had stopped scratching itself and was watching them intently over the railings and the rows of crooked little crosses. Its bell was completely mute.

'You villagers seem to have a lot of contact with the clinic,' he went on. 'Most of the bierstube's clients are patients there, aren't they? I recognised quite a few of them last night.'

'Really?' she said with weary irony.

'Customers with plenty of money and not much else to spend it on.'

'You're absolutely right there. What are you getting at?'

'I presume most of the businesses in the village make a living from the clinic's patients. It's a big clinic, after all. There are probably more people there than there are in the village itself? And some of you villagers must work at the clinic? In the kitchens, cleaning and so on.'

'Of course. That's obvious.'

'The clinic management is good to you, letting you use the gym, the library and pool. In return you're good to them, letting them know if anyone tries to escape. And you never give lifts to anyone who wants to leave. Am I right?'

She laughed and shook her head as she wrapped the cheese in its greaseproof paper.

'I don't know what you're talking about.'

'You're the first friendly person I've met here,' Daniel went on. 'Everyone else has been distinctly unfriendly. No one else has been willing to help me.'

She was sitting still with her hands on the wrapped cheese, staring at him with an expression of utter bewilderment. The cow had tired of them and had gone back to grazing the meadow.

'Help you? With what?'

'You think you're talking to Max, don't you? You know him? Do you remember the long-haired bloke with a beard who was sitting next to Max in the bierstube last week? His brother?'

She nodded hesitantly. She looked scared.

'I'll explain.'

And he did.

She fiddled with her bracelet and glanced at him from the corner of her eye.

'Twins?' she said.

He nodded.

'You do believe me, don't you?'

'I don't know. It would explain why you're talking so weirdly. And you are actually very different. Your manner, I mean.'

'You have to help me get away from here, Corinne. No one else believes me. How far is it to the nearest town?'

She laughed.

'A long way.'

'Have you got a car?'

'I can't even drive.'

'But you must know someone with a car?'

She gazed at him sadly.

'It wouldn't work. I wish I could help you. Believe me. But only the doctors can get you out of here. The doctors make the decisions.'

'Do they make decisions for you as well?'

She bit her lip and said nothing.

He leaned closer and repeated his question:

'Do the doctors make decisions for you as well, Corinne?'

She lowered her head and said quietly:

'For me as well. They decide everything.'

Daniel wanted to object, but before he could say anything the clear air was shredded by a terrible howl. It came from up by the trees, and was so concentrated, raw and tremulous that it could hardly have been made by a human being.

26

'What was that?' Corinne whispered.

A cow would seem the most logical answer, but the pale brown cows on the meadow didn't appear to be missing one of their number, and were still grazing, entirely unconcerned. (Which might have been proof of Corinne's theory that they were stone deaf.)

Then there was another howl, this time more shrill.

'It's human,' Daniel declared, standing up. 'There must have been an accident.'

He looked off towards the trees and felt Corinne's hand on his.

'Don't go,' she said firmly. 'I'll call for help. Just don't go up there.'

She dug about frantically in her bag and pulled out her mobile phone.

'Don't go,' she repeated as she dialled a number, then pressed the mobile to her ear, all the while clinging on to Daniel with her other hand.

The man – Daniel could tell that it was definitely a man – was roaring non-stop from inside the forest now.

He freed himself from her hand and started to run up the hillside.

It took a few seconds for his eyes to acclimatise to the shift from the sunlight of the meadow to the gloom of the fir forest. At first he could only see one of the two men, standing with his legs wide apart and his cowboy hat pressed down firmly over his forehead. Daniel recognised him as Tom, the crazy wood carver.

It took him another few seconds before he saw the second man, who was tied to a tree trunk, completely naked. His skinny and very hairy body might almost have blurred into the bark of the tree had it not been for the dark red blood that was flowing freely from several wounds, down his torso and legs.

The scene looked like a prehistoric display of primitive religious worship and human sacrifice. It was appalling, and unreal.

'And now to mark the eighth block of wood,' Tom intoned solemnly, slowly moving his knife towards the fettered man's stomach.

He tickled him gently with the point of the knife as he studied the upturned, howling face, then withdrew the knife once more.

'Why are you screaming? I haven't touched you yet.'

The bound man looked down quickly at his stomach, then with a burst of laughter Tom cut him just below the navel. The body stiffened in a fresh howl that sounded dry and cracked, like a broken instrument.

Daniel stood there transfixed. Neither of the men seemed to have noticed him.

The cows were very close. Daniel couldn't see them, but the hard, metallic clang of their bells merged with the man's screams. It was like a terrible dream.

'You took fourteen pieces of wood, didn't you?' Tom cried. 'Fourteen, wasn't it? Or was it more?'

He's utterly mad, Daniel thought. Who had Corinne called? Was there a policeman in the village? Probably not. And there was no point expecting any help from the lethargic, withdrawn villagers. Had she called the clinic? The man was losing blood fast. And at any moment Tom was capable of dispensing the blow that would finish him off instantly.

The cowbells and screaming drowned out the sound of Daniel's footsteps as he crept around behind the men, under cover of the trees, stopping behind a dense fir tree close to Tom. He inadvertently knocked one of the branches, making it swing. Tom spun round, landing with both legs bent like a frog. He stared intently at the swaying branch. Daniel stood absolutely still.

Through a gap in the foliage he could see Tom get closer, then hold out his hand to grab the branch. Any second now his hiding place would be revealed. He felt as though he was about to pass out.

But Tom's mind followed its own path. He seemed more interested in the swaying branch itself than what had made it move.

'Fir twigs,' he said thoughtfully, tugging gently at the branch. 'Of course. I think I'll cut out your innards and stuff you full of fir twigs.'

For a moment Daniel thought Tom was talking to him, that he had seen him after all. He was preparing to raise his hand to ward off the knife when Tom suddenly let go of the branch and turned back towards the man tied to the tree.

'Yes, that's what I'll do,' he declared firmly, as though he had just had a brilliant idea. 'Bloody hell, yes. Fir twigs. That'll look great.'

Tom went on chattering in a ceaseless torrent while Daniel watched him through the foliage. He noted that Tom's grip of the knife got looser the more animated he became, until it flew out of his hand in the middle of one particularly expansive gesture.

Daniel estimated the distance between Tom and the knife on the ground. Tom moved with the agility of a young person, lithe and quick, but his grey hair and the creases on his face suggested he was in his sixties, and he didn't look especially strong. How long would it be before he picked up the knife again? A matter of seconds. Then it would be too late to save the bound man. And possibly too late to save himself as well.

Daniel stepped out between the branches and in a few quick strides was behind Tom's back. Tom had no time to notice anything, and was still chattering and gesticulating when Daniel put his left arm round his neck and wrestled him to the ground. His hat flew off and his long grey hair whipped at Daniel's face, surprisingly soft, gentle as lamb's wool.

Daniel sat astride his spindly chest and tried to trap his arms with his knees. Tom was writhing beneath him, spitting and snarling. It felt to Daniel as if he had caught a wild animal. A very wild, dangerous, and cunning animal.

And the next moment the animal had a claw, red from the blood of its prey. Tom had got hold of the knife.

Daniel leapt up and stamped as hard as he could on Tom's hand. There was a crunch, like a twig snapping. The knife flew out of his hand and fell beside them, and Daniel kicked it away into the trees. He dropped on top of Tom once more and pressed his sinewy body to the ground. Tom spat in his face, the bound man was howling, and the cowbells rang out.

'OK, let's all just calm down now,' an authoritative voice cried.

Daniel looked round, still holding Tom's arm tight. Men in uniforms were approaching out of the trees from all sides, pistols drawn.

'Nobody move. Stay exactly where you are.'

The bound man let out a hysterical sob of laughter. It was impossible to tell if it was relief at being rescued or the irony of the command he had just been given, but he was still laughing after he had been cut down from the tree and carried off on a stretcher.

Tom was sitting on the ground now, staring at his right hand as it lay limp in his lap. He was stroking it gently with his left hand as if it were a wounded baby bird.

'You hurt my hand,' he whispered, looking up at Daniel accusingly. 'Something's broken. My working hand.'

Two of the uniformed men grabbed hold of Tom and pulled him to his feet. He howled like a dog when they handcuffed him.

'My hand, my hand!' he yelled. 'Mind my working hand. It's hurt!'

Daniel said nothing when they put handcuffs on him. He was so surprised and shocked that he couldn't speak. In the world he was currently in, absolutely anything could happen, he realised that now.

The men led him out of the forest. Corinne was standing a short distance away on the meadow, talking into her mobile. She looked pale and alert. When Daniel passed her with a uniformed man on each side, she held the phone to her shoulder and called out to him:

'I saw the whole thing. I'll be a witness. Don't worry.'

The meadow, so peaceful a short while ago, was now teeming with uniforms, and up on the road stood several vehicles, both pickups and smaller cars.

The man with the stab wounds was laid in one of the pickups, which drove off quickly. Tom was put into another one, and Daniel in a third. He found himself in a windowless space with seats on either side. Even though his hands were cuffed, they still – to his utter amazement – secured him to the seat with a belt round his waist, locking it with a small key. Two police officers sat down in the seats opposite him. They *were* police officers, weren't they? How else would they have this sort of power?

Daniel stared at the locked belt and exclaimed:

'Why are you arresting *me*? *I* was the one who—'

One of the police officers waved his hand to stop him.

'We can deal with that later. Right now we just want a bit of peace and quiet in the valley.'

The back doors were closed from outside and a strip light came on in the roof. At first the light was feeble and ghostly, but flared up to full strength when the engine started.

Daniel tried to stop himself panicking. Maybe getting arrested would turn out to be a good thing. Finally he was being taken out of the valley. He might not have envisaged that it would happen in handcuffs, but at least he was going to be taken to the police station in the nearest town, where the whole matter would be investigated. Corinne and the knifed man would speak in his favour, and evidently Tom was known locally to be a madman.

It was unsettling being driven in something with no windows. Daniel felt sick. And he had a strange feeling that the vehicle was turning left the whole time, which had to be an illusion.

The vehicle stopped and the back doors were opened. They were in front of a large building. It didn't look much like a police station. Daniel turned round and saw the park stretching out towards the floor of the valley, and in the distance the sheer, yellow-white cliffs with the dark water-marks.

Then he suddenly realised that not only did he recognise the men's uniforms, but the men themselves. Two of them, anyway. They were the guards who had taken him and Marko off to the care centre.

He was still in the valley. He was at Himmelstal's rehabilitation clinic. This was the building where he had come to see Doctor Obermann on . . . yes, how long ago was it? Yesterday! God, it was yesterday. Odd things happened to time in Himmelstal.

'He's here now,' the second man said into his mobile.

The glass doors in front of them slid open.

27

An assortment of men and women were gathered round the conference table, shuffling their papers. When Daniel, escorted by two hosts, came into the room they all looked up at him as one, with expressions that seemed interested, expectant, and possibly – Daniel wasn't quite sure – friendly.

One of them stood up and came towards him. Gisela Obermann, more smartly dressed than when he had last seen her. She had done something with her hair as well, he couldn't say what. With a glance she indicated that the two hosts should leave the room, and then she gently touched Daniel's arm in welcome. She invited him to sit down on the vacant chair next to her, then turned to address her colleagues.

'Most of you have met Max before, of course, and are aware of his background. The reason I've asked him to come here today is partly because of an incident that occurred a couple of hours ago, and partly as a result of a process which has been going on for a while and which I believe could be of interest to us. I'm very happy you could join us today,' she went on, facing Daniel, 'and that you're willing to help us with our research.'

Daniel gave her a cold look. She made it sound as if he was attending voluntarily. When the truth was that he had been brought back to the clinic in handcuffs and had spent the last hour in a waiting room. He had sat there reading German and American magazines while a nurse looked in on him every now and then, bringing him juice and sandwiches, and asking him to wait a bit longer. Then two men in pale blue hosts' uniforms had suddenly appeared and politely asked him to accompany them up to the doctors' floor.

'Can you start by telling us your name?' Gisela Obermann said.

'What sort of nonsense is this?' an older man interrupted. Daniel recognised him from the clinic's inspection rounds. Doctor Fischer. Director of the clinic, and its chief consultant. Hair like a metal brush.

'Please, just listen. This might be more important than you think, Doctor Fischer.' Gisela turned back to Daniel again. 'What's your name?' she asked with exaggerated lip movements, as though she were talking to someone who was hard of hearing.

'Daniel Brant,' Daniel replied in a firm, clear voice. 'Max's twin brother.'

'Exactly.'

Gisela looked at the other participants round the table in triumph. The man next to Doctor Fischer was smiling cautiously. He was the only one in the room wearing a white coat. And the only one with dark skin. Indian background, Daniel guessed. Someone raised a pen and opened his mouth to say something, but Gisela had already turned back to Daniel:

'You've been unsettled these past few days. You asked the hostesses to call a taxi, because you wanted to leave Himmelstal. Is that right?'

'My visit is over. So naturally I want to leave Himmelstal,' Daniel said irritably.

'Naturally,' Gisela Obermann nodded. 'You've explained how you came to be here to me and the hostesses. Would you mind telling my colleagues?'

Daniel took a deep breath and composed himself.

'We'll listen to you with open minds and without any preconceived opinions,' Gisela added.

He repeated the story as briefly and factually as possible. But Gisela wanted more detail:

'Why did Max want to get away from here?'

Daniel explained about his brother's dealings with the mafia, and the threat against his Italian fiancée.

'And how did ... er ... Max receive news of this threat?' a man with a short red beard wanted to know.

'He got a letter.'

'A letter? Here, in Himmelstal?'

'Yes. At least that's what he said. Somehow they had found out that he was here.'

'And where is this letter now?' the red-bearded man asked.

No one was looking down at their papers or gazing at the magnificent view from the window any longer. All eyes were on Daniel.

'I've no idea. I assume he got rid of it. But I know where the photograph is.'

'What photograph?' two of the doctors asked at the same time.

'They sent a photograph of a girl they'd beaten up. To make him understand they were serious. It's down in the cabin if you want to see it.'

Gisela was nodding intently.

'So Max got out of Himmelstal, and you were left behind?'

'Yes.'

'That wasn't very nice.'

'No, but that's what he's like. Although I suppose something could have happened to him as well.'

185

Several hands were in the air now, but Gisela ignored them.

'I'm sure you all have plenty of questions, but I propose that we move on to what happened earlier today. You were on an outing with a girl from the village, is that right? Could you tell us what happened?'

Daniel recounted the whole nightmarish episode with Tom and the wounded man tied to the tree.

'So you crept up on him and disarmed him?' Gisela summarised. 'Why?'

Daniel looked at her, taken aback.

'To stop him, of course. He was harming a bound man. Torturing him. It was the worst thing I've ever seen.'

An older woman spoke up. She looked like someone's grandmother, with old-fashioned glasses, her hair in a bun, and a shawl around her shoulders.

'Did you know how dangerous Tom is?' she asked quietly.

'Well, obviously I could see what he was doing to the man tied to the tree. He's mad!'

'Weren't you worried you might get hurt?' the grandmotherly woman went on.

'I was terrified.'

The grandmotherly woman nodded, then made some notes.

'Had you met Tom before?' someone asked, Daniel didn't see who.

'I met him a few days ago when I was trying to get a lift out of here. I realised even then that he was crazy. But I didn't know he was so violent.'

'Did you have any dealings together, you and Tom?'

This came from the man with the red beard. He looked up eagerly, almost cheerfully, from a notepad covered in writing.

'Dealings?' Daniel said. 'What sort of dealings?'

'Concerning wood. Or anything else?'

'No,' Daniel laughed. 'I wouldn't have any dealings with someone like him.'

'Did you have any dealings with André Bonnard?' the red-bearded man went on.

'Who?'

'The man who was being tortured,' Gisela explained.

'No. I have no idea who he is.'

The red-bearded man turned a page of his pad and wrote quickly, like a stenographer.

Daniel looked at the men and women round the conference table. He had been waiting to meet these respected doctors, and here they were, all together. A gathering of idiots.

'I saved the life of that Bonnard, or whatever his name is. But I was treated as if I'd escaped from a madhouse, then brought back here in handcuffs by some sort of guards. And the other day I was locked in a ward and almost died in a fire because your hospital has such atrocious safety procedures. I'm considering suing you.'

'Just a moment,' Gisela Obermann said. 'I haven't been told about any fire?'

She looked around questioningly.

'A minor incident during routine testing,' Doctor Fischer clarified. 'A fire in a mattress. A discarded cigarette. It was quickly dealt with by the staff.'

'A minor incident? We could have died!' Daniel said angrily. 'Marko passed out from the smoke. I tried to drag him out. The whole room was full of smoke.'

'Your patient's exaggerating,' Doctor Fischer said to Gisela Obermann.

'I should still have received a report.'

'There was nothing to report. He's only trying to pretend he was a hero.'

'But this is of great interest to me,' Gisela said, her cheeks now starting to burn. 'This is extremely interesting.'

'Are we done with this now?' Daniel said. 'If we are, perhaps I can go.'

'Of course,' Gisela Obermann said. 'You've been through a very unpleasant experience and need to get some rest. You don't have to worry about Tom from now on, I can assure you of that.'

Daniel snorted.

'I'm not remotely worried about Tom. For God's sake, haven't you realised you've got the wrong patient here? You let a sick man go and you're holding a healthy one. *You* ought to be worried about *that*.'

'We've got plenty of time to discuss that,' Gisela Obermann said.

'You might have, but I haven't. I'm getting out of this place right now.'

'By all means. You're welcome to return to your cabin if you wish.'

'Obviously I mean I'm leaving the clinic.'

He stood up and tucked his chair in.

The red-bearded man stopped taking notes and sat there with his pen poised, as though he were waiting for some fresh remark. There was a faint sound of snoring from the Indian doctor, who appeared to have fallen asleep in spite of his upright posture. Doctor Fischer cleared his throat loudly and the Indian snapped his eyes open like a doll.

'Goodbye,' Daniel said, and left the room.

28

The night was beautiful and still.

Daniel was at the eastern end of the valley, crossing the bridge. On the right-hand side the water flowed as sluggishly as an old river. To the left it threw itself down steep rocks and carried on its course deep between the walls of a narrow, impenetrable ravine, dramatically lit by moonlight as if in some nineteenth-century Romantic painting.

He followed the road on the far side of the rapids, and now had the vertical wall of the mountain with its water stains to his left.

On the opposite side of the valley he could see the village with its church tower and, higher up the slope, the clinic. Above him the sky hung like a dark blue, semi-transparent canvas strung up between the two mountainsides. There was a smell of earth and grass and water.

He had realised that the road for vehicle traffic followed the oblong shape of the valley in an elliptical, closed circuit. Like a loop. A noose.

But the loop wasn't entirely closed. It joined another road, it must do, because how else would anyone ever get into the valley?

His plan was to avoid the road on the north side of the river where the village and clinic were. Instead he would stick to the south side, and follow the road along the vertical cliff he called the Wall. The way the taxi had come when he arrived. Unfortunately he had been asleep for the last part of the drive, so didn't know exactly where they had entered the valley and joined the loop. Probably either just before or after they had been stopped by the guards with the metal detector. Where the mountain was covered with ferns. Or had the ferns been part of his dream? Oh well, sooner or later he had to reach a junction where one of the roads would lead out of the valley.

He was better prepared this time, and had packed his rucksack for a long hike. His plan was to get as far as he could under cover of darkness. If a vehicle approached he would take cover until the coast was clear. When he got tired he would rest in an old barn or in the shade of a tree, maybe get a few hours' sleep. Then he would continue his hike. He wouldn't try to get help from anyone, or ask for directions. He couldn't expect anything from the villagers, they were all in the pocket of the clinic one way or another, even the lovely Corinne. The amount of respect she had for the doctors was fairly absurd. He came to think of old Swedish spa resorts with their complicated, double-edged loyalties.

The valley broadened out and he could make out fields and small clumps of deciduous trees between the road and the mountainside. He couldn't see any animals in the fields. Maybe they sought shelter in amongst the trees at night. Assuming there were any there in the first place. Because what animals would allow themselves to be penned in by such a ridiculously simple barrier – a length of nylon wire strung up scarcely a metre above the ground?

There were signs hanging from the wire at regular intervals.

They swayed gently in the night wind. When the moon peered out he grabbed hold of one of them and read 'Zone 1'. The next one said 'Warning' in three different languages. Every other sign said 'Zone 1', interspersed with those that said 'Warning'.

Daniel looked at the grassy slope on the far side of the barrier. He could see nothing to suggest the need for any warning. No shooting range, no building site, no sign of human activity at all. Just grass and trees and the rock face.

He heard a car engine in the distance. The car was coming towards him from behind, from the direction of the clinic. He ducked quickly under the wire and hurried across the meadow towards a clump of trees. He wondered about the warning, but the approaching car constituted a clear and immediate danger, whereas the warning was incomprehensible and vague, and possibly no longer even accurate. He stood still in the darkness between some thickets of hazel, waiting for the car to pass. But instead of going past, it pulled up and stopped. Two clinic guards got out.

The next moment a car approached at speed from the other direction and pulled up alongside the first one. Another two guards got out and after a brief exchange all four of them ducked under the nylon wire and fanned out across the meadow. Two of them hurried off towards the rock face, and two made their way towards the clump of trees where Daniel was hiding.

He pulled back deeper into the trees, well aware that he couldn't go much more than fifty metres. After that the mountain got in the way. Then he was forced to proceed westward along the rock face, hoping that the trees would carry on, to protect and conceal him.

Now he could see the far side of the meadow: the signs hanging from the wire fluttered like big white moths in the darkness.

The uniformed men were behind him. The cones of light from their powerful torches exposed the tree trunks, signs and rock face in brief, incoherent images.

'Can you see him?' one of them called.

'No, but he's got to be here.'

He quickly ducked under the wire.

The next moment something terrible leapt up from the grass and hit him, cutting through his skin and muscle.

PART TWO

29

One by one the members of Himmelstal's research team came into the conference room. Squinting against the morning sun flooding in through the plate-glass window, they sat down in the seats that had become theirs over time, opened their briefcases and took out their notebooks and plastic folders.

Gisela Obermann was standing at the head of the table, smiling anxiously at her colleagues as they arrived. When they were all there she closed the door.

'I hope you have an extremely good reason for calling this meeting,' Karl Fischer said as he irritably opened a bottle of mineral water and poured himself a glass. 'Max,' he read from the summary that Gisela had left at all their places. 'Again. What's he come up with now?'

'I'm sorry to call a meeting at such short notice this morning,' Gisela Obermann said. 'But of course that's the advantage of our all being in the same place. Things happen, and we can meet at once to discuss them.'

'What's happened?' Hedda Heine wondered. She leaned across the table and peered over the top of her glasses like a worried mother owl.

'Has he done any more heroic deeds?' Karl Fischer said tartly.

'I'm about to tell you what's happened. But first I'd like to remind you of yesterday's meeting. You remember that we sat here yesterday and listened to Max? You remember what he claimed?'

'That he was called something else,' Hedda Heine said.

'Daniel Brant,' Brian Jenkins read with his forefinger on his notes. 'Max's twin brother. They'd changed places.'

'Yes, dear God,' Fischer said, taking a large sip of mineral water.

'You also remember the reason for yesterday's meeting?' Gisela went on, pretending not to have noticed Karl Fischer's derisive tone. 'He risked his own life to save another person. Would you, with all your experience and knowledge of Max, say that this was characteristic behaviour for him?'

'No,' several people muttered.

'He wants attention, that's all. And he certainly got it,' Karl Fischer said. 'Besides, we don't know exactly what happened.'

'What happened was exactly what he told us. The guards have confirmed it. Well, his behaviour certainly surprised *me* a great deal. It made me think about what he told me before. That he's Max's twin brother, physically almost identical, but a completely different person.'

'I honestly don't see why you're making such a fuss about this,' Karl Fischer said. 'Lying is part of these people's personalities. As far as I understand it, this particular individual lies more often than he tells the truth. It's hardly anything new.'

Gisela nodded.

'That's what I thought as well. But this is so well thought out, so carefully planned and executed. Those of you who have met Max before know that his lies blossom instantly and are abandoned shortly thereafter. Of all the untruths he's tried to get me to believe, he's never repeated a single one of them. He simply gets fed up of them. He's far too quixotic and impatient to be able to stick to a lie with any degree of consistency. This time he's done precisely that. For four days now, he's been telling exactly the same story to different people.'

'I dare say his imagination is running dry,' Fischer muttered. 'Even the best storytellers repeat themselves sometimes.'

'The question we must always ask ourselves,' Hedda Heine said, 'is: what does the person in question stand to gain by this? These people do nothing without it benefiting them somehow.'

'He's already explained that very clearly. He wants to be released,' Fischer interrupted abruptly. 'Naturally that's impossible, but hope is always the last thing to die. And you're far too experienced to let yourself be manipulated, Gisela. So why are you taking up our time with this?'

Gisela took a deep breath, composed herself, then said:

'As we speak, Max is lying in intensive care with burns to the right side of his body. He went into Zone 2 last night.'

There was a moment's silence around the table. Doctor Fischer was drawing geometric patterns on his pad.

'Is he badly hurt?' Hedda Heine asked.

'It was dark, and the security staff didn't find him immediately. He was left lying there rather too long. But he'll be OK.'

Brian Jenkins was leafing through a bundle of papers with a look of concentration.

'Wasn't he the one who . . . Yes, here it is.' He tapped his finger at a line he had just found. 'August last year. The culvert.'

Gisela fixed him with an intense stare.

'Precisely! Max went into Zone 2 almost a year ago. Don't you see what that means?'

The others looked at her rather uncertainly.

'This is extremely significant. After all, we usually say that no one goes into Zone 2 more than once,' Doctor Pierce pointed out.

'Exactly!'

Gisela's cheeks were red. The others were still looking thoughtful.

'There's something that doesn't make sense with this man,' she went on. 'I've felt it since my conversation with him on Tuesday. I sat up last night studying the recordings of our meetings.'

She paused, then looked hesitantly at Doctor Fischer, who was whispering something to Doctor Kalpak. The others waited. Hedda Heine gave her a gesture of encouragement and she went on:

'I compared our most recent meeting with previous ones. And that only confirmed my suspicions. Something was very different. His gestures, posture, choice of words, facial expressions, the way he moved his head, the way he walked and sat down. All the things that are so characteristic of a person, the things that are so obvious that neither the person themselves or anyone else actually thinks about them. This simply isn't Max, I thought. It's Max's body. But there's someone else inside it.'

30

Like a magnificent ship, Gisela Obermann's balcony seemed to be drifting through the air. From the ground below them came the smell of pine needles, moist grass and glacial meltwater. The sky was overcast and veils of cloud glided at low altitude through the valley.

Gisela Obermann tucked the blanket more tightly around him, then sat down in the adjacent recliner and asked:

'What do you know about Himmelstal, Daniel?'

'It's a luxury clinic in a beautiful but dangerous setting. The staff seem crazier than the patients. But the native inhabitants of the valley are craziest of all. And there's practically no communication with the outside world. Every time I try to get away from here, I get yanked back by some invisible rubber band. That's pretty much everything I know.'

He buried his chin in the blanket the doctor had wrapped around him. It had a faint smell of her own perfume.

It wasn't really cold, but the thermostat controlling his body temperature seemed rather erratic, and without warning an icy chill could rise up from the injured parts of his leg and upper arm and spread through his body with a shiver. The next moment the cold could be replaced by heat. He had been told that this was good, a sign that the nerves were undamaged.

'So you don't know anything. This place must seem extremely odd to you.'

Daniel let out a bitter little laugh.

'To put it mildly.'

'It's occurred to me that I'm going to have to regard you as a new arrival here in Himmelstal. And tell you all the things I usually tell new arrivals.'

Gisela Obermann sat herself more comfortably in the recliner.

'I should probably take it from the start. It takes a while to explain.'

Daniel shrugged his shoulders under the blanket.

'I've been here almost two weeks. I can stay a little while longer. Take as long as you like.'

'OK. You know what psychopathic behaviour is, don't you?'

'Sure, how do you mean? A psychopath is an individual with no conscience. An evil person.'

'That last phrase isn't a term used by professionals, obviously. But of course by definition evil is precisely the act of causing innocent people to suffer without feeling any guilt. But if we are to call a person evil, then this person has to have the chance to make a choice. And the person making the choice has to know what they are choosing between, naturally. But a psychopath doesn't know the difference between good and evil.'

Daniel protested.

'I'm sure they do.'

'Intellectually, maybe. They know that lies, theft and violence are evil, in the same way that someone colour-blind knows that tomatoes, blood and sunsets are red. But just as a colour-blind person will never experience with their own senses what we mean when we say "red", a psychopath will never experience what we mean when we say something is "evil". Concepts such as good and evil, love and guilt are words without any meaning. It's a definite lack, but the psychopath him or herself doesn't suffer from it. It's the world around them that suffers. The worst violent crimes are committed by psychopaths . . . '

'Forgive me,' Daniel interrupted, 'but where are you going with this? Which psychopath are you talking about here?'

Gisela Obermann looked at him in surprise, and seemed close to laughter. She looked down at her lap for a few seconds, apparently composing herself, then raised a perfectly serious face to him.

'You'll soon understand, Daniel. Be patient. So, as I was saying, the worst violent crimes are committed by psychopaths. People who commit such crimes are obviously given very severe punishments. But . . . ' She held a finger in the air and raised her eyebrows. 'What if the people committing these crimes have a small medical abnormality that make their brains different to ours? What if their brains lack the capacity for empathy? Is it then right to demand that they show empathy, and punish them because they can't? Isn't that just as wrong as demanding that a paralysed stroke victim should walk? Or that someone with learning disabilities should solve complex logic puzzles? They simply *can't*. They don't have the brain that's required to do it.'

'Do you have any scientific evidence for this, or is this something you've worked out entirely on your own?' Daniel asked.

'A bit of both. We've accumulated substantial research evidence showing that psychopaths' brains are different to other people's, but not enough for us to understand the full extent of the difference. We might be able to solve the mystery next year, or in ten years' time. Or maybe never. But what is obvious is that psychopaths' brains demonstrate clear abnormalities. There are very definite differences in their frontal lobes and amygdalas, unusual brainwaves in response to emotional stimuli, an overactive dopamine system and a number of other things. The differences are physiological and measurable. If these people act the way that they do as the result of a physical handicap, can it be right to punish them, Daniel? Locking them up in terrible prisons or, as in some states, executing them?'

'I'm against capital punishment,' Daniel said, scratching his chin.

He hadn't shaved for several days, and his beard was starting to grow again. He couldn't help feeling it. It was like a source of security in the midst of all the confusion. A cuddly animal that was always with him.

'But obviously society needs to protect itself from dangerous criminals,' he went on. 'Whether or not they've had unhappy childhoods or have weird brainwaves or whatever else. There's no place for them in society.'

Gisela Obermann seemed satisfied with his answer.

'Exactly. Every attempt at treatment and rehabilitation thus far has failed. The reoffending rate among psychopathic criminals is alarmingly high. Psychopathy remains incurable. So: punishment instead of treatment.'

She put her hand in her pocket and pulled out a case containing long, narrow cigarillos.

'Unless,' she said, lighting one of them, 'there's a third option.'

'Do you really want some sort of moral, philosophical discussion?' Daniel said. 'I think you're going to have to find someone else for that. I'd rather you just explained what happened to me in that meadow. I've never come across an electric fence strong enough to inflict actual physical burns before. What sort of animals are kept there? Elephants?'

202

Gisela held the case of cigarillos out to Daniel. He shook his head. She leaned back in her chair, took a few thoughtful puffs, and let the smoke sail off over the railing of the balcony.

'A third option,' she repeated, as if she hadn't heard Daniel's interruption.

Maybe she was deranged? It wouldn't be that unusual for a psychiatrist.

'What third option?' Daniel asked.

She carried on smoking in silence for a while, then went on:

'A brief history lesson: fourteen years ago there was a big European conference in Turin about psychosocial personality disorders, popularly known as the Psychopath Conference, where a whole load of neurologists, psychiatrists, politicians and philosophers met up. They shared research findings, held debates, argued. They struggled round the clock with the question of how we can protect ourselves from these extremely dangerous individuals in an ethically defensible way. After rigorous debate, gradually a vision emerged that they could all unite around. Some form of long-term – probably lifelong – isolation was deemed essential, but not in an institution like a prison or a mental hospital. It had to be an environment that offered decent living standards and freedom within certain very limited boundaries. Somewhere people could live a reasonable life. The place would have to be fairly large, seeing as it would have to house a lot of people, and would constitute its inhabitants' whole world for the rest of their lives. What they had in mind was a life that was as normal as possible. The inhabitants should have private accommodation, they should have some sort of occupation or other meaningful activity. They should be able to run businesses, study, take exercise, and be given the opportunity to develop different skills. In short, an entire little society.'

'That all sounds nice and cosy,' Daniel said.

'That depends how you look at it. The place would obviously have to be completely isolated from the outside world. Everyone was careful to stress how different it would be to the way similar groups had been treated historically – leper colonies and so on. This wasn't about shunting people out of sight and forgetting about them. On the contrary, the place would be a centre for research, and would offer a unique opportunity to study psychopaths under controlled conditions in a relatively normal environment. Not to punish, not to provide care. But to study. Research, observe, measure. With the intention of finally uncovering the mysteries of psychopathy, identifying its causes and developing an effective treatment. That was the goal, albeit a distant one.'

'A colony of psychopaths,' Daniel said with a little whistle.

Gisela Obermann reached over the balcony railing and tapped the ash from her cigarillo.

'Exactly. The conference delegates were agreed on all this. The problem was the location. A lot of people thought an island would be the obvious choice for an experiment of this nature. A working group was set up to investigate the feasibility of various islands. But it turned out that the supply of isolated islands with the conditions for a reasonable life was distinctly limited. Any that fitted the requirements had long since been settled and exploited. Those that remained had no drinking water or natural harbour, or were far too rugged to be safely inhabited. Officially the project got no further than that.'

She broke off, turned towards Daniel and said with sudden suspicion:

'Is this really new to you?'

'Yes, but I don't see why you're telling me all this. What happened to the project?'

'There was a report. Which got lost among the many other

reports in the archive.' She reached over the balcony railing again and sent more ash through the air. 'That was the official version. But one of the delegates, a neuropsychiatrist, couldn't let go of the idea. An acquaintance had told him in passing about a motoring trip in the Swiss Alps, where he had ended up in a narrow, depopulated valley full of ramshackle barns and an abandoned clinic building. The psychiatrist – my current boss, Karl Fischer – visited the valley and discovered that it was absolutely perfect for the purpose. He set about getting funding, and a few years later Himmelstal was set up as an isolated area for psychopaths, where they could live and be studied. We don't have any official status, but the authorities in most European countries are aware of us and send us patients.'

'So I've ended up in a clinic for psychopaths?' Daniel let out a raw laugh. 'That explains why the villagers prefer to keep their distance. But not everyone in the clinic is a psychopath, are they? If I've understood it correctly, there are plenty of patients suffering from stress-related problems, exhaustion, depression, that sort of thing.'

She looked at him, then smiled.

'Oh, Daniel, I . . . I'll come back to that. There's more to explain first. These zones, for instance, do you know about them?'

'I haven't managed to avoid finding out about them. Particularly the rather unfriendly Zone 2,' Daniel said bitterly, with a gesture towards the injured parts of his body. 'But you're welcome to explain more. It would be fascinating to know why you subject innocent visitors to electrical torture and serious burns.'

'That wasn't intentional and I'm very sorry you were so badly hurt. You didn't know about the zones, otherwise you wouldn't have wandered off into them. You should have been told about the risks. *I* should have told you about them,' she corrected herself. 'I should have been more alert, and I should have paid more attention to what you were saying when we spoke. It was unforgiveable of me not to warn you.'

'Warn me about what?'

'As I said before, the area had to be completely cut off from the outside world. Obviously there's a natural geographic boundary already in the form of the steep mountains surrounding the valley. But of course that isn't enough, more barriers are needed. Walls and fences don't fit the profile of the project. With Zone 2 we've created an invisible but very effective barrier. The zone runs in a loop around the entire valley, and the ground is mined with electrically charged cables. The strength of the charge is too low to be fatal, but it does make it impossible for anyone to get through.'

'It was certainly enough for me, at any rate.'

'You fell and were left lying in the live area. The guards were a bit too slow getting to you and didn't manage to cut the current in time. No one's supposed to suffer the sort of burns you were subjected to.'

'So what is supposed to happen, then?'

'That people are scared off. Stopped. Conditioned. And rendered unconscious if they carry on further into the zone. The charge is weakest at the edge, and stronger further in.'

'And Zone 1?'

'A warning zone. So that no one wanders into Zone 2 by mistake. It runs in a loop between the authorised area and Zone 2. Zone 1 is saturated with cameras and motion sensors. If you ignore the warning signs and carry on into Zone 2 regardless, you set off an alarm and one of the patrolling security vehicles will arrive shortly afterwards to pick you up. Hopefully before you make it into Zone 2, but if the car's some distance away when the alarm goes off, then what happened to you can be the result. Then of course there's a Zone 3 as well.'

'Of course,' Daniel said sarcastically. 'And a Zone 4, and a Zone 5.'

'No, no. There are only three zones. Or three shells, as we usually say. Himmelstal is like an egg with three shells.'

Gisela drew an oval shape in the air.

'Zone 3 is another warning zone. Facing outwards, towards the outside world. So that no poor mountaineer or lost tourist wanders into Zone 2. Zone 3 is a large area surrounding the other zones, and it consists mainly of inaccessible mountains. It's not particularly likely that anyone would arrive that way, but we've still put up signs saying that this is a military area, out of bounds to the general public, and that trespassers risk life-threatening injury.'

'A military area? Why bother to lie?'

'Himmelstal is . . . well, not exactly a secret project, but not quite public either. We hope to become more open when we can demonstrate more research. If we went public today, we'd have to spend all our time and energy explaining and defending it. We can't afford that. We have official bodies in every EU country behind us, so there's nothing untoward going on. But for the time being we prefer to work with a certain degree of secrecy.'

Daniel looked at Gisela Obermann. She was sitting upright now, and there was a feverish glow in her eyes. In an odd way she seemed happy. As if she had just seen salvation. Of all the patients he had encountered at the clinic, none of them had radiated as much madness as this woman. Was there any truth in what she was saying, or was it all her imagination? Maybe she was actually a patient who for some bizarre reason had managed to gain access to one of the doctors' rooms?

He gazed out over the valley. Veils of cloud were drifting like smoke in front of the giant figures on the rock face to the south. That was where he had made his nocturnal escape attempt through the pale green meadows and leafy woodland.

That was where the guards had pursued him towards the mountain while their shouts and torches cut through the darkness. He knew all of this with absolute certainty. And he knew something else: there had been something terrible in amongst that vegetation. Something that had made him lose consciousness and had given him these burns.

'These zones . . . ' he said, huddling up under the blanket.

'Yes?'

'You can get here along the road without any problem.'

'If your arrival is expected, yes. But not otherwise. The road is well guarded where it passes through the three zones. If an unwelcome visitor fails to heed the warning signs and makes it to the final zone, a patrol car will soon be there to warn them off. It happens sometimes with tourists who've taken the wrong turning.'

'So what about welcome visitors, then?'

'Anyone who has a legitimate reason to come to Himmelstal – staff, goods lorries, visiting researchers and relatives – has to inform us of their arrival in advance. Their approach is picked up in good time by the surveillance cameras, and they're stopped by the guards before they reach Zone 2.'

Daniel recalled his arrival in the valley. The dark blue van. The men in uniform who had searched him with a metal detector and gone through his bag.

'If everything's OK, the current and alarms along the road are switched off so that the vehicle can enter,' Gisela went on. 'As soon as it's through, the current is switched on again and the ring around the area is complete once more.'

'An electric gate opening and closing,' Daniel said quietly.

Gisela nodded and stubbed her cigarillo out on the railing.

'Exactly. Invisible, but effective. Like the system of zones as a whole: invisible, but effective.'

She took out the little case again and put the remains of the cigarillo in beside the fresh ones.

'Himmelstal's inhabitants don't have to look at an ugly fence. Nevertheless they know that the barrier is there, and they respect it. Quite a few have wandered into Zone 1, either by mistake or out of some spirit of adventure, and have been stopped there. A few have got through the net and made it into Zone 2. But no one who has ever been in Zone 2 goes on to repeat the experience! That's what's so remarkable. Here I'm talking about people prone to taking huge risks, people governed by instinct, the way most psychopaths are. People who quickly forget an unpleasant experience and are utterly incapable of learning from the past. *Yet no one has ever entered Zone 2 more than once.*'

Gisela paused and waited for Daniel's response. He looked at her questioningly. She leaned forward and went on:

'An electric shock is the sort of thing that goes straight into the body's memory.'

She was staring intently at Daniel to make sure he was listening. She was so close he could feel her quick, shallow breathing.

'That's the most effective conditioning there is, as any researcher working with animal testing knows. You can be the most deluded person in the world, rearranging your past as much as you like, and therefore making the same mistakes time and time again. But you can't erase an electric shock. It's etched into your memory for the rest of your life. And this is exactly what we need, in order to set limits for psychopaths: an unambiguous message that speaks directly to the body, ignoring the manipulative nature of consciousness. An experience that a psychopath can never forget or pretend never happened. It's the type of thing that isn't susceptible to that sort of process. It's a primitive form of awareness that embeds itself very deeply.'

'Once bitten, twice shy,' Daniel muttered. 'A reliable old pedagogical strategy. I have to confess, it's an experience I could easily have done without. But every cloud has a silver lining. Since I got that electric shock your attitude towards me has changed. You're explaining things to me, you're calling me by my real name. It actually looks as though you've finally realised who I am.'

She put her hand on Daniel's blanket in the place where she thought his hand was.

'I'm sorry I didn't realise before,' she said, with genuine regret in her voice. 'I had my suspicions, but I wasn't sure.'

'So what was it that convinced you?'

She laughed.

'I just told you. No one ever goes into Zone 2 more than once. Max went into Zone 2. Then you did. That proves that you're two different personalities.'

Her choice of words confused him.

'Max went into Zone 2 as well?'

'Sorry, of course you wouldn't know that. It was sometime last summer. He tried to escape through a culvert by the rapids. He picked a time when the water level was low, sawed through the grating and crawled in. He must have assumed that the zone was only active above ground. But there's another grate further inside the drain. There are several more, as a matter of fact, but he got no further than the first because that one's electrified. The patrol car happened to be nearby and they pulled him out immediately.'

Gisela Obermann paused and looked at Daniel with sudden anxiety.

'How does it feel when I tell you this?'

'I'm surprised.' Daniel gulped to clear the lump that had come to his throat. 'And this happened last summer? I didn't know Max had been here that long. I thought . . .'

'What did you think?'

'Never mind. The important thing is that you finally realise that I'm not Max. It's been horrible, being mistaken for him

210

the whole time. Being accused of lying and manipulating. For a while I thought it was going to drive me mad.'

To his own surprise he found himself letting out a dry, croaky laugh, and at the same moment he felt a tear running down his cheek. He quickly pulled one hand out from under the blanket and wiped it away.

Gisela smiled at him sympathetically.

'You're much nicer than Max,' she said.

'But Max is your patient. It must be a problem for you that he's finally managed to escape.'

'That's nothing you need to worry about. Leave that to us. How are you feeling? Are you tired? Burn injuries take a lot out of the body, even if they are relatively superficial. And what I've just told you must be fairly disconcerting. Would you like to return to your room?'

Daniel shook his head firmly. He had no desire at all to go back to the little room in the care centre where he had spent the past few days. He would have liked to believe he was dreaming. But the air was so fresh that every breath felt like drinking a mouthful of cool water. Surely you couldn't experience air that way in dreams? The burned skin on his leg and shoulder ached and stung. He was more awake than he had ever been before.

Gisela Obermann glanced at her watch.

'It's high time for lunch. Shall I order some food to be brought up for us?'

31

With the help of two crutches Daniel left the balcony, hopping through the sliding doors on his uninjured leg into Gisela Obermann's spacious room. Lunch had been set out for them on the table: two plates of lamb fillet and root vegetable mash, and a bottle of red wine. A silver-coloured serving trolley was parked alongside. Daniel realised that lunch had been delivered from the restaurant, not the patients' canteen.

Gisela pulled out a chair for him and helped him sit down.

'Do the doctors here usually invite their patients to lunch in their offices?' he wondered, cutting a piece of pink, thyme-scented meat. The knife sank through it as easily as if it were butter.

'Not usually, no.'

'Did you and Max used to eat lunch here?'

Gisela Obermann laughed and put down the wine glass she had just picked up.

'Max? No. He hardly ever wanted to come here. He hated talking to me. You're completely different, Daniel. The evening after you were last here I stayed up late reviewing recordings of previous meetings with Max. I compared them with the film of our conversation. And I could see immediately that everything was different with you. The same body. But still different.'

'Haven't you ever heard of twins, Gisela?'

'According to our records, Max doesn't have a twin brother. Then there were those incidents with the fire and Tom. You risked your life to save other people. Max would never have done that. That reinforced what I was thinking. My colleagues didn't believe me. They assumed you were manipulating me. But once you went into Zone 2, there was no denying the facts any more. That was the proof.'

She smiled triumphantly.

'Proof of what?' Daniel wondered.

'That your personality is genuine. It's all-encompassing. If there had been the slightest trace of Max left in you, you wouldn't have been able to go into Zone 2. But you've erased him completely. I don't know how it happened. It probably has something to do with your first electric shock . . . '

'My *first*?'

'Last summer.'

'But that happened to Max,' he protested.

Gisela nodded quickly.

'Exactly. That was when you were still Max. You lost consciousness on that occasion as well, lost your memory for a short while. You soon recovered, but something had happened to you. You were quieter, more withdrawn. When your brother came to see you, you adopted his personality. Absorbed his whole body language and open manner. And when he left, you believed you were him. You *became* Daniel. A pleasant, empathetic, selfless man. It might only be temporary, but it's wonderful nonetheless.'

She smiled, her eyes twinkling.

'This is the first time we've been able to observe a change

in any of our residents. A positive change, no less. This is incredibly hopeful for our research.'

Daniel felt giddy. He put his knife and fork down.

'That's what you think?' he exclaimed. 'That I'm suffering from multiple personalities?'

'I'm not sure I'd say suffering. In your case it's a purely positive development. Even if Max comes back, you'll have Daniel inside you, and he's the one we need to focus on and try to draw out. This could be the breakthrough we've been waiting for.'

'So you don't believe a word I've told you? You don't believe Max has escaped and that I'm his twin brother?'

Daniel was so upset that he tried to stand up, but the pain in his leg made him slump back down again.

Gisela Obermann dabbed carefully at her mouth with her linen napkin.

'I believe that story is real for you, Daniel,' she said diplomatically. 'You don't remember anything of your life as Max. Memory loss is more the rule than the exception in cases of dissociative identity disorders.'

Daniel was close to tears of despair.

'But you are going to let me leave, aren't you?'

'Leave?'

Gisela Obermann was studying him with a shocked expression.

'No, I'm afraid not. Definitely not. You're the golden egg. Our first evidence of progress. We're going to watch over you day and night and make sure you feel absolutely fine. Would you like coffee?'

She reached for a flask and two cups on the trolley.

Daniel shook his head. As she poured herself a cup she said:

'I'm going to be having a meeting with my colleagues tomorrow, and that's when I'm going to present my theory about your case. And this time they're going to believe me.'

She smiled momentarily down into her cup of coffee. Her cheeks were glowing and her voice had risen to a falsetto.

'I hope I won't have to attend this meeting?'

'Attend? Daniel, you're going to be the star attraction!'

She held out a plate of chocolate macaroons. He didn't see it.

'So when will I be able to leave?'

'When we've solved this mystery,' Gisela said, quickly popping a macaroon in her mouth before putting the plate back on the trolley. 'You could become our first fully treated case. The first cured psychopath. When we no longer need you for our research, then ... ' She shrugged. 'Well, it's perfectly conceivable that you would be the first person in history to be discharged from this clinic.'

She paused, as though she were listening to what she had just said, and found it so remarkable that she scarcely believed it. Then she lit up.

'Discharged? Yes. Why not? *Why not?*'

'When?'

'Oh.' Her smile became more subdued. 'Not for the next few years, of course. Serious research takes time, as you know. But we're going to take very good care of you here, you can be sure of that.'

She reached across the table and patted him gently on the cheek. Daniel twisted his head away.

She *is* mad, he thought. I don't have to pay any attention to anything she says. He had noticed it the first time he saw her. Little glimpses of something dark and broken in her eyes. Like a face appearing briefly in a window, then pulling back as soon as you spotted it.

Then a different thought occurred to him.

'You keep talking about psychopaths. Do you mean that Max is a psychopath?'

215

'He wouldn't have ended up here in Himmelstal otherwise, would he?'

'But there's no real evidence for that diagnosis, is there? He's burned out. Manic depressive. A bit crazy sometimes. That doesn't make someone a psychopath, does it?'

Gisela Obermann burst out laughing.

'Manic depressive and a bit crazy? Maybe. But that's not why you're sitting here, my dear Max–Daniel. Wait a moment, I'll show you something.'

Gisela got up and went over to a small filing cabinet behind her desk. She opened one of the drawers and returned with a bundle of photographs that she laid on the table in front of Daniel.

'Do these pictures mean anything to you?'

He looked at the top picture. A semi-naked man, lying in a pool of blood on a bathroom floor. The next one: a close-up of the dead man's face, half of which had been smashed in. A solitary eye stared blankly from the mess of congealed blood. Horrified and disgusted, Daniel looked up to see Gisela observing him closely.

The next picture showed a woman with the top half of her body bare. She wasn't dead, but had been badly beaten. She was facing away from the camera, showing a back and upper arm that were covered with cuts and bruises. A hand reached into the picture, lifting her long, dark hair so that her injuries were visible. There was also a full-frontal picture of her, and a close-up of her beaten face. Police pictures.

Daniel picked up the picture and studied it carefully.

Gisela leaned over him.

'Is that someone you recognise?' she whispered.

'No. Who is it?'

'Someone who got in Max's way. They both encountered Max.'

'Who's the woman?'

'A young Italian girl that Max had a relationship with. She left him and met someone else. This man.'

Gisela picked up the picture of the man's shattered face. She held it in front of Daniel for a few seconds until he looked away.

She spread the pictures out over the table.

'What are you feeling?' she asked.

'Take them away. It's disgusting,' Daniel said.

'You asked who the woman was, yet you weren't curious about the man. Are you more interested in her?'

He shook his head violently, but avoided looking at the pictures.

'Of course this wasn't the first time he'd done something like this, was it?' she went on.

With trembling hands, Daniel gathered the pictures together and turned the pile face down.

'Max didn't do that,' he said firmly. 'He's never been violent.'

'No? How well do you really know him?' Gisela Obermann asked as she put the pictures back in the drawer.

He sat without speaking for a few moments, then shook his head and repeated:

'Max couldn't have done that.'

She was looking at him intently, waiting for him to say something else, but he chose not to comment further on the photographs.

'So this is a clinic for psychopaths?' he said instead, trying to make his voice as neutral as possible.

'Yes.'

'Surrounded by an invisible barrier?'

She nodded.

'But the zones go round the whole valley, not just the clinic. How does that work for the people in the village?'

She looked at him uncomprehendingly.

'Or do you mean to say that the people in the village . . . '
Daniel gulped. 'That *they're* patients as well?'

'Not patients. We prefer to say residents. Everyone in
Himmelstal is a resident. Some live in the clinic buildings or,
like you, in cabins in the grounds of the clinic. Others live
down in the village or in their own houses around the valley.
It all depends what people prefer, and what the clinic's management think most suitable.'

Daniel considered this for a moment, then said:

'The older woman at the bierstube. Hannelore. She's a . . .
resident . . . too?'

Gisela nodded.

'What did she do? Why did she end up here, I mean?'

Gisela thought for a moment before saying:

'We don't usually talk about other residents' backgrounds.
But obviously you're a special case. And as far as Hannelore
and her husband are concerned, the whole valley knows
about them already anyway. And plenty of people outside as
well, for that matter. They were in the newspapers all over
Europe ten years ago or so. Hannelore and Horst Fullhaus.
You've never heard of them?'

Daniel shook his head.

'They had eight foster children, and murdered six of them.
Their own son was also involved, but he was never found
guilty because he was a minor.'

'She murdered six children?' Daniel gasped. 'How? No,
don't tell me, I don't want to know.'

He was trying to take in what Gisela had just said. Could
it really be true? Now that he thought about it, he had read
about the Austrian couple many years before. A child chained
up in a dog kennel, was that it? And something about a
tumble drier.

'What about Corinne?' he went on. 'The girl at Hannelores Bierstube, is she a resident as well?'

'Like I said: everyone except the clinic staff and the research team is a resident. This isn't a hospital in the usual sense. It's a society in which each person has their own role. Corinne serves drinks and provides the entertainment at the bierstube. A talented girl. You like her?'

'What did she do?'

Gisela hesitated.

'I don't think Max knew. And in that case I can't tell you either.'

Suddenly he felt violently sick, and for a moment he thought he was going to throw up over the table, but it was only his racing pulse threatening to suffocate him.

She put her arm round his shoulders.

'All this is too much for you, isn't it? You need to rest. I'll call someone to take you back to your room.'

Gisela went over to the phone and made a call. She helped him up from his chair and passed him his crutches.

'You were about to say something about the woman,' she said as he hopped towards the door on his crutches.

'What woman?'

He turned and suddenly caught sight of the coat hook that Gisela must have been given by – or more likely had bought from – Tom. The carved face glared at him with its staring eyes and silently screaming mouth.

'On the pictures I showed you. You recognised her, didn't you?'

'No,' he said firmly. 'I've never seen her before.'

He was lying. He recognised the woman from the photograph that Max kept under his mattress. The same woman, the same injuries. The picture had probably been taken on the same occasion.

32

'Well, what do you think?'

The image on the white screen faded away. For a moment the conference room was dark. Gisela Obermann touched a button and with a whisper the curtains glided open. Squinting eyes peered at the light flooding in, as if a new film, gentler but grander, was starting up on the vast picture window.

'The first video was recorded in my room on 3 May this year. The second is from 14 July,' Gisela said, turning her back on the natural scenery outside. The sky above the mountains was blue in that transparent, fresh way that always made her feel thirsty.

'Astonishing,' Hedda Heine exclaimed. 'I see what you mean, Doctor Obermann. It's the same man. He's even wearing the same top on both occasions. Nonetheless: a completely different person!'

'The body language is certainly different,' Doctor Pierce muttered as he leafed through his bundle of papers.

Philip Pierce had spent most of his life in the world of research, and hardly had any clinical experience. He was always quiet, careful, excessively cautious. Gisela couldn't quite understand how he managed to get by as well as he had. No one questioned his research, even though it was ridiculously expensive and produced meagre results. The only explanation had to be that he had no natural enemies. He was too bland for anyone to want to sink their teeth into him. A researcher like that could last a lifetime at Himmelstal.

'As you heard, the man in the later recording claims to be Daniel, Max's twin brother,' Gisela pointed out. 'It is significant that he does really have a brother, even if they aren't twins, and that this brother visited him three weeks ago.'

A middle-aged woman with masculine hair and clothing held up a finger.

'Doctor Linz?'

'How long has he claimed to be Daniel?'

'Max's brother visited him three weeks ago. He claims that they swapped places with each other then.'

'Did you meet the brother, Doctor Obermann?'

'No, we don't usually meet visitors. But of course some of the hosts met him. They just remember that he had a thick beard, shaggy hair and glasses. Looked a bit bohemian. When he checked out he was wearing a woolly hat. Naturally it's difficult to see the features of someone with a beard and a lot of hair, especially at a distance. But no one I've spoken to was struck by any great resemblance.'

'And Max doesn't actually have a twin brother,' Karl Fischer pointed out, nodding towards the blank projection screen. 'We can ignore that story. He's simply lying. Putting on a performance. It's good, I'll give him that. But our residents have had a whole lifetime to practice lying and manipulation. Lying is part of their characters.'

'You talk of lies,' Gisela Obermann said. 'However I have a feeling this is something different. I'm starting to think that our client really does see himself as a different person.'

'Dissociative personality disorder? Multiple personalities? Is

221

that what you mean?' Hedda Heine said, peering intently at Gisela.

Gisela nodded eagerly.

'In this case we're not talking about a switch between various personalities,' she said quickly when she saw Karl Fischer's derisive smile. 'The cases I have been thinking about are those in which the person in question finds themselves in an insoluble situation and can't see any way out. Yet they simply can't bear being who they are. They leave debts, family conflicts and disgrace behind and reappear somewhere else as an entirely different person, without any memory of their former life. We all know how unhappy Max was in Himmelstal. He never reached the stage of acceptance, getting down to some sort of serious activity the way most of our residents do. You are familiar with his repeated attempts to bribe and charm us into letting him leave. His desperate attempt to escape through the drains. Part of him, the sensible part, finally realises that there is no way out. He has lost his freedom because he is who he is. But another part carries on looking for an escape route. And one day he simply runs away from himself. Into a person who would never have ended up in Himmelstal. A person who is friendly, selfless, law abiding. He's had the model in front of his eyes for several days, and has known him since childhood: his own brother. When his brother leaves, he recreates him and takes over his personality.'

The faces round the table were like a tableau of all the responses she had prepared for: scepticism, confusion, interest, derision. Only Doctor Kalpak seemed unconcerned, just sitting there with his almond-shaped eyes lowered. She fixed her gaze on the most positive, a young, male visiting researcher that she didn't know, and added:

'This is an unconscious process, not conscious. And it is made easier by him claiming that his two-year-older brother is actually his twin.'

'A fascinating theory, Doctor Obermann,' Karl Fischer said, his stern voice wrapped in silk. 'And what makes you think that the process is unconscious?'

'Because it's such a thorough transformation. It encompasses his whole being. As you saw for yourselves.'

'Hmm,' Fischer said thoughtfully.

He waited until he had the complete attention of everyone else, then went on in a slow, low voice, speaking very clearly, like a school teacher addressing a class of first years:

'Everything you mention is part of an actor's repertoire. Max is an astonishingly good actor. He has a natural talent for it, and a lifetime of training. You saw him in that play last winter, didn't you? I have to say that I was impressed. It was as if we were watching an entirely different person, wasn't it? The way he moved and spoke, everything was different. He's doing the same thing now. And he is fully aware of what he's doing. Study him when he doesn't know he's being observed. He'll probably have reverted to his normal pattern of behaviour.'

'That play . . .' Doctor Pierce interjected cautiously. 'I seem to remember it was about someone pretending to be two people, one bad and one good, and managing to fool everyone. Max could have got the idea for this deception from that.'

'As I said: he's deceiving you, Gisela,' Karl Fischer sneered dismissively.

Gisela Obermann pretended not to have noticed that Doctor Fischer had dropped her title, in contravention of accepted practice within the walls of the conference room.

'Doctor Fischer,' she said, with strained politeness, 'we are all capable of being deceived. The day we consider ourselves too smart to be deceived is the day we are most at risk. We must always be on our guard, and I am grateful for your reminder. Max's exceptional acting talents are obviously something we need to bear in mind. However, what has convinced me isn't his physical mannerisms but his selfless behaviour in recent weeks.'

'What exactly do you mean, Gisela?' Hedda Heine said, peering amiably above the frame of her glasses.

'That I believe him. He hasn't deceived me. He's deceived *himself*. Many of our patients have, of course, successfully managed to convince themselves that they're perfectly normal, decent people. Max has gone a step further. His desperation to get away from here is so strong that his natural talent for acting has allowed him to create a new personality for himself.'

'Dissociative personality disorders are extremely rare when it comes to our residents,' Doctor Pierce pointed out. 'I don't think we've ever had a diagnosed case. And nothing in Max's history points in that direction. He's always been very stable in his identity.'

Hedda Heine nodded in agreement, and said:

'Multiple personalities are extremely unusual in any circumstances. I've never come across a case in all the time I've been practising, only read about them.'

She had a shawl covered in large roses fastened round her shoulders with a brooch. As she spoke about multiple personalities, Gisela thought she looked like one of those Russian dolls, and that if you opened her up at the middle you'd be able to pull out smaller and smaller versions of the same old woman in a shawl, until you finally ended up with a tiny, solid Hedda.

'The phenomenon has been widely debated,' Doctor Linz said. 'Some people claim that these strange personalities don't arise spontaneously, but are conjured up by the therapist during hypnosis. That they are an undesirable side-effect of treatment.'

Gisela eyes shone.

'That's exactly what occurred to me! That this is a side-effect of treatment. But a *desirable* side-effect.'

The others looked at her uncomprehendingly.

'I was thinking of the Pinocchio Project,' Gisela said in a low voice. 'Doctor Pierce, what's your opinion?'

Karl Fischer groaned and shuffled as though he were in actual physical pain. Pierce glanced at him anxiously before turning towards Gisela:

'I'm sorry, Doctor Obermann. The project you're referring to doesn't work that way. Behaviour is only affected very temporarily. At best. No profound personality changes have ever occurred. I wish . . . But no. I haven't been able to prove anything similar to what you have been talking about.'

'Up to now, maybe. Perhaps this is something entirely new. We might be on the right track towards a breakthrough,' Gisela said optimistically.

Doctor Pierce smiled sympathetically.

Gisela Obermann looked around to find support and interest in any of the others. Instead they all seemed rather bored, even the young visiting researcher. Brian Jenkins was impatiently clicking a ballpoint pen as he stared at the alpine landscape outside the window.

Gisela let out a sigh of resignation.

'Well, it was just something that struck me. That there's been a change. And that all change offers the hope of improvement.'

'There's no change, Gisela,' Doctor Fischer said. He sounded weary. 'And there is, sadly, no hope.'

'So what's the point of our research then?' Gisela Obermann exclaimed angrily. 'If we don't believe in the possibility of change? Isn't that what we're doing here? Keeping our eyes and ears open for the slightest change and using that to identify the germ of a solution? Otherwise we might as well all go home and employ camp guards instead.'

'Perhaps that's exactly what we ought to do,' Doctor Fischer said, glancing at the time. 'After nine years in this place, I'm starting to lean more and more towards that opinion.'

'Doctor Fischer,' Gisela said, 'you ought to be ashamed of yourself.'

She turned to the others.

'Let's take a break. We'll meet back here in half an hour. Then you'll get the chance to meet Daniel again.'

She stood up and looked out through the picture window. Two large birds were hovering close to the rock face. They were circling back and forth in front of the black marks, as though they were trying to decipher them. They seemed to be some sort of bird of prey.

33

When the doctors returned to their seats, Daniel was already there. He had been collected from his hospital room by two hosts, and was sitting next to Gisela at the end of the table. He felt like a prisoner who had been dragged to his trial from his cell. He could only see the men and women round the table through a sort of fog. The box of contact lenses was still in the cabin and no one had fetched it for him even though he had asked more than once.

Gisela welcomed him, then immediately set about questioning him like a lawyer.

'You and Max are twins, if I've understood you correctly?'

'I've said so plenty of times now.'

Everyone around the conference table was watching him with the greatest interest, except Doctor Fischer, who was pointedly looking up at the ceiling.

'Can you tell us who you are?'

As Daniel was talking, Doctor Fischer stifled a yawn, turned to Gisela Obermann and said:

'Gisela, my dear. Why are you taking up our time with this nonsense?'

'We have to listen to what he has to say. I think it's quite clear that we're dealing with a new personality here. He has no memories of his life as Max,' Gisela said.

Hedda Heine asked to speak.

'If Doctor Obermann is right, we're facing a moral dilemma. Shouldn't we be concerned for his safety? He is clearly what certain of our residents call a "lamb". Shouldn't he have some sort of protection?'

'Absolutely not!' Karl Fischer snarled, slapping his hand down on the table. 'He's here for the same reason as all the others and he won't be getting any more protection than anyone else. He's a particularly devious, calculating individual who has read up on psychiatric disorders and is now trying to play us off against each other.'

'Doctor Fischer!' Gisela exclaimed. 'Choose your words carefully. Remember that the resident in question is present.'

'Take him out, then. I don't think we require his presence any longer. He keeps saying the same thing. To be honest, I'm sick of him.'

Gisela stood up abruptly and nodded to Daniel.

'I'll come with you to your room,' she whispered.

'Well, that's that,' Karl Fischer said as soon as Gisela Obermann and Daniel had left. 'You must make allowances for Doctor Obermann. She's highly ambitious and works hard. I'm afraid everything has got rather too much for her recently. Does anyone have anything to add, or can we end this meeting now?'

'On an entirely different subject,' Brian Jenkins said, waving a sheet of paper. 'This list of researchers who have been invited to visit. There's one name here, Greg Jones. Who the hell is that? I've never heard of him.'

Karl Fischer ran his fingers through his short grey hair. He thought for a moment, cleared his throat, and said:

'As you all know, we have a very generous anonymous benefactor who has given a great deal of money to Himmelstal. Well, that's this Greg Jones. He would rather I didn't say so, so I must ask you to keep it to yourselves. His fortune is based on a cosmetics company founded by his grandfather. His sister was kidnapped by a madman when she was eleven years old. The family was prepared to pay a huge sum in ransom but there was a misunderstanding and the kidnapper didn't get his money in time. The girl was found in a rubbish bin with her throat cut. Greg Jones wants to solve the mystery of psychopathy. Thanks to his support, we might one day succeed. The least we can do is grant his wish to visit Himmelstal and show him round. Because he doesn't want to make a fuss, he'd rather join a group visit. I've promised him the very greatest discretion. He is to be treated exactly the same as our other guests.'

Brian Jenkins let out a whistle.

'A modest dollar billionaire. Unusual. Greg Jones isn't his real name, is it? Fine. As long as he invests his money in Himmelstal he can call himself whatever the hell he wants.'

With her arm in a maternal hold round his back, Gisela Obermann led Daniel off to the lift, then through the corridors.

'I'm having trouble persuading the others to agree with my theory,' she said. 'Most of them think you're manipulating me. And Doctor Fischer can be rather blunt at times. I hope it didn't upset you. Am I walking too fast for you?'

Although Daniel had abandoned the crutches, he was still limping slightly. He missed the contact lenses. He suddenly realised what it must be like to be old, to have difficulty walking and seeing. Gisela slowed down.

'Considering what I've had to put up with in this place, a few blunt words don't matter much,' Daniel said. 'By the way, what does "lamb" mean?'

'It's Himmelstal slang. That's what the residents call the rest of us. People with consciences and the ability to empathise. We're lambs. They regard us as stupid, lesser creatures, but simultaneously as rather attractive, I think. Pure, innocent. They see a sort of beauty in us. Mind you, us doctors aren't regarded as proper lambs. Nor are the clinic staff. Because we're on our guard, we know too much. Real lambs are probably what's missing in here.'

Daniel thought about Samantha, and something suddenly struck him.

'There are both men and women in the valley.'

'Mostly men,' Gisela said. 'Eighty per cent. Which doesn't necessarily mean that psychopathy is more common in men, but it does tend to manifest itself in acts of greater violence, which makes them more liable to criminal and medical investigation. And we get most of our residents through the legal system.'

'But there are women here as well,' Daniel pointed out. 'Residents of both sexes spend their whole lives in Himmelstal, interacting freely with each other. Yet I haven't seen any children so far. Not in the village, nor anywhere else in the valley either. Not a single child!'

'We want everything to be as natural as possible in Himmelstal. There's no ban on sexual relationships. But obviously we can't have any children here. Everyone, women and men alike, are sterilised. It's done as soon as people arrive.'

She said this calmly and matter-of-factly, as though she were talking about vaccinations against flu.

'So Max has been . . . '

Gisela nodded.

'Everyone has. And because you and Max share a body, that applies to you as well.'

She's talking about Max. Not me, Daniel said to himself. This doesn't involve me.

'To start with we feared that the women would be taken advantage of. However the women here in Himmelstal can bite back. So people are free to pair up as they wish. That's the best way. As natural as possible. Some were couples before they even arrived. Like Hannelore and her husband at the bierstube. There are a number of fleeting relationships. And some homosexual relationships as well, of course. And in all likelihood prostitution too.'

They had reached the ward where Daniel's room was. Gisela tapped in a code and the doors slid open for them.

'But we don't really know much about that, that's all part of the residents' private lives. Everyone gets tested for sexual infections. It's done as soon as a resident arrives. Tests, then any necessary treatment. So here there's no need for anyone to worry about anything. No pregnancy. No sexually transmitted diseases. A free-love paradise, I suppose.'

They stopped at the door to Daniel's room.

'Well, here we are,' Gisela said, opening it for him.

Daniel didn't move.

'Hang on a moment. I know identical twins have the same DNA, but if Max was sterilised, you must be able to see that I'm not him. That can be checked, can't it?'

Gisela laughed.

'Probably. That's not really my area of expertise. I imagine I'd have to get Doctor Fischer's permission for such an unnecessary investigation. But everyone here knows who you are. You're the only one who doesn't.'

She gestured towards the room.

'Go and get some rest now. I hope you'll be able to return to your cabin soon. Until then, you can read through this.'

She handed him a printout with an alpine mountaintop on the cover.

'Some information about Himmelstal. We usually give it to

231

new arrivals, and I suppose that's how we have to regard you. And Doctor Heine was right, you need protection, Daniel. I'll see what I can do. A piece of advice: don't tell the other residents that you're Daniel. To them you're still Max, OK? The social structure in Himmelstal is strictly hierarchical, and Max enjoyed a degree of respect.' She winked conspiratorially at him and whispered: 'Just pretend to be him.'

34

Daniel lay on the bed in his hospital room, reading through the brochure Gisela Obermann had given him for the tenth time. Someone had finally picked up the box of contact lenses from the cabin for him.

There was a knock at the door. Without waiting for an answer, Karl Fischer walked in and sat down on the edge of Daniel's bed.

'So, how's our patient doing, then? You're mending nicely, I hear. I'm pleased, Daniel. You are still Daniel, aren't you? Or has another interesting personality popped up that I don't know about?' he said scornfully, giving Daniel a gentle slap on his burned leg, making it jump with pain.

Karl Fischer had never visited him in his room before. Apart from the nurses, Daniel had only had contact with Gisela and a pale, skinny doctor who was an expert in burns.

'Where's Doctor Obermann?' he asked.

Fischer didn't reply, and looked around the hospital room as if it were entirely new to him. His pale blue eyes moved like little fish in a net of wrinkles, and somehow seemed several decades younger than the rest of him. Then he caught sight of the brochure resting on Daniel's chest. He picked it up, slapped it against the palm of his hand with a smile, and said:

'Doctor Obermann has been stripped of responsibility for you. That was the unanimous decision at the end of our last meeting.'

'What for?' Daniel asked in surprise. 'I got on well with Doctor Obermann.'

Karl Fischer laughed and slapped the brochure back on his chest. Daniel felt an intense dislike of the man.

'I'm sure you did, Daniel. You managed to twist her round your finger wonderfully, didn't you? But no one else believes this rubbish about a new personality, you need to understand that.'

Daniel sat up in bed a bit too abruptly. His side hurt and he had to close his eyes for a moment and take a few deep breaths.

'I haven't said anything about a new personality,' he snapped. 'I've simply said that I'm not Max but his twin brother.'

Doctor Fischer pressed his palms together like a saint, touched his fingertips to his thin lips, and gave Daniel a sly look.

'There is no twin brother, my friend.'

'No? So who was it who came to visit and wrote their name in the ledger in reception?'

Karl Fischer winked secretively with one eye.

'That was your two years older brother, wasn't it?'

Daniel groaned in despair.

'Max gave you the wrong date of birth. I don't know why, but he must have done. Even so, surely the staff noticed how similar we are. Surely someone spotted that we're twins!'

Karl Fischer shrugged his shoulders and idly inspected one of his fingernails.

'Don't ask me. I never saw your brother. As I understand it, you've both got dark hair. But you're the one who's my patient, your brother doesn't interest me. He's gone, and I'm going to be *very* restrictive when it comes to future visitors for you. It only seems to give you peculiar ideas. You've ended up here at Himmelstal for very good reasons, and you're going to be here for the rest of your life. The sooner you accept that, the better you'll feel.'

Daniel gasped and grabbed hold of the bed as if Doctor Fischer were trying to shove him into a deep pit.

'I want a proper telephone,' he said. He tried to keep his voice steady. 'I want to call Sweden.'

He didn't know who he wanted to call, he didn't really have any friends. Someone who could confirm that he was who he said he was. The school where he worked? There would be no one there during the summer. The population registry?

Doctor Fischer tapped the brochure.

'Residents don't have access to external phone lines,' he said drily.

'I'd like to talk to Doctor Obermann.'

Daniel wished he could stop shaking. He didn't want to break down in front of Doctor Fischer. In front of Doctor Obermann, maybe, but not Doctor Fischer.

Fischer smiled tolerantly.

'From now on you're my responsibility. You won't be seeing Doctor Obermann again. You'll be staying here for another week. If your injuries carry on healing well and you don't come up with any more nonsense, you'll be allowed to move back to your cabin. But I don't want to hear any more rubbish about twins,' he added in a sharp tone of voice. 'Nothing like that.'

He leaned across Daniel's injured side and whispered close to his face. His breath smelled of ozone, like the air immediately after a thunderstorm.

'The next time you go into Zone 2, you'll be moved to downstairs. Is that understood?'

Daniel didn't understand. Nevertheless he thought it best to nod.

PART THREE

35

A lamb among wolves, Daniel thought as he stood in front of the care centre with the park laid out before him.

July was turning to August, the grass on the slopes was still improbably green, but there was something in the air that told him that autumn was on its way.

He had been desperate to get out of his hospital room, but now that he was standing here, healed and discharged, he felt as if he had been banished and wanted to go back inside. The short walk to the cabins at the top of the hill suddenly seemed a long and dangerous hike.

He turned towards the care centre, and saw the blue sky and racing clouds mirrored in its glass façade.

Then he took a deep breath, grasped the shoulder straps of his rucksack tight – as if it were carrying him and not the other way round – and headed quickly through the park, eyes forward, not even risking a sideways glance, and on up the slope. As on previous occasions, he encountered people on their way to the pool, tennis courts or canteen. But he no longer thought they looked like tourists at a luxury hotel. He now knew that every single person he met who wasn't dressed in a pale blue uniform was a predator in human guise. Ravenous beasts longing to set their teeth into a real lamb.

He had intended to walk calmly, but couldn't help running the last twenty metres to the cabin. His neighbour Marko was nowhere in sight, for which he was grateful.

With his hand trembling, he unlocked the door. He went straight over to the alcove containing the bed and drew back the curtain. No one there. No one in the bathroom either. The cabin looked the same as when he had left it. He locked the door firmly from the inside, then sank on to one of the wooden armchairs, panting as if he had been on a march. He was safe. For the time being.

Daniel spent the next few days like a prisoner in his cabin. The tins of baked beans kept him fed, and he drank tap water. He kept the door locked and let the patrols use their own key to open it when they checked on him every morning and evening. The smiling hosts who, according to the information brochure, 'should be regarded primarily as staff, at your disposal'. But who, for 'safety reasons', were equipped with tasers and always went round in pairs. (That was true, Daniel had never seen any host or hostess alone outside the clinic buildings. But he had yet to see a taser. He presumed they hid them under their pale blue jackets.)

He kept the curtains drawn so that the cabin was in a permanent state of semi-darkness. Whenever he peered cautiously through them, he saw Marko glued to the outside wall of his cabin each evening. Why was he in Himmelstal?

His neighbour spent most of the day inside, but sometime around seven o'clock his shuffling steps could be heard out on the porch, then a thud as he slumped down. Then he would sit there all evening. Whenever Daniel got up in the night to go to the toilet, he would nudge the curtain aside and see him sitting there, staring out into the darkness like a large, motionless, nocturnal animal. During the day, when he wasn't there, you could make out a darker patch on the wall where he usually sat.

What did Marko see while he was sitting there? Because even if it was dark and most people were presumably asleep, the clinic grounds weren't entirely deserted at night. According to the rules, you had to be in your room at twelve o'clock at night and eight o'clock in the morning so you could be checked by the patrol. 'What you do in between is up to you,' Max had said.

And, oddly enough, this appeared to be true. The time around half past eleven was always unsettled, with people hurrying through the park and up the hill to get to their cabins and rooms. When everyone was in their place a period of strange calm and quiet descended, only broken by the hum of the approaching electric buggy and the hostesses' knocks and cheery cries in the neighbouring cabins.

Then, after another half-hour of quiet, the grounds seemed to come to life again. More subdued than during the day. Cabin doors opening slowly, voices whispering in the darkness, shadows scuttling across the lawn. Occasionally you could hear discreet knocks on the doors of other cabins, and once, to his horror, his own door. 'Psst!' someone hissed, like a big insect, then slowly and quietly tried the door handle several times. Daniel lay still behind the curtain, hardly daring to breathe. There was an irritated snort followed by silence outside.

Daniel hadn't noticed this nocturnal activity before because he had slept so soundly. Now, however, he often lay awake long into the small hours, fretting and worrying, and if he did nod off, his sleep was fragile as glass and he would be wide awake at the slightest sound.

One night he got up and lifted the mattress to take out the photograph Max had shown him the night before he left. He was sure it was the battered woman in Gisela's pictures, and that the pictures had been taken at the same time.

But it was no longer there. He removed the whole mattress. The picture was gone. The clinic staff must have found and removed it.

When he returned from the ward he had discovered four emails waiting for him on the computer. One from Father Dennis, and three from Corinne. He didn't open them. Max's mobile rang several times, but he let it ring.

One rainy afternoon, when he had been shut inside the cabin for five days, the mobile rang so persistently that he had to get it out and look at the screen. If it was one of the doctors or staff, he would answer it.

He missed the call, but saw it was from Corinne, and that he had eleven missed calls from her. Just as he was about to switch the phone off altogether, she rang again. He pressed the button to answer it, and said:

'I don't want to talk to you.'

'Don't hang up,' Corinne said. 'You don't have to be scared of me. Do you hear me? You don't have to be scared of me.'

She was talking calmly and firmly, as though she were talking to a child. He could see her before him. Her animated brown eyes, the sharp tilt of her jaw. So much had happened over the past few weeks that he had almost forgotten that face, but hearing her voice brought it all back to him. He experienced a momentary glow of recognition. Then he said:

'I'm hanging up now.'

'No, wait. You have to listen to me. It's important. I've spoken to Gisela Obermann. I know what's happened to you. It's good that you're suspicious. It's good that you're staying indoors. It's the right thing to do. But if you isolate yourself completely you'll go mad. And at some point you're going to have to go out and get food.'

He said nothing. She was right. His cabin was like a besieged town, and his food supply had almost run out.

'You should avoid the others,' she went on. 'Don't hide yourself away though. Do you understand? You mustn't show any fear. They can smell your fear through the walls of the cabin. Are you still there?'

'Yes,' he said quietly.

'We have to meet.'

'I don't want to meet anyone.'

'Good thinking. But in your situation, you won't survive on your own. Listen, Daniel: you're new here. You're a lamb. You're surrounded by enemies. What you need is a mentor.'

He gulped and said:

'You're a resident of Himmelstal. How can I trust you?'

'You don't have any choice, Daniel. Without a mentor you're lost. And believe me, I'm the best you can get here. There are plenty of worse choices. Far, far worse.'

'I'd rather not leave my cabin.'

'You don't have to. Open the door. I'm right outside.'

He went over to the window and peered through the curtain.

There she was, dressed in an orange anorak with her mobile pressed to her ear under the hood. She seemed small and pathetic in the pouring rain. She was looking straight at him, and through the window he saw her lips move, as the voice on the mobile half-pleaded and half-commanded:

'Open the door now.'

He opened it. She pulled off her anorak and draped it across two chairs, then sat herself down neatly on one of the wooden armchairs as she shook her wet hair like a dog. Daniel sat opposite her.

'So you've spoken to Gisela Obermann,' he said. 'Is she your psychiatrist?'

'Yes.'

'Is it good practice for a doctor to discuss their patients with another patient?'

243

'Don't get hung up on silly details. You can't afford that. Your situation is serious.'

'Did Doctor Obermann tell you I'm suffering from multiple personalities as well?'

Corinne nodded.

'And do you believe that?'

'No. But as a theory it might actually work to your advantage. It's made her better disposed towards you. She thought she'd discovered something important. All the research staff in Himmelstal dream of discovering something important. Only now Gisela has been taken off your case and Karl Fischer has stepped in. That's not good. But you'll have to make the best of it.' She shuddered as if she were freezing. 'A cup of tea would be nice.'

'Sorry. I haven't got any tea. I've got tins of baked beans, and water.'

She stood up and dragged a chair over to the kitchen counter, clambered nimbly up on it and pulled down a large box of teabags that Daniel hadn't noticed before from the top shelf.

'Max didn't like tea. I bought him this box so he'd be able to make tea for me when I came,' she said as she filled the kettle with water. 'Do you want some?'

'Yes please. So you've been in this cabin before, then?'

'A few times. Mostly we'd meet at mine.'

She got out two mugs and put a teabag in each. Daniel waited for her to say something more about her relationship with Max, but she didn't elaborate.

'I feel like a guest in my own home,' he said as she put the mug of tea on the table in front of him.

'Isn't that what you are here in Himmelstal?' She gave him a wry smile. 'A guest?'

'Who can't go home,' he said bitterly.

She took a careful sip of the hot tea, then leaned back and said:

'So. Gisela has told you what sort of place this is. Now do you understand why I seemed so uninterested when you asked for my help to get out? I can't get you out of Himmelstal. I can't get myself out of here.'

'If Max comes back ...'

She waved her hand dismissively.

'He won't. I know him. You were his chance, and he took it. The doctors make all the decisions, so they're the ones we have to convince. They have their weaknesses, same as everyone else. They're vain, desperate to make their careers, they're competitive, and ridiculously fascinated by psychopaths. They see us as exotic animals, and Himmelstal is their very own Serengeti. Anyone doing research into psychopaths dreams of getting a grant to come here as a guest researcher. With the monsters right outside the door.'

'I'm not a psychopath,' Daniel said angrily.

He stood and began to pace around the cabin. Recently he'd been unable to sit still for any length of time.

'Nor me,' Corinne said.

He stopped and looked at her.

'So why are you here, then?'

'It's a long story, I'll tell you some other time. Let's just say someone made a mistake. But this is about you, Daniel.'

'You're here by mistake, and I'm here by mistake,' Daniel snapped. 'How many of us are here by mistake?'

'Not very many. The diagnoses were perhaps a bit sloppy in some cases. But even if they aren't all one hundred per cent psychopathic, you'd do better to assume that they are. Just to be on the safe side.'

'I'm going to get out of here!' Daniel roared, banging his fist on one of the beams. It hurt, but he went on thumping it as tears streamed down his face. His sudden fury took him by surprise.

Corinne seemed unconcerned by his outburst. She drank

her tea, then, when he had calmed down and sank back on to his chair, she said:

'Obviously you're going to get out of here. But it might take a while. Until then it's a matter of survival. I promise to help you, and the only help I've got to give is good advice. Don't frown that way. Good advice could be the difference between life and death for you.'

'I didn't say anything.'

'No, but I saw the look on your face.'

'I'm listening,' Daniel said meekly.

'OK.' She put her mug down hard, straightened her back and took hold of her left thumb. 'First: keep to yourself. Don't let yourself get drawn into any deals, pacts, friendships or love affairs. But you mustn't hide away. Go to the canteen every day and eat lunch. Sit on your own, but *go*. Do your shopping down in the village. Have a beer in the bierstube. Stand tall. Don't try to avoid people's gaze. Reply politely but don't say much if anyone speaks to you. Don't start any conversations yourself. Never show that you're afraid or weak, but keep your distance if there's ever any trouble. It was brave of you to overpower Tom and save Bonnard's life, but to be brutally honest I don't think he was worth it.'

'Isn't every person's life worth saving?'

She looked up at the ceiling in despair.

'Bloody hell, Daniel. André Bonnard raped and murdered little girls, the youngest one was three years old. The value of such people's lives is worth discussing, and I'll be happy to have that discussion another day. But you need to be careful. Getting caught up in fights is dangerous. Being a witness to fights can be equally dangerous. See nothing, do nothing. You have to be selfish. Is that clear?'

He kept quiet and simply nodded.

Corinne took hold of her left index finger and said: 'Then you have to think about your body. Eat properly. And exercise.

246

Hard. You never know when you might need a strong, agile body. You might end up in a situation where your life depends on your physical condition. There's no need to let anyone else know what good shape you're in though. So don't go to the gym. I never do any exercise there, as you can probably imagine. Women are in short supply here in Himmelstal. You don't want to stand there in a vest and hotpants twisting your body this way and that among a crowd of rapists and sadists. The clinic management fully understand my attitude, and let me have a little gym in my flat in the village. It's not much, mostly weights, but it works well enough for me. You're welcome to come and exercise there if you like.'

'Thanks.'

His anger had subsided and he was now listening intently to everything she was saying.

'That's the body done. Then there's your soul.' She let go of her index finger and grabbed her middle finger instead. 'You need to take care of that as well. I understand that you read a lot?'

'How do you know that?'

She smiled.

'You can't even have a beer in the bierstube without reading at the same time. I don't think I've ever seen one of our clientele with a book before. And there's a book on the table now.' She nodded towards the paperback. 'You were sitting here reading when I rang, weren't you? It's from the library, so you've already found your way there. Good. Keep it up. I have a different method of getting away from it all.'

'What?'

'The church.'

'You're religious?'

She threw her hands out.

'Call it what you like. There's a Mass every evening at six o'clock, and I go there on days when I'm not performing.

We're a small but dedicated congregation, we sit in the pews as far away from each other as possible, listening to the priest, singing hymns, lighting candles.'

'The priest?' Daniel said. 'Is that the Father Dennis who puts his sermons on the Himmelstal website?'

Corinne nodded.

'He might not be a theological genius, but we don't have a lot of choice. I don't go for his sake anyway. The inside of the church is actually very nice. You could come with me one evening if you want.'

'No thanks. That sort of thing's not for me.'

'You might change your mind. What else? Well, be careful, obviously. But you are already. Keep your door locked. Don't open it if you're not expecting anyone. Don't go out at night. Don't hang around on your own in lonely places. And of course, I don't suppose I have to say: don't tell anyone who you are. We need to convince the doctors of your true identity. But as far as the residents of Himmelstal are concerned, you're Max.'

She stood up and pulled on her anorak. It was at least three sizes too big.

'Oh, yes. One more thing,' she said, putting her boots on. 'Has Samantha been to see you?'

'Here? In the cabin? No,' Daniel said.

She looked at him and sighed.

'You need to get better at lying if you're going to survive here. You're blushing like crazy.'

'That was a long time ago. I actually thought it was a dream,' he muttered with embarrassment.

'I'm not begrudging you, but like I said: be careful.'

She unlocked the door, pulled her hood up, then turned towards him with her fingers on the door handle.

'See you,' she said, then slipped out into the rain.

36

The next day was sunny, and the snow-capped mountaintop was glistening in the west. Daniel had decided to heed Corinne's advice and eat lunch in the canteen. With his back straight and his eyes fixed firmly ahead, he walked down the slope and through the park, which smelled fresh after the previous day's rain.

Outside the care centre there was plenty going on, as usual at this time of day. People were hurrying along the footpaths, alone or in groups. Two hostesses were heading off towards the village, one of them talking animatedly on her mobile. But nowhere could he recognise any of the faces he had seen around the big table in the conference room. He hadn't heard anything from the doctors since he had been discharged from the ward. Not from Doctor Fischer, nor Doctor Obermann, nor any of the others.

He looked up at the imposing edifice of the care centre and tried to identify which room he had been in. The conference room was on one of the upper floors. Gisela Obermann's room was right at the top. The ward in which he and Marko had been locked for tests had to be on one of the lower floors.

And the ward where he had been treated for his burns was probably somewhere in the middle.

But the glass façade was so impenetrably shiny that he couldn't even identify any floors or windows from where he was standing. All he could see was a mirror image of the valley: sky, treetops and the rock face opposite.

In the canteen he chose to sit outside on the paved terrace. He had selected the table carefully before he even went in and joined the queue with his tray. There were only a few diners sitting outside, and the table wasn't too close to them, but not too isolated either.

He had no sooner started eating than someone sat down at the next table. Daniel recognised the village barber. His shirt was unbuttoned down to his chest, and his fringe had been blow-dried to a reddish-brown, untidy mop that partly covered the wrinkles on his forehead. The barber took a cautious taste of his lasagne and let out a groan of delight.

'This is how lasagne should taste. Loads of cheese. There's no need to go to the restaurant to get good food. Because most things are just as good down here in the canteen, don't you think?' he said to Daniel.

'Yes, absolutely.'

Daniel had made up his mind to agree to everything that was said, or at least not to protest.

The barber tasted his wine – one glass was included with lunch, for those who wanted it – then smacked his lips together. Daniel caught a whiff of aftershave as the man leaned towards his table and winked conspiratorially over the rim of the glass.

'We don't have it so bad, do we? Out there . . .' He gestured with one hand at something vague in the distance, and snorted derisively. 'Nothing but problems! I don't want to go back out there.'

The chair scraped on the slabs as he moved it closer to

Daniel, hurriedly dabbing his mouth with his napkin to catch some melted cheese.

'People think you go to Hell if you kill someone. If only they knew that you end up in Himmelstal instead. If people could see us, then every last fucker out there would be a psychopath.'

'Maybe.'

'When I committed my first murder, I ended up in prison. Awful place. Terrible people, terrible food. We worked in a laundry, washing hospital sheets soaked in blood and shit. Disgusting! When I committed my second murder, they said I was ill and I ended up in hospital. A madhouse, basically. Not a nice place, but better than prison. We were made to sew and listen to Mozart. After my third murder they said I was a psychopath and I got sent to Himmelstal. Now I've got a nice two-room flat down in the village. With a view of meadows and the river. My own barbershop. I only work mornings these days. I spend the afternoons lying by the pool or playing a bit of tennis. In the winter I strap on my skis and set off down the slopes. I'm not complaining, definitely not.'

'No, I can understand that.'

'I wonder where you end up after the next murder? The Bahamas?'

He let out a shrill laugh.

'Well, good to see you,' Daniel said as politely as he could, then stood up with a stiff smile.

'Oh, don't go,' the barber said, grabbing his arm. 'Look, you haven't finished. You should never leave a lasagne like this on your plate.'

He pushed Daniel down on to his chair again, moved his own chair even closer and said in a low voice:

'I know what you think of me.'

'I really don't think anything.'

'Yes, of course you do. You think I'm a spy, don't you? An infiltrator.'

'Certainly not. What do you mean, a spy?'

'There are spies in the valley, surely you knew that? They get close to people. Find things out.'

'I didn't know that. Who are they spying for?'

'The doctors, of course. They make out they're tough. Boasting about how many people they've murdered. But it's easy to be tough when you can call for backup whenever you want, isn't it? You know Block, the one who disappeared? A hired thug, mass murderer and all the other things people said he was. Used to hang around with Kowalski and Sørensen. Soon as things got a bit heated, a car full of guards would show up. Conveniently for Block. Do you think that was coincidence? I don't.'

'How do you mean, that it wasn't coincidence?'

'He *called* them. Not with his mobile, obviously. But somehow.'

The barber quickly finished his wine and glanced suspiciously over his shoulder. Then he leaned closer to Daniel again and whispered:

'He had a *gadget*.'

'What sort of gadget?'

'It looked like an MP3 player or somesuch. Every time the guards came, he'd been fiddling with it just before. And the guards were there instantly. As if they'd been hanging around nearby.'

'And now he's disappeared?' Daniel said carefully.

The barber nodded.

'Exactly. And isn't it funny that the guards spent so long looking for him, really thoroughly? I mean, people go missing here every now and then, but they don't usually make such a fuss, do they? They count on a certain number of losses. But when Block disappeared, it was as if the doctors

252

had been hit by an earthquake and the guards searched through every resident's home. No, Block wasn't one of us. He was one of *them*.'

'You might be right.'

Daniel made a fresh attempt to stand up with his tray, but the barber put his arm round his shoulders and whispered:

'I knew it all along. There was something fake about him. We spoke once. About killing and so on. He pretended to know what I was talking about, but he didn't have a clue, I could tell. Not a clue. A mass murderer?' He snorted in Daniel's ear – a hard little puff of breath against his eardrum – then pulled him even closer and hissed: 'He's never killed so much as a hamster. You can tell that sort of thing, can't you?'

He leaned back and looked at Daniel with renewed interest.

'If you want to keep that hairstyle, it'll soon be time to get it cut again. I presume you'll choose a professional this time? And what's this? Have you stopped shaving?'

The barber stroked his cheek gently. Daniel had to stop himself from knocking his hand away.

'I like it like this,' he muttered.

'Are you going to grow a beard? You should know that a well cared for beard demands professional attention. As does a slightly longer haircut.'

He smiled and playfully tousled Daniel's hair, but suddenly stopped with the palm of his hand on his head.

'What's this?' he said, standing up and leaning over Daniel's head. 'I could have sworn you were anti-clockwise.'

'What?' Daniel said, confused.

'That the hair on your crown grew anti-clockwise. Hmm,' he said, sitting down again. 'I must have got it wrong. That's what happens when you abandon your barber.'

He laughed.

A group of people sat down at the table next to them. The barber let go of Daniel and turned towards them.

'I see you chose the lasagne. Wise choice. There's no point eating in the restaurant when the canteen is such good quality, is there?'

Daniel took his chance and got up. On his way to leave his tray in the rack, he had to stop himself from breaking into a run.

37

Behind his drawn curtains Daniel was waiting for the evening patrol. He was tired, and was reading a book to stay awake. He didn't really need to sit up and wait. They had their own key, after all, and if he did go to bed early they'd let themselves in and quickly and quietly check that he was behind the drapes covering the bed. But he always found it rather uncomfortable when the drapes were pulled aside and the torchlight crept across the walls of the alcove. He preferred to open the door himself and greet them while he was still dressed.

He must have been very tired, because he hadn't heard the electric buggy approaching, and the firm rat-a-tat of the knock startled him. It had the same rhythm as an old advertising jingle that he vaguely remembered. A girl's voice, shrill and naïve like some sixties pop song, called out exactly what he knew she was going to say:

'Hello, hello, anyone at home?'

He knew it was the little dark-haired hostess. She always knocked that way, and always called out the same thing. With a weary smile he got up and opened the door.

And there stood Samantha, dressed in pirate's trousers with her blouse tied just below her bust. He went to close the door a second after he had opened it, but that was a second too late. She had already put her foot out to stop it, and slid through the gap like a cat.

'Fooled you,' she laughed, throwing herself down in one of the wooden chairs with her leg over one armrest, and taking a cigarette out of her handbag.

'You have to go,' he said. 'The evening patrol will be here any minute.'

She shook her head firmly as she tried to get her lighter to work.

'They're starting in the village tonight. They won't be here for another twenty minutes. We've got time for a quickie,' she said with her cigarette bobbing on her lower lip. She was still trying to light it, but her lighter wasn't working. 'Fuck. Have you got any matches?'

'Please, just leave,' he asked.

She found a box of matches over by the hearth, lit the cigarette, and turned to walk slowly towards him with rolling hips and a lazy smile. There was something creepy about her; every movement seemed exaggerated, out of control. As she got closer he could see from her eyes that she was clearly under the influence of something.

'Hello, Lambkin,' she said softly, stroking his cheek. 'I haven't seen you for ages. You gave that Tom a real seeing to, I heard. Good work.'

'I had to do something,' Daniel muttered, taking a step away.

'You crushed his hand, darling. People all round the valley are talking about it. I don't think you have to worry about any reprisals. Tom isn't exactly popular. Everyone knows he's an idiot. His head's full of mashed potato.'

She tapped her own head and pulled a face.

'But I dare say Tom wasn't too pleased. You're not going to find it easy to get hold of any wood. There's a fair chance you'll freeze to death this winter.'

Winter? The thought of being stuck in Himmelstal that long made him shudder. She laughed and patted him comfortingly on the arm.

'Take it easy, Lambkin. For the time being, someone else is taking care of the wood. Tom probably won't be back for a while.'

'Where is he now?'

'In the Catacombs, I suppose.'

'The Catacombs? Where's that?'

'Don't really know. Not a nice place. Underground. Like Hell, pretty much. Mind you, Hell doesn't exist. Maybe the Catacombs don't either. The problem with such places is that everyone talks about them, but no one ever comes back and says what they're really like.'

He remembered that Karl Fischer had mentioned something about 'downstairs'. Could that be the same place?

He peered through the curtains for the evening patrol. Samantha knocked on the table behind him: rat-a-tat-tat. He turned round and she laughed.

'They'll be a while yet. We've still got time.'

She came and stood next to him, cupped her hand over his groin and squeezed gently as she slowly blew smoke out of her mouth. Her pupils seemed to be overflowing with a black, sludgy liquid. Disgusted, he pushed her away from him. It was a gentle push, but she reeled as if she were on a high wire.

'What's the matter? Waiting for someone else, maybe? A little sailor girl? A little shepherdess? Is that the kind of thing that turns you on?'

Strange. Women were in the minority in the valley, and the only attractive ones he had met seemed to be fighting over him. He didn't even have to leave his cabin, they just forced their way in. And they each seemed to keep a remarkably close eye on what the other was doing.

'Do you know who she is really? Do you know what she did?'

'Who?'

'The little sailor girl. The shepherdess. Ding-a-ling.' She pretended to ring an invisible cowbell. 'Has she told you what she did, before she came here? Do you know, Lamb-kin?'

'Don't call me that. My name's Max.'

Slowly she shook her head and wagged a long, red-varnished fingernail at his chin.

'You've already told me all about it, have you forgotten? You're his stand-in. Don't be scared, Lambkin. It's a wonderful secret, and it's perfectly safe with me.'

She smiled, and the look in her eyes drifted off into a dark pool.

'I'd like you to go now, Samantha.'

'Don't you want to know what she did, your little shepherdess?'

Finally there was a knock on the door, the same rhythm he had already heard that evening, and the same cheery cry. The lock turned and the little dark-haired hostess was standing in the doorway twittering:

'How are you, Max? Had a good day? Samantha, hurry up. We'll be at your cabin in a few minutes.'

Samantha tilted her head back, shaped her mouth and very carefully blew out several parting smoke rings before she pushed the hostess aside and slid out into the night.

Long after she and the evening patrol had gone, the smoke swirled around under the beams in the ceiling, thick and suffocating, like fog from a swamp. Daniel wished he dared open the window to air the room.

He was annoyed with himself for having been so credulous and opening up to Samantha. And he should have reacted quicker when he saw who it was. Shoved her back and closed the door again. He had to get quicker, smarter, stronger.

He dug out his mobile and called Corinne.

38

It was early in the morning, and the little square was still shaded by the mountain. The bell on the door to the bakery kept ringing as people emerged with fresh loaves, and on one balcony a man in a vest was watering his window boxes. There was nothing to suggest that the village was anything but a perfectly normal village, with carefully maintained houses and industrious inhabitants going about their business.

Corinne was sitting on the side of the well, wearing a jacket with the hood pulled up. As soon as their eyes met she gestured almost imperceptibly with her head and started to walk off. Daniel followed her through the narrow village streets, then up a flight of steps on the side of a building. They stepped through a door under the ridge of the roof into a dark, claustrophobic hall leading to another door with a coded lock.

'Your door's more secure than mine,' Daniel said.

'That's because I'm a woman.'

She let him into a large, gloomy attic space where the walls and ceiling were made of rough wood, with only a few tiny windows.

'Well, this is where I live,' Corinne said as she went round turning on the lights, mainly table lamps and small strings of fairy-lights.

It was certainly an unusual home. The walls were adorned with fantastical masks, puppets and posters for theatre performances. The bed was covered with an Indian throw and, like an island in the middle of the room, there was a group of red velour armchairs. A third of the space had been transformed into a gym, with weights and equipment and a large mirror on the wall.

Daniel stopped and looked at the masks.

'My former life,' Corinne explained. 'And my current one.'

She gestured towards the gym part of the room.

'OK,' she went on before Daniel had time to ask any questions. 'So you've realised that you need to get in shape. Let's start by warming up.'

She pulled off her jacket and threw it aside. Under it she was wearing a red vest. She went over to the equipment, took out a skipping rope and slowly began to skip.

'You can have the bike.'

Daniel walked in a curve around the flailing rope and sat on an exercise bike. It required quite an effort to get it going. Some years ago he had done plenty of exercise, jogging and going to the gym, but his depression had broken the habit and he had never got back into it again.

'What have you been up to since we last met?' Corinne asked.

'I've been writing letters,' he panted. 'Can you send letters from here?'

'Sure. You hand them in at reception in an unsealed envelope. Before anything is sent, it gets read by the clinic staff to assess its suitability.'

'Suitability?'

'Obviously letters mustn't contain threats or anything else unpleasant. And you're not allowed to say too much about Himmelstal. Officially it's a "special psychiatric clinic", nothing more specific than that, and we're expected to maintain that image.'

Corinne did a few extra high jumps, spinning the rope twice while she was in the air, then resumed a gentler tempo again.

'And you're not allowed to write to anyone you like. The addressee has to be checked and accepted first. Who have you written to?'

'The population registry and passport authority in Sweden,' Daniel panted. 'The Swedish Embassy in Bern. I want to have my identity confirmed. I don't have the exact addresses, but I was hoping someone could help me with that.'

Corinne broke off her skipping and laughed out loud.

'Those letters will never get out of Himmelstal.'

'What about incoming post?' Daniel asked. 'Is that censored as well?'

'Yes. Everything gets read. And the sender is checked out.'

'That's odd,' Daniel said.

He had stopped pedalling and was sitting still on the bike.

'How do you mean?'

'Max received a letter before I got here. The contents were distinctly threatening.'

He told her what had been in Max's letter from the mafia.

'Did you see it?' Corinne said.

'No. But I did see the photograph they sent. Of a woman they'd beaten up.'

'That letter didn't come in through official channels, that much is obvious.'

'How would it have got here, then?'

'How should I know? A lot of things come into Himmelstal that shouldn't be here,' Corinne said.

She hung the skipping rope on the wall.

'Drugs?' Daniel asked.

'Has anyone offered to sell you some?'

'A bloke in the canteen implied as much. And I've seen people who've seemed to be under the influence.'

'Samantha?'

They certainly keep an eye on each other, Daniel thought. Who had seen Samantha at his cabin? Only the hostesses. Who might have told Gisela Obermann. Who might then have told Corinne during a therapy session.

'I thought it was the evening patrol,' he said by way of excuse. 'She was high as a kite. I got rid of her at once.'

Corinne seemed satisfied.

'There are drugs in the valley,' she admitted as she wrapped her hand with a long strip of black cotton. 'Not much though. Enough to satisfy demand, but little enough to keep prices high. I'd estimate that the amount available is exactly calculated for the number of users in a population of this size to keep maybe two or three dealers in a life of luxury.'

'Who are they? The bloke in the leather waistcoat?'

'He's a small-time dealer. But if you head west in the valley you'll find a couple of really nice houses up on the right. The people living there don't have very special jobs. They must have other sources of income.'

'So who lives there?'

'Kowalski lives in the villa at the top of the slope. Sørensen lives in the one lower down.'

Kowalski and Sørensen were the men who usually played cards by the pool.

'But how do they get the stuff in?'

'Good question. Everything coming in gets thoroughly checked. It ought to be impossible.'

'Does the clinic management know there are drugs here?'

'Obviously.'

'Why don't they intervene?'

Corinne looked at him in surprise.

'And do what? Call the police? Make sure the guilty parties are prosecuted? Punish them? They've already been convicted and punished. Everything that can be done has already been done. They're beyond courts and prisons now. There are no further sanctions available. The only thing that remains is the accurate and scientific study of what happens.'

'So they study the drug trade but they don't stop it?' Daniel exclaimed.

Corinne wound the last of the cotton strap around her hand and fastened it.

'Of course they don't want drugs here. But they're here, in which case they have to be taken into account in any research. Who the dealers are, who the runners are, and who ends up buying. Who gets rich from the trade, and who ends up poor. What method of payment is used: money, goods, services, prostitution. There's a sociologist here, Brian Jenkins, the one with the red beard, who's interested in this sort of thing.'

'What research methods does he use? Does he stand there taking notes as the deals are done?' Daniel asked as he slowly began to pedal again.

'He interviews residents in his office. Talks to the staff. Gathers information. A bit here, a bit there. Some residents can be extremely helpful if they think there's anything in it for them.'

'Grasses?'

'I think they're called informants.'

'What do you get by passing on information?'

Corinne pulled on a pair of boxing gloves.

'You get a gold star in your case file. It's important to keep in with the research team.'

'But you'd hardly get a gold star from Kowalski and Sørensen?'

'You can't please everyone. Look, we're cooling down now. Come on. You can have the bench press.'

Corinne set about gently hitting a punchball. Daniel watched her in fascination. As she shifted her weight from one leg to the other she increased her speed. The ball slapped rhythmically against its wooden base as her bracelet of coloured stones rattled about against the edge of the glove.

'What's the matter with you? Haven't you ever seen a woman box before?'

'Not wearing a bracelet, no.'

She ignored his comment and went on punching. Daniel struggled on with the exercise bike.

'Do you want to try it?' she asked after a while.

He got off the bike and she wrapped his hands the same way she had done her own a short while before, then pulled on the gloves, still damp with her sweat, and fastened the velcro straps. Daniel felt like his mum was putting his mittens on so he could go outside and play in the snow.

She showed him the various blows: jab, right and left hooks, and upper cut.

'Who taught you to box?' he asked.

'I did a bit of training before I came here. But I'm mostly self-taught. There are plenty of people here who could teach me more. But I don't want to be dependent on anyone else. My training is my little secret. It's best that way.'

Daniel gave the bag a punch, then leapt clear as it swung back towards him, and hit it again.

'Hey,' Corinne said. 'Don't break my punchbag. It was hard enough to get hold of as it is, and the clinic management will never get me another one. Not so hard. That's it. And let your body roll with the punch. Good.'

He carried on, and found a rhythm, but it was much harder than it looked, and after a short while he gave up.

'You've got talent,' Corinne said. 'Ask the management for a pair of gloves. Then we could practise sparring together.'

Daniel laughed breathlessly. His top was drenched in sweat.

'Doesn't all this exercising bother your neighbours? It must make a fair bit of noise,' he pointed out as he pulled the gloves off.

'I'm on my own in the building. The ground floor is used as a storeroom for the shops. And the first floor is vacant at the moment. It's nice being by myself. But on the other hand, if I do ever get into trouble, no one will hear me screaming,' she said with a smile. 'Do you want to take the weights, or shall I?'

Daniel held up his hands.

'I think that's enough for today.'

'The shower's over there by the front door,' Corinne said as she lay down on the bench under the weights.

When he emerged from the bathroom with Corinne's bath towel round his hips, she had prepared a jug of rhubarb cordial with ice and had changed into a towelling dressing gown.

While she showered he sat down on the red sofa and poured himself a drink. He looked around the large, strange room. On one chair were her sweaty gym clothes. On impulse he put his hand into the right pocket of her jogging pants and pulled out her mobile. He glanced quickly at the bathroom door, then checked for received messages. Completely empty. The same with sent messages. Evidently she erased everything straight away.

But in saved messages he found something: one solitary message from someone identified only as 'M'. He opened it and read: *I feel happy every time I see you. Be careful.* It was sent on 21 May. He looked round for a pen to write down the phone number, but the water had stopped in the bathroom and he quickly put the phone back.

Corinne came out. She was holding the dressing gown shut with one hand as she squeezed the water from her hair with the other.

'Am I the only person in Himmelstal who's seen you exercising?' Daniel asked.

'Yes,' she said, sitting down in the armchair, then added: 'Apart from Max, of course.'

She poured herself a glass of rhubarb cordial and drank it thirstily.

'Did you exercise together?'

Corinne laughed.

'You really don't know your brother very well, do you? He hated getting sweaty. He'd never attempt any sport more strenuous than fishing.'

Daniel hesitated for a moment.

'I realise it's none of my business, but what sort of relationship did you have?'

'Me and Max? Well. It would be wrong to say we were friends. You don't have friends in Himmelstal. But we used to spend time together. We could talk to each other. It started in the drama group, where I was the director. We put on a production of *The Good Woman of Setzuan*. A shortened adaptation that I'd been involved in myself before I came here. Max played the pilot. He was good. He understood whatever I said at once. He could have been a fine actor if he'd chosen that path. The production was a great success, and after that he often came down to Hannelores Bierstube and chatted to me while I worked. Sometimes he came home with me afterwards.'

She noticed the way he was looking at her and quickly clarified:

'We didn't have a sexual relationship. Neither of us was interested in that. We just sat here like this, talking.'

'How come you dared to bring him home? You were the

267

one who told me not to open my door to anyone. Did you trust him?'

Corinne thought for a moment.

'Well, obviously I was exposing myself to a degree of physical risk. But there's a different risk in Himmelstal, and when Max arrived in the valley that risk was starting to feel more and more of a threat: going mad. Mad with suspicion, isolation and anonymity. I was so tired of always sitting here alone in the evenings, staring at the remnants of my old life.'

She glanced at the theatre posters and masks on the walls.

'I longed to be able to talk about myself, to share my thoughts with another person. Nothing particularly deep or important. Only enough that someone would know who I am. I used to get that feeling when we were rehearsing *The Good Woman* and Max and I would talk about the play. And I didn't want that feeling to stop. So I went on spending time with him, and I asked him back here with me so we could talk freely without everyone in the bierstube listening in. He was entertaining, nice. He made me laugh.'

Daniel felt a pang of jealousy.

'Did you know he'd beaten women up?'

Corinne nodded.

'Gisela had warned me. Only I didn't care if he killed me. Rather that than being as isolated as I had been.'

'You and Gisela Obermann seem to know each other pretty well?'

Corinne said nothing for a few moments.

'I like her,' she finally said. 'And I think she likes me. But she's a doctor. You can't talk openly with a doctor. It's a completely unequal relationship. She has total control over me. One careless word from me and she could send me to the Catacombs.'

There it was again, that word.

'The Catacombs?'

'Did I say that? Oh, it's Himmelstal slang for harsher treatment.'

'Like what?'

'Withdrawal of privileges. Heavy medication. A secure ward. That sort of thing.'

'So there is a secure ward here?'

'Yes. If a resident gets too violent and dangerous, they have to be able to isolate him from the others. Lock him up and pump him full of drugs. Otherwise the residents would kill each other and there wouldn't be any research material left.'

She stood up and fetched the jug of rhubarb cordial from the fridge and refilled their glasses.

'Why is it called the Catacombs?' Daniel wondered.

'As you know, there used to be a convent here. Only the Leper Cemetery is left from that time. The nuns themselves weren't buried there, or in the village. They're supposed to have had an underground crypt beneath the convent. In other words, beneath what is now the clinic. People joke that that's where difficult residents are put, in the Catacombs. Himmelstal humour. I shouldn't have used that expression.'

'Are you at risk of ending up in the Catacombs, Corinne?'

'No, it was just a way of saying that the doctors have complete control over us. It's what people say here, that's all. Don't take it literally. Gisela is my therapist and doctor, not my friend. You can't expect to find friendship here. But if you get the chance to grab a bit of human contact, you take it. That's what I've tried to do.'

'Is that what you're doing now? Grabbing a bit of human contact from me?'

She smiled in amusement.

'I get the feeling that for the first time here in Himmelstal I might be able to hope for . . . a bit more than that. I don't trust you entirely, Daniel. And you don't trust me entirely. And you shouldn't, either. Not yet. But we can get to know

269

each other better. And when we know each other, maybe we can trust each other. And become friends. Would you like to be my friend?'

She said this with a quiver in her voice, as if she were asking something huge, and was afraid of being rejected.

'I'm very choosy when it comes to picking my friends. But out of everyone I've met so far in Himmelstal, you're the strongest candidate,' Daniel said.

Corinne lit up.

'That's exactly the way to think of it. OK, I've got a few things I need to do now. See you at the bierstube, maybe? Or at church?'

'I'd prefer the bierstube. Thanks for letting me use your gym.'

'You're welcome to come back whenever you like.'

She went with him to the door and gave him a quick hug. He could feel her wet hair and the smell of soap. He put his fingertips round her wrist, very softly and gently, but the touch made her start and pull her arm away.

'Don't you ever take off this bracelet?' he asked.

'No.'

'It means something special to you, doesn't it?'

'It reminds me of who I am,' she said. 'See you.'

On the way home Daniel hesitated, unsure whether to take the shortcut through the patch of fir trees or follow the road up to the entrance to the clinic. Fir trees brought back unpleasant memories. But still he chose the path through the woods. It looked as though most of the residents used the path, it was well trodden and littered with cigarette butts and rubbish, and Daniel didn't want to appear different, or afraid. He would rather have run, but he forced himself to walk calmly and quickly. He even tried whistling.

Suddenly he caught sight of someone sitting amongst the

trees, ten metres from the path. He calmed down when he saw that it was a woman on her own.

There was nothing violent or unsettling about the scene. The woman was sitting on a mossy rock, smoking. She was staring into the middle distance, and didn't seem to have noticed Daniel. She had kicked off her high-heeled shoes, which lay on the ground in front of her.

'Doctor Obermann,' Daniel said, surprised.

She gave him a weary glance, then looked away. The smell of her cigarillo merged with the smell of sap and firs.

'I'd like to talk to you,' he went on, walking towards her.

'You're no longer my patient,' Gisela Obermann said curtly.

'I know. I'm Doctor Fischer's patient. But I'd rather have you back.'

She let out a short, odd laugh. Without looking at him, she said:

'So you think you've got a choice?'

A ray of sunlight found its way through the branches of the trees and was illuminating her face. Daniel was taken aback when he saw how tired and worn she looked. Her skirt had slid up over her thighs, revealing a ladder in her tights, large as a spider's web.

'No,' he said, 'but I find it easier to talk to you than Doctor Fischer.'

'Go away,' she said coldly. 'Do you hear me? You're not my patient and I've been forbidden from talking to you. I'm not allowed to have any contact with you.'

'But you've got to help me. I need to contact the Swedish authorities to get confirmation of who I am. You have to talk to your colleagues.'

Daniel was talking quickly and animatedly. He crouched down beside her on the moss.

Gisela Obermann tossed her half-smoked cigarillo aside and

stood up abruptly. She took a few steps backwards in her stockinged feet, holding her mobile phone in front of her like a crucifix to ward off a vampire.

'If you don't leave at once, I'll call the guards,' she hissed. 'I'll press the emergency alarm. Have you got that?'

Daniel looked at her in horror, then hurried back to the path.

39

'There are days when I think life in Himmelstal is pretty OK, in spite of everything,' Corinne said. 'When I imagine I could probably manage to live my life here.'

They were sitting on the grass close to each other on Corinne's spread-out jacket. On the other side of the rapids the swallows were circling their nests in the rock face, and off to the west the snow-clad mountaintop seemed to be floating on pillows of cloud in the clear air, like an independent world with its own natural laws.

'I've got these wonderful surroundings, I've got my singing and my performances. And now I've got you, Daniel. You coming here is probably the best thing that's happened to me since I arrived.'

She took his hand and squeezed it. He squeezed back, but thought that it certainly wasn't the best thing that happened to *him*.

'I've always thought I could live a decent life in Himmelstal if there was only someone here I could rely on. A single person I could feel safe with.'

'I'm not going to be staying here, you know that,' he said firmly.

She looked past him at the snow-capped mountain, smiling serenely as if she hadn't heard him.

'But,' she went on after a pause, turning to face him, 'there's still one thing I miss terribly. I didn't think about it to start with, but I'm missing it more and more. Do you know what it is?'

Daniel could think of so many things. He shook his head.

'Children.' She said the word with a whispering sigh. 'For years now I've heard nothing but adult voices, mostly men. Never any shouts from children playing, or toddlers screaming, or babies gurgling. Their laughter! Oh, I'd give anything to hear children laughing. You know, that chuckling, unstoppable laughter. Complete, unadulterated joy. Without the slightest doubt that life is anything but completely good.'

Her voice broke and she hid her face in her hands, and he saw her shoulders shake with silent sobbing. It was a heartbreaking sight.

He wrapped his arms round her and held her. And as she cried against his chest, he realised that she wasn't just missing children in the abstract.

'Do you have any children on the outside?' he asked gently.

'No.' She was so close to him as she muttered her reply that he could feel her lips moving against the cotton shirt over his nipple. 'But I really like children.'

And then she cried some more. For children she had never had, and would never have.

The clanging church bell began to ring. Off to the west a bird of prey was silhouetted against the sky. It circled higher and higher until it finally vanished over the top of the Wall.

A minibus was driving along the road. It slowed down and stopped, but no one got out.

'Whose vehicle is that?' Daniel asked.

Corinne looked up. She wiped the tears from her eyes so she could see better.

'That,' she snorted. 'That's a safari bus. Full of psychopath-tourists. We've probably got fifteen pairs of binoculars pointing at us right now.'

'Fuck you!' she said to the minibus, giving it the finger.

The vehicle set off again and carried on through the valley.

'Guest researchers from all over the world come here to study us. Mostly they just sit in the safety of the conference rooms or visitors' accommodation. But sometimes they go out on an adventure in that minibus. With bulletproof windows that they're under strict instructions never to open.'

Corinne glanced at her watch as she wiped away the last of her tears.

'Mass starts in half an hour,' she said.

And the light came on in her eyes again. Not at full strength, more like the distant glow from a city at night. She put her hand on his shoulder and said:

'Come with me to church, Daniel. I'd really like that. You only have to sit there. Do it for me.'

The light filtering into the church was subdued and coloured by the stained-glass windows. At first glance it gave an old-fashioned impression, but the windows clearly dated from the second half of the twentieth century. The style was clumsily naturalistic, and the colours garish.

The windows made him think of the rumours he had heard in the bierstube: that Father Dennis was a paedophile who had violently assaulted his Sunday school pupils in the name of Christ, and was guilty of murdering one of them.

One of the windows depicted a handsome Jesus with two children dressed in loose togas that looked as if they might fall off at any moment. A flaxen-haired girl leaned longingly against Christ's hip while a small boy appeared to be struggling to get off his lap, as if he were having doubts. His toga had ridden up, revealing his stubby little penis. The motif seemed to have been chosen specially by Father Dennis himself.

The second window depicted a lamb which was very skilfully holding a large wooden cross between its crooked front legs. A patch of red which may have been blood spread out around its hooves. This window also had unpleasant associations for Daniel. The lamb was staring blankly and stupidly ahead, and he could hear Samantha's hoarse whisper: 'Lambkin.'

The third window showed a collection of fat cherubs dancing in a circle like a swarm of marzipan pigs with wings. Lots of peach-coloured flesh, pouting lips and dimpled buttocks. Father Dennis's idea of heaven?

They sat in a pew right at the back. Recorded organ music streamed out of a pair of loudspeakers. Daniel counted eight people in the pews apart from them. They were all sitting alone, at some distance from each other.

Shortly after they sat down Father Dennis appeared in his priest's robes. He looked very distinctive. His forehead had a deep depression in it, and the skin of one cheek was pale pink and stretched. These were the scars from two assaults. Child abusers were loathed and persecuted everywhere, and Himmelstal was no exception.

In Father Dennis's way of looking at the world, however, this persecution had been elevated and now showed that he had been specially selected. It was a form of martyrdom comparable to that of the saints. He didn't even balk at drawing comparisons with the suffering of Christ himself, and believed that the derision of the rest of the world gave him a greater understanding of what Our Saviour had gone through. He accepted every insult, every hate letter, every punch as a sign that he was blessed, a sign of his solidarity with He-who-was-most-hated-and-derided.

For understandable reasons, the priest lived a retiring existence. He had a room in the actual hospital building itself, from which he communicated with the outside world through his page on the valley's intranet, and through enthusiastic use of group emails. Every day he was escorted to and from the church on one of the hosts' electric buggies. Father Dennis's religious activity was seen as important in the valley, which was why the clinic's management had seen fit to extend this level of security to him. It made him even more hated among the other inhabitants, who couldn't count on the same level of protection.

A long, narrow box of fine sand ran along the top of the altar rail like a window box on a balcony. The sand contained a few burned-out candles surrounded by a ring of melted wax. Father Dennis placed a row of new candles in the sand and lit them one by one. With each candle he muttered a short prayer and made the sign of the cross.

'For the dead,' Corinne said with her head bowed.

They were on their knees in the pew, their hands clasped together. Daniel glanced at her.

'Which dead?'

'Residents of Himmelstal who've died.'

The priest took a few steps back and stared ceremoniously at the lit candles while a Bach fugue rumbled out of the speakers. Daniel counted the candles.

'Twenty-four. How many of those died a natural death?' Daniel wondered.

'That depends what you mean by natural. In Himmelstal it's natural to die from murder, suicide or overdose,' Corinne muttered, looking down at her clasped hands. To anyone watching it would have appeared that she was praying. 'There are probably far more than twenty-four. But some are never found. They simply disappear.'

The organ music fell quiet. Father Dennis had climbed up into the pulpit.

In his emailed sermons he had two favourite themes to which he kept returning. One was *the Lamb*: the innocent sacrificial lamb, so white and pure. The Lord taking care of his flock. The Good Shepherd.

The others was *Wounds*: Christ's miraculous bleeding wounds. The wounds of the martyrs. Father Dennis's own cherished, painful wounds that he wore like jewellery.

Sometimes he combined these in a sermon about *the wounds of the Lamb*.

Daniel wondered which of these themes he'd choose for today's sermon.

Father Dennis cleared his throat and began:

'Let us for a moment imagine that we are angels.'

'You'll have to imagine pretty hard,' Corinne said quietly to herself.

'Wonderful, pure angels with snow-white wings, floating up in the sky. We're drifting high above the Alps, and see them below us. It must look beautiful, mustn't it? And then we drift over Himmelstal, and do you know how that looks? I can tell you. The landscape is mountainous, no great peaks, but a few ups and downs, like the hair on an animal's back. Then suddenly: a cut! A wound in this back. Narrow. Deep. *Painfully* deep. And this is Himmelstal. *A wound*. Carved by the icy knife of a glacier. My friends: *we live at the bottom of a wound!* You and I are maggots living in that wound. We infect it, keep it open, make sure the pus keeps flowing. That's our lot. Living at the bottom of a wound.'

The priest's voice was intense, almost breathless.

Daniel felt sick.

'You'll have to forgive me, but I can't handle any more of

this,' he whispered to Corinne. 'And I'd like to get to the library before it shuts.'

He squeezed her hand in farewell and crept out.

As he headed back towards the clinic he passed one of the guards' vans parked up at the side of the road. The guards themselves were walking slowly along either side of the rapids, with long poles sunk into the swirling water.

Watching them, he felt the ground beneath his feet tremble slightly. A faint, barely perceptible movement that made the bellflowers sway gently on their stalks in the breezeless summer evening. As if the valley were shuddering.

40

The library was silent and deserted. There was no one else in sight apart from the librarian. Daniel went up to the counter.

'I'd like to read something about falcons.'

The little bald man adjusted his glasses and led him over to one of the shelves.

'Here. *The World of Birds of Prey*,' the librarian said, handing him a large book with a golden eagle on the cover. 'Anything else?'

'That's all, thanks. This was exactly what I was looking for. Thanks for your help,' Daniel said, turning to leave.

'Nothing about the Second World War? We've got plenty of interesting books here.'

Daniel stopped. The Second World War was something of a passion for the librarian. In his flat in the village he had maps pinned with the positions of German and Allied troops, and he kept a careful eye out for any new books published on the subject, and made sure that the Himmelstal library had as good a selection of books on the topic as any university library.

Daniel also knew that the little bald man had another

passion: garrotting innocent people with nylon thread. He was said to be very skilled at this difficult art, and his murder weapon of choice was easily accessible in the shop selling fishing supplies in the village.

'The Second World War is always interesting, of course,' Daniel therefore replied amenably. 'What would you recommend?'

'Oh, there's so much to choose between. Follow me, I'll show you,' the librarian boasted. He hunched his shoulders and screwed his eyes up mischievously, making his steel-framed glasses bounce.

Daniel followed him hesitantly in among the bookcases, glancing over his shoulder towards the door. How much longer were they going to be on their own in there?

The librarian was talking about his favourite subject, but was soon drowned out by a shrill siren, followed by a dull rumble that made the shelves shake. The same trembling that Daniel had felt a short while before down in the valley, but much stronger.

'What was that?' he asked.

'They're blasting,' the librarian said calmly as he searched with his finger along the spines of the books. 'On the building site.'

'They're building something new?'

The librarian nodded.

'A residential complex. Right at the top of the hill. Six floors. Single and double-room flats. Balconies with views of the valley. I'm thinking of applying. I'm not happy in the village. Do you live in the village?'

'No,' Daniel said, and to avoid having to say where he lived he quickly added: 'When's it due to be finished?'

'Next summer. Of course it might only be for new arrivals. Another two hundred are going to be coming next year.'

The librarian climbed up on to a stool and peered at the books on the top shelf through his reading glasses.

'Two hundred?'

'Yes. Himmelstal is expanding. Have you read this, about the British Secret Service?'

He climbed down from the stool with the book in his hand. Daniel wanted to take it and go, but the librarian started to tell him what it was about, and was soon sounding so enthusiastic that he might have been trying to sell it to Daniel instead of lending it out. He was so eager that his bald head was shiny with sweat. Daniel regretted arousing this passion, and was worried that if it got strong enough it might awaken the librarian's other obsession.

He didn't calm down until he saw Pablo, a former thug from the Madrid underworld, wander in and take a seat to read some motorcycle magazines as if he owned the place. Pablo was known for his brutality, but at least he was a witness, and the librarian was as scared of him as Daniel was, if not more so. The Spaniard's arrival was like a bucket of cold water over the little man's overheated senses, and his voice sank to a whisper as his eyes grew uncertain and fluttering.

Daniel breathed out. The world of birds of prey. A sparrow relieved when an eagle chases away a hawk.

'Thanks very much. I'll take these home and start reading,' Daniel said quickly. 'Oh, one more thing. You seem so well informed. I saw some guards down by the rapids. It looked as though they were searching for something?'

'Yes,' the librarian said, nodding solemnly.

'Is it . . . Has a resident gone missing?'

'Oh, no.' The librarian smiled. 'The guards don't bother to search for residents.'

He glanced towards the Spaniard and lowered his voice to a whisper:

'It's one of the hostesses.'

'The little dark-haired one?'

Daniel hadn't seen her for a while, and had been wondering where she'd gone.

The librarian nodded almost imperceptibly. This was a subject he didn't want to talk about.

'Thanks again for your help,' Daniel said. 'I'll bring the books back as soon as I've finished them.'

'Keep them as long as you need them,' the librarian said with a generous sweep of his hand. 'I'll come and find you if anyone asks for them. You live in one of the cabins, don't you?'

Daniel muttered something vague that could have been either a yes or a no.

'I need to know where my best friends are, after all,' the librarian said with a smile.

'The books, I mean,' he explained, pointing at the books under Daniel's arm.

That night Daniel dreamed of Father Dennis's snow-white angels floating high above Himmelstal. He was up among them, as weightless and free as them. The valley lay below him, green and fresh, with the winding river and the little village. The bell in the church was ringing and the sound rose up to them, sounding crisper and clearer in the air.

Then he suddenly noticed that the angels were no longer white, but dark. They'd turned into big birds of prey, circling round and round as they peered down at the valley floor. Thick yellow pus was running through the valley now instead of water, and the birds weren't looking for mice or smaller birds but the huge white maggots crawling around on the grass.

Of course, that makes sense, Daniel thought in the dream. He felt strangely calm, as if the unpleasant things he was seeing didn't upset him at all, merely confirming his suspicions.

And the crisp ringing wasn't from the church bell – how could he have thought that? – but the little bells that were tied to the birds' legs with leather straps.

At the same instant he realised something else, and the thought was so strong that it wrenched him from sleep.

He lit the lamp in his alcove, pulled his mobile phone down from the shelf and sent Corinne a text message.

41

'I think I know how it works,' Daniel said in a low voice as he leaned over the table.

They were sitting in the restaurant on the first floor of the main building. They had just finished their dinner of venison fillet with wild mushrooms.

The waitress came over to their table with a tray. She poured them coffee and left a plate of chocolate macaroons – the same sort that Gisela Obermann had offered him in her room.

When the waitress turned away another memory popped into his head: Max had slapped her on her broad backside. At the time, about a month before – was it really no more than that? – Daniel had still believed Himmelstal was a luxury clinic and that the broad-hipped waitress was some decent woman from an alpine village. Now he knew that she was from Holland, and that she had lured her husband into the bomb shelter of her parents' villa, barricaded the door and left him to starve to death inside while she watched television upstairs.

'How, then? Who brings the drugs in?' Corinne asked once the waitress had disappeared into the kitchen.

'Someone who can get into the valley and drop it off without any hassle with electrified zones, guards or sniffer dogs.'

'And who might that be?'

'Falcons.'

She looked at him sceptically as she dabbed at her mouth with her napkin.

'On one of my first days here I met a man with a tame falcon,' Daniel went on quietly.

'Adrian Keller,' Corinne said, pouring some milk in her coffee.

'You know him?'

She nodded.

'He lives in an isolated cabin at the far end of the valley. He used to be a thug for the Colombian drug cartels. Utterly ruthless. He's supposed to have spent several years living with an Indian tribe in the jungle. He keeps to himself, never sets foot in the village or clinic grounds. He's got a load of traps set out. Only the van from the shop and the guards making their morning and evening checks ever go out there. And even they hardly dare get out of their cars. Yes, he's got falcons. He hunts with them. The clinic management let him because it seems to mean so much to him. He's obsessed with his falcons and hunting. Sometimes that's what you have to do, Gisela says. Channel the evil into a harmless hobby.'

'Possibly quite a lucrative hobby? The other evening I read that the Allies used falcons during the Second World War, to bring down German carrier pigeons. It didn't work very well because the falcons couldn't distinguish between German carrier pigeons and Allied ones, and killed them all indiscriminately. But it struck me that falcons might be able to carry things themselves. They're trained, they always return to their master. Let's suppose Keller has a contact outside, and that the falcons fly over the mountains to the contact, who ties a little parcel to their leg before they fly back.'

Daniel sounded enthusiastic, but Corinne shook her head.

'The clinic management have actually looked into that possibility. They've spoken to falconers and ornithologists. They all say the same thing: it's impossible. Falcons are useless at carrying messages and objects. They don't work as carrier pigeons. Although their speed and sight is vastly superior to other birds, they haven't got the same brilliant sense of direction that pigeons have.'

'Oh,' Daniel said, disappointed. 'It was just a thought. Have you got a better theory?'

Corinne opened her mouth, then decided against it.

'We've got company,' she said, nodding towards the door.

A group of four people had walked in, and were being led to a reserved table by the window. Daniel recognised Doctor Fischer, Doctor Pierce and the Indian doctor who hadn't spoken during the meeting. The fourth man was wearing a baseball cap. Daniel couldn't recall ever having seen him before.

'Probably a visiting researcher,' Corinne said. 'There are a lot of them here at the moment.'

'The ones watching us from the safari minibus?'

Corinne nodded.

'Presumably this one wasn't happy with that. He wants to see the animals get fed,' she said bitterly. 'That's always popular. It's a shame for him that we've already finished. If he'd come ten minutes earlier he could have watched us devouring a deer.'

Daniel glanced at the man in the baseball cap, who was studying the menu intently.

'He seems more interested in his own food,' he said, then went on in a lower voice: 'What were you about to say? About how the drugs get in?'

'We're in a hospital, aren't we? Hospitals have drugs. And psychiatric hospitals have drugs that affect the mind. I think the answer's there somewhere.'

'From the hospital? You think the staff are dealing drugs? Or are they being stolen by a resident?'

She shrugged.

'It could be the staff, or it could be residents. Or it could be both of them, working together.'

'But I've heard that you can buy cocaine here. That's hardly psychiatric medicine,' Daniel pointed out.

'They're always getting deliveries of legal drugs. If there are a few illegal drugs hidden among them, maybe no one would notice.'

'In that case the staff have to be involved. Do you suspect anyone in particular?'

'No. It depends what their motives are. Money's the usual one, of course. Then again, I can imagine other reasons why someone would want to bring drugs into the valley.'

'Such as?'

'Academic greed. Brian Jenkins, the red-haired sociologist, might as well pack his bags and go home if there were no narcotics in the valley. His study of the effect of narcotics on the social structure here would be completely pointless and he'd lose his funding.'

'Couldn't he just change the focus slightly? Himmelstal before and after drugs?' Daniel suggested. 'Any other motives?'

'Love,' Corinne said. 'Psychopaths can be extremely charming. It's not impossible to imagine a resident having an affair with a hostess. Or a nurse.'

The group by the window had got their drinks. They drank a toast, and the man in the baseball cap, who was evidently American, told a funny story that made the others laugh.

'The hostesses always work in pairs,' Daniel pointed out. 'To stop anything like that happening. And the nurses are never alone with patients either.'

'In theory, yes. But not in practice, as you know. You must have been on your own with a nurse at some point when you were being treated for those burns? And who knows what you and Gisela got up to in her office?'

Daniel smiled.

'You're right,' he said. 'It's a possibility.'

Still, he wasn't ready to let go of the idea of falcons flying in and out over the mountains, completely free and unchecked.

As soon as they got outside Daniel could tell that something had happened, or was about to happen.

The park was full of that peculiar vibrant atmosphere he had come to recognise during his time in Himmelstal. There were small groups of people standing around in the darkness, talking rapidly in low voices. An electric buggy pulled up over on the path, and Father Dennis stuck his head out like a timid but curious animal peeping out of its burrow.

Then there was the sound of an engine on the road. The crowd of people was lit up by headlights, and a van drove into the clinic grounds at high speed and stopped outside the care centre. Staff in white coats came streaming out of the building towards the van.

'Go away. There's nothing to see,' the guards shouted, pushing back the residents who were gathering round the vehicle.

A stretcher was lifted out and carried quickly towards the door of the building. As it went past Daniel had time to see its occupant: an unconscious young man with handsome features and a large wound to his forehead. The blanket covering his body was bloodstained.

'Raped. Found in the woods,' someone whispered.

'He's a fucking idiot,' someone else snorted.

'Is he alive?'

'Looked like it.'

Father Dennis was approaching from the electric buggy in full regalia. He stopped at a respectful distance from the others, crossed himself and muttered a quick prayer. With his floor-length Mass robes flapping round his legs he hurried back to the buggy and disappeared in the direction of the village.

The stretcher had been carried into the care centre and the van drove off. The crowd dispersed, everyone heading home now that the performance was over.

'God, he was only a boy. A teenager,' Daniel said, upset.

Corinne shrugged her shoulders.

'Everyday life in Himmelstal. The worst thing is that you get used to it. At the start I thought it was terrible. Now I'm just glad it wasn't me. And you start to worry what it might lead to. If someone's going to want revenge. Sometimes an event like this can unleash a whole chain of violence. But this was probably nothing more than an ordinary sex attack. No more will come of it.'

Daniel clenched his fists.

'I'm getting out of here,' he said in a hoarse voice. 'This is worse than a madhouse. Worse than prison. I'm going to talk to Karl Fischer tomorrow.'

'You can always try. Thanks for dinner, by the way. It's a long time since I ate in the restaurant. It's no fun going up there on your own, and I haven't had anyone to go with before now.'

'I'll walk you home,' Daniel said.

'You don't have to.'

'Yes I do. There's no way you're walking to the village alone.'

'If you walk me home, then you'll have to come back on your own afterwards. It's better for me to go now, while there are other people heading in that direction. I won't be alone. Goodnight, and thanks for this evening.'

She gave him a quick hug, then hurried to catch up with the group heading down the slope. A few metres behind them she slowed her pace and maintained that distance the rest of the way to the village. She was surprisingly brave, Daniel thought as he watched her go.

'Have you two been to the restaurant? Smart move.'

Daniel turned round and discovered Samantha standing by the bushes, smoking. She'd probably been there for a while, but there had been so many people around that he hadn't noticed her. Now she was the only other person left. She wasn't wearing any makeup, and was dressed in bulky jeans and a polyester tracksuit top. With her short hair, she looked like a teenage boy hanging around a street corner waiting for his gang to show up.

'What did you say?'

'I said it was smart of you to choose the restaurant. You're avoiding the bierstube, aren't you? I'd never drink beer if she was serving it.'

'Who?'

Samantha took a long drag on her cigarette and peered at him slyly through the smoke. She tilted her head, jutted out her elbow in a contrived posture, and dangled her hand.

'Ding-a-ling,' she said slowly.

Corinne was still doing her performance as a shepherdess, but it had been a while since Daniel had seen it. He thought about her taut, muscular body and her lightning reflexes when she was hitting the punchbag. Her secret, strong side, a long way from Samantha's mocking parody.

He turned his back on Samantha to walk off to his cabin but changed his mind. A sudden curiosity, impossible to contain, made him ask:

'Why wouldn't you drink beer if she was serving it?'

'Because of what she did.'

'What did she do?'

'You don't know?'

Samantha leaned against the lamppost, looked out into the darkness and pretended to think.

'Hmm. Maybe I shouldn't tell you. I wouldn't want to spoil your idyllic image of the little shepherdess.'

Daniel could see that she was desperate to tell him. He waited.

'OK,' she said eventually. 'She poisoned little children.'

'You're lying.'

'She was a paediatric nurse. She put something in their bottles.'

'She wasn't a paediatric nurse. She was an actress.'

'To start with, yes. She got pregnant, then had a miscarriage, and couldn't get pregnant again. After that she was obsessed with babies. She got a job in a maternity ward. Did a lot of overtime. Knitted blankets and clothes for the babies. Was always there, never took any breaks. When the kids started dying like flies there was an investigation. She managed to kill nine kids before she got caught.'

Daniel gulped. He thought about what Corinne had said: what she missed most in the valley was children.

'But what the fuck,' Samantha said with a shrug. 'What is it Father Dennis always says in those emails? *We shouldn't sit in judgement.* Quite right. You're not sitting in judgement, are you? Me neither. But I wouldn't drink any beer served by her. That's not a judgement. That's self-preservation, pure and fucking simple.'

She took a last greedy drag on the cigarette, then tossed it into the bushes and glided off across the lawn.

42

The wind was surprisingly mild. From somewhere over by the care centre came a faint, unidentifiable, metallic rumbling sound, and far in the distance he could hear the engine of the guards' car driving its endless circuit. Otherwise it was quiet.

Marko had shown no surprise when Daniel went out again after the night round. Leaning back against the wall of his cabin he had raised his hand in a limp, wordless greeting and Daniel had responded in kind before setting off quickly down the hill.

As he walked through the small patch of woodland that separated the clinic grounds from the village, he reflected on the fact that what he was doing was extremely dangerous, completely unnecessary, and not at all like him. He could easily wait till morning. There was no need for him to talk to Corinne right away.

But his desire for certainty – immediate certainty – was stronger than his fear. He could only remember one previous occasion in his life when he had been similarly desperate to know the truth: when he suspected that Emma, his former wife, was having an affair he took the day off and spent the morning frantically going through her drawers and pockets, and then tailed her to a meeting with her lover. He recalled how irrational and shameless his actions had seemed, but also the feverish excitement and – above all – the *urgency*.

He jogged through the poorly lit village streets and went up the steps to Corinne's loft apartment.

'It's me, Daniel,' he shouted, so as not to scare her by knocking.

When she eventually opened the door, her face was streaked as if she had been crying. Then he realised it was sweat and that the furrow in her brow came from her annoyance at being interrupted. She was dressed in shorts and a vest, salsa music was coming out of the speakers and she was holding her boxing gloves under her arm.

'What is it? Has something happened?' she asked.

'No. I wanted to talk, that's all.'

'Now?'

'Now.'

She let him in.

'Can you wait ten minutes?'

He nodded and sat down on the sofa. Corinne drank some water from the tap, pulled her gloves on and carried on training. Her shepherdess outfit was on a hanger by the wall, clean and freshly ironed.

Daniel watched her as she set about the punchbag. She was muttering aggressively, as if she was talking to an imaginary opponent, and he couldn't tell whether it was sweat or tears running down her cheeks, or possibly a mixture of both. There was a spotlight shining on her from the ceiling. The rest of the large room was dark, apart from the strings of red, green and blue fairy lights.

Daniel felt as though he had been left behind in a room where a party had just come to an end and something else was about to happen. An unpredictable after-party for a few select people.

His heart was still racing from his rapid walk and the strange, intoxicating anxiety. Once again his thoughts wandered to Emma and the last terrible weeks of their marriage. He had squeezed the truth out of her like a tube of toothpaste, and no matter how hard he squeezed there was always a little bit left that he couldn't get at. He had followed her, caught her red-handed, confronted her. Then came the relief and pain of knowing for certain. And the frustration at still not knowing everything.

There was a half-full bottle of wine on the kitchen counter. He pulled out the cork and poured himself a glass without asking, then sat back on the sofa as his pulse slowed down. The wine, the salsa music and the regular thud of the punch-bag filled him up and settled like a smothering blanket over his febrile thoughts. He watched Corinne's fight with the black, lumpy monster that took each blow with an unconcerned swing. She was so slight, yet so strong and stubborn, and utterly furious.

Exhausted, she staggered back, sank to her knees and pulled off the gloves.

'What did you want to talk about?' she panted.

'Not yet. After you've had a shower.'

As the water ran in the bathroom, he wondered how to frame his question. His thoughts, which had been sharp and clear a short while ago, as though lit up by a sudden flash of lightning, were now mired in doubt. When she emerged shortly afterwards with her open, girlish face, her dripping hair and a bath towel wrapped tightly round her body, he had almost forgotten why he was there.

'Well?' she said. 'Have you had another idea about the drug deliveries?'

'No.'

'Then what was so important that it couldn't wait till tomorrow?'

She was standing with her arms folded, her legs set slightly apart as she looked at him from under her wet, absolutely straight fringe. A little girl in a dressing gown that was too big for her.

All his urgency vanished. That business with the babies didn't matter. Odd. But that was how it felt. Maybe it was a lie, maybe it was the truth. It didn't make any difference. If it was true, it must have been temporary insanity, a wound in a psyche that was otherwise completely healthy and beautiful. He didn't want to know. Some things were more important than the truth. Such as the fact that she was the only person in Himmelstal who had shown him any friendship and warmth. The only person he could talk to.

Suddenly the worried look on her face cracked into a smile. And at that moment it was as if a switch had been flicked and thousands of tiny, silvery lights had come on inside her irises, all directed at him. How does that happen? he thought in amazement. Where does the light come from?

'Well, tell me!' she said. 'What was so urgent?'

'This,' he said, getting up from the sofa and cupping her face in his hands. He brushed her wet hair back and kissed her.

She pulled away with a jerk and put her hand over her mouth as if to shield it.

'No. We mustn't,' she said.

'Why not?'

She folded her arms again, tucking her hands under her arms as if she were cold, and looked away without speaking.

'Don't you trust me, Corinne? I trust you. Do you hear me? *I trust you.* You're the only person here I trust. And I'm the only person *you* can trust.'

She was staring at the wall and shaking her head with her jaw clenched, like a stubborn child.

296

Daniel swallowed and went on:

'I don't know what you've been through, what you've done or what you used to be like. But right now we're here, you and me. Whatever happened before belongs in the past, I don't care about any of that. I love you the way you are now.'

'Oh, God,' she sniffed. 'Shit.' She ran her hand quickly over her eyes, and added: 'I love you too. I have done ever since that picnic at the Leper Cemetery.'

'In that case, this may well be the only love that exists in this valley,' he said seriously. 'Have you thought about that?'

She considered what he had said.

'You're probably right.'

He moved his face so close to hers that their noses were touching, and kissed her again. This time she didn't pull away. They tasted each other, curiously and carefully at first, like some new food they'd never tried before, then with increasing passion. He took a step back and undid the towelling belt around her waist, all the while looking at her face, ready to stop if she gave any sign. But she just looked at him, smiling and trusting, and he opened her dressing gown and gently stroked her girlishly small breasts with two fingers. She stood there motionless with her eyes closed and her nipples stiffening. Then she opened her eyes. The shower of light was flowing with full force. A dangerous, edgy glow.

'This is impossible,' she whispered. 'It shouldn't be happening.'

43

During the weeks that followed they made love as often as they got the chance. In Corinne's flat after training. In Daniel's cabin. On one occasion outdoors under a pine tree, and several times in an abandoned barn. The awareness that they were surrounded by enemies egged them on, and the brutal environment formed a sharp contrast to their own heightened senses, like ice on hot skin. Daniel hadn't felt so virile since he was a teenager.

At the same time it was a welcome respite after his constant adjustments and suspicions, to be able to sink into a warm embrace and put himself in someone else's hands. A flight from the valley, into lust and forgetfulness.

He told Corinne about his childhood with his mother and her parents in Uppsala, about his chaotic birthdays with Max, and their complicated relationship as twins. And Corinne talked about growing up in Zürich, about her admiration for her father, a mountaineer who died on a climb when she was thirteen years old, and the theatre group she had belonged to, and an unhappy love affair with a married director. She never mentioned any babies, and he didn't ask.

They spent almost all their time together. Every night after the patrol had been he would creep down to Corinne's flat in the village. Love had emboldened him, and he now dared to move about after dark. The whispering voices out there were no longer anonymous. Thanks to Corinne, he knew who the shadows were, and what they wanted. Most of them were completely uninterested in Daniel and left him alone. The ones you had to watch out for lived beyond the clinic grounds and village. The basic principle seemed to be that the further you got from the village, the crazier and more dangerous people were.

But obviously he mustn't let his guard down. When Daniel handed his books back to the library, the librarian had given him an ambiguous look, tapped the cover of *The World of Birds of Prey*, and said:

'I presume you read that the mating season is the most dangerous time for their prey. The reaction time of voles, for instance, decreases by a third when they're on heat.'

'Yes, that's supposed to be true,' Daniel had replied nonchalantly.

But he was secretly grateful for the warning. So there were people in the valley who were aware of his relationship with Corinne.

Every morning and every evening he and Corinne had to part in order to be in their respective homes when the hosts called. Daniel thought it was ridiculous. But when the hosts made their checks, you had to be in your registered abode. That was one of the ground rules in Himmelstal.

He had suggested to Corinne that he move in with her and register there instead. He had understood that that sort of thing happened occasionally. Corinne had told him, for instance, that Samantha had been Kowalski's official lover, and that she had registered as living in his villa.

But Corinne had no desire to legitimise their relationship

in that way and get it sanctioned by the clinic's management. On the contrary, she was very careful about none of the doctors and psychologists finding out about it. Daniel had to promise to keep it secret, and she wouldn't hear of him registering at her address. So Daniel always had to leave Corinne's flat in good time to be home in his cabin at the distinctly antisocial hours of eight a.m. and midnight.

One morning he woke up unusually early. The theatre masks were staring with their empty eyes in the gloom. He got up and dressed, gave the sleeping Corinne a gentle kiss goodbye, and left the attic flat.

A strange quiet was resting over the village. The first few hours after the goodnight patrol could be pretty lively hereabouts, but by this time, not quite dawn, everyone seemed to have settled down.

There was plenty of time before the morning patrol showed up, so he decided to take the longer but safer route, along the road. He'd be able to spot any potential enemies at a distance.

The bottom of the valley was still immersed in the darkness of night, but over to the east the sky was clear and cobalt blue. Daniel was freezing in his summer jacket, and speeded up.

There was a sudden sound in the silence. At first he thought it was a bird calling. A creaking, whining sound that rose and fell in the cold air. Daniel stopped to listen. A short way ahead of him the road curved round some bushes. That was where the sound was coming from.

The creaking got louder, it was like a tune. Suddenly he remembered where he had heard it before. It was Adrian Keller's bicycle cart.

Daniel had no desire to meet him on his own out in the valley at dawn. He quickly left the road and hurried across the frosted grass of the meadow to an old barn with a collapsed roof. He stood in the shelter of the wall peering out at the

300

bend in the road. He saw he had left indistinct footprints in the frost and hoped that Keller wouldn't notice them in the early morning gloom.

The creaking melody cut through the silence and a moment later the man appeared at the bend in the road. Daniel held his breath. The cart was loaded with the same wooden box as last time.

Adrian Keller followed the road eastward for another fifty metres, then stopped. He climbed off, lit a cigarette and sat down on the edge of the trailer.

The snow-capped peak was glowing rosy red while at the same time a bright star twinkled in the darker part of the sky. The sound of the circulating guards' car could be heard far in the distance.

Keller smoked his cigarette without hurrying, then opened the sliding door of the box. There was a flutter of wings and he took a few steps back.

When Daniel peered out from behind the wall of the barn again, Adrian Keller was standing on the frosty grass with the falcon on his arm. Fog was rising like smoke from the rapids.

A small, dark cloud was sweeping rapidly in from the east and as it came closer Daniel saw that the cloud was a flock of pigeons. Quickly the man freed the falcon from its hood and set it loose. At the same moment the flock of pigeons scattered and the hunt began high up in the glassy air. Daniel shaded his eyes against the rising sun as he tried to follow the falcon through its twists and turns.

Another falcon shot up from the bottom of the valley, and now there were two of them hunting. One of them returned to its master, who quickly grabbed the pigeon from its talons and sent the falcon back up at once without letting it taste its prey.

Adrian Keller leaned over the pigeon and it looked as though he were freeing it of something, before tossing it in a

301

sack. The second falcon was already on its way down and the man received this new bounty as well, fiddling with it intently as the falcon flew off again. The flock of pigeons was no longer visible, but the falcon vanished over the edge of the rock face and once again it returned with a pigeon in its claws.

When the falcons failed to find any more prey, Keller emptied the pigeons from the sack and let the falcons loose on them while he lit another cigarette.

Then he put the hoods on the falcons, shut them in their box and cycled back with his trailer the way he had come.

Daniel waited a good while after the squeaking sound had vanished. He left the barn and went over to where the man had been standing. The half-eaten pigeons lay on the ground in drifts of blood-stained feathers.

Daniel crouched and inspected the shredded bodies of the birds. One foot lay on its own, claws outstretched, some distance from the other pieces. Around the ankle was something black that looked like a scrap of insulating tape.

He poked the bloody remnants with a stick. He discovered that each of the pigeons had sticky marks or fragments of tape tightly wound around their legs.

Suddenly Daniel realised how the whole thing worked: these pigeons were prepared by someone outside the valley and sent in at dawn just as Adrian Keller let his falcons loose. The falcons caught the pigeons, and Adrian Keller got hold of the cargo that was tied to their legs. And the pigeons that survived flew back to their dovecote outside the valley, the way homing pigeons do, meaning that their valuable load was returned to the sender. Nothing got wasted. They just had to count how many pigeons went missing and send the bill.

Daniel walked on towards the clinic. By the main building he passed the hosts, who were laughing and chatting as they got ready to set out in their electric buggies. They were wearing blue wool coats over their normal uniforms.

He unlocked his cabin door and sat down to wait for the patrol while he considered the best way to make use of his discovery. Should he tell Doctor Fischer? Another member of staff? Would telling anyone actually be to his advantage? He'd talk to Corinne about it.

But now he suddenly felt very tired. As soon as the patrol had gone, he thought he might grab a couple of hours' sleep before going to see her.

It seemed the patrol must be starting in the village that morning and working its way up. He yawned and hoped he wasn't going to fall asleep in his chair before they arrived. He always tried to be awake when the patrol came, but occasionally they caught him by surprise when he was asleep. Once he had almost hit one of the hostesses out of reflex. She had parried his blow with a surprisingly quick karate move, then laughed as if it happened a lot.

He had to wait another twenty minutes until he heard the familiar hum outside, then the knock and the door handle turning.

'Good morning, Max. Did you sleep well? You've already made your bed, I see,' the hostess said with a glance towards his untouched bed, clearly visible behind the open drapes.

She obviously realised he had spent the night elsewhere, but seemed merely to find this amusing. Daniel didn't reply.

The hostess was on her way out to her colleague when she turned round and, with her hands in her coat pockets, said:

'Oh, yes. Your brother's here. You knew that, didn't you?'

44

Daniel wondered if he had heard right.

'He's *here*?'

'Yes,' the hostess said. 'He was asking after you in reception yesterday. Didn't he get hold of you?'

His heart was beating wildly, but his face remained expressionless. He had become very good at keeping his facial muscles under control.

'We must have missed each other,' he said. 'I was out all day yesterday, and my mobile was switched off. When did he get here?'

'Sometime yesterday morning. I wasn't on duty then. Check with reception.'

The hostess went out to join her colleague. Daniel hurried to open the door again, stuck his head out and asked:

'Where is he now?'

'I suppose he spent the night in one of the guestrooms. I'm sure you'll find him.'

As soon as the morning patrol had left he went over to Marko's cabin and banged on the door.

'It's only me. Your neighbour,' he shouted.

There was a groggy noise from within in response.

'Did you notice if anyone was trying to get hold of me yesterday?' Daniel asked through the closed door.

The groggy noise sounded like 'no'.

'No one knocking on my door?'

'No.' Clearer and more annoyed this time.

No, of course not. Marko was a nocturnal creature who spent all morning asleep.

Daniel went back into his cabin and switched on his mobile. He had several missed calls and three voicemails from a number he didn't recognise. With sweating fingers he tapped in the code to listen to his messages, then held the phone to his ear and waited breathlessly.

'Hey, bro.'

It was Max's voice. He could tell instantly.

'Where are you? I've been sitting on your step for two hours now and I'm starting to get fed up. Look, I'm really sorry I was gone so long. But I've had terrible problems. I'm just happy I survived in one piece. I'll tell you all about it later. I'm never going to have anything to do with the mafia again. Hope you haven't been having too bad a time. Well, I suppose you've worked out what sort of place this is now. Maybe I did sketch over the details a bit, but you'd never have agreed otherwise. And it really wasn't supposed to take as long as this. What was I going to say? Oh yes. I'll sit here for a bit longer, then I'll push off.'

There was a click and the message was over. Daniel had hardly caught his breath before the next message began, received an hour and a half later. The same familiar, strained voice said:

'Do you know what I really hate? People who always have their mobiles switched off. It's so *fucking* arrogant. Well, I'm with a bloke called Adrian Keller. Maybe you know him? He's the only person I socialise with here, actually. Big on

305

nature. Falcons and stuff. A bit reserved. He hates the rabble in the village, just like me. Anyway, that's where I am at the moment. Can you come out here, Daniel? Right at the end of the valley. The way we cycled, you know. Just a bit further on. Call me when you're on your way and I'll come and meet you. The guy's got loads of traps and stuff around the house, so you have to take care. Stick to the road.'

The third message had been received at quarter past two at night, and the tone was very annoyed:

'Where the fuck are you? I'm starting to get worried about you. Come out here so we can get this sorted.'

Daniel checked the number of the incoming calls. He called it. There was no answer.

He had no desire whatsoever to visit Adrian Keller's isolated house. But if that was where Max was? His brother was capricious. He could quickly change his mind and leave again. If he really did intend that they should switch back again, it was best to hurry.

45

Daniel was crouched over the handlebar of one of the clinic's mountain bikes, pedalling through the valley so hard that the sweat was pouring off him. He passed the Leper Cemetery with its crooked crosses at high speed, along the forest road that led up to Tom's cabin, until he came to a bridge that crossed the river at the point where it reached the valley floor.

He was now in the wild, western part of the valley where the loners lived, where you only came at your own risk. The hosts never patrolled out here with their electric buggies. The patrols were handled by armed guards who did their rounds in vans.

Daniel had a rough idea where Adrian Keller's house was. During the course of a long day out with Corinne she had showed him the narrow track that led to his house, and warned him against going up there. She had also pointed out the two large villas at the top of the grass slope. The top one, the larger of the two, was Kowalski's. The one below was Sørensen's. Beside each house was a garage, Kowalski and Sørensen both had cars. Not the latest model, admittedly, but still. Private cars. No other residents in Himmelstal had cars.

Bicycles and flatbed-mopeds were the commonest form of transport here. Most people had no transport at all and simply borrowed the clinic's bikes when they needed to. Cars were mainly the preserve of the staff.

He stopped at the end of the track leading to Keller's and rang the number he had been called from. No answer. Were they still asleep? It was a few minutes after nine o'clock. Max had evidently been up late last night, judging by the time of his final message, and of course Keller had been out with his falcons at dawn. So maybe they were tired now.

If Max had left Keller's cabin and returned to the clinic, Daniel would have bumped into him. Unless he'd taken the track at the very top of the slope. But why would he do that? He'd asked Daniel to come to Keller's house, after all. He ought to have rung if there were any changes. Although with Max you could never be sure.

He put his mobile away, swung his leg back over the bike and steered it on to the track and up the winding slope that led to Adrian Keller's house.

The day that had started so clear and frosty had turned grey. Veils of wet mist were sweeping the valley, making his clothes damp.

He jumped off the bicycle and stopped thirty metres away. Kowalski's black Mercedes was parked in front of the house. Adrian Keller's reputation as a recluse seemed to be something of an exaggeration.

In a large cage covered with chicken wire the falcons sat on dead trees shrieking loudly and mournfully into the fog. Maybe their cries announced his arrival, because while he was standing there wondering if he ought to go any closer or turn away, the door suddenly opened and Adrian Keller peered out.

Daniel led the bicycle a bit nearer. He was careful to stick to the middle of the track.

'Is my brother here? He rang and said he was with you,' he called.

Keller didn't answer, but gestured to him to go in.

Daniel hesitated. Then he made his way to the house, leaned the bicycle against the railing and went up the steps towards Adrian Keller.

It took a while for his eyes to get used to the gloom inside, because the shutters were closed. Unlike most of the buildings in the village, the house hadn't been built recently in a picture-sque old-fashioned style. It seemed properly old, had probably been here since before the start of the Himmelstal project.

Kowalski and Sørensen were sitting at a table under a low-hanging lamp. In front of them were plastic bags of white powder and a set of scales. Sørensen looked up.

'You're in so much of a hurry you had to come up here?'

'I got a message from my brother. He said he was here,' Daniel said, his voice wavering.

Sørensen looked at Kowalski and Keller.

'What's he mean?'

Keller shrugged his shoulders.

When Daniel glanced to his left he saw a large, horizontal wall-mirror that reflected the whole room like a picture. He could see them all inside the gold frame: Kowalski and Sørensen in the limited light from the lamp, Keller as a fuzzy figure away in the gloom, and he himself, at the moment staring wildly out of the centre of the picture, red and sweaty after the bike ride. The scene made him think of a seventeenth-century Dutch painting, of characters caught at a fateful moment, where every detail is loaded with meaning.

Kowalski pulled down the glasses that had been perched on his head, placed a fold of paper on the scales and poured out some powder from one of the bags. He was squinting through his glasses in concentration, peering at the scales and carefully tapping out a bit more powder. The stone in his ring reflected the light from the lamp in tiny red sparkles.

'I don't know what you're talking about, but you'll have to wait,' he said calmly. 'We're not done here yet.'

He opened a small, self-sealing plastic bag, carefully poured the measure of powder into it, and closed the bag. Daniel realised this was the morning delivery from the pigeons and falcons, being divided up into portions to sell on. He shouldn't have seen this. But it was too late now.

'How much do you want?' Sørensen asked.

'I don't want any. If my brother isn't here, I think I'd better go.'

Wrong answer.

Kowalski raised his eyebrows, leaned across the table and said with genuine curiosity in his voice:

'What do you really want?'

Asking for Max had been a mistake. Daniel had to change tactics.

'What does it cost?' he said, taking out his wallet.

'What?' Kowalski wondered in a friendly tone of voice.

'That,' Daniel said, pointing.

'I don't know what you mean. There's nothing here.'

Kowalski had put the bag down on the table and pushed his glasses up on to his forehead again. Sørensen grinned and massaged his shoulder.

'Unless you can see something?' Kowalski went on.

Wrong again. Daniel shook his head and put his wallet away.

'Cocaine? Is that what you were thinking of?'

Daniel turned his head to avoid seeing the white bags, and once again was met by the mirror image of the room. The men with their scales, he himself in the middle and Keller in his corner.

But something had changed since the previous picture:

310

now Keller was holding a large hunting knife in his hand. He was holding it limply, it wasn't a threatening gesture. Maybe he'd had the knife in his hand the whole time without Daniel noticing.

Kowalski put his glasses down on his nose again, put the fold of paper back on the scales and, with great concentration, began to pour a trickle of powder from the bag. The falcons were crying in their aviary outside. Short, hoarse cries, full of angst and despair.

'There's a chance that someone might offer you the opportunity to buy something like that sometime,' Kowalski said thoughtfully as he opened a fresh self-sealing bag. 'But I don't have a clue what it costs.'

'No,' Daniel muttered.

'And it certainly doesn't come from here.'

Kowalski looked at him over the frame of his glasses, stern and serious as an old schoolteacher.

'No, no,' Daniel repeated.

He thought he could hear laughter. Or was it crying? It must be the falcons. But the sound didn't seem to have come from the aviary outside. It appeared to be coming from inside the house, somewhere to his right, close but still muffled. If it weren't impossible, he would have sworn it was coming from the mirror.

His eyes darted round the room. At one point on the wall he saw a mass of small splattered stains, as if a shower of dark liquid had hit the wall and dried there.

'I have to go,' he whispered. 'Excuse me.'

He walked towards the door. The men at the table watched him in silence. Slowly and carefully he walked past Adrian Keller, who was standing there like a cardboard cut-out with his knife. Daniel looked at the short, broad blade. He felt weightless and unreal.

And then he went completely rigid. Outside the house

311

echoed a scream that was unlike anything he'd heard before. Full of angst, heartbreaking, and very high, as if it came from something very small.

'A child!' he gasped. He turned towards the three men in the room. 'That was a child crying!'

The men looked back at him with no change in their expressions. It wasn't possible that they hadn't heard it. Adrian Keller's eyes sparkled like small grey-blue lamps above his high cheekbones.

Daniel tumbled towards the front door and rushed out. The crying had changed to an urgent whining. Where was the child?

A branch in the undergrowth was swinging, dropping a shower of yellowed leaves.

Bewitched, Daniel stared at the wriggling body dangling among the foliage. A hare. Caught and strangled in one of Adrian Keller's snares.

Keller came out of the house. He was still holding the knife in his hand, and very calmly, as if this had been his intention all along, he raised it and cut the hare down from the branch.

He went over to the falcons' cage, opened a door in the mesh and left it wide open. The falcons stayed where they were on the bare branches. They sat there hunched, their heads twitching.

With a flick of his hand Keller sent the hare flying into the yard. The falcons flew out instantly, landed on their prey and began tearing and pulling at it at once. A couple of them contented themselves with watching the others from the roof of the aviary. Maybe they were the pair that had eaten their fill of pigeons for breakfast.

Keller stood there motionless, watching the falcons eat.

'Just a hare,' Daniel said to himself, taking hold of the bicycle.

He was still trembling, and his legs felt soft as clay. Keller didn't seem to be paying him any attention.

Out on the track he pulled his mobile out and tried to call Max again.

No answer. But he thought he could hear a weak tune somewhere nearby. From inside the house. Or the grounds. The ringing tone from his mobile stopped at the same time as the tune. He called again, pressed the mobile to his chest to muffle it and listened to the sound from outside that resumed as soon as he dialled the number. Although it was faint, he was able to recognise it: Schubert's Trout Quintet.

So, Max's mobile was somewhere within earshot. But for some reason he wasn't answering.

Daniel sent a text: *Didn't see you at Keller's. Cycling back to cabin*.

The distinctive bleep of a text arriving was much clearer than the Schubert tune. Now he could tell where it was coming from: not from the house but the woods.

Instead of returning to the cabin he set the bike down in the ditch, walked back along the track and into the woods.

'Max?' he called urgently.

He moved slowly and carefully through the trees, watching his feet the whole time. It was dangerous to walk here, the ground was mined with traps and snares.

He could sense the falcons as dark shadows over the forest. One of them darted down towards the trees, disappeared into the rustling leaves and climbed up into the sky again as if it had taken a dip in the greenery.

He stopped, looked around and called out once more.

All he could hear was the faint sound of the wind and the short, strange cries of the falcons as they circled above the trees. They were right over him now. He leaned his head back and looked up at the foliage where the falcons were making their dive-bombing swoops.

And now he realised what had caught their interest. High above, hidden in the canopy of leaves, swung a man's body, dressed in a check shirt and jeans.

Whoever it was hanging up there had made the same mistake as the hare.

With his heart pounding he crept closer. With each step he inspected the ground before putting his foot down. When he reached the tree he looked up at the snared body to try to see its face. But where the face ought to have been was nothing but a mass of dark mincemeat. Daniel couldn't even hazard a guess as to what the person had looked like when he was alive.

He took out his mobile and with trembling fingers pulled up the number Max had called from. He hesitated and glanced up at the swinging body, where a falcon was dive-bombing a greedy crow. With a shudder he pressed to make the call, then stood and listened without raising the mobile to his ear.

A moment later Schubert's melody rang out through the forest.

But it didn't come, as Daniel had feared, from the dead body up in the tree.

He turned round.

There, in the middle of the woods, on a carpet of fallen leaves, stood Karl Fischer, staring at the screen of his ringing mobile phone with a frown. He was dressed for a hike, with a short coat, a green woolly hat and heavy boots.

'Ah, there you are in person,' he said, looking up. 'What a coincidence. Well, we won't be needing this then.'

He clicked to silence the phone and put it in the inside pocket of his coat.

Daniel was staring at him in astonishment. He hadn't heard anyone approaching. How had Karl Fischer got there? To judge by the way he was dressed, he had walked. Daniel now saw that he had a walking stick in his hand.

'Was that *your* number I just dialled?' he asked, thoroughly bewildered.

'Of course, what did you want? It's been a while since we last spoke, but I've been tied up with a group of guest researchers. Well, at least we've met now.' Doctor Fischer walked quickly towards him, swinging his stick. 'Very unusual to see you in this part of the valley. You've been paying Adrian a visit, perhaps? I was thinking of calling in to see him myself. So, what's on your mind, my friend?'

'There's something ... I mean *someone*, up there,' Daniel said in an unsteady voice, pointing up into the tree.

'Really?'

With his hand raised against the sky, Karl Fischer peered upwards.

'Goodness, look at that! Isn't that Mattias Block?' he exclaimed, sounding as if he'd just bumped into an old friend on the street. 'So we've found him at last!'

When Daniel returned to Keller's house with Doctor Fischer, Kowalski and Sørensen were standing by the car, ready to leave. Keller was inside the cage, taking care of his falcons.

Daniel felt slightly giddy. The sight of the dead body had been a shock, but at the same time he was relieved it wasn't his brother.

'Good morning, gentlemen,' Karl Fischer said. 'Our friend here has made me aware that one of our residents is in the vicinity. It would appear that he had the misfortune to tread on one of your traps, Adrian. From what I could tell, it must have happened some time ago. You haven't noticed anything?'

Adrian Keller carried on with what he was doing without answering.

'Obviously we need to get the poor fellow down. I'll send the guards. Well. I don't think there was anything else.'

He turned to Kowalski and Sørensen.

'Perhaps one of you gentlemen would be so kind as to drive me and Max back to the village?'

The black Mercedes meandered slowly round the bends on the hill towards the bottom of the valley. Sørensen was driving, with Karl Fischer beside him. Daniel and Kowalski were sitting in the back. Kowalski smelled strongly of aftershave, something herbal and flowery, almost feminine. Daniel glanced at him. Kowalski was looking ahead with a neutral face, and kept his hands folded over a flat briefcase which Daniel assumed contained the small bags of cocaine.

'Isn't it strange?' Karl Fischer said enthusiastically. He wasn't wearing his seatbelt and kept turning to face the back seat. 'We're such creatures of habit in the way we see things. How we've searched for him! All over the valley. But no one ever thinks of looking up, do they?'

46

The girl in reception smiled at Daniel.

'How can I help you?'

It was the hostess with the black-rimmed glasses, the one who had been in reception around the time Max disappeared.

'The morning patrol told me my brother arrived yesterday. He was asking after me here in reception. Perhaps you were the person he saw?'

'No. Sofie was on duty then. But there ought to be a message here somewhere.'

Daniel waited impatiently while she looked round behind the counter.

'Ah, here it is.'

She had spotted a note pinned up on a noticeboard, adjusted her glasses and read it out loud:

'*Max Brant's brother visiting. Can't get hold of Max. Ask Max to come to reception.* The message isn't signed. But it must have been Sofie who wrote it. Her shift starts at two o'clock. Come back then.'

*

As Daniel emerged from the main building one of the guards' vehicles arrived. It stopped in front of the care centre, and a small crowd of residents had gathered before the guards even had time to open the rear doors. A moment earlier the park had been as good as deserted, but now they were here, some fifteen people, staring at the doors of the van as they were pulled open and the stretcher lifted out.

He had seen this before. Whenever anyone was brought to the care centre, wounded or dead, there would be a handful of spectators already in position, and more of them gathered like flies drawn by some imperceptible smell. And there was always someone who knew what had happened and who the injured or dead person was, even in cases where the body was covered up and invisible, as it was on this occasion.

As he walked past them he heard the name being whispered: 'Mattias Block'. He looked at the gathering of residents and wondered what they were feeling. But all he could see were unconcerned faces. The whispers seemed merely to be a statement of fact.

Daniel went to the canteen for lunch. At five minutes to two he was back in reception.

Sofie, a doe-eyed, slender creature, was standing behind the counter sorting something out. Her hostess's outfit was slightly too large for her and looked more like a school uniform.

'You were here when my brother arrived yesterday, weren't you?' he said.

She looked up and shook her head firmly.

'No visitors arrived while I was on duty.'

'So it wasn't you who wrote that note?' Daniel said, pointing at the noticeboard behind her.

She took the note down and read it.

'No,' she said solemnly. 'It wasn't here during my shift. Someone must have pinned it up later.'

'And who was on duty after you?'

'Mathilde.'

'Mathilde? She's the one I spoke to a little while ago, isn't she? She didn't write the note. She said it must have been you,' Daniel said, taken aback.

'We were the only two working in reception yesterday. How odd. Hang on, I'll just have a look in the register.'

She opened the green ledger where Daniel had signed in when he first arrived. That felt like a lifetime ago.

'We haven't had any visitors for the past two weeks.'

She closed the ledger, shrugged, then added breezily:

'Looks as though someone's joking with you.'

She was about to crumple the note up when Daniel held out his hand.

'Could I have that?'

It had been Max's voice he had heard, he was convinced of that. The range of the local mobile network was restricted to the valley. It wasn't possible to call in from outside. Max had been somewhere nearby. And for some peculiar reason, it looked as though he had used Karl Fischer's mobile phone.

Daniel recalled the only Midsummer's Eve the brothers had celebrated together. Anna and their father had rented an old pilot's cottage on the Bohuslän coast for the summer and invited Daniel and his mother for the holiday. The whole family had played hide and seek in the overgrown garden. When it was Max's turn to hide they couldn't find him. In vain they searched all the likely hiding places – the patch of fruit bushes, the outside toilet, the woodshed and vegetable store – then expanded the search to cover the jetties, fishing huts and cliffs. When they found an old well with a rotten wooden lid in the neighbouring plot their anxiety increased still further. Someone hurried home to get a ladder and a torch, but found Max sitting in his room upstairs eating the last remnants of the cake. He had simply got fed up of the game and gone inside. From his window he had watched the others searching for him, amused at their concern.

Was he sitting laughing somewhere this time too?

There was no answer when he knocked on Corinne's door, and she wasn't answering her mobile. She couldn't be at the bierstube because it wasn't open yet. Daniel started to get worried.

A short while later he found her in the church. It was a long time until Mass, and she was completely alone in the large building. Daniel stopped in the archway by the door and watched her, without letting her know he was there.

Corinne was standing in front of the oblong box of candles on the altar rail. A ray of sunlight was filtering through the cherubs in the stained-glass window, colouring her face pink. She stuck a candle into the sand, lit it and crossed herself, the way he had seen Father Dennis do.

She stood for a while, looking at the candle, then went over to a small painting of the Madonna and Child. She inserted another candle into the holder in front of the picture and lit that as well.

Daniel took a few careful steps into the church. She turned round in a flash, her hand frozen in the middle of crossing herself. The candle flickered.

'God, you scared me,' she gasped, dropping her hand. 'What are you doing, creeping about like that?'

'Sorry. I didn't want to disturb you,' he said, stopping in the aisle. 'I was wondering where you were. Do you want me to leave? If you'd rather be alone . . . '

'No, no. I just wanted to call in here before I start work. Come here.'

She held out her arms to him and he hurried over and kissed her. Her cheeks were damp and warm, as if she'd been crying.

'Anyway, where have *you* been? I was worried about you,' she said. She was holding his face in her hands and looking at him sternly. 'Have you heard? They've found Mattias Block.'

'I was the one who found him.'

'You?' she exclaimed in surprise.

He told her about that morning's strange events.

'Can I see the note?' Corinne asked.

He took it from his pocket, smoothed it out and handed it to her.

'Do you recognise the handwriting?'

She held it closer to the candle in front of the painting.

'This isn't anyone's handwriting,' she said thoughtfully. 'This has been spelled out with exaggerated neatness. Like a birthday card. Someone making a real effort.'

She glanced at her watch.

'I have to go home and get ready,' she said, putting the note in her pocket. 'Karl Fischer's bringing the visiting researchers to the bierstube this evening. It's their last day in Himmelstal.'

47

The mood seemed excellent as Daniel sat down at his favourite table in the corner.

Corinne sang her ever-popular song about cows and rang her bell, and her accompanist, the man in the Tyrolean hat, then sang a duet with her that Daniel had never heard before.

The visiting researchers, who were excited and slightly drunk, were seated at two tables that had been pushed together close to the stage. They joined in the simple chorus 'falleri, fallera' and stamped their feet in time, making the whole floor shake. They were at the end of an intensive week. From morning to evening they been confronted with evil and suffering in a highly concentrated scientific form. But now, in the expert company of Karl Fischer and with a few guards discreetly spread out around the room, they felt secure and relaxed.

The music fell silent and the performers left the stage. The visiting researchers cried out for an encore but Corinne waved them off with a smile. The Tyrolean man disappeared in the direction of the kitchen, and Corinne sat at Daniel's table. With beads of sweat on her brow she gratefully accepted the tankard of beer that Hannelore's henpecked husband put down in front of her.

'They make me sick,' she said in a low voice with a sideways nod towards the researchers, then went on:

'I checked out that note. Compared it with other handwritten notes.'

'What notes?' Daniel asked.

'All sorts. Notes written by the staff at the clinic. I couldn't find anything that resembled your note. But like I said, I don't think whoever wrote it used their own handwriting. However, I did find something else interesting.'

She put her hand in the pocket of her apron and discreetly slid a folded sheet of A4 across the table. Daniel unfolded it on his lap and looked at it. It was a handwritten lyric.

'The Shepherdess,' he read. '*When the sun goes up . . .*'

'The other side,' Corinne said.

He turned the sheet over.

'What's this?'

'Max's medical notes,' she said quietly. 'A copy of the first page.'

It was hard to read in the dim lighting, but it did actually look like an extract from a patient's records.

'How did you get hold of this?' he wondered in astonishment.

'I haven't got time to explain right now. It was a printout that was produced when Max was admitted here. Personal details and background information. One thing's particularly interesting. Look at the top, the patient's date of birth. Then further down, under the heading *Family background*. Max and his brother Daniel have the same date of birth. Same day, same month, same year. Twins, in other words.'

Daniel looked up.

'All this is correct. So why are Gisela Obermann and Karl

323

Fischer claiming that Max doesn't have a twin? Haven't they read his notes?'

'That's what I thought as well,' Corinne said. She leaned over the table and said in a whisper: 'Which is why I logged into Max's notes and took a look at what they say now.'

Daniel stared at her. The beads of sweat were shimmering on her brow, but the misted tankard of beer was still standing untouched on the table.

'How can you get access to another resident's medical notes?'

Corinne made a sign that he should keep his voice down. She looked over her shoulder. One of the visiting researchers had stood up and seemed to be delivering an improvised speech to Karl Fischer.

'Never mind about that,' she whispered. 'So, I checked Max's current records to see what they look like. And compared them with the printout that was produced when he first arrived. Obviously his file is much more comprehensive now. But his personal details are the same. With one exception: Max's date of birth. It's been changed from 28 October 1975 to 2 February 1977. Max is now two years younger.'

'Why would anyone change that?'

'That's exactly what I'm wondering.'

'Are there many people here who have access to the residents' medical notes?'

'Only the staff. The doctors, psychologists and other researchers. Some of the nurses.'

'And you,' Daniel added pointedly.

She pretended not to hear him. She leaned forward again, squeezed his hand under the table and whispered:

'You have to get out of here, Daniel. Himmelstal is a dangerous place, and I believe there are things happening here that shouldn't be happening. The staff aren't much better than the patients.'

'But now they'll have to let me go. However you got hold of that old printout of Max's records, it shows that I've been telling the truth all along. Max and I are twins, and this makes my story credible.'

Corinne glanced at the visiting researchers, who had just got another round of beer. Then she turned to Daniel and went on in a low voice, still holding his hand.

'We've got even stronger evidence than that. I lit two candles in the church today. One was for Mattias Block, my friend who met his death in the valley. The other was a candle for life. For the first time, life has been created in Himmelstal.'

'What do you mean?' Daniel said, bewildered.

'I'm pregnant,' she whispered.

His head was spinning.

'You can't be. You've been . . . '

He couldn't bring himself to say the word 'sterilised'. It sounded so harsh and final.

Corinne shook her head slowly. She squeezed his hand hard under the table.

'I'm as fertile as you. We're going to have a child, Daniel.'

At that moment the drawn-out notes of the accordion echoed round the room. The man in the Tyrolean hat was standing on stage again. Corinne pulled out a lipstick and hastily applied some to her lips, then adjusted the lacing of her dirndl. As the visiting researchers applauded enthusiastically, she walked over to the stage and began to sing, with gently swaying arms:

'*Im grünen Wald dort wo die Drossel singt.*'

The visiting researchers cheered. The man in the baseball cap raised his huge tankard and Karl Fischer tapped out the beat on the table.

Daniel paid and left the bierstube. The leaded windows

were open wide and the singing and accordion music followed him down the alley.

He recalled what Samantha had said about Corinne's background. Was she really pregnant, or was this just wishful thinking, madness?

If it was true, then she was no ordinary resident. So who was she?

PART FOUR

48

Nothing was visible from the outside except a tall, dense fir hedge. If you looked between the branches you could make out a heavy steel fence immediately behind it. There were two gates in the hedge: a large one, wide enough for vehicles, and, in the side facing the clinic buildings, a smaller gate where Daniel had seen a group of doctors emerge early one morning, then walk over towards the care centre in formation. That was when he realised that the area inside the fir hedge contained the doctors' housing.

He rang the bell beside the gate. A young male voice answered over the speaker. Daniel leaned towards the entry phone and said:

'My name is Daniel Brant. I'd like to see Doctor Obermann. It's important.'

'Sorry,' the voice said. 'No visitors are allowed in here. You'll have to try and find her in her office.'

'I've already tried there. But apparently she's at home. Please, tell her I'm here, and that it's important,' Daniel said with as much gravity and authority he could muster.

'One moment.'

The speaker fell silent. In the distance came the noise of the diggers preparing the site for the new buildings further up the slope. After a few minutes there was a bleep and the gate opened automatically and incredibly slowly.

Inside he found himself in a different world.

There were a dozen or so single-storey bungalows surrounding a lawn with a fountain at its centre. There were flowerbeds with a few solitary late roses, trees with yellowing leaves, and a brick barbeque.

It was a peaceful, secluded place. It made Daniel think of the walled palace gardens of the Orient, lying like hidden treasure, protected from prying eyes in the midst of bustling cities.

'She'll be with you shortly,' the young guard said, leaning out of a small lodge beside the gate.

Daniel waited. The fountain splashed and the fir hedge softened the noise of the diggers to a distant murmur.

Then the door to one of the bungalows opened and Gisela Obermann came towards him on the paved path. She wasn't wearing any makeup, she was dressed in jogging pants and a T-shirt, and her hair looked like it hadn't been washed recently.

'Welcome, Doctor Brant,' she said, holding her hand out to him.

'Everything OK?' the guard wondered.

'Fine,' Gisela said.

She turned towards Daniel with a broad smile:

'I've read your report with interest, Doctor. Come with me, let's go inside.'

The guard disappeared into his lodge as Gisela led Daniel back to her house.

Her smile vanished the moment they were inside the door.

'You must be completely mad to come here,' she hissed, walking ahead of him into a living room, beautifully furnished but astonishingly messy and reeking of smoke. Books, bundles of papers, empty bottles and dirty plates were spread out everywhere. The blinds were drawn and a small reading lamp by one of the armchairs illuminated the gloom.

She cleared another armchair so that Daniel could sit down. When she came closer he noticed that she smelled of alcohol.

'The guard's new, so he doesn't yet recognise everyone in the valley. I managed to persuade him that you're one of the visiting researchers who's stayed on. If it had been any of the other guards you'd never have got in. What are you doing here? You're no longer my patient, and I'm forbidden to have any contact with you.'

'I know. But I have to talk to you. I tried to reach you at your office but was told that you're ill.'

She made a noise that was something between a laugh and a snort.

'Karl Fischer's put me on sick leave. He thinks I'm mentally unstable. According to him I'm exhausted. I need rest. I ought to get away from here, but I've got nowhere to go. My old flat in Berlin isn't there any more. None of my old life is there. Himmelstal is all I've got.'

She reached for a wine glass lurking among the piles of paper on the table, drank the last dribble and fetched a half-full bottle from the bookcase. She filled her glass with a quick, careless gesture as she went on:

'Apart from the guard we're completely alone. All the others will be at the care centre at this time of day. But some of them come home early, so you can't stay long.'

She forced the cork back into the bottle with clumsy fingers, then stopped.

'Would you like a glass? I can open another bottle. This Mosel is really lovely.'

'No thanks. I came because I need the answer to a question. Who is Corinne? She's not just an ordinary resident, is she?'

A movement on the other side of the room made Daniel turn his head. He saw a large white Persian cat lying on a pile of clothes on a chair over by the window. It blended in with the pale fabrics so well that he hadn't noticed it before. The cat stretched, dropped to the floor and crept silently across the room. Without looking at it, Gisela reached down to the floor, picked it up and put it on her lap. Daniel couldn't recall ever seeing the cat in the clinic grounds or down in the village. He assumed it was never let out of the doctors' private compound.

Gisela stroked the cat's fur and said:

'Corinne is your cricket.'

'My what?'

'Your cricket. I shouldn't be telling you this. But I'm no longer connected to your case. In fact I don't consider that I have any responsibilities any more. No rights, and no responsibilities.'

She let out a hoarse laugh.

'My cricket?' Daniel repeated, bewildered. 'What does that mean?'

'Have you ever read Carlo Collodi's story about Pinocchio? The wooden puppet who comes to life and becomes a boy? He moves and talks like any other boy. There's just one thing missing: a conscience.'

'I've seen the Disney version,' Daniel said.

The look she gave him told him that didn't count.

'Instead of a conscience, Pinocchio has a cricket who sits on his shoulder and whispers to him if something is right or wrong. In the end, after he's been through a lot and has had constant advice from the cricket, Pinocchio gets a conscience of his own and becomes a real person. In academic language, you could say that the cricket's whispers are *implemented* in him. Do you understand?'

'To be honest, no.'

She leaned towards him and whispered with exaggerated lip movements:

'*Corinne acts as your conscience.*'

Daniel laughed.

'She's never given me any moral advice.'

'Of course not. That wouldn't be very effective. It's all much more subtle than that. You're one of a group of eight subjects who each have a cricket. A chip has been implanted in your brain. With the help of a little gadget, your cricket can affect your behaviour.'

'Conditioning?'

Daniel tried to sound nonchalant, but he was shuddering inside. A chip in his brain? That wasn't possible. When could it have happened? Gisela was rambling. He remembered that she was on sick leave, for exhaustion. Besides, she was drunk.

'If you like. We're not talking about electric shocks or anything as coarse as that. This is an extremely finely-tuned instrument that emits electromagnetic radiation at low frequency. Don't look so worried. It's no more dangerous than mobile phones, according to Doctor Pierce. If the test subject does something manipulative or displays a lack of empathy, the cricket can press a button and make them feel a degree of discomfort. Not pain, just a vague sense of unease, a slight anxiety. When the person is being helpful, unselfish and sympathetic, the cricket can use the gadget to give him gently comforting feelings.'

'And how do they know that the subject's helpfulness isn't put on? What if he's only lying, pretending?' Daniel pointed out sceptically.

'The crickets would see through that. They've been well trained for the job.'

'So they manipulate their test subject?'

He didn't believe a word of what she was saying.

'Of course. You could say that they use the subject's own

333

weapons against him. There's really nothing odd about it. It's no more than what we all do to each other every day. Even if most parents would never admit that there's anything manipulative about the way they're raising their children. A worried frown when a child does something wrong. A smile when it does the right thing. Entirely unconscious, of course. You see it between bosses and their subordinates, teachers and students, between couples and friends. Tiny signals in the form of facial expressions, body language and tone of voice. And it works. Do you know why?'

'No.'

'The brain has particular nerve cells, the mirror neurons, whose main purpose is to reflect the emotions of our fellow human beings. This reflection is what makes us empathetic and socially mature. In psychotherapy we started consciously using the phenomenon of mirroring long before we knew about its biological basis.'

'Surely using an implanted chip to manipulate someone is entirely different to raising a child, or psychotherapy?' Daniel said. 'It's a form of abuse.'

Gisela nodded thoughtfully as she turned the cat on to its back like a baby and stroked its stomach.

'It is different, that's true enough.' She was slurring slightly. 'What I was describing is the way it works for normal people with normal neuron systems. Many of our residents here in Himmelstal have completely undeveloped mirror neurons. We don't know why. But there's a definite abnormality. Do you remember what I said the first time I told you about Himmelstal? That demanding empathy from a psychopath is like commanding a lame person to get up and walk? He simply doesn't have what it takes. His mirror neurons are as feeble and undeveloped as a lame person's leg muscles.'

'I remember you saying that. Do you mind if I open a window? I'm sorry, but it's a bit stuffy in here.'

He moved a couple of piles of paper from the windowsill and pushed one of the windows open.

The space in front of the houses was empty, except for the guard who was leaning against his lodge smoking. A couple of sparrows were picking at some crumbs by the barbeque.

Daniel took a few deep breaths of the autumn air, then returned to his armchair and said cautiously:

'You said something about a chip?'

Gisela Obermann nodded.

'Because psychopaths aren't affected by their parents' frowns and aren't receptive to therapy, we have to use more concrete methods,' she explained, reaching for her glass.

The cat slid sideways on her lap as she leaned forward, but it seemed to be fast asleep, hanging like a limp rag over her thighs. She moved it back into place again.

'Straight to the source,' she went on, tapping her head. 'We insert a chip that picks up tiny signals sent by the cricket, which sets the brain's own system of reward and punishment into action. Our hope is that the mirror neurons will be stimulated by this and that we'll be able to wake them up. But we haven't reached that point yet. So far it's just a form ... well, a form of subtle training, I suppose you could say.'

She paused and drained her glass.

'Obviously, residents aren't supposed to know any of this. Doctor Fischer would throw me out of the valley at once if he knew I'd told you about the Pinocchio Project. But he's probably going to do that anyway, I'm afraid.'

'So Corinne works for you? Her job is to manipulate residents?'

'Her job is to manipulate *you*,' Gisela said, pointing a shaky index finger at Daniel. 'No one else. There are other crickets whose job it is to manipulate other residents.'

'Who are the other crickets?'

She shook her head and waved her hand defensively.

335

'I've already said far too much. Are you sure you don't want me to open another bottle of wine. It's so *refreshing*. I'd never have survived in Himmelstal without this wine.'

Daniel shook his head.

'I don't get what sort of people these crickets are. As I understand it, Corinne has been here in the valley for several years.'

'You know perfectly well how long she's been here,' Gisela said irritably, shuffling so that the cat's soft body rippled in her lap. It seemed to be completely unconscious.

'Oh, don't try that business about not being Max. Your multiple personalities were just a trick, weren't they? It was stupid of me to fall for it.'

'That was entirely your idea, Gisela. I've never said a word about multiple personalities,' Daniel reminded her calmly. 'So Corinne is some sort of psychologist, a doctor? And that's why she has access to Max's medical records?'

Gisela laughed.

'Corinne's an actress, didn't you know? The crickets come from all different backgrounds. They've been carefully selected and tested, and they've been given thorough training by the clinic. It takes special skills to be a cricket. Insight, being a good listener, social competence. But they also have to be very tough. Corinne came here with the sole purpose of being your cricket. She's got all the information about you, and her task is to live as an ordinary resident, living and working in the village, and making friends with you.'

Daniel gulped hard.

'Love? Sex? Is that part of the job description?' he asked.

'Absolutely not. The crickets are supposed to get close to their residents, but never to get intimate with them. The crickets are instructed to punish any sign of a sexual approach by triggering feelings of unease.'

'And if that doesn't work?'

'Then they call for reinforcements. All the crickets have a direct line to the main security office.'

Daniel considered this.

From outside in the garden he could hear the bleeping sound as the gate opened, followed by the guard talking to someone. Presumably one of the doctors who had got home from work early.

Gisela didn't seem to have noticed. She was lying back in her armchair, slightly crooked, and her body seemed as fluid as the cat's.

'This chip,' Daniel said. 'When did you insert it into my brain?'

'Just after you entered Zone 2,' Gisela replied calmly.

Daniel tried to control the urge to panic. He had been unconscious after the electric shock. Unconscious, then maybe sedated? He remembered having a terrible headache when he woke up.

He hadn't noticed any scars from an operation on his head. But perhaps a tiny chip wouldn't leave much trace? He felt through his hair with his fingertips. He could see the chip in his mind's eye as a minute metallic flake, sharp as a razorblade, and he imagined it cutting into the tissue of his brain. He swallowed and said:

'So I've been walking around with a chip in my head for two months?'

'No, no. You've had it for . . .' Gisela closed one eye and tried to think. 'It must be about a year. More or less. Getting residents into the care centre is a problem, they always resist, so we took the opportunity when you were already there. You were pretty far gone when they found you in the drainage tunnel.'

Daniel burst out laughing. He was so relieved that he couldn't stop. Gisela laughed along with him, drunkenly.

He wiped away his tears of laughter and stood up.

'Thanks for the information, Doctor. Well, I won't disturb you any longer. It was nice to see how you all live, here in your peaceful little oasis.'

'Peaceful little oasis? Here?' Gisela was glaring at him with unfocused eyes. 'Oh, please! This is a *snake-pit*. We're busy eating each other. If I had anywhere to go outside I wouldn't stay a minute longer. But I've burned my boats. I've staked everything on this fucking valley.'

She sniffed, lifted the limp cat under its front paws and rubbed its head against her eyes like a big, white handkerchief.

As Daniel walked through the garden he tried to keep his face turned away from the two doctors who were sitting in the autumn sunshine on one of the terraces. If they saw that a resident had got inside their protected enclave he'd be in serious trouble.

But the men were so busy talking that they didn't notice him. Fragments of their agitated conversation reached him as his hurried along the fading rosebed.

'See you again, Doctor Brant,' the guard said with a smile, then bowed as the gate slid open.

How much of what Gisela had said was true?

He remembered what the barber had said about Mattias Block having a 'gadget'. Was that the sort of instrument that Gisela had been talking about?

Daniel tried to remember all the times that he and Corinne had met, but he couldn't recall her ever holding anything that could be called a 'gadget' in her hand.

The bracelet! The bracelet with the flat, coloured stones that she never took off. Not even when she exercised, practised her boxing or made love. The bracelet she had toyed with when he had got too close. '*It reminds me of who I am.*'

338

49

Considering that he was director of the clinic and its senior consultant, Karl Fischer had a surprisingly modest room. It lay at the far end of the doctors' corridor, and was considerably smaller than Gisela Obermann's. Because it didn't face the valley but rather the slightly depressing Gravel Quarry mountain, the architect hadn't thought it necessary to put in a picture window. With just its desk, a half-empty bookcase and a few hard chairs, the room gave an almost ascetic impression. No curtains. Nothing on the walls.

'I'm pleased that you could see me,' Daniel said. 'And I'd like to apologise for coming so late.'

He had tried to see Doctor Fischer several times during the day, but only now, at eight o'clock in the evening, had he been informed that the doctor was in his room.

The doctor moved one of the hard chairs from the wall and set it in front of the desk.

'Good to have you here, my friend. Sit yourself down. To what do I owe this pleasure?'

'To start with, this.'

Daniel put the sheet of paper on the desk. Karl Fischer

pulled his glasses from his forehead on to his nose and glanced through it quickly.

'I see,' he said. 'Your file.'

'This is the first page of Max's medical notes, the way it looked when he was admitted to Himmelstal,' Daniel explained. He was excited and slightly out of breath. 'Do you see the personal details right at the top? The date of birth? If it's not too much trouble, I'd like you to read it out loud.'

The doctor glanced at him curiously over the top of his glasses. Then he read in a clear voice:

'October 28, 1975.'

'Thank you. And a little further down. Under *Family background*. His brother's date of birth.'

'Is this some sort of party game?'

'Please, just read it, Doctor.'

'October 28, 1975.'

'Exactly. Max and his brother were born on the same day. In other words, they're twins. And, seeing as I am Max's twin brother, I can confirm that this information is correct.'

'But . . .'

' . . . this isn't the information *you* have, Doctor Fischer? No, because after Max was admitted, someone changed his date of birth in the records.'

Doctor Fischer looked at the sheet of paper with renewed interest.

'Everything else is the same,' Daniel said. 'Only the date of birth has been changed.'

'Where did you get this?'

'I'm afraid I can't tell you that.'

Daniel reached quickly across the desk and snatched the copy of the notes out of Karl Fischer's hands. He folded it up and put it in the inside pocket of his jacket.

'So, Max and I are twins.'

The doctor took off his glasses and began to polish them

with his shirt sleeve. He seemed suddenly bored. But Daniel went on:

'That was the first thing. The second thing I wanted to tell you is that I'm going to be a father.'

'Really?' the doctor said. He raised an eyebrow but went on polishing. 'And who is the lucky mother?'

'You'll find out soon enough. Aren't you going to congratulate me? Isn't it great news?'

'Great news? It's a miracle,' Doctor Fischer said drily.

'You're absolutely right there. Every child is a miracle.'

Karl Fischer nodded solemnly.

'But you've been sterilised, which makes the whole thing much bigger. Even if the surgeon was having a bad day and you're still fertile in spite of the operation – which does happen, once in a thousand cases – then it's hardly likely that he would have made the same mistake with another resident. And ...' he looked at his glasses, breathed on them and resumed his polishing, '... even if that were the case, the chance of the two of you taking a liking to one another is still infinitesimal. So I would prefer to regard it as a miracle.'

He put his glasses back on again, turned to his computer and tapped at the keyboard. Text scrolled down the screen.

'Here it is,' he cried happily, tapping his finger at one detail on the screen. 'Max Brant. All snipped and dealt with.'

'Which proves that I'm not Max,' Daniel said calmly. 'If necessary, the mother is prepared to have an amniotic fluid test to prove that I'm the father. That was the second thing. The third proof that I'm not Max is easily checked with your magnetic imaging camera. Max had a chip inserted in his brain after he entered Zone 2. There's no chip in my brain. Didn't you notice that when you scanned my brain in that contraption?'

Karl Fischer seemed properly surprised now.

'That wasn't something we were looking for at the time. Who have you been talking to?'

'That isn't important,' Daniel said, pleased to see at least a hint of uncertainty in the doctor. 'But I want you to check my brain again. If you don't find the chip, then you're keeping the wrong person locked up here, and you'll have to let me go.'

Doctor Fischer took a deep breath. He pushed his glasses up on to his forehead, rubbed his eyes and pulled a face.

'You've talked to Doctor Obermann, haven't you? She's told you about the Pinocchio Project? Oh well. No matter. It's been something of a failure, if you want my opinion. But the sky is supposed to be the limit here in Himmelstal, and we're meant to try unconventional methods. The Pinocchio Project is Doctor Pierce's pet project. He's been fighting for it for years, and in the end I let him go ahead. You had a chip inserted, that's true. We've still got the images of your last MRI scan, so we don't need to repeat that. Shall we go down and take a look now, to get it over and done with?'

'If you don't find a chip in my brain, will you believe me?' Daniel asked as they waited for the lift.

Doctor Fischer gave him a look full of wounded pride.

'I don't deal in belief, my friend, I deal in certainty. If you don't have a chip, then you can't be the person we operated on, can you?'

They got into the lift. Doctor Fischer pressed the button and they glided down through the transparent tube. On one side of the glass walls the floors rushed past at speed, and on the other the shiny stone floor of the lobby got closer and closer. Daniel could see the guard leaning against one of the pillars.

But, to his astonishment, instead of slowing down the lift carried on downwards. Through the floor of the lobby. They

342

were no longer in a transparent glass tube but a dark shaft, and the lift was illuminated by a small lamp that he hadn't noticed while they had been surrounded by the light of the lobby.

This was wrong. As far as Daniel could remember, the scanner was in a room on the ground floor. They should have got out there, then gone down the corridor further into the building.

He looked at Doctor Fischer in surprise, but before he could think of how to phrase his question the lift stopped.

Doctor Fischer held the door open for him.

50

The freshly polished linoleum floor shone under the fluorescent lights.

'We need to walk a bit further down the tunnel,' Doctor Fischer said, marching quickly ahead of him through the windowless passageway towards a junction.

'Where are we going?' Daniel asked, bewildered.

'To my room.'

'But weren't we in your room just now? Up in the doctors' corridor?'

The doctor seemed to be in a great hurry all of a sudden, and Daniel almost had to run to keep up with him. Beneath them their reflections flitted along like hazy ghosts in the shiny floor.

'I have another room. We're taking a shortcut. We're under the park now. If you turn right here' – and without stopping Fischer pointed at the passageway leading off from the junction – 'you reach the library. You can get to all the buildings in the clinic through these tunnels. If you know the codes for the doors, that is. It's very practical in the winter. But we mainly do it for security reasons, as I'm sure you can appreciate.'

That explained why the doctors were so seldom seen outside.

They carried on along the passageway, passing other turnings every now and then. Occasionally there were staircases and metal doors marked with letters and numbers. Daniel guessed that one of these passageways connected the doctors' residential compound with the clinic. Only once, on that sunny morning, had he ever seen the doctors walking through the park as a pack, on their way to work in the care centre. It was clear that they had to have a different way of getting there.

'Well, here we are,' Doctor Fischer suddenly said, tapping a code on to a keypad beside a steel door.

Inside was a small room, with another door that the doctor opened with an ordinary key.

'Can I offer you a cup of tea?' he asked.

Several lamps came on simultaneously around the room. They were in a fairly large, heavily furnished room with Oriental rugs on the floor. The walls were lined with bookcases and pictures, and in one corner there was a narrow bed covered by a red bedspread. The room was so cosy and so comfortably lit that you hardly noticed that it was underground and had no windows. Daniel looked around at the inlaid bureau, the neatly made bed and the cardigan with patched elbows hanging on the back of a chair. There was no doubt about it: this was Karl Fischer's home.

But it was also an office. A large desk with a computer on it faced out into the room, and the bookcase beside it was full of files and journals. That explained why Fischer's room in the doctors' corridor had been so bare and impersonal: he only used it on the rare occasions when he saw his patients. The bulk of his work was done in this underground lair.

The doctor went over to the desk and switched the computer on. While it started up he went into a kitchenette. Daniel heard him running water.

'I have some Indian tea that I really do recommend,' Fischer called. 'I usually have a couple of cups when I need to wind down. Do you take milk?'

'No, thanks.'

The kettle started to rattle as Doctor Fischer got out the pot of tea and some cups, whistling a little tune. It was obvious that he felt at home here.

Daniel stood in the middle of the room, letting his eyes roam over the spines of the books, mostly psychiatric and neurological textbooks, a few prints of old buildings, and a couple of framed photographs. These caught his interest and he took a step closer.

The first was a group shot of the Himmelstal research team. If they could actually be called a team. Daniel had a feeling that they were a group of very distinct individuals. But here at least they were standing shoulder to shoulder with Doctor Fischer at their centre in front of the main building, smiling confidently. Gisela Obermann looked surprisingly alert and happy.

The other framed picture was also a group photograph. It was taken indoors, six men and two women, most of them young, lined up like a football team. None of them was smiling. They looked determined and focused. Apart from one of them, a blond-haired man. He wasn't looking into the camera but had his face turned towards one of the women, with a rather tender expression. Daniel had never seen him before, but he recognised the woman. It was Corinne. He recognised some of the others as well, from the village, the bierstube and the canteen. At the edge of the group, like a teacher or coach, stood Doctor Pierce.

'Here we are,' Karl Fischer said, coming out of the kitchen with two steaming cups. He passed one of them to Daniel.

'I added a splash of milk anyway. Just a touch. This sort of tea can easily taste a little bitter otherwise.' He nodded towards the photograph. 'Doctor Pierce and his newly hatched crickets,' he said by way of explanation.

'Who's that?'

Daniel pointed at the blond man who was staring at Corinne. It looked as though he couldn't take his eyes off her. Or else he had happened to turn his head to say something at the very moment the picture was taken.

'That's Mattias Block. Handsome, wasn't he?'

Daniel looked at the gentle, soft face and suddenly recalled the message on Corinne's mobile phone, from 'M': *I feel happy every time I see you. Be careful.*

'The poor bastards had no idea what they were getting into,' Doctor Fischer said with a cold laugh. 'Three months of intensive physical and mental training on the fourth floor. Never going out at all. Then they were given their instruments and implanted into the valley as newly arrived residents and told to make contact with their targets on their own. Courageous men and women, don't you think?'

'What sort of people are they?' Daniel asked.

'A mixed bag.' Doctor Fischer pointed at them one by one: 'A former spy. An advertising guru. A confidence trickster. A hypnotist. An expert in animal communication. And an actress. I don't remember the other two.'

'What does an expert in animal communication do?' Daniel asked. Doctor Fischer had been pointing at Mattias Block.

'Talks to animals. He was supposed to be able to, anyway. Talking to people's dogs and other pets about their problems. Doctor Pierce thought that would be a particularly useful skill in these circumstances. He handpicked these individuals with great care.' Fischer sighed and shook his head, and with that he seemed to regard the matter as concluded. 'But my dear fellow, *do* take a seat. We were going to look at your brain, weren't we?'

Daniel sat hesitantly on one of the wing chairs. The doctor settled down at his desk, adjusted his glasses and began to search the computer's database.

'Here it is,' he said happily, turning the screen so that Daniel could see it. 'Beautiful, isn't it?'

A bisected brain was spinning on its axis, shimmering blue like the earth from space.

'Is that mine?' Daniel asked.

'Your very own brain,' Doctor Fischer confirmed.

He turned the screen back again and used the mouse and keyboard to mark off and enhance one part of the brain. He enlarged it, twisted it this way and that, then enlarged it even more. Fascinated, Daniel watched what the doctor was doing from behind his chair.

Karl Fischer seemed to be playing with his brain. He made it turn somersaults and rolled it like a ball to the left, then the right. He cut it into manageable sections, like slices of watermelon. He made the slices even thinner, fanned through them like a pack of cards, lifted them out one at a time and inspected them, then bundled them all back into their original shape.

Daniel's brain disappeared from the screen and the doctor went and sat down in one of the armchairs as he stirred his cup of tea in silence.

'Did you find a chip, Doctor Fischer?' Daniel asked cautiously.

'No.' The doctor sipped the hot tea, then put the cup down on the saucer. 'But then I wasn't expecting to.'

'No? But you were so sure a little while ago. So now you realise that I can't possibly be Max?'

The doctor nodded.

'I've known that all along.'

51

Daniel looked at him in astonishment. Doctor Fischer was without any shadow of a doubt a bewildering character.

'In that case, I don't understand why you've been keeping me here.'

'Because I'm not finished with you yet, my friend. You interest me a great deal, you know. In fact I find you the most interesting of my patients. My favourite patient, if you like.'

He chuckled happily over the rim of his teacup.

'But I'm only here by mistake,' Daniel objected.

The doctor shook his head firmly.

'Oh, no. Oh, no. That was no mistake. You see,' he said, putting his cup down, 'I was interested in you the moment I found out that you existed.'

'And when did you find that out?'

'When Max was admitted here. I saw in his file that he had a brother with the same date of birth, a twin, in other words. As I'm sure you know, twins are a dream come true for anyone researching human nature. If they're identical twins, of course, and I soon found out that that was the case with you.'

'How?' Daniel asked, with a growing sense of unease.

'I have a wide network of international contacts. I can find out most things about our residents and their relatives. It's part of my job. I found out that you had no criminal convictions, and had a decent career, which made me even more interested. You ought by rights to have inherited the same characteristics as Max. Why is he a psychopath when you aren't? Or . . . ' Karl Fischer leaned forward, frowned in mock sternness, and pointed at Daniel, ' . . . are you just better at hiding it?'

Daniel gasped, insulted.

'So you're suggesting . . . '

'No, no, no. It's far too early to be suggesting anything. But the possibility exists that you're a *different sort* of psychopath. One who doesn't act rashly and impulsively. Who has the patience to wait for the right opportunity, and is calm enough to tidy up after himself and conceal what he's done. Who can calculate reward and risk. And who therefore never gets caught for any crime, so we in Himmelstal never get to see psychopaths of that sort. This is the most interesting type of psychopath, and hardly any research has been done into them.'

Daniel snorted.

'I've heard so much rubbish since I got here that nothing surprises me any more. How do you know that that sort even exists if they never get caught? Have you ever met one?'

Doctor Fischer leaned his head back, appeared to reflect for a moment, then said:

'In my whole life I've met only two, possibly three, psychopaths of that sort. They're very difficult to recognise. And the reason why I couldn't unmask them was quite simply . . . ' – he gestured apologetically – ' . . . that I myself am one of them.'

'You have an odd sense of humour, Doctor Fischer.'

The doctor shook his head.

'I'm completely serious. I had the typical childhood for a psychopath: I stole money from my mother's purse, I hit my friends if they didn't do as I said, and I took great pleasure in torturing toads, cats and any other animals I could get hold of. I'm practically a textbook example. It seemed perfectly natural to me. I assumed that everyone was like me.'

'None of that is particularly unusual among children,' Daniel said in a well-intentioned attempt to alleviate the doctor's unpleasant supposition.

But Karl Fischer persisted:

'That type of behaviour is *extremely* unusual among children who grow up in comfortable circumstances. Of course I soon learned that such behaviour led to punishment, and wasn't beneficial to me in the long term. As a result I had to: one – select actions that would truly be to my advantage. And: two – carry them out in complete secrecy. You've hardly touched your tea. Don't you like it? The taste is a little unusual, but once you get used to it it's easy to get rather addicted to it.'

'I like it,' Daniel said, obediently taking several large sips.

Karl Fischer looked happy.

The taste *was* unusual. It tasted of Christmas – cinnamon, cloves, cardamom – and something else, something dry and bitter that was hard to identify.

Daniel wasn't at all sure how to read Karl Fischer. Did he mean what he was saying, or was his astonishing confession merely an expression of some dark professional humour? Either way, he didn't seem to be the right person to talk to, and Daniel made up his mind to conclude the visit as quickly as he could.

But the doctor leaned back and went on:

'When I was young my parents were terribly worried about me, however once I started school they became extremely proud of me. Everyone said I had "matured". I was very intelligent, got moved up two classes, and outside school I carried on my own studies at a level that astonished everyone around me. I studied mathematics, biology and chemistry, but what interested me most was medicine. How human beings are constructed. The skeleton that holds us up. The heart that pumps life into us. The brain that produces thoughts, memories and dreams, then hides them away in its nooks and crannies. It fascinated me immensely. I believe I was seeking an answer to who I was in all of this. Because it was abundantly clear to me that I wasn't the same as everyone else.'

With growing surprise Daniel listened to his doctor. He didn't know what to think.

'Empathy, love and compassion were alien emotions to me. I kept hearing about them. As concepts they were as familiar to me as the jungles of Africa. I knew what they looked like, but I had never been there, so to speak.' The doctor went on calmly: 'And I realised that I was never going to get there. At the same time, it was quite clear to me that these strange ideas were regarded as entirely natural by everyone else. Like someone who can't read, I learned various strategies to hide my shortcomings. I became good at watching and imitating other people's behaviour. I learned when you were supposed to cry, comfort someone, or tell them you love them. During my early teenage years I was regarded as a bit odd and edgy, but I smoothed off most of the rough edges over time. When I was studying medicine the other students would say that I was spontaneous, charming, even sensitive. You're looking at me so oddly, Daniel. Is there something you recognise in what I'm saying?'

Daniel shook his head in amazement.

'I've never heard anything like it.'

Karl Fischer smiled.

'And even if you did recognise something, you wouldn't

admit it, would you? This is the last thing anyone would admit to. This is the big secret. *That one isn't a proper person.*'

'You still seem to have done well in life,' Daniel said.

'Naturally. I've built up a magnificent career. Without feelings, one has so many more opportunities, of course. Research findings can be falsified. Competitors can be got rid of. A drowning accident, a fall from a balcony during a rowdy party, an unexplained fatal mugging late one night at a conference. Not to mention the drugs that a doctor has access to, and which in high doses can lead to tragic cases of suicide.'

Daniel gasped, but before he could say anything Karl Fischer had leaned over and put a reassuring hand on his shoulder.

'Those are merely examples, my friend. Possibilities. You're not getting any facts.'

The doctor fell silent and reached for his cup.

Daniel became aware of a ventilator rumbling somewhere, and clung to the idea of fresh alpine air being pumped down to them.

Fischer sipped his tea, then went on quietly:

'When I was young I committed a number of serious crimes. Physical abuse, and property crimes. I was never found out. When I got older I lost interest in doing that. The reward seldom matched the risk. By that time I had also discovered a subject that absorbed all my time and energy: psychopathy. I realised that most people studying this area had no idea what they were talking about. They concentrated on the impulse-driven trouble makers, while the quiet, clever ones were ignored. Does it upset you, my discussing this sort of thing?'

While the doctor was talking Daniel had been feeling colder and colder. He was thinking of the two doors that Karl Fischer had had to unlock when they arrived.

52

'If you don't mind, I think I'd rather talk about something else,' he said. He was trying not to look at the door. 'So, you know I'm not Max, and that you have no right to hold me here. I came here because Max wanted to see me ...'

'No, no, no,' Karl Fischer interrupted with a wave of the hand. 'Completely wrong. You came here because *I* wanted to see you. Your brother hadn't expressed any such desire. But when I saw that Max had a brother I decided to get you here to Himmelstal.'

'*You* decided, Doctor Fischer?'

'Of course. It's common knowledge that inherited factors play a role in psychopathy – there's a certain amount of dispute about just how great a role. I said earlier that I've only met two or three psychopaths of the perfectly controlled variety. One of those was my own father. He hid it well, and was a well-regarded eye specialist with an impeccable reputation. But there was something about him that I recognised, and the older I got the more sure of it I became. Now, if father and son can bear the same inheritance, surely that should apply in even greater measure to identical twins?'

He paused, screwed up one eye and peered slyly at Daniel with the other.

'You said you were the one who got me here,' Daniel said. 'How?'

He leaned forward as if he was interested in what the doctor had to say, but he was actually looking at the door. The outer door had required a code to get in. Did it need a code if you wanted to get out as well? That would obviously be crazy from a fire-safety perspective. But Daniel had already discovered that fire safety wasn't a particular priority here at the hospital.

'I was done with Max,' Karl Fischer said abruptly. 'After just a few conversations with him I realised that he was rather uninteresting. His history before he arrived here and various incidents with other residents suggested that he was an impulse-driven trouble maker who turned to violence without any thought of the consequences. And we've got plenty of those here. You were the one I was interested in, but obviously it was impossible for me to bring a law-abiding, decent member of society into Himmelstal. When I saw some recent pictures of you on the internet I was struck by how similar you were. So I decided to switch the twins over. It wasn't hard to persuade Max. He was overjoyed at my plan, and wrote you that letter. When I read it I let it go out with the staff's mail rather than via the censor.'

'And you changed the date of birth in his notes?'

'I did that soon after Max arrived. Evidently you've managed to get hold of an earlier printout. Can I ask how you got it?'

Daniel remained silent.

'Well, it doesn't matter now. In those pictures on the internet you had a beard and fairly wild hair, and glasses, which cheered me up, because of course Max had no beard and didn't wear glasses. I encouraged him to carry on shaving and getting his hair cut really short so that the fact that you were twins wouldn't be too obvious when you arrived. And it all worked perfectly, didn't it? Max got his freedom and I got the twin I really wanted. And officially nothing had happened, apart from Max having his older brother to visit for a few days. The fact that he behaved slightly oddly after that and began to make bizarre claims is exactly the sort of thing you'd expect in a place like this, isn't it?'

Daniel nodded mechanically. He was having trouble concentrating on what Doctor Fischer was saying. He was tired and his thoughts had started to wander in a peculiar way, beyond his control, the way they usually did before he fell asleep. What was the time, anyway? How long had he been sitting here listening to Doctor Fischer? And where was 'here' exactly? For a moment he got the idea that he was in the home of an older colleague whose flat he had once visited in Brussels. Then he realised he was staring at the books on the other side of the room, convinced that they belonged to his grandfather, the professor of linguistics, and that if he left the room he would find himself on Götavägen in Uppsala.

'You look tired,' Doctor Fischer said. 'I'm something of a night owl, this is when I'm at my most alert. I tend to forget that not everyone is like that.'

'Yes, I wouldn't have any objection to going back to my cabin now. What you've told me has left me feeling rather disconcerted, Doctor Fischer. I need to digest it,' Daniel replied.

The doctor nodded.

'That's entirely understandable. We're almost at the end of our conversation. To which *you* took the initiative. Not me,' he added, pointing his forefinger at Daniel with a slight smile.

Then he saw that his teacup was empty and stood up.

'Shall I top you up as well?'

'No, thanks.'

When Doctor Fischer disappeared into the kitchen, Daniel walked quickly over to the door. He tried the handle and found that it was locked. Doctor Fischer went on talking from the kitchen:

'Seeing as Gisela Obermann had been in charge of Max, obviously she became responsible for you as well. A strange woman. When she popped up with her silly ideas about multiple personalities it was time for me to take over. She seemed to have become rather obsessed with you, and had lost her professional focus.'

When Doctor Fischer appeared again, Daniel had just sat back down in his armchair.

'Gisela is far too weak a character to work in Himmelstal, and recently she's been exhausted and nervous. I ought to have sent her home a long time ago, but she's had problems in her private life and has nowhere to go. I do hope things are going to work out for her,' the doctor said, settling himself down again.

'What about Max?' Daniel wondered. 'Where is he? Is he here in the valley?'

'Here?'

Karl Fischer burst out laughing.

'Oh, no. He won't be returning here of his own volition, you can be sure of that. I've got no idea where he is.'

'But I heard his voice in those phone messages,' Daniel pointed out. 'The mobiles can't receive calls from outside. He must have been in the valley if he was able to reach me.'

'I recorded his messages before he left Himmelstal. I've got a number of others that he read out for me, but I used the couple that were most suitable when I called you. Max said you usually keep your mobile switched off, only turning it on every now and then to check your messages and missed calls.'

Daniel was staring at him in astonishment.

'Why did you do that?'

'Because you, if you don't mind me saying, were a fairly dull subject for study. Apart from your attempt to escape, which I was obviously expecting, you were behaving in an exemplary fashion. You hardly ever went anywhere, and the one person you spent any time with was your secret guardian. Your "cricket", as the imaginative Doctor Pierce prefers to call them. The only time you resorted to violence was when you went to the defence of a helpless resident who was being tortured, thus giving you hero status with the more credulous of my colleagues and prompting poor Gisela to make a complete fool of herself with her silly ideas. I had you taken into the care centre and performed a couple of tests that turned out to be a severe disappointment to me. The MRI scan showed no abnormalities in your brain activity upon emotional stimulus. Your brain didn't react at all like a psychopath's brain. In other words, it responded to emotional triggers as if they were cognitive. And my practical test with the fire disproved my theory entirely.'

'Test? So the fire wasn't caused by Marko smoking in bed?'

Karl Fischer held out the palm of his hand.

'I helped him a little. Stronger sleeping pills than usual, a lit cigarette placed in his bed when he was asleep. A smoke machine from the theatre made the whole thing look worse than it was. You behaved like a proper little boy scout. A great disappointment, as I said. So I led you to Keller to see if anything would happen there. There's usually always something happening at Adrian Keller's.'

'So you were at Keller's?'

'Of course. Kowalski and Sørensen drove me up there. As you've probably worked out, I have rather good relations with those gentlemen. They help me with my research, and I help them with certain matters in return. Plenty of things have happened in Keller's house that are of great interest to a behaviourist with my speciality, and occasionally – but only when he himself wants to, because he's a man of great integrity – he allows his living room to be used for experiments. The mirror in his living room is a one-way window. My observations there have led me to write a number of completely unique research papers about what people are capable of doing to one another. Obviously I can't publish them under current circumstances.'

Daniel's anger had woken him up and he had to stop himself from attacking Karl Fischer.

'A one-way window? So you could *see* me?'

'I had a front row seat. But sadly you left the stage earlier than anticipated. You were interrupted by a hare, wasn't that it? And you thought it was a child.'

He chuckled, then stopped himself and said seriously:

'A child, ah yes! Of course. You're going to be a father. But you haven't said who the mother is?'

He leaned forward, blinking expectantly.

Daniel hesitated before replying. Instinctively he felt that he shouldn't reveal his relationship with Corinne. Possibly to protect her. Or simply because it seemed to be the only thing that Karl Fischer didn't know about him. He wanted to hold on to that card for a while longer.

'That'll come out in time.'

'Hmm. Yes, things usually do,' Fischer said thoughtfully. 'But what if she's deceiving you? Maybe she isn't pregnant at all? Have you seen the result of the pregnancy test?'

Daniel said nothing. What if the doctor was right?

'Let me guess who it is.'

Karl Fischer leaned his head back against his chair, closed his eyes and pretended to think.

'Samantha?' he suggested.

Daniel remained silent. Fischer took that as confirmation.

'I thought as much,' he chuckled happily. 'Perhaps I ought to tell you that Samantha usually gets pregnant about ten times a year. Of course she's about as fertile as a bullock, but in her imagination she's always getting fertilised, and to make the whole thing seem more realistic she makes sure to have an active sex life with various men. Do you know her background, before she came to the valley?'

'No.'

'It's rather tragic. At the age of sixteen she ran away from home with her boyfriend, who was considerably older, and a violent drug addict. Samantha was pregnant but didn't want an abortion. In the eighth month the boyfriend kicked the foetus to death in her stomach and she was forced to give birth to a dead child. In conjunction with that she suffered a severe psychotic episode and was admitted to a psychiatric ward where they pumped her full of drugs and discharged her without giving her any actual treatment. She moved back in with her parents, broke off all contact with the boyfriend and started work as a nursing assistant in a maternity ward. She seemed utterly charmed by the babies, constantly fussing over them, never wanting to take her breaks. Then there were several sudden deaths among the babies. Then a few more. But only in Samantha's ward. The staff were put under surveillance and Samantha was found out. She smothered the first one with a pillow. Then she slipped drugs into their bottles. Hasn't anyone told you this?'

'Yes, now that you come to mention it,' Daniel muttered. 'But I never realised . . . '

'You don't like to believe it, do you? Samantha's a very attractive young woman, after all. In the prison she ended up in she flirted outrageously with the male staff, practically throwing herself at them. For one of them the temptation evidently got too much, because in spite of the fact that she had only received visits from her mother, she fell pregnant. She was made to have an abortion. She put up violent resistance and had to be taken to the abortion clinic under sedation. It wasn't long before she was pregnant again. This time she managed to conceal the pregnancy until it was too late for an abortion. She gave birth under strict guard, and immediately after the birth the child was taken away from her. She went mad on the ward, got hold of a pair of scissors and stabbed one of the nurses in the jugular, and a heavily pregnant patient in the stomach. Shortly after that she was brought to Himmelstal. My psycho-dynamic colleagues see her nymphomania as a sign of her desperation to get pregnant. But obviously she's been sterilised, like everyone else here. So if I were you, I'd wait a while before opening the champagne.'

'What a sad story,' Daniel said.

He was secretly feeling very relieved. He remembered what Samantha had said about Corinne and the babies. So she had actually been telling him her own story.

'But can she really be diagnosed as a psychopath?' he added with a yawn. He was far too tired for a conversation like this.

'Of course not,' Doctor Fischer said with a snort. 'This valley is a dumping ground for all sorts of detritus that no one wants on the outside. That's the problem with our dual role as a research centre and a secure enclave. As researchers, we want cases that are as clear-cut as possible. Unfortunately, in order to get funding, we have to accept a fair number of patients who don't belong here. We can't afford to be too choosy, Daniel.'

He laughed, a hard, short laugh, and went on in a matter-of-fact tone:

'To be honest, Samantha – like most of my female research colleagues – is here because of gender quotas, and not on merit. We have a large surplus of men in the valley, and an attractive woman with nymphomaniac tendencies solves a practical problem. As I'm sure you agree,' he added with a wink.

'Either way,' Daniel said, unwilling to be reminded of his

own experience of Samantha's nymphomania, 'I don't understand why you want to keep me here. I clearly haven't fulfilled your expectations. You were wondering if I was a "concealed" psychopath, and you've got your answer: I'm not. So now you can let me go home.'

Doctor Fischer rubbed his forehead anxiously.

'The problem is that I can't do that. Not without revealing that I have consciously been detaining an innocent person here for two months. I'm sure you can see that's out of the question. I'd have to resign as director of the clinic, and I'd lose all my research grants. I'm afraid I'm going to have to keep you here as Max as long as I can.'

'As long as you can?'

'Yes, but that probably won't be much longer. Sooner or later your brother will come back.'

Daniel took a deep breath to respond, but Fischer pre-empted him.

'Oh, not voluntarily, of course. But he'll do something stupid out there, I'm convinced of that. He was so full of hate for that Italian girl. It upset him hugely that he only managed to kill her fiancé and that she survived. All he wanted was to kill her, that was the main reason he wanted to get out of Himmelstal. And if he gets caught we'll have him back again. Which will be rather confusing. Because of course we already have one Max here! There'll be an investigation and I'll be found out. So we've got a problem here, Daniel.'

'It doesn't necessarily have to be a problem,' Daniel said. 'Just get me out of this place before Max is sent back. I can leave the valley discreetly. I'm sure you could help me with that. Everyone will think I've had an accident or been murdered by another resident. Like Mattias Block. Or one of the others who've disappeared in the valley and never been found.'

Karl Fischer lit up.

'What an excellent idea! That's exactly what I'll say. That you've vanished without a trace. Like Mattias Block. Poor man. The victim of Doctor Pierce's insane experiment. The idiot sent him in as Adrian Keller's cricket. Sent him right into the lion's den to subdue the beast with a ridiculous little gadget. Not really the same as talking to dogs, is it? And he didn't know that Keller was *my* lion. When I discovered he'd selected Keller it was too late, the chip was already in place. Not that I have much faith in Doctor Pierce's attempts at conditioning. But if Mattias Block actually had managed to tame Keller, the performances in his living room would have been useless for my research. No more of those highly interesting torture scenes. I'd have been left sitting behind the mirror and yawning while my object of study did crosswords and watered his pot plants. I did think about bringing Keller in for an operation and removing the chip, but it was actually easier to remove Block. Admittedly, he did succeed in escaping from his execution in Keller's house, only to find a different version in one of his snares.'

Daniel was hardly taking in what the doctor was saying. A thick fog had settled over his mind. Like the fog in the valley it parted every now and then to let in what was going on around him in short, distinct sentences and images.

'So you're going to let me leave the valley?' he asked.

'No, that would be far too risky. You could cause me a lot of trouble when you got out. And I'm not done with you yet. I haven't even started. You can disappear from the valley, though – that's an excellent idea. In fact, you can disappear today. Actually . . . ' – he looked at his watch – 'you *have* already disappeared.'

'How do you mean?'

'It's twenty past twelve. Isn't it surprising how quickly the time goes when you're having fun? The evening patrol will have found your cabin empty and sounded the alarm. The guards' vehicles might already be out looking for you. And they'll carry on tomorrow. But not too long. As you yourself said, everyone will think Max is dead.'

'But . . .' Daniel began in lame protest. He tried to find the rest of the sentence, but it had been swallowed up by the fog before he had time to get it out.

'Of course, I understand. You need to sleep,' Doctor Fischer said helpfully.

That wasn't at all what Daniel had been about to say, he was sure of that. He had been on the point of saying something else, something important, only now it was gone.

'You're tired, aren't you? Let me look at your pupils.'

Doctor Fischer took hold of his chin and looked into his eyes.

'Exactly,' he said. 'Very tired.'

Daniel was on the verge of denying this when it struck him that he *did* feel very tired. In fact he felt more tired than he had ever done in his entire life. He had no idea how he was going to have the energy to walk back through the passageways, across the park and home to his cabin.

Doctor Fischer stood up and went over to a drape hanging over the wall at the far end of the room. He pulled it aside and opened a steel door that had been concealed until then.

'I'll show you to your room. Come with me.'

Slowly Daniel stood up and walked, step by step, over to the doctor, then stopped in the doorway.

In front of him was yet another of the underground passageways. But this one was rather different to the others. It was narrower and the roof was lower. From somewhere he could hear cries and something banging on metal. A guard who was leaning against the wall glanced at them quickly and incuriously.

'Where are we?' Daniel asked warily.

His heart was beating so fast that he felt sick.

'In a different part of the tunnel system,' Karl Fischer said. 'When the clinic was built I and our American sponsor made sure it was equipped with a few extra areas that weren't marked on the plans.'

He gave Daniel a gentle shove in the back, making him tumble forward into the corridor, then quickly locked the door behind them.

'I dare say you've heard about this ward. The residents talk about it a lot. They've even given it a nickname.'

53

'The Catacombs?' Daniel whispered.

Doctor Fischer nodded.

'Personally, I think the name is a rather poor choice. There was supposed to be an underground crypt here when the convent was at its height. But there's probably nothing left of that these days. In any case, what we have here, as you can see, is a very modern set-up, and everyone down here is alive.'

Daniel gazed in amazement at the row of metal doors that presumably opened on to prison cells. Each door had a small round window made of extremely thick glass at head-height. In some of the windows faces could be seen against the glass. Although several of them were moving their lips as if they were talking, maybe even screaming, not a sound could be heard. Their silently gaping mouths and the thick glass made Daniel think of fish in an aquarium.

'This part of Himmelstal's activities isn't so well known,' Doctor Fischer said as they passed the doors. 'A small and dedicated group of us conduct research down here. Our task masters seldom visit. I inform them of anything I feel they should know. To be honest, I don't think they actually *want* to know too much. All they want is results.'

'What sort of activities?' Daniel asked.

They had stopped in the middle of the corridor and Doctor Fischer was looking thoughtfully through one of the windows.

'Cutting-edge research,' he said. 'At the very forefront of neuropsychiatry.'

He called one of the guards over.

'Please check this patient,' he said, tapping a fingernail against the glass. 'That doesn't look like ordinary sleep to me.'

With a sense of unreality Daniel observed the faces as they passed by. The faces staring at him through the little windows resembled creatures from another world. Their heads were either fully or partially shaved and their eyes were either overflowing with emotion or completely empty.

He knew that what he was seeing ought to make him angry, that he ought to protest. But he was exhausted, not just physically, but his thoughts and senses too. All he really wanted was to get some sleep, and what worried him most right now was that the corridor was so long and that the floor seemed to slope oddly to one side, as if they were on a boat. The porthole-like windows only increased this impression, and Daniel started to feel slightly seasick.

The room the doctor had mentioned, a room with a bed where he could spend the night, no longer seemed such a bad idea. There was no way he could make it back to his cabin. The fact was he needed a bed immediately. He stumbled and the doctor grabbed hold of his arm.

'Not far now. Can you walk?'

Daniel nodded. To his right was a woman's face, held like an old photograph in the round, riveted metal frame. A thin, porcelain face, very pale, with blue rings under the eyes and dark, shadowy stubble on her bald head. Alien, inhuman, yet simultaneously peculiarly familiar. He'd seen the face before, close to his own. Was it his mum? No, of course not. His mum was dead. But maybe this woman was dead as well?

He turned and looked back in bewilderment at the row of doors they had passed. Maybe all these people were dead? Or, if not dead, then at least ... Well, they certainly weren't alive, no matter what Doctor Fischer might claim. After all, they *were* in the underworld.

He remembered the strange, heavy book his grandfather had in one of the bookcases in his home in Uppsala. Daniel had felt a mixture of fear and delight whenever he looked at the pictures: it was Dante's *Inferno*, with Gustave Doré's engravings. Naked, contorted bodies, tormented by serpents, fire and unimaginable horrors. Doomed to eternal suffering.

'How are you feeling, Daniel?' Doctor Fischer said close to his ear.

'I'm a bit dizzy,' he whispered.

'Shall I send for a stretcher?'

'No, I'm not ill.'

He straightened his back then, with Virgil holding his arm, he staggered on through the underworld.

'It's just over there,' Doctor Fischer said encouragingly.

In front of them a guard was holding a door open. Fischer and Daniel went in.

They were hit by a strong smell of disinfectant and urine. The room was small, and painted with very shiny white gloss paint that cast harsh reflections from the fluorescent lights. There was a bed and a tabletop, both fixed to the wall, as well as a stool shaped like a steel cylinder with a black PVC seat.

'Nice,' Daniel muttered in confusion, pointing at the minimalist design of the stool as he sank on to the bed. He was so tired that he hardly knew where he was.

'And practical,' Doctor Fischer added, demonstrating how the seat could be lifted so that the stool became a toilet.

'Fantastic,' Daniel said, and closed his eyes.

'Now you must get some sleep, my friend. I don't think you'll have any trouble. The medication I added to your tea was fairly strong.'

The light was reduced to a pleasant semi-darkness, and the door closed with a brief sucking sound that make Daniel open his eyes again. Through the little window Karl Fischer gave him a last, paternal look. Then he was gone.

Daniel let go of consciousness. Faces drifted past, bobbing about as if they were floating in goldfish bowls. The thin, strangely familiar porcelain face stopped in front of him, forced its way out of the glass and leaned over him. It was lit from below, as if by a pocket torch.

Suddenly he knew who she was. The realisation burrowed its way out of his deep sleep and made his limbs twitch in a desire to take flight. He didn't manage to wake up, but he still knew: it was the little dark-haired hostess. The one who disappeared, the one the guards had been searching the river for. Skinnier and without any hair she looked very different. But it had definitely been her, staring at him through the round window in one of the doors.

54

'So he's missing?' Hedda Heine said in a worried voice. 'Since when?'

'The host patrol informed security headquarters at ten past twelve last night,' Doctor Pierce explained. 'And they contacted Ms Simmen.' He gestured towards Corinne, who was sitting next to him at the conference table. 'But she knew nothing about it.'

'The last time I spoke to him was the day before yesterday, that evening in Hannelores Bierstube,' Corinne said.

Outside the picture window the clouds were hanging between the walls of the valley, heavy and grey-white, like a layer of padding in a box. She wasn't often up this high. She usually met Doctor Pierce in a small treatment room on the first floor of the care centre.

'Recently Max has always been in his cabin for the hosts' patrols. We haven't had any problems there. Which is why it's so unusual that he wasn't there last night,' Doctor Pierce went on. 'We were hoping he'd turn up of his own accord during the night, but his cabin was still empty when the morning patrol checked. The last sighting we have of him is from the guard on the door of the care centre. According to him, Max took the lift up to the doctors' floor at nine o'clock in the evening. He was going to see you, Doctor Fischer.'

'That's right,' Doctor Fischer said. 'He insisted on seeing me even though it was late. I agreed to see him because he was so keen. He seemed rather confused. He was making ridiculous claims.'

'What sort of claims?' Pierce wondered.

Karl Fischer pulled a tired face.

'The same old thing. That he isn't Max but his twin brother. Somehow he'd managed to find out about the Pinocchio Project. I suspect he may have met a certain female colleague of ours who is currently on sick leave and ought not to have any contact with residents. Either way, he knew that Max had had a chip implanted and wanted me to check the results of his MRI scan to see if he didn't have a chip. That was supposed to prove that he isn't Max. It seems to have become something of an obsession for him. He was extremely persistent, so to resolve the matter once and for all I agreed to his request. We went down and looked at the scans. I showed him the chip. He became distraught.'

'I hope you told him that the chip is completely harmless?' Doctor Pierce said. 'The radiation is no worse than you get from a mobile phone.'

'Yes, but I don't think that was what was worrying him. I think he was distraught at discovering his true identity. That this marvellous twin brother was an invention. He's been deceiving himself, and now he was forced to realise the truth. Or else the whole performance was just put on. But it was certainly late, and I was eager to get rid of him. So I took him through the tunnels and let him out through the library building. That was the shortest route back to his cabin.'

'And what time was that?'

Fischer shrugged.

'Ten, maybe.'

'Did you see which way he went after that?' Hedda Heine asked.

'No. I assumed he went straight home.'

'Then you were the last person to see him,' Pierce concluded. 'Did he seem particularly upset?'

Fischer rubbed his unshaven chin, making a rasping sound.

'Well, I suppose so. But I thought he'd calm down overnight.'

'Are you quite sure you saw a chip?' Pierce asked, staring intently at Karl Fischer's face.

'Of course.'

'It couldn't be that you expected to see one, and made a mistake because you were tired?'

Fischer gave him a scornful look.

Pierce went on:

'Because I've been down to the MRI unit myself and asked Sister Louise to bring up the images. And I didn't see a chip.'

Karl Fischer was about to protest, but Doctor Pierce wouldn't be interrupted.

'And Ms Simmen has something to say that I think will be of interest to all of us.'

He turned to Corinne and gave an almost imperceptible nod of encouragement.

She looked round at the people sitting at the conference table, straightened her back and said in a steady voice:

'I'm pregnant. With the resident you believe is Max. But who can't possibly be him.'

The scientists looked at each other in bewildered silence.

Hedda Heine leaned forward:

'Are you absolutely sure, Ms Simmen?'

Corinne nodded.

'I've taken two pregnancy tests.'

'And there's no one else who ... could be the father?'

'No,' Corinne said firmly.

Karl Fischer was looking at her without saying anything.

'You're the resident's cricket, aren't you?' Brian Jenkins said. 'As I understand it, there are strict rules governing the behaviour of crickets. Close, but not too close, and so on. Am I wrong, Doctor Pierce?'

'I know perfectly well what the rules are,' Corinne said irritably. 'But over the past few months there's been something about my client that hasn't made sense. He's been completely unreceptive to the instrument.'

She held up her arm and showed her bracelet.

'I brought it in to check it, and made some adjustments,' Doctor Pierce said. 'Ms Simmen claimed that it still wasn't working, so I assumed she was using it wrongly and wanted to replace her with a different cricket. But Ms Simmen refused to be replaced. She claimed that Max was very different and that she had a duty to protect him.'

'Which he immediately exploited,' Karl Fischer said with a scornful glance at Corinne's stomach.

'Not at all,' Corinne said angrily. 'Daniel isn't Max. He doesn't exploit anyone. Everything he's been telling us is true. He's Max's twin brother, and Max was the one we let out after the visit back in July.'

'Max doesn't have ... ' Doctor Fischer began.

'Yes, he does!' Corinne said, waving a sheet of paper. 'The other day I found a page of the material I was given during my training. I know we weren't supposed to keep anything on paper. But one of my colleagues taught me the lyrics to a song and I wrote them down on the back of a sheet of paper which I then kept. It turned out to be Max's admission documentation. And from this it is quite clear that Max has a twin brother. Someone must have altered his medical records after he was admitted.'

373

She passed the copy round.

Doctor Pierce looked in his briefcase, took out some stapled sheets of paper and passed these round as well.

'Ms Simmen is right. I checked what she said with the population registry in Sweden. And we've got the wrong twin. Now he's missing, and I'm extremely worried about him. I suggest that we send the guards out at once.'

His colleagues stared at him, and Hedda Heine said:

'I quite agree. What do you say, Doctor Fischer?'

'Yes, that would probably be best. They can search the valley,' Fischer said disinterestedly, passing the documents to the person next to him. He had hardly looked at them. 'Well, that's agreed, then. They go out and look for Max. Pierce will contact security headquarters.'

'They go out and look for *Daniel*. Not Max,' Corinne corrected him.

Doctor Fischer stood up with a glance at his watch.

'I've got a lot to do, so I hope you'll excuse me,' he said.

As soon as he left the room a heated discussion broke out around the table.

Corinne sat in silence. The discussion was partly about her and she felt superfluous in a rather unpleasant way.

Doctor Pierce called security headquarters on his mobile. He was the only person she knew in the room and he was the one who had brought her along. As soon as he finished his conversation she was planning to say goodbye to him and sneak out.

But just as he was putting his mobile back in his pocket there was a knock on the door and a hostess came in, holding a phone in her hand.

'Sorry to interrupt. I've got a call from the Italian police. They want to talk to the director.'

'Doctor Fischer has just left,' Pierce said. 'Try him on his mobile.'

'He's not answering.' The hostess waved the phone, at something of a loss. 'They said it was urgent.'

'I'll take it,' Pierce said.

He took the phone and went across to the big window to speak in private.

When the conversation was over he turned round:

'The police in Naples are wondering if Max Brant is still in Himmelstal. Four days ago they arrested a man for the brutal assault of a woman, and they think it's Max.'

55

Daniel took the two pills the guard was holding out to him, along with a small plastic cup of water. His head was aching and his tongue felt rough and unpleasant, like a foreign body in his mouth. He hoped the pills would alleviate his physical discomfort and ease the terror and claustrophobia that were slowly building up inside him.

The pills had the precise effect he had hoped for. His senses dulled to a pleasant disinterest and he had almost fallen asleep again when the guard returned to lead him to a shower room to have a wash. Everything seemed to be happening in slow motion.

'We're underground. We're underwater,' he thought as he glided along the corridor, freshly showered and dressed in the same black-and-white tracksuit as the other patients.

His body and thoughts alike seemed to be swimming about.

A skinny figure with a shaved head was walking ahead of him. Like Daniel, he was being led by a guard. The man was moving jerkily, and kept stopping to comment on his sur-roundings.

'Nice, quiet place, this. But it's too cramped. Ought to be made a bit wider.'

He stopped and slapped the walls. His guard waited patiently. Daniel and his guard were forced to stop because of the blockage in the corridor.

'And those ugly people in there,' the skinny man snarled, pointing at one of the round windows containing a man's contorted face and a fist banging soundlessly against the glass. 'I can't stand to look at them any more. Get some better-looking ones instead. Some decent birds. That would be better. Wouldn't it?'

He turned towards Daniel. It was Tom, the violent wood carver. He smiled broadly before the guard pulled him away.

Then Daniel was back in his cell again, and a short while – or possibly a long while – later three people were standing in the doorway of the cell. Doctor Fischer, the Indian doctor, and a man in jeans and shirtsleeves that Daniel didn't recognise at first because he wasn't wearing his baseball cap.

'Good morning,' Doctor Fischer said. 'I hope you slept well. We're just going to take some samples from you. You can stay lying down. Please roll your sleeve up. You'll hardly notice, Doctor Kalpak is very good. I'll be right back, I'm need to show Mr Jones out.'

The Indian doctor stroked the inside of Daniel's elbow with two silky fingertips before sinking the needle into a vein. It felt warm and tickly as the blood ran out into a small tube that Doctor Kalpak was holding.

Several tubes of dark, almost black blood had been filled and stacked in a little stand by the time Doctor Fischer returned. The Indian doctor sealed the tubes, put a plaster on Daniel's arm and withdrew with a discreet bow.

'Doctor Kalpak is my personal surgeon. Incredible dexterity. His sister plays first violin with the London Symphony Orchestra,' Doctor Fischer said.

'Who was the other man?' Daniel asked.

'Mr Jones, you mean?'

'Yes. Is he a doctor too?'

'He's one of Himmelstal's biggest sponsors.'

Daniel sat up. The pills had made him calm and unafraid.

'He's American, isn't he? There are rumours that he's from the CIA.'

Doctor Fischer shrugged his shoulders.

'There are lots of rumours in the valley.'

'And most of them have turned out to contain a degree of truth. What is this place? What are you going to with all the people you've got locked up down here?'

'Help them.'

'Help them?'

'Yes. And not just the people *here*. My goal is to help all people.'

Daniel almost laughed out loud. Doctor Fischer was well and truly mad.

'How?'

'I'd be happy to explain it to you, Daniel. But I suggest we move to my little abode. Now that Doctor Kalpak has taken those blood samples, there's nothing to stop you having a bit of breakfast. I haven't actually had time for any myself yet. How about some tea and toast back at my place?'

Daniel, who would have given anything to get away from the stinking cell, if only for a short while, gratefully accepted the offer.

Doctor Fischer adjusted the velvet curtain in front of the steel door and switched on the lights in his cosy apartment. The corridor with its hermetically sealed cells immediately seemed completely unreal, even though they had only just come from there.

At the doctor's insistence Daniel sank into the same armchair he had sat in the evening before, and as the doctor toasted some bread and laid the table he got a strong feeling that he must have fallen asleep there in the armchair and that the events of last night and that morning had been a nightmare. But his black-and-white tracksuit and the plaster from Doctor Kalpak's blood tests told him otherwise. In spite of the pills he felt alert and tense, and he had trouble swallowing the toast with rhubarb jam that Doctor Fischer prepared for him.

'I enjoy inviting my patients in for a cup of tea and a chat. Well, not all of them, obviously. But patients like you, Daniel.'

Daniel glanced towards the curtain on the left-hand side of the room which, if his memory served correctly, concealed the door through which they had come the previous evening. Leading to the official tunnel network. That was right, wasn't it?

'I always appreciate having someone intelligent to talk to. Now eat, my friend. Is something troubling you? Ah, the door over there. You need both the code and a magnetic key card to get out that way, and there's usually a guard nearby. So you can drop that idea. You take your tea without milk, don't you, if I remember rightly?'

Doctor Fischer poured some milk into his own cup and stirred it.

'There's nothing else in it,' he said, gesturing towards Daniel's untouched cup. 'You've had all the medication you need for the time being. I hope I got it right. Balanced and harmonious, but clear-headed enough to hold a decent conversation.'

And, as if he were sharing a secret with Daniel, he leaned forward and said in a low voice:

'Do you know, I'm not terribly keen on psychotropic drugs. Too primitive and clumsy. In the future we'll be using much more finely tuned methods.'

Daniel took a cautious sip of his tea.

Karl Fischer nodded happily, cleared his throat and said:

'Well, as you've seen, there are a lot of different research projects underway in Himmelstal. The idea was for us to work on a number of fronts until we found the causes of psychopathy and how it could best be cured. You know about one of the projects, the one based on Doctor Pierce's Pinocchio model, where the psychopath is viewed as a wooden puppet that is almost but not quite human. As you've no doubt realised, I don't subscribe to Doctor Pierce's puppet theory. Is a psychopath any less human because he doesn't have a conscience? Well, that obviously depends on how you define the concept of humanity'

'What project are you working on in there?' Daniel interrupted, not terribly interested in definitions of any sort.

Doctor Fischer leaned back in his armchair and went on calmly:

'You think I'm being too philosophical? The fact is that philosophy, medicine and psychiatry are getting closer and closer to one another. Why has evolution equipped human beings with a conscience?'

Daniel couldn't tell if this was a rhetorical question or if he was expected to answer it. To hurry things along, he chose the latter interpretation:

'To restrain aggressive and egotistical impulses. Without a conscience we would kill each other and wipe out our species.'

'Would we?' Karl Fischer exclaimed, pretending to be shocked. 'Do rats have consciences? Do snakes?'

This time Daniel decided to stay quiet.

'Hardly. A conscience isn't essential for the survival of a species. So why do we have one?'

Daniel didn't respond. Karl Fischer wasn't remotely interested in having a conversation. He just wanted an audience.

'Presumably,' the doctor went on, with a dramatic pause

designed to keep his audience on tenterhooks as he calmly sipped his tea, 'presumably it arose so that the strongest member of the tribe wouldn't eat the others' food. The survival of the group was more important than that of the individual, and hungry, pleading looks became triggers for unselfish behaviour. In this primitive form the conscience wasn't much more than an animal's reaction to the whimpering of its young. A sort of instinct, an inner voice. But human beings, unlike animals, have the capacity to *resist* their inner voice. As a result, they have also been equipped with a means of limiting their behaviour that they alone possess: guilt. A thermostat that kicks in whenever someone deviates too far from the programme. That probably worked perfectly well in the Stone Age. But today? Do we live in tribes in the middle of a wilderness, Daniel? No, we are individuals who interact and compete in a marketplace. Conscience and guilt are no more essential to our survival than having an appendix. The truth is that we would manage perfectly well, and probably much better, without them. As a species, I mean, of course. Naturally certain *individuals* would not survive, but of course that's the price you pay for evolution.'

He drank some more tea and Daniel took the opportunity to interject:

'If I understand you correctly, Doctor Fischer, you've no interest in *curing* psychopaths? You regard their lack of a conscience as an *advantage*?'

'It's true that I don't look at psychopaths the same way as the other researchers here in Himmelstal,' Doctor Fischer agreed, nodding solemnly. 'To continue in terms of evolution: psychopaths aren't a throwback to an earlier, more primitive state, as some people believe. Quite the contrary. The reason why this deviation occasionally arises is precisely the same as with other deviations: nature is testing out new models. If they are functional, they survive and give rise to more of the same model. The fact is that the number of diagnosed psychopaths in Himmelstal increases with each passing year. When Himmelstal was first established we had to go out and actively seek study material. Today we are drowning in applications from every country in Europe. We can only accept a fraction of the cases that people want us to take. So, from an evolutionary perspective, the psychopath model is very successful.'

'I can't see any evolutionary advantages to an increase in the number of murderers, rapists and thieves,' Daniel protested.

'No, there are no advantages to that, you're quite right there. Himmelstal is overflowing with impulsive, violent idiots. Because the majority of psychopaths don't merely lack a conscience. Unfortunately they also lack patience, perseverance and self-discipline, which renders them useless in most contexts. As plenty of mafia bosses and terrorist leaders have had cause to regret. Their dream is the controllable psychopath. Emotionless, but unshakeably loyal to his employer. Unafraid, but cautious when necessary. Intelligent, but without any independent creativity. In short: a robot. You can imagine how useful someone like that would be in certain situations.'

Karl Fischer paused and looked intently at Daniel, as though to check that he was keeping up with his reasoning. Daniel nodded solemnly and said:

'Is it possible to create someone like that?'

Fischer threw out his hands.

'Maybe.'

'Is that why Mr Jones is here? Are you working for the CIA?'

'That's certainly what the CIA believe, yes,' Doctor Fischer said with a chuckle. 'Americans! They've got it into their heads that I'm creating human missiles that they can use in one of their never-ending wars. And as long as they keep pumping money into Himmelstal I have no intention of disabusing them of that notion. We would never have been able to expand to the extent that we have without their money. Take my own research department, for instance.' He gestured towards the curtain covering the door they had come through. 'That would never have been set up without Mr Jones's generous donations. Which is why I have to put up with him scampering about like a rabbit in the tunnels down here. I let him see some of the experiments, and send him the occasional confidential report. Naturally, he has no idea of what I'm really doing. He thinks I'm taming monsters. Which is completely wrong. My project is much bigger than that.'

'What is your project?'

'The happy human being. A world without suffering,' Doctor Fischer said with a modest shrug of the shoulders.

'Wow. And how are you going to achieve that?'

'Most people's unhappiness is caused by the fact that they have more emotions that they need.'

'So you want to shut off people's feelings?' Daniel exclaimed. 'You want to turn everyone into psychopaths? Is that what your project is about?'

In spite of the pills he was becoming so angry that he could hardly sit still.

Karl Fischer put a firm hand on top of Daniel's and said:

'Let me finish. I don't want to shut anything off. I simply want to lower the volume.'

He gave Daniel's hand a light squeeze and smiled reassuringly before he let go and continued:

'When I was a student I did a placement in a psychiatric clinic, and I was astonished at the amount of guilt exhibited by the patients. Often utterly pointless guilt. Guilt about things they couldn't possibly have had any control over. Guilt about things it was too late to do anything about. Painful emotions, and completely unnecessary. The more I listened to these patients, the more surprised I became. Because I myself had never experienced anything like that, it fascinated me. All that angst. All that suffering. People with healthy, functioning bodies who could have been absolutely fine if it weren't for all those *feelings*.'

He spat out the word as if it had a bad taste.

'But isn't it our feelings that make us human?' Daniel protested with a lump in his throat.

'And who decides what a human being is? Is it something that's fixed for ever? "Man is a rope tied between beast and Superman", as dear old Nietzsche put it.'

Daniel opened his mouth to comment but Doctor Fischer went on quickly:

'Is there some law that says mankind must always suffer? In my surgery I would prescribe medication to suppress anxiety as a temporary reprieve. A plaster on the wound. But I'm not satisfied with sticking plasters. I won't settle for smoothing things over. I want to *remove* the source of the evil. Imagine that, Daniel: that we can remove evil for ever. Wouldn't that be fantastic?'

'I don't understand how . . . ' Daniel attempted, but Fischer wasn't about to let himself be interrupted and went on in the same excited tone of voice:

'Think about how much evil guilt has caused! You're talking to a German, don't forget.' He wagged his finger sternly. 'We're *experts* at guilt. After the First World War we were broken and humiliated. And as if that wasn't enough, we had to pay vast reparations, we lost our colonies and our armaments. Most humiliating of all, we were forced to sign an admission of guilt where we accepted responsibility for the war. So we were guilty of our own suffering! No one can handle that sort of guilt. That was what caused the greatest bitterness, and caused us to long for redress. In other words, another war. Guilt causes suffering, suffering causes more guilt. It's a vicious circle. I say: break it! Get rid of guilt!'

'I still don't think I would want to have anything to do with someone who couldn't feel guilt,' Daniel said quietly.

'But if everyone was the same? In my world there won't be any oversensitive pedants like you. Don't look so shocked. How much happiness have you derived from being so sensitive? Your depression – did that make you happy?'

'How do you know I've ever been depressed?' Daniel exclaimed in surprise, but Karl Fischer ignored the question.

'You're lumbered with a Stone Age soul in a highly technological society, that's your problem, Daniel. The world needs people who are ambitious, competitive and tough. The unions and the state won't take care of you any longer. You need to be able to fight for yourself. Most people aren't capable of that. They become unemployed, confused wrecks, making profits for psychologists, drink companies and the pharmaceutical industry. Do you know, Daniel, I am *utterly* sick of all the people who make money from suffering. Psychotherapists, pill-pushers, faith healers. Priests, authors, artists. All the parasites living off people's sensitive consciences, their suffering souls!'

Karl Fischer had worked himself into a frenzy of ecstatic rage and Daniel wanted to object, yet he felt strangely hollow. He knew Fischer was wrong, but he was incapable of raising an objection. Maybe that was because of the pills he'd been given.

'I still don't agree with you,' he said lamely.

Doctor Fischer smiled amiably and composed himself.

'Of course not. You're part of all this, and can't see it from the outside the way I can. But believe me: mankind's exaggerated sensitivity is a remnant from a previous stage of development. Like body hair. There's no longer any need for it, so it would do no harm to remove it.'

The notes of the Trout Quintet began to ring out from Doctor Fischer's breast pocket. He interrupted himself and took the call.

'Excellent,' he said, and put the mobile back. 'That was Doctor Kalpak. Your blood test showed that everything is in order and that you're in excellent health. There's nothing to stop us proceeding with the treatment as soon as possible.'

'Treatment? What treatment?' Daniel wondered anxiously.

'It would take too long to explain it to you now. In brief, you could say it's like the Pinocchio Project, only in reverse.'

Daniel took a deep breath, then, in a voice that sounded considerably calmer than he felt, he said:

'So you want to make a wooden puppet out of a human being?'

'I'm not sure I'd describe it quite like that. But evidently the puppet imagery appeals to you. "A puppet with someone else's hand inside you" – wasn't that how you described yourself?'

Daniel stiffened.

'Where did you hear that?'

'Apparently that's what you told your psychiatrist. When you sought treatment for depression, I think it was?' Doctor Fischer said as he walked over to the bookcase and searched the row of files.

'I don't understand how you managed to get hold of that sort of information.'

'I have an extensive network of contacts. And we doctors have to share our material if progress is ever going to be made.'

He returned with a file and made space for it on the table, pushing the teacups and saucers aside.

'Medical records are confidential,' Daniel objected.

'Sometimes the good of the many has to take precedence over the good of the individual,' Fischer muttered as he searched through the file. 'At least, that's what your psychiatrist thought once I'd explained that I knew about the affair he was having with one of his female patients. Information that could do serious damage to his career and marriage if it got into the wrong hands. From your conversations with him it would appear that you ... ah, here it is: *you have a weak sense of self and you have felt dominated by your brother throughout your life.* Yes, you even seem to have regarded yourself as *a pale imitation of him.* Very interesting. You've tried to find your own role in life, but without your brother you have always felt *empty and hollow, ready to be filled up by the first person who came along. Like a puppet.* That was it.'

He closed the file noisily.

'When I read that I knew that you'd be of great value to me. You weren't the sort I'd been hoping for. But there's every chance that you will be.'

56

The operating room gave the impression of being makeshift and primitive, as though it had been prepared in haste to take care of the victims of some catastrophe: unopened cardboard boxes, equipment shoved in a corner, and a plastic bucket full of dirty cotton wool balls.

To his astonishment, Daniel wasn't especially worried. He assumed this was because of the injection Doctor Kalpak had given him. The surgeon had whipped the syringe out quickly, without any warning, as if he'd had it up his coat sleeve, and in the middle of a gentle, lilting sentence he had plunged it into Daniel's arm. It must have contained the same substance he had previously been given in tablet form, because once again he had a sense of swimming or treading water. He was docile and obedient and the two guards barely had to use any force at all as they pushed him down into what looked like a modern dentist's chair placed at the centre of the operating room. It was covered with green paper which didn't seem to have been replaced since the last patient, because it had dark stains on it and was torn in a few places, as if the patient hadn't been able to keep still.

Doctor Kalpak moved a buzzing object towards Daniel, who actually burst out laughing with relief when he saw it was an ordinary electric shaver. Doctor Kalpak laughed too, revealing a snow-white row of teeth as he ran the shaver over Daniel's scalp, sending tufts of his newly grown dark hair falling to the floor.

'Just like at the barber's, eh?' he called out breezily.

Karl Fischer appeared on the other side of Daniel. Between his thumb and forefinger he was holding a small metal rod, five or six centimetres long. Daniel looked at it in bemusement.

'What have you got there?' he wondered.

Fischer twiddled the rod between his fingers as he appeared to think about a suitable response. Finally he said:

'See it as the hand that's about to fill you up.'

Daniel wasn't happy with that answer, but before he had time to say anything else a rumble like thunder rolled through the ground, making the instruments and bottles rattle on the shelves.

'Dear God, they're blasting again,' Doctor Kalpak cried. 'We'll have to wait. I can't operate when everything's shaking.'

'It's already stopped. No problem,' Doctor Fischer said calmly.

'No vibrations! Absolutely no vibrations!' Doctor Kalpak insisted anxiously. 'It mustn't be out by even a millimetre!'

'And it won't be. You're going to put it in exactly the right place.'

The two doctors looked at each other from either side of the chair while they waited. The only sound was the hum of the air vent.

Fischer nodded in encouragement and Kalpak shaved the last of Daniel's hair from his scalp. With a bee-like buzz the backrest was lowered until he was lying flat, then the whole chair was raised to a comfortable working height.

Doctor Kalpak folded something down across Daniel's forehead – a sort of metal frame that fixed his shaved head and stopped him turning it to either side.

The doctors looked at each other again. Fischer's left eyelid flickered in an almost imperceptible wink.

'What are you planning to . . . ?' Daniel began.

A moment later his head exploded in a shower of sparking pain. He heard a scream, possibly his own, and his consciousness was torn apart like a strip of burned film.

57

Absolute darkness, Daniel thought in alarm. Dense and compact, like a physical substance, it surrounded him on all sides, forcing its way into his mouth and nostrils. No hint of light anywhere, no nuances in the black. It was as if he now found himself inside a new element, with no idea of what was up or down. Drifting in space. The fact that the North Pole is up and the South Pole is down is simply a prejudice, why do we say that? Up and down in relation to what?

Obviously he was dead. Up and down no longer existed. He had nothing from which to get his bearings. However if that were the case, could he be thinking these thoughts? And there *was* something for him to get his bearings from. Something heavy and hard pressing on his right leg and hip in a distinctly real and painful way. He tried to move away from the weight, or push it away, but discovered that he couldn't actually move very much at all. Where were Doctor Fischer and Doctor Kalpak?

Then he realised what must have happened. The blasting on the building site. Doctor Fischer's underground research facility wasn't part of Himmelstal's official activities and wasn't included on any of the plans. So they wouldn't have taken it into account when they were working out what explosive charges to use. The room he was in, and possibly the whole underground research facility, had collapsed.

Buried alive! The thought was there even if he didn't want to admit it.

He tried shouting, but that caused more pain than noise as his throat filled with concrete dust and forced him into a fit of agonised coughing.

In the middle of coughing he heard something. A machine? A human voice? Drawn out notes, vibrating and squeaking. He lay still and listened hard. He recognised the tune. Wasn't that 'The Star-Spangled Banner', the American national anthem? But it sounded very odd. Like a human voice trying to imitate an electric guitar.

'Tom!' he called out. 'Is that you?'

At an increasing rate, the peculiar voice switched between loud cries and a low bass rumble, and after a long crescendo it broke off with a click as a tiny flame flickered into life.

Tom appeared out of the darkness. He was holding a cigarette lighter in his hand, his skull-like face and shaved head glowing in its feeble light. His guitar imitation had evidently been tiring, he was breathless and had a dribble of saliva at the corner of his mouth, but he seemed completely uninjured.

'Can you help me, Tom? I seem to be stuck,' Daniel groaned.

'Yes, it's far too cramped here,' Tom sighed, without moving a muscle.

In the weak light Daniel could now make out collapsed blocks of concrete and jagged metal supports. He was lying on the floor with the upturned operating-chair on top of him.

'Tom,' he groaned again.

Tom came closer and lit up his face with the lighter. He took a couple of steps back, inspecting him thoughtfully as he ran his hand over his bare head, then finally declared:

'All that crap has to go. It's blocking the view.'

'I completely agree with you,' Daniel hissed. 'But I'm a bit stuck. Do you think you could help me?'

Tom moved closer again and took a look at the situation. He crouched down next to Daniel and handed him the lighter:

'Hold this.'

He put his shoulder against the lump of concrete and pushed as hard as he could, but failed to budge it at all.

'Can't do it,' he declared. 'You'll have to keep it like this. It doesn't look nice though.'

'Maybe if you tried to pull me out instead?' Daniel whispered.

Tom sighed, and it sounded as if he was getting fed up, but he did at least take hold of Daniel's arms and, with a hard, irritable jerk, succeeded in moving him a short distance. Which meant that the whole weight ended up on Daniel's shin instead of his hip. He roared with pain, but somehow managed to crawl forward and pull himself completely free. He rolled over and clutched his ankle as he panted for air.

'You look much better without all that crap,' Tom said approvingly.

Daniel stood up and checked that nothing was broken, then looked round with the lighter. They were trapped in a small pocket, completely surrounded by collapsed concrete and reinforcing bars.

Tom whistled and pointed at something. From beneath the concrete an arm in a white coat sleeve was sticking out. The hand was dark-skinned with a paler palm, the fingers long and slender, like flower stalks.

'Doctor Kalpak,' Tom said.

He leaned over, pulled gently at the long fingers and tutted sadly.

'He could have been a great guitarist.'

'His sister plays first violin for the London Symphony Orchestra,' Daniel muttered as he tried to find a pulse in the still warm wrist.

He looked at the pile of concrete that reached all the way to the ceiling. Doctor Fischer was probably somewhere under there.

'Where were you when the tunnel collapsed?' he asked Tom.

'In the waiting room. I was going to be operated on after you. I went to the toilet and the guard waited outside. Then something happened when I flushed it. I must have pressed the wrong button. What about you? Were you in the middle of your operation?'

He pointed at Daniel's freshly shaved head, and Daniel suddenly became aware of something warm and sticky running down his temple and on to his cheek. With a gasp of horror he put his hand to his scalp, then stopped and gently touched a sensitive area just above his right ear.

Tom grabbed the lighter and shone it close to Daniel's head.

'Flesh wound, that's all. You probably got hit by a bit of concrete,' he said, then added apologetically: 'Well, I must be going now.'

He turned away, leaving Daniel in darkness. Then, with the lighter in one hand, he began scrambling up the heap of collapsed concrete with surprising agility.

'Be careful it doesn't collapse any more!' Daniel cried as Tom darted from piece to piece like a mountain goat.

Where did he think he was going?

'Too damn cramped here as well. This ought to go,' he snorted. 'And this.'

Tom was standing at the top of the pile of concrete, holding out his hands as the little flame from the lighter flickered in the darkness.

'There's a lot that ought to go, Tom.'

It got darker, and to his horror Daniel saw that Tom was about to disappear between the blocks of concrete.

'Wait, where are you going?' he called, terrified at the thought of being left alone in the darkness.

'That's it. This is better,' Tom's voice said from above Daniel.

Tom's head and the hand holding the lighter stuck out from an opening between the concrete and the roof.

'Are you coming, or are you going to stay there?' he called.

'What's on the other side?' Daniel asked anxiously as he scrambled up the collapsed concrete wall.

'I don't know if you're going to like it. But at least it's not so fucking cramped,' Tom said.

'Is it a treatment room? Corridors?'

'Something like that.'

'Is there anyone there?'

Tom turned away, the hand holding the lighter vanished and it went dark. His voice echoed strangely from the other side of the rubble:

'No. Or yes. Sort of.'

'Hang on. Bring the lighter back!' Daniel said as he stumbled.

He fumbled for a foothold in the darkness. Tom reappeared with the lighter and Daniel saw to his horror that he had almost slipped down between two great lumps of concrete.

'Could you hold the lighter there until I get up, please?' he asked.

Tom sighed impatiently but did as he was asked, filling in the time with a few electric guitar riffs.

Once Daniel had clambered over the last block, Tom pulled back so that he could get through the opening. It seemed impossible at first, but Tom had managed it. Even if Daniel wasn't as skinny as Tom, he had to try at least. What other choice did he have?

He scraped his wounded head against the concrete and

trickles of sticky blood ran down his face. With his teeth clenched against the pain he tumbled out on the other side.

The first thing that struck him was that it smelled completely different. The dry smell of concrete dust was overpowered by a cold, damp odour of earth and stone. It was equally dark on the other side, but something told him they weren't in an examination room or hospital corridor. He had the feeling of being at the bottom of a deep well.

'Tom!' he called out. 'Where are we?'

His voice was thrown back at him off stone walls. In the distance he could hear the echo of water dripping slowly.

'If it wasn't so cold, I'd say we were in the Vietcong's underground tunnel system,' Tom said from somewhere in the darkness.

'You sound like you're a long way away. I can't see anything. Have you got the lighter there?' Daniel called.

There was a click and the flame flared up with a hiss as it hit the damp air. Tom was standing some ten metres away from him in a narrow passageway with an arched stone roof. His breath was clouding.

'Didn't you say you saw people here?' Daniel reminded him. Tom shrugged.

'I saw *those*,' he said, holding the lighter closer to the wall.

Daniel realised that the stone wall contained horizontal niches, almost like pigeonholes. He moved slowly closer to the niche that was lit up by Tom's outstretched lighter.

He had a fair idea of what he was about to see, having come across something similar in Rome and Paris, but the sight of the brown cranium and empty eye sockets still made him gasp. It was too dark for him to see inside the other niches, but he knew they too would be full of skeletons, lying there on their built-in bunk beds.

'The Catacombs,' he whispered. 'So they really do exist.'

'Looks that way,' Tom said, then added in a sudden burst of

rational thinking: 'We need to save the fuel. Have a quick look. Then we'll go on in darkness.'

Daniel grabbed a couple of broken reinforcing rods from the heap of concrete. If they were going to go on through the darkness they'd need sticks to test the way. He didn't want to stumble over anything without warning.

The lighter went out and they headed off through pitch-black darkness, Tom first, then Daniel. With one hand Daniel kept a firm grasp of Tom's tracksuit, and with the other he ran the metal rod against the walls where the skeletons lay in their open graves half a metre away from him.

There was a clatter as Tom's pole struck stone.

'What is it? Have we reached the end?' Daniel asked from close behind him.

Tom took out the lighter and they saw that the tunnel continued beyond a right-angled corner. It became narrower and lower.

The lighter went out again and they carried on through the darkness, crouching down as Tom kept his spirits up with a frenetic electric guitar solo. Daniel hit his head on the roof several times. He yelled out whenever the stones scraped against his wounded scalp, and the blood poured down his face. Tom took no notice of him and just carried on, making his weird electronic noises.

Suddenly he stopped in the middle of a long, reverberating note.

'Another wall?' Daniel asked.

Without getting the lighter out he moved aside and Daniel saw why he had stopped. A short distance ahead of them they could see a thin sliver of light.

'I knew it had to come out somewhere,' Daniel exclaimed. 'It's a door.'

But when they reached the strip of light it was no door but a solid brick wall, with a vertical crack at the corner.

'Well, at least it's an outside wall,' Daniel said.

He tried to peer through the crack. The light was so bright that it blinded him at first. Was that really ordinary daylight? He waited a moment, let his eyes get used to it, then looked again. But the crack was too narrow and the light still too bright. He couldn't see anything but white emptiness out there. A room? An empty examination room with white tiled walls and fluorescent lighting?

No, the cold draught coming through the crack wasn't from a room. And the smell, the wonderful, fresh smell of outdoors! That was the valley out there. Freedom.

He realised how ironic his situation was: the valley he had previously thought of as his prison now felt like freedom. And the way out was a crack a centimetre wide. What a joke. He'd die in here, together with crazy Tom, and they'd end up sharing their grave with the other skeletons.

He put his mouth to the crack and shouted for help. It was like shouting at a wall. The sound came back at him and he doubted anyone would be able to hear him, even if they happened to be standing right outside. The crack was far too small to let any sound out.

'You look fucking awful,' Tom said in disgust, pointing at Daniel's blood-streaked face.

'Sorry about that,' Daniel said.

To his amazement Tom unzipped his tracksuit top and took it off. Then he took off his vest, baring his scrawny, hairy chest.

'What are you doing?' Daniel wondered. 'You'll freeze to death.'

With a few quick tugs Tom tore his vest into shreds. Daniel stared at him. For a moment he was struck by the touching notion that his comrade was going to bandage his wounds. But instead Tom rather roughly rubbed the blood from his head and face.

'That'll do,' he nodded, staring with satisfaction at the bloody rag he was holding up.

Daniel slumped down by the wall. He held his hand up to the sliver of daylight that fell on the darkness like a narrow thread. He brought his thumb and forefinger together as though he could grab hold of it. He went on with this pointless game for hours until he was so cold he could hardly feel his body any more.

Tom walked up and down in the darkness, muttering nonsense and practising his guitar solos. Daniel tried not to listen to him. He was concentrating on the strip of light as it grew steadily paler and thinner.

58

With a crash the great stone door hit the ground, throwing up clouds of what Daniel first assumed was dust. He was surrounded by happy, jubilant voices. Someone wrapped a blanket round his shoulders and led him out. He stood there, blinded, as he rubbed his eyes and blinked tiredly, like a bear woken from hibernation.

A moment later he realised why he hadn't been able to see anything through the crack, why everything outside had been so white and silent.

Himmelstal was completely covered in snow! In soft, flowing layers it covered the fringe of trees at the top of the Wall, the rooftops over in the village, and the banks of the frozen river.

But where in the valley was he? Confused, he stared at the black railings and the crooked stone crosses that looked as if they'd been decorated with whipped cream.

'You were lucky,' a guard panted, leaning exhausted against the railings. 'That door probably wasn't meant to be opened before the Day of Judgement.'

Daniel turned round. The fallen door was embedded in the

snow, and behind it gaped the dark entrance to a temple. Bloody hell, he was in the Leper Cemetery! The mausoleum. He'd come back from the grave!

Two other guards led him towards the vans that were parked down on the road.

'What about Tom? Where is he?' Daniel asked, turning to look at the opening to the monument again.

'Tom?' the guards said in surprise. 'Is *he* here somewhere?'

At that moment Tom appeared out of the darkness. The usually ultra-stoical guards couldn't help a gasp of terror as Tom slid out of the door to the grave, half naked, head shaved, peering suspiciously around him like a ghost fleeing from Hades.

After a second or so the guards recovered from the ghostly apparition and, with their usual speed and efficiency, hand-cuffed Tom, threw a blanket over his naked shoulders and led him off towards another of the vans.

Another van arrived and before it had even stopped Corinne leaped out of the passenger side. Red-cheeked and wearing a fur-brimmed hat she padded towards Daniel through the snow. She hugged him hard, then kissed him on the cheeks, mouth and chin.

Then she took a step back and looked at his head.

'You're going to need a few stitches,' she declared.

Daniel would never have imagined it could feel as good as this to get into one of the guards' vehicles. He and Corinne sat down in one of them, while Tom was put in another.

'What a stroke of luck that we managed to get you out of that awful grave,' she said as the engine started up and the van rolled off along the recently cleared road.

She took off her hat, crept in under his blanket and rested her head in the crook of his neck.

'Am I going to the clinic now?' Daniel whispered.

At least that was what he was thinking, but he wasn't sure if the words had passed his lips. His consciousness was coming and going like something with a weak battery.

For a brief moment he had an out-of-body experience, and could see the van from above, describing its elliptical path around the narrow, wintery valley. Round and round, with a short stop at the hospital building, then round again. A merry-go-round that always took him back to the clinic. Where everything began again. There was no way out. Maybe there was no world outside the valley. And never had been.

'Only to get you patched up,' Corinne said, gently nuzzling his head. 'I'll be with you. God, I'm so glad you're here. We've been searching like mad. The guards would never have found you if they hadn't seen that red flag against the white snow.'

'Flag?' Daniel said uncertainly. 'Oh, that was Tom's vest, with my blood on it. He tied it to a metal rod and managed to squeeze it through a crack. I thought he'd gone mad.'

'Of course he's mad. But he saved your life,' Corinne said, rubbing her face against his neck like a cat.

59

In the guest suite of the old main building Daniel and Corinne were lying together in a double bed for the first time.

'Are you sure we can leave here tomorrow? Both of us?' Daniel said.

Corinne was lying against his shoulder. Outside the tall windows with their open velvet curtains, snowflakes the size of feathers were falling through the darkness.

'No one's going to keep us here,' she said. 'They've no right to. Doctor Pierce has got hold of all your personal details from Sweden and he'll have you out of here as soon as possible. Didn't he say when you spoke to him?'

'He said they're launching an investigation into Fischer's activities, and that they'll need to talk to me later. If that's true, they're going to have to come to me,' Daniel said, banging his fist against the mattress. 'Once I've left Himmelstal, I'm never setting foot here again. And I want to be gone by the time Max arrives.'

'You will be.'

She stroked her hand over his cheek and temple, and the bandage covering the stitches on his shaved head.

'It'll be lovely to get away from here,' she whispered.

'I don't understand how you could stay here voluntarily,' Daniel said. 'What was the attraction?'

'The excitement, I think. My dad was a mountaineer. It's in the blood.'

'What about the power? What was it like, controlling someone else's brain by remote control?'

'It was . . . fascinating,' she said hesitantly.

'I can imagine. Making the bad good. Playing God.'

'Yes. I suppose it was a bit like that.'

She curled up under his arm and they lay there together in silence, watching the snowflakes fall outside.

'How well did you know Mattias Block?' Daniel asked after a while.

He noticed a change in her body when he mentioned the name.

'He was the one I got on with best when we were training. We became good friends,' she said in a faint voice, as if the memory pained her.

'Just friends?'

She sighed.

'You're not going to get jealous of a dead man, are you? We were in love with each other. But relationships between crickets were strictly forbidden. When we were let out into the valley to carry out our tasks, we weren't allowed to have any contact at all. I can't forgive Doctor Pierce for assigning Mattias such a dangerous subject as Adrian Keller. He was the wrong person for that.'

'What about Max? Did he ever try to seduce you?'

'Of course.'

'And you stopped him with your bracelet?'

'Yes. When he got too close . . . click.'

She held out her arm and pressed the index finger of the other hand to her wrist, as if she was pressing a button, only pretending because the bracelet was no longer there.

'He used to say it was my freckles. As soon as he saw them, he lost the urge.'

'It must have been fun to be able to toy with a man that way?'

Corinne leaned on her elbow and kissed him.

'It's every woman's deepest wish,' she whispered as she playfully ran her finger down his chin, neck and chest. 'Being desired, but being able to put a stop to it whenever you want. That's so obvious for men, but not for women. If we show any kind of interest, we have to follow through, don't we? All these stupid alarms and sprays that you clutch in your pocket on the way home at night. Deep down, you know they don't work. This worked.'

'Not on me, though,' Daniel said. 'You've got no defence against me.'

He pulled her back down, kissed her, and put his hand on her stomach.

'It's too early to feel anything moving,' she said.

But he left his hand there. Like a protective dome it rested above the life that had blossomed against the odds in that wicked place. And within a couple of minutes her deep breathing had lulled him into the deepest and most relaxed sleep he had ever experienced in Himmelstal.

60

Snow was falling gently between the mountains.

The diggers that had stopped work on the new site when the snow started were once again in action as a team of men fought to dig people out after the collapse.

The collapsed part of the tunnel system had come as a great surprise to the works manager, seeing as the system didn't stretch that far, according to the plans he had been given. To his horror he had discovered that the entire hillside was riddled with passageways like a rabbit warren, something that his explosives experts had obviously been unaware of.

Daniel was sitting ready to leave in the lobby of the clinic together with Corinne. Her suitcases were over by the entrance. He himself had no luggage. The heat from the open fire had made them take off their coats and put them across the sofa. He was fidgeting impatiently.

'Why isn't the car here?'

'It'll be here as soon as they've ploughed the road into Himmelstal,' Corinne replied calmly, taking the glass of glühwein that one of the hostesses offered her. She offered one to Daniel as well, but he declined with a shake of the head.

'And you're sure it's going to take us out of the valley?' he said. 'I won't believe that until I see it.'

He looked up at the stuffed fox head on the wall. The firelight was reflecting off its teeth, giving them a red glow.

Another hostess leaned over the counter of the reception desk with a phone in her hand and called out:

'They've found two more. Only minor injuries.'

Eight bodies had been recovered from Doctor Fischer's underground clinic so far, including Doctor Kalpak and Fischer himself. Twenty people had been found alive in their cells and had been moved to the real care centre above ground. Among them was the hostess who had gone missing, as well as two nurses who had worked for Karl Fischer before, as everyone assumed, resigning without notice and going home.

At the time of the accident the clinic's sponsor, Greg Jones, had been in one of the guestrooms. He had been so shocked by events that he immediately sent for his private helicopter and left the valley.

Daniel stood up, went over to the entrance and looked out. He didn't like all this snow.

The phone at the desk rang. The hostess took the call, then turned towards them and said:

'The road's open now. The car will be ready to leave in five minutes. Have you got everything?'

When they came out the snow was still falling, very lightly and slowly. The car wasn't some old van but a comfortable BMW that was used for driving visiting researchers in and out of the valley. The driver put their bags in, then opened the back door with a calm, sweeping gesture. Everything seemed to be happening in slow motion, as if the snow were slowing things down. For a terrible moment Daniel was convinced it was all a dream and that he was going to wake up and discover that there was no car ready to drive him away from here.

'Are you really going to drive us out of Himmelstal?' he asked anxiously.

'Of course,' the driver said.

Corinne got into the back seat and adjusted her hat, which had been knocked askew when she climbed in. Daniel got in beside her, and she took his hand and smiled at him encouragingly.

With sloth-like slowness the car rolled down the slope and into the woods, where snow-heavy branches formed a tunnel around them. He realised that the driver couldn't drive faster with the road in this state, but the slowness was still exasperating.

They reached the bottom of the valley and falling snow surrounded them like billowing lace curtains. The mountains were vague, scarcely visible, and inside the car it was grey and dark.

'If it carries on this way, the roads will get blocked again and we'll have to turn back to the clinic,' he muttered.

'Don't worry. The snowploughs will be working non-stop,' Corinne said.

But there was a great deal of snow on the road, and the car had to slow to a crawl.

They passed the Leper Cemetery. The broken entrance to the tomb gaped empty, dark and frightening, like the portal into the underworld that it actually was. Further up the slope they could see the search team looking for more survivors in the collapsed tunnels. He gave Corinne's hand an involuntary squeeze, and she gave him a kiss that tasted of cinnamon and warm wine.

Slowly they made their way through the valley. The snow had made the landscape unrecognisable. It was hard to believe that these sleeping white fields had only recently been green with lush grass.

Suddenly Daniel remembered something.

'That time we lay in the grass and you talked about children. When you said what you missed most in Himmelstal was children. You were crying. Was that all an act?'

Corinne gazed out into the milky haze. In the gloom inside the car her brown eyes looked almost black.

'I had to play my part,' she said quietly. 'If it had got out that I wasn't a proper resident, I'd have been taking a huge gamble. There were so many rumours about spies working for the doctors. I don't think anyone ever suspected me, but Mattias obviously got unmasked somehow, and he paid a terrible price. I don't know what Keller did to him. He must have fled the house in panic, otherwise he wouldn't have run straight into one of those snares.'

She was drowned out by a clattering noise, and the inside of the car was lit up by orange light as a snowplough came up behind them. The driver pulled as close to the edge of the road as he dared, stopped and let the snowplough pass. They drove on, sticking close behind it, and its rotating light lit them up as if they were in a disco.

'You sounded so genuine when you were crying,' Daniel said. 'You were distraught.'

He looked at her face, flickering yellow and red as she replied:

'I'm an actress, Daniel.'

'So how much of you has been real, and how much has been an act?'

'It's hard to say. Do you want a percentage?'

'What about our love? Is that an act for you?'

They had reached the far western edge of the looping road. Another road led off it, with an illuminated sign flashing a warning in red that they were entering Zone 2.

Ahead of them the snowplough carried on round the curve, back towards the clinic.

'God, no,' she said. 'You mustn't think that.'

The driver stopped at the junction with the other road. The windscreen wipers were going at top speed.

A guard emerged from a concrete hut. He was clutching the collar of his uniform together, huddled against the snow. He glanced inside the car, then went back into the hut.

A moment later the sign flashed green and they drove on. Corinne was sitting up straight and motionless as she stared ahead through the windscreen.

The alpine world lay in front of them. When Daniel leaned down and peered up through the car window, he could just make out the imposing mountaintops behind the curtain of snow. Neither of them said anything.

Shortly afterwards they reached another warning sign that switched to green as they approached. A barrier slid open and the snow that had settled on it slid to the ground in a long, thin sausage. Slowly they drove through and the barrier sank down again behind them.

They were out of Himmelstal.

Corinne leaned her head against his shoulder and the car drove on along the winding road, like a tiny toy in the immense landscape.